Joy to the Worlds

Mysterious Speculative Fiction for the Holidays

Maia Chance, Janine A. Southard,
Raven Oak, and G. Clemans

Grey Sun Press

SEATTLE, WA

Joy to the Worlds: Mysterious Speculative Fiction
for the Holidays

Copyright © 2015 by Maia Chance, Janine A. Southard, Raven Oak, & G. Clemans. All rights reserved.
Printed in the United States of America.
For information address Grey Sun Press, PO Box 99412, Seattle, WA, 98139
WWW.GREYSUNPRESS.COM

"Odysseus Flax & the Krampus" and "Mr. and Mrs. Mistletoe" © 2015 Maia Chance
"Hunting for Justice" and "Death Node" © 2015 Janine A. Southard
"Ol' St. Nick" and "The Ringers" © 2015 Raven Oak
"Bevel & Turn" and "Escape from Old Yorktown" © 2015 G. Clemans

Cover Design: Andrea Orlic

Bell Arch from *Gleanings from Popular Authors Grave and Gay* © 1882
Festive Bell from *Art and Song: a Series of Original Engravings...* Edited by R. Bell © 1967
Gothic Snow Globe © 2015 Raven Oak
"Jolly Old Saint Nicholas" © 1881 Benjamin Hanby
"We Wish You a Merry Christmas" © 1935 Arthur Warrell
"It Came Upon a Midnight Clear" © 1849 Edmund Sears

ISBN 978-0-9908157-6-1

Library of Congress Control Number: *2015949042*

CONTENTS

WILD HUNT

BY JANINE A. SOUTHARD

"In 'Wild Hunt,' Janine layers Germanic myth and a hardboiled detective's voice to spin an astonishingly clever romp of a tale. Delinquent pixies, mistletoe like 'milky miniature eyeballs,' and quirky clues lead Tyson Wallenstein—a preternatural sleuth in polarized sunglasses—on a hunt through a kitschy, snowbound landscape. With a little skill and a lot of tingling in his dead bones, Tyson might crack the case...unless he kills the perpetrator and eats his soul instead."   —Maia Chance

What do you hunt, little lamb, little lamb?
When the night darkens early
And ghosts roam the land.
What do you hunt?

My dead bones rumbled, signaling a supernatural crime nearby. The miniscule vibrations were barely shivers but still evident. No long-timer in our company would bother with such a tiny tingle, but it could be my chance. I'm Tyson Wallenstein, the newest member of the Wild Hunt. Just died last year.

So when we rode past a cottage on the snowy forest's edge—black horses galloping in the black night, our black dogs baying and howling—I paused. The rest of the Hunt slowed with me.

A few old ones snorted, and no Hunt dog trotted up to join my investigation. King Herla, however, said only, "Good luck, Tyson. We'll check in with you at the next mid-night."

Then the rest of the Wild Hunt galloped away, leaving me alone at my crime scene. They were after larger game, on the trail of some delinquent pixies whose families had begged King Herla for his help. Of course he'd agreed. King Herla was on a crusade to make the Hunt more useful to the supernatural community. Even if those pixies were just spray-painting winter gardens or eating the life force of one little farm's sheep, he was hunting them down and bringing them to justice.

In the old days, the Wild Hunt had chased beautiful women and trolled disrespectful human men. So they told me. These days, we recoiled from stalking unwilling ladies or "gifting" plague-ridden carcasses to anyone who didn't lower their eyes when we passed.

We still have to hunt *something*. Changing times have meant changing prey, and now we're the best detectives you'll ever meet.

At least, the others are. I've only been with the Hunt a year, so I'm still learning. The fact that they left me alone on this case...either King Herla believes I'm going to prove myself worthy, or none of the long-timers want to hitch their star to my blazing comet.

I left my centuries-dead horse to stamp his black hooves alongside the disappearing human footprints in the snow. My rumbling bones had led me to a wooden cottage, and I stepped inside a classical-Christmas party zone.

Next to an antique sideboard bearing a sticky punch bowl, an old-fashioned Yule log crackled in the brick fireplace. The oaky smoke gave a Christmassy texture to the décor even if the place was clearly warmed with central heating. Strings of lights dripped from the ceiling highlighting the nutshells abandoned on the wooden floor. Pinecone wreaths adorned every single door, and red-and-white stockings hung over the fireplace.

And the ubiquitous mistletoe? It was stuffed in a dead man's mouth.

The body lay on the leather couch under a nubby blanket, and I checked him out as best I could without moving him too much. Some human investigator might be along later, and I didn't want to mess up the crime scene before a forensic scientist had a chance at it.

If only I had my own forensic scientist! Someone who could do DNA typing or, failing that, some fingerprinting. But I was with the Wild Hunt, not some city's police department. I didn't have a crime lab backing me up. What I did have was a single day, so I had to get to it. No use wishing for mundane intervention that wasn't coming.

Other than the mistletoe weeping translucent berries onto the floor like milky miniature eyeballs, nothing on the body seemed immediately out of place. The victim's red button-up shirt bore amber stains at the cuffs, and a naked toe peeked out from underneath the blanket's fringe. I sniffed at the shirt's stains and reared back with eyebrows that could've crinkled my brain with how far up they flew. The spots carried the sickly sweetness of black rum, but black rum was *black*. It was kind of a defining characteristic. That meant something serious mixed into the punch had changed its hue. But whether it was poison, tequila, or food coloring, I had no idea.

A Hunt dog could've done more with the stains—smelling or licking—but it was just me on the scene. Just Tyson Wallenstein, the newest member of the Wild Hunt.

On the table next to the body lay a tumbler half-full of potent amber liquid. Next to it a white plastic inhaler mocked the victim's permanent inability to breathe. It certainly looked like an accident, like a boring human had died of asthma in his sleep after too much drinking and foolishly putting mistletoe in his mouth. *The berries are toxic, buddy.* Not that it mattered when he was already dead.

But it couldn't be an accident. Not with the rumbling in my bones...not with my reputation among the Hunt at stake. If I couldn't solve this crime, I'd be mocked at best. At worst, I'd be shunned from the investigative arm and join the subset of Hunter who could never touch the ground again without crumbling to dust.

But if I did solve it, I might get my own hound. Clearly King Herla believed I had a chance, or else he wouldn't have left me here while he chased the delinquent pixies.

I knelt down to look under the table for more clues. Beside seven more old fashioned tumblers, I caught my first real clue: a burgundy leather wallet. I flipped it open—my year-dead fingerprints wouldn't muddle any non-supernatural investigation—to reveal a driver's license, student ID, health insurance card, three credit cards, a bus pass, and twenty-six dollars.

The victim—a Sandy McGrath—didn't have much cash, but he did have a number of receipts for fast food and expensive liquor. I'd never drunk forty-year Laphroaig, but I knew connoisseurs probably cared about it. The rest of the alcohol on the list, however, was Pabst and boxed wine. I had to hope that meant he'd planned to save the Scotch for himself and serve the rest to party guests.

...which would explain the truly staggering number of glasses and nutshells, too many for one man with any sense of cleanliness.

I ducked back under the table to see what else I could find.

Five empty bags of potato chips. The bags crackled as I smoothed them and stacked them to the side in order to get further back. My eyes adjusted to the dimness under the oaken tabletop where the smoky sparks from the Yule log couldn't reach.

Yes! They revealed my second clue, one far more promising than a wallet. A prosthetic leg. Someone at the victim's party had left it behind, and I hoped that someone would be anxious to get it back. Though it did beg the question: what sort of person left a leg behind when abandoning a party? Perhaps the owner and the victim had a vicious fight, and the owner had left in a hurry.

A fight would be motive.

I fished the leg out and wiped crumbs and dust off the waxy surface. The limb bore carvings and whorls that suggested wings rising up from the ankles. It looked more like a boot than a prosthetic at this distance and bore an *avant garde* high heeled shoe that I was sure matched the owner's wardrobe. The leg's owner—female, by the style of shoe and slenderness of calf-shape—had spent money for artistry.

Maybe it belonged to a mythology student, one who wanted to emulate Hermes with feathered feet. A mythology student could be a killer. Our Cinderella would be steeped in crimes of passion.

And she couldn't have gotten far, not one-legged.

A knock came from the door. Then a giggly shrieking, and the cabin door creaked open, washing me with sharp-cold air and yellowing dawn light. I was keenly aware of my position, crouched on the floor next to a dead body with an artistic leg-bludgeon in my hand. I straightened, knowing the damage was already done.

But I supposed I looked no weirder than the couple at the door. My first, best, only suspect—for how many one-legged ladies would come to this cottage, fighting through the falling snow in the earliest hours of the day?—clung to a broad shouldered college boy. They both looked young to me, freshmen or sophomores on a Christmas-break party tour. Her thick black hair hung over his arm like King Herla's horse blanket.

My skin pricked from the chill, but my supernatural bones stayed quiet.

The blond boy was easy with his smiles, possibly still drunk. That'd probably clear up once the couple got far enough inside to see the body hidden by the couch arm. "Hey there." Or maybe he was sex drunk, from the rasping edge to his words. "Greg Doran. This is Kiana Mahelona."

"Tyson Wallenstein," I introduced myself and stuck out a hand to shake.

Kiana slithered to the floor and propped herself against a wall, freeing Greg to complete the introduction ritual. "Oh!" She noticed what I held in my other hand and made come-hither motions for her leg.

As a piece of evidence, it was only good as proof she'd been there, and now I didn't have to hunt her down. Easily I handed it over.

She slipped her thigh into the bootlike top, and bent over to adjust some buckles. "Please don't make any 'pulling my leg' jokes." Kiana raised her head enough to roll her eyes in solidarity with me against such jokesters.

9

"I would never." I let her get back to her comfortable place before springing the question. I wanted an honest reaction, not one tainted by strange neck positions. Then: "Could you tell me how you knew the victim?"

"What?!" She flew upright, flailing arm knocking into Greg's shoulder. *Is he her boyfriend? Hookup?* "Ohmygod. Whatsisname is dead?!" Kiana tottered, quickly supported by her trusty Greg; he settled her into the crook of his arm.

Wow. She'd left a leg here, and she didn't even know the guy's name. That said something about something, but I wasn't sure what. I really could've used another Hunter on this, but that's what happens when you take a case no one else wants and stake your entire afterlife on it, I guess. I went fishing; "If you've never met him..."

The boy answered, thank goodness. "Oh, we've met him. We were partying here earlier tonight, along with a few other cottage campers. But Kiana and I...we...that is, she finally decided..." After taking an elbow in the ribs from the woman in his arms, Greg settled on, "We left early and only came back to get Kiana's leg."

I hadn't been sure the Hunt's magic would work for me until this guy started answering my questions. By rights, he should've called the police and accused me of being the killer. Instead, he treated me like a law enforcement officer. "And you just *left* her leg here?" It still seemed weird to me.

Greg pulled his lady-love tighter against his side. "We were in a hurry, and it wasn't like she was using it at the time."

"Ohmygod," Kiana said again, sound muffled in her palm-shield. "I wanna clean my leg and go home."

Her lover stroked her hair. "It'll be okay," he whispered, though my preternatural ears picked him up just fine. "I'll be right here with you."

"Not back to my mistletoe-infested cabin. *Home.*"

The boy clutched at her. "Hey, no, it's gonna be okay. This nice detective is going to figure out what happened, and we're all going to be fine. Right, Detective?"

I was more interested in the infestation. "You don't like mistletoe?"

The guy shrugged. "We think the proprietor's been putting mistletoe in everyone's cabins for us. Like, we didn't buy any, y'know, but he's got keys to all the cabins, so it makes sense."

Kiana sniffed. Her smooth cheeks had salty tear tracks, like striped sheets or tiny pixie handprints. "I've got a dog. It's not safe for him to be around it. I was thinking of going home if the mistletoe didn't go away, but then I met Greg."

He gazed down into her eyes and spoke in an intimate whisper, "I'm so glad you stayed. We still have another two weeks."

I was pretty sure he'd forgotten I was there.

"Not if there's a killer!"

These college kids were way too interested in sex and alcohol to expend the energy for murder. Besides, if they were telling the truth, and the victim—Sandy—had been alive when they'd left for their *nocturnal activities*, then they couldn't have killed him. And if they were lying about that, then they still had alibis. Even if those alibis were each other.

Before poor Greg could argue his position with Kiana, I asked, "Did the deceased have any enemies?"

Greg rolled his eyes. "The guy was the master of parties. Everyone loved him. Free beer!"

But Kiana was more thoughtful. Slowly she said, "My cabin's the closest one to here. That's why Greg and I went back to my place for our hookup last night."

Greg frowned at the word *hookup*.

"I didn't think anything of it at the time—" Kiana bit her lip. "—but I overheard him arguing with someone yesterday. Something about keeping to the deal. But then my dog started barking, so I didn't get more than that. He hates loud noises. Loves playing with balls and birds but not if they're squeaky toys, you know?"

I thanked them for the information and shooed them off. I wasn't sure about this mysterious deal, but I'd keep an eye out. Maybe the cottages' owner would know who had grievances against Sandy McGrath.

The morning sun sparkled on the snow drifts, and I fished polarized sunglasses from my saddlebags before swinging onto my midnight-maned mare. Overnight snowfall had undoubtedly closed the pass, and I'm sure we were both glad to be already dead in this brutal cold. The pair of us set off for the owner's cabin, whose location I'd plotted on a camp map at the victim's chalet.

The owner, a Mr. Davies according to his name placard, wasn't at his cabin.

Maybe he'd run off in the night while I'd been inspecting McGrath's cabin. Maybe the victim was a terrible tenant and the owner'd had enough of loud parties. Maybe I'd catch up with the perpetrator at the pass, capture him, judge him, kill him, and eat his soul.

Well, more likely I'd give his soul to King Herla when the Hunt returned from finding the missing pixies. My king would accept the proof that I deserved to be a full-fledged member before he committed the final execution. Maybe I'd get a Hunt dog of my own, a deep black hound to howl my rage and share its centuries of experience.

That all depended on finding my suspect.

What were those pixies *eating* anyway? I shook my head. Well, that wasn't my investigation, and the rest of the Hunt knew what it was doing. They'd probably traced some short-lived cows or sheep by now, their little pixie problem well in hand. I needed to do the same with my case.

My horse and I cantered toward the other cabins, weaving between pine-scented trees and their inconvenient roots until the wooded quiet was broken by a *pfft pfft pfft*.

Hunting the sound, we came across a stooped man in a tattered down jacket spritzing a broken tree. It was a little late in the season for that kind of maintenance; he should've sealed the trees before the snow fell. Splintered branches piled at his side, and his face bore the lines of exhausted age. My bones shivered in sympathy, which meant he'd been touched by the supernatural somehow. Maybe it was related to my case.

"Freeze!" I said, only realizing afterward how ridiculous it sounded. I wasn't a real cop; he wasn't running away. And it was already pretty frozen out.

He flung the spray bottle in the air and whirled to look up at me. "Augh!" he said, startled. When I didn't move, he brought a hand up over his heart and squinted. "Who are you? What do you want? No, I'm not fixing the hot tub. Been too tired to get around to it, just like the pre-winter pruning."

It had been over a year since I'd enjoyed a hot tub. I pressed my lips thin to make my expression stern. "I'm here about the dead body in one of your cabins."

"What? Who was it?" He tilted his head at me, then shook it. "Terrible thing. No one's going to want to stay where there's been a murder. Have to call someone to get the body."

That sounded like the opposite of motive. But I knew he still had the means, and he was too calm. Either that or exhausted, like a pixie had stolen his energy away. "Some of your guests mentioned you've been using your cabin keys to hang mistletoe. Is it true you can get into every cabin?"

Davies grumbled and bent, excruciatingly slowly, to reclaim his tree spray.

I tacked on, "And the victim was Sandy McGrath."

He snorted and walked away from me at a surprising clip, moving on to the next broken tree on snow-sure feet. My horse trotted behind him, and we kept up easily. "Course I have keys, but I haven't been in any cabins this year. Kids've been vaguely talented at holding onto their keys when they get drunk. I gave 'em to Sandy at one point, even. He was *supposed* to help me clear out the stupid mistletoe. That stuff is toxic, you know." Davies stressed *supposed* with all the sarcasm a disgruntled old man could muster.

"I take it he wasn't good at mistletoe cleanup."

Davies had his back to me, spritzing the tree. "We had a deal. Little **mumble** loved decorations too much, though. Wouldn't do it. So I made him give 'em back. Brat must've died just to spite me. *Tch*. Bad enough that dog's been hanging around. This was one of the last places people saw the Wild Hunt back in the '20s, y'know. If we got deaths *and* giant black dogs, I'm going to go broke."

The irony wasn't lost on me.

Mr. Davies was made of exhausted old age and probably wouldn't fix that hot tub before he died himself of natural causes. He couldn't have killed the victim. Not only was it bad for his business, but he didn't have the strength for a quick kill.

I didn't have the kind of luck that would make his dog sighting an actual Hunt dog. Too bad. I could've used the help because now I was stuck. From what I could tell so far, other than the feeling in my bones, this looked like an accident. With only half a day to go before the Wild Hunt returned to collect me, I had no suspects, no clues, no way to prove I deserved anything other than an eternity on horseback, isolated from all but the worst assignments. King Herla would not be pleased.

"Hey! Hey!" Davies gained a bit of energy and took off at twice his walking speed. He shook a fist at a black dot in the distance in a manner that I'd never seen happen in real life. "You!"

I took off after him, spurring my steed. When I passed him, he bent over double and rasped, "You take care of it," before heading back to his damaged trees. Good, that would leave me unfettered.

In a clearing, I caught up with Kiana's sleek inky dog. I pushed up my sunglasses to look him over without polarization. His eyes were smaller than a Hunt dog's, less piercing, and his twitching ears cocked toward the copse from which I'd plunged. He stood shorter as well, barely up to my thighs if I'd been on the ground. His paw prints made stark impressions in the snow coat, and a clump of mistletoe waited at his feet.

The mistletoe dripped with white berries whose black spots made me shiver; it was as though they were watching me. The bunch was in disturbingly good condition for having been carried in a hound's mouth. Even the blood-red ribbon that held the stems together appeared perfect and unrumpled from my vantage point.

14

I slid from my horse and grabbed a bone from my saddlebag, tossing it to the dog in front of me. The canine's head swung, following the movement, but it remained where it was. I approached on slow feet.

A bark rang through the glade. I did not falter but continued my advance. Another bark and my bones hummed. Close enough, I darted forward and snatched up the green-white-red bouquet. I ran my fingers over the velveteen ribbon, letting the texture fill the wrinkled spaces in my dead skin.

The thickly muscled dog dashed to the tree line, yipped, then ran back to nose at my hip.

I couldn't help myself. "You want to fetch?" I threw the bundle a few yards, and he chased after it.

Strange that a dog should be so attracted to a wad of poisonous flowers. Perhaps I should've switched out the mistletoe for something less doggy-deadly. Wouldn't it rather have an old-fashioned stick? My playmate pranced back to my side and dropped the plant at my feet.

"Go long," I said and faux-threw it.

The dog dashed off, fooled, and I sighed. At least I had these last few moments on the ground to remember before King Herla consigned me to horseback forever. All I'd managed to do was clear suspects and play fetch with a bunch of mistletoe.

I loosened my grip on the leaves in my grasp and smoothed the round green fronds back out, not worried about the poisonous oils. I was already dead. What could happen?

They didn't need much smoothing.

This mistletoe reminded me of the one in my victim's mouth. It could have been an optical trick, but...I counted the stems and checked their lengths against my fingers. As far as I could tell, this was exactly the same posy as my first clue.

It couldn't be coincidence.

But if no guests had brought the mistletoe and if Mr. Davies hadn't provided it, then how had it gotten here? It had to be from a supernatural source, because my bones still made those sympathetic vibrations, and there was no one around except for me and the dog.

And the mistletoe.

Loudly, making sure my voice would carry all the way to the trees, I announced, "That's odd." I felt silly talking to the empty woods. "I think I'll dissect this plant for clues."

The vibration in my femurs turned to a shudder in my hands, and I pitched the mistletoe just as it changed form. It returned like a vicious boomerang, one bearing needle-shaped teeth. A pixie!

It screeched and charged me. Those opaque white berries had turned to pinprick eyes. I ducked out of its path, but green leaves had become wing blades that clipped my cheek beneath my sunglasses. First blood.

"Hunter," the pixie accused in the glade's silence. "Where is your justice for my dead sister?"

I cast my mind back to the crime scene. A man had been dead—no one's sister—with his inhaler beside him. His teeth had gripped the mistletoe firmly in his mouth. Mistletoe. Just like the shapeshifter in front of me. "Did she murder that man?" A sleeping asthmatic's pathways were delicate. It could have been an accident.

A thorn-sharp nail punctured the tip of my nose, and I reared back. "We won't leave! This is our home. *Our* hunting lodge."

Our?

The pixie warbled, half out of my hearing range, then it rushed me once more. Again I dodged, but it rounded and hissed in my ear, "The humans don't need all that life breath." I swatted at it, protecting my lobes from soul-sucking piercings. A pixie fed on breath, cutting short its victim's lifespan. Usually that victim was farm-raised livestock, but a deep stab could give it the chance to suck even my magical-self dry, like a vampire bat on a baby.

It warbled again, which turned into a chorus. Then into a discordant symphony.

I was surrounded by pixies. Buried in flapping wings and the smell of old age and mothballs and cheap liquor.

Buried in biting teeth that made tiny rents in my flesh. Then punctures inside those rents.

I ran for my horse, not that I had a weapon or a cage handy, but maybe I could escape. Each step was danger. They were herding me, swarming me. One bounced off my sunglasses, creating a crack in the world. I ran and dodged and sank into the Yule-time snow.

My mouth opened to suck in air, and a pixie flew nearly inside to stop my panting. Like my murder victim had, I chomped down.

I spat the pixie's carcass to the harsh white ground, making brown and green streaks on the snow. Immediately, another sneaked into my mouth to take its place. Bite, spit. And another and another.

A great warble rose up, a higher pitch. A faster vibration. Anger but not retreat.

My first nemesis closed in. "Why won't you die already?"

I inhaled to answer, and the lead pixie flapped its wings backward. It stole my breath.

Like it was stealing its victims' lives. The perfect crime: eat the years from the end of a human's span, and no one would notice if the human got a little tired and died before its time. Unless the pixie got greedy enough to drain a whole life at once...or was accidentally bitten by a desperate asthmatic.

But it couldn't suck *my* life along with my breath. I snatched the pixie out of my mouth and held it still, heedless of its shrieks. "I'm already dead," I told it.

I forged ahead toward my horse, and my swarming enemies followed. This was why we had horses. This was what the Hunt was made for: triumph over our prey!

It was the work of mere minutes to incarcerate them in my saddlebags, starting with the one grasped in my hand. I may not have expected pixies, but I could give them to King Herla with pride. I'd found my suspects and solved the murder.

Of course, I had to wait for King Herla and the rest of the Wild Hunt to come back to me. By the time twilight fell, I'd checked and rechecked the victim's chalet for anything incriminatingly supernatural. Then I sat out on the frozen wooden doorstep with my eyes on the path we'd all taken before I was left to my solitary investigation. The purple night was turning quickly to pure raven-black.

The cabin's front door bore a holly wreath, and the pine trees dropped pinecones in the cycle of life. But no mistletoe berries or rounded leaves. There wasn't a single sprig of mistletoe anywhere around as far as I could see.

Those pixies were burning a metaphorical hole in my saddlebags. All I had to do was give them to my king and get my commendation, but the dark wasn't black enough yet for the Hunt to arrive. I was ready to prove my worth.

Soon.

Two people approached through the cold wind. They came on foot and without hounds. This wasn't the Hunt.

"Hello there, detective!" Greg called out. He smelled of too much cologne, and his breath came in white puffs that evaporated into nothingness like the pointless talk they were.

Kiana, far more observant than her holiday hookup, noticed the fullness of my saddlebags. "You're leaving?" Her voice ticked up in pitch, nervous. "You can't go before you're sure of what happened."

I was sure enough for the Wild Hunt's justice. My bones sat quiet.

Greg patted her shoulder and frowned when she shook him off. "It's safe now, right? Kiana shouldn't leave, right? Especially while the pass is still closed, right?"

Kiana abandoned him, striding toward me on steadier-than-organic legs. "Don't let Greg put words in your mouth." Her order was as implacable as King Herla's.

But it was true. She really didn't have to go unless she wanted to. The pixies weren't coming back. "I'm satisfied that he died of natural causes," I told her, gently and firmly. Our eyes met, and I made mine as sincere as a Hunt hound's, though I was telling her lies. My intent was true, if my words were not. "This was an unfortunate accident brought on by the combination of alcohol and asthma. Nothing for you to worry about." That was probably what human justice would find.

Her head cocked as she evaluated my answer and my motivations.

"Actually, your dog helped in my investigation," I said. She preened a bit, her shoulders shifting under her down jacket. "He had a mistletoe clump that he shouldn't have been gnawing, and we figured out that it was the kind with berries to choke on."

Greg's fingers curled in Kiana's jacket from behind, and she let herself be reeled into his embrace, secure in her pseudo-knowledge. He said, "Thank you so much for your work, Detective. We appreciate it."

Kiana twined her gloves with his. "So many people get scared about Rex because he's so big and black."

A big, black dog was my dream. I couldn't remember a time when it hadn't been, even if I'd died only a measly year ago. "You can tell all your friends how helpful your Rex was."

Kiana nodded, exaggerated and resolute. "Have a good night," she bade.

Greg trailed in her wake as they disappeared, undoubtedly off to celebrate their newfound safety.

As soon as they left, the woods filled with howling and baying. The Wild Hunt had returned to reclaim their own, and they filled the gaps in the clearing surrounding my victim's chalet with torches and a blackness that ate the night like fire. Hooves stamped at the packed ground.

King Herla's steed, taller than the rest, pressed through the crowd to whicker before me. "Fill me in as we ride," he ordered. "The delinquent pixies I promised to find are more slippery than expected. My reputation fails with every day they go unseen." He cursed. "I still feel them nearby..."

Helpless to obey, I slid a foot into the stirrup and swung up to sit beside him on my own mount. I couldn't help the smile that ached in my jaw joints, though my fingers mushed sweatily on the reins. "Maybe the pixies in my bags are the ones you're looking for."

19

The lines in his timeless face all shifted position, rippling like a lake. "You have my pixies?"

"Maybe." I explained the mysterious death and the shapeshifting mistletoe as our horses stamped the snowy ground. "And I even got in a perk for our grim dog PR too."

King Herla raced to the front of our column, and his horse reared—a victorious silhouette against the moon. "Tomorrow you may eat, drink, and make merry," he called to us. "But tonight..." I heard the smile under his beard. "Tonight we ride!"

With a great howl, we streamed into the evening's cold. We rode to return the wayward members to King Herla's pixie-clients; the perpetrators would be sentenced to justice. The Hunt had fulfilled its duties in this region. Once the exchange was made, we would move on to another location, another injustice in our busy Yule season.

A Hunt dog dropped into place beside me, black as the inside of a snowed-in cave and all mine. I was ready to work the next case with my new partner.

The original title for this story was "The Mistletoe Did It." Not only because no one would believe the conclusion was in the title, but because it would be funny. This was going to be a whole running joke that spurred sarcastic lines like, "Yeah, right. Next you'll tell me the mistletoe did it." Until my SO came up with the pixies-as-mistletoe concept, that was all I knew about the story. (My SO has been known to have brilliant plot ideas.) From there, everything flowed.

I'm still sad no detective gets to shout, "The mistletoe did it!" at a mysterious dinner party.

Janine A. Southard

ESCAPE FROM OLD YORKTOWN

BY G. CLEMANS

Do you remember those field trips in school where you visited a "real life" working medieval village? A place full of characters strumming lutes, juggling knives for the king, and functioning in tight corsets? Take that memory and make it a working Victorian village, then lob in a runaway teen and a rising revolution. If you've ever worked a faire or living village, you'll recognize the sarcastic bite and humor to this story, and if you haven't, well...you'll learn to appreciate those who do!   —Raven Oak

We wish you a Merry Christmas, we wish you a Merry Christmas..." Lizzie struggled to put spirit in her voice as she harmonized with the rest of the young women. The yellow gas-glow of a streetlamp couldn't melt the snowflakes that settled on their capes and mantles. For once she was grateful for her green velvet bonnet. Passersby paused on the sidewalk to listen to the carolers before ducking into the various charming shops that lined the street.

Lizzie snuck her I.G. datapad out from her white muff. No Inter-Galactic texts. Of course. Sometimes she wondered if this backward planet's policy of scrambling I.G. waves was set up just to make her life miserable.

Beside her, Meghan (Little Miss "I'm So Authentic") jabbed an elbow into Lizzie's side without missing a note. Lizzie glared down at the petite, ash-haired girl. What was up with Meghan's sickeningly angelic face?

She must practice in a mirror making her mouth into a perfect, lovely O.

Lizzie shoved her pad back into the muff, faked a smile, and finished the song with the rest of the group. "...*And a Happy New Year!*"

Mrs. Harader, the round-faced, round-bodied entertainment manager, smiled at the tourists. "Thank you for visiting Old Yorktown where the spirit of Victorian Earth is alive and well. Please stop by our seasonal Christmas boutique. Enjoy your evening!"

The plump woman's red plaid dress swished as she turned back to the choir of teenage girls. "Thank you, ladies. Break time. Be back here in thirty minutes."

Thank the freakin' stars. Lizzie found her best friend Cab and linked arms with her. Sure, it was officially recommended behavior for Yorktown employees to stroll arm in arm—it looked all quaint and chummy for the tourists—but she and Cab did it because it was the best way to quietly mock everything around them.

They sauntered right down the street, avoiding the sidewalk crowded with visitors who came to the faux Victorian village for holiday shopping and old-fashioned (boring) fun. Even though Lizzie had moved to Earth over three years ago after her mom had gotten the job as town manager, she still couldn't believe how many people came from around the galaxy for a glimpse into old timey life.

Lizzie's heavy green skirt pushed against Cab's sky blue one. She dropped her voice. "Hey, you wanna go have a smoke? I nicked some cigs from the tobacconist shop."

Cab grinned at her, flashing the space between her teeth that Cab hated but Lizzie loved. It kept her from looking too perfect. Even the ridiculous sky blue bonnet worked on Cab, framing her blue eyes and blond hair. Lizzie had to admit Mrs. Harader had chosen Cab's costume well.

Still, Lizzie couldn't stand the way they were dressed up like dolls. Mrs. Harader had chosen the green for Lizzie because "it brought out her auburn hair and hazel eyes." Disgusting.

They were all just part of the scenery, figurines in a life-sized diorama that was completely irrelevant to the big, exciting universe out there.

Cab whispered, "Why, Elizabeth Braynor, smoking? I am so shocked I practically have the vapors."

The cardinal rule was to stay in character while at work. And smoking was definitely not in character for Victorian ladies.

Cab continued, "But seriously, you know Mrs. Harader would smell smoke and then dock us for costume cleaning. And I'm really close to having enough money for an I.G. transport ticket." She paused. "Sorry, Lizzie. I really wish you could escape for a while, too."

"Me, too, but I'm broke. Besides, you know my mom never wants me to go anywhere." Lizzie sighed. "Although sometimes I wonder if she'd even know if I took off, she's so busy with Yorktown business. She's like this weird combination of overly protective and totally absent mom."

"It takes a lot to run this place, I guess."

They stopped in the middle of Main Street, the intersection of the T-shaped town. Main Street ran along the top of the T; visitors entered from the west, taking shuttle busses from the flight station a few miles away. The long vertical of the T led south to Queen's Bridge and into the village green beyond.

"Let's not talk about the formidable Harriet Braynor for a while," Lizzie said. "How about we go out to the green and pretend we're on a planet far, far away. I'm going bonkers tonight."

They waited for a horse-drawn buggy to roll by, then hurried across the street and down the narrow road to Queen's Bridge. The long, timbered span, rife with icy patches, took a while to cross.

Stepping off the bridge, they strolled toward the gazebo at the edge of the village green. During Post Fusion Reconstruction, the town planners had done it right, creating a perfect sightline from the center of Main Street, across the bridge to the gazebo, and out to the field beyond. It was all so goddamned picturesque.

They walked onto the snowy field. The cold seeped further into Lizzie's laced-up boots. In summer, a country faire (yes, faire with an "e") was held here, but now it was just a flat expanse of white, bordered by a row of trees on the far side.

"I know all this gets to you," Cab said, "But it really is a beautiful night."

The snow had stopped falling and white stars peeked through the clouded night sky. Lizzie missed her home planet, Kepler. She missed electric raves and flightpod travel. She missed lightweight, temp-controlled, form fitting outfits. She missed hanging out with people who had new opinions and galactic perspectives.

But Cab was right: Earth was a beautiful planet. Beautiful. Quiet. Boring.

A line of yellow lights burst into view, flashing in and out of the clouds at a distance. Lizzie gasped, "What the hell is that?"

"An Inter-Galactic transporter? No, way too small for that. Whatever it is, it's right in the middle of our no-fly zone."

"How did it get through?"

"I don't know but it's coming closer. Fast."

They stumbled backward toward the gazebo. The yellow lights careened toward the village green. Lizzie could now make out the shape—an individual flightpod, like a tiny, pudgy glider. It zoomed lower and lower at a steep diagonal, barely clearing the row of trees.

It was oddly quiet. No sound of a motor, just the whooshing of air. Lizzie glanced back toward Main Street, which seemed so far away now. No one noticed that a glider was about to crash land in a no-fly zone. Everyone continued on with their goddamned jolly business. Even if she yelled, even if they could hear her, what could anyone do?

"Lizzie, run!" Cab grabbed her hand and pulled her up into the gazebo, as if the white filigreed structure would offer any protection. Not when the glider was going to crash right into them.

The glider pulled up, bringing its belly parallel to the ground. It bumped down a few times and skidded along the snow, leaving a dark furrow behind it. Metal flaps popped up from its wings—the pilot was trying to slow down. It slid and slid until finally, the small white flightpod shushed to a stop just a few feet from the gazebo.

Lizzie said, "Holy freakin' stars."

They hurried down the gazebo steps and approached the small glider. The tinted cockpit dome clicked open on one side and a gloved hand pushed the dome all the way open. Inside the cockpit sat a young guy with a crooked grin.

Lizzie gasped. She knew him. Well, she recognized him. Everyone would, even in this deliberately backward town. The pilot was J.D. Plisskin, the teenage son of the President of the Galaxy.

They stared at him. He stared at them, grinning. Was he in shock?

J.D. smiled even wider. "I haven't traveled back in time or anything, have I?"

Both girls laughed, despite the warning bells that clanged in Lizzie's head. This boy had a bad reputation. He partied. He flew around the galaxy like he owned it. She was not going to be wowed just because he was famous. And cultured. And—oh, stars, why not admit it?—very, very cute.

Lizzie reined in her smile and busted out her sarcasm. "Welcome to Old Yorktown, Earth, where misplaced sentimentality and technological repression are alive and well."

He chuckled and tilted his head. "I made it all the way to Earth? Huh. Old Yorktown sounds familiar. It's one of those living history museums set up during Reconstruction, right? Supposed to be really authentic."

Lizzie tried to be subtle as she rolled her eyes at Cab, but the boy noticed.

"What? What did I say?"

Cab intervened. "Oh, nothing, it's just that when you live here and work here, the whole 'authentic' thing starts to get really annoying. Especially for Lizzie."

The boy nodded at Lizzie. "Well, Lizzie, thank you for the warm welcome. I'm J.D." He turned back to Cab. "And you are?"

"Cab. Don't ask what it's short for."

"You girls are sassy. I like it."

Lizzie didn't even try to hide her eye roll this time.

He laughed and reached for his harness buckle. As he bent his neck, he winced in pain. Cab, once again proving she was a better person than Lizzie, stepped forward. "Are you okay? That was quite a landing."

J.D. tilted his head from side to side. "Neck's a little tender, but I'm fine." He shrugged off the harness and climbed out of the cockpit. He was slim and tall, taller than Lizzie had expected. How in the Galaxy did he fit into that tiny cockpit?

He looked back at the long furrow in the snow. "It was quite a landing, though, right? I'm kind of a tech guy, so all that was totally unexpected. I was aiming for whichever off-grid zone was closest—not exactly yours—I guess my controls got screwed up. I lost my lift."

Lizzie said, "I'm no aviation expert, but isn't taking an interplanetary, nighttime flight into an off-grid zone really dangerous in that little thing?"

He leveled a mock-serious look at her. "Why, yes. Yes, it is."

"So, what were you thinking?"

"I was thinking it would be fun to take a really dangerous interplanetary, nighttime flight into an off-grid zone in this little thing." He grinned and circled the glider, looking for damage. "Looks okay, I guess."

J.D. faced them again. "So. I have a big favor to ask. I wasn't exactly supposed to go out tonight. And I kind of ditched my security teams." He shot an embarrassed glance their way. "Um, I don't know if you know who I am."

Lizzie actually felt kind of sorry for him. She smiled. "Well, we are cut off here, but we get the occasional news of your...adventures."

He ran a hand through his unruly brown hair. "All right, all right. Every once in a while I get away from my crazy father and try to have some zippin' fun. But someone always recognizes me, and then everyone swarms with their datapads, and photos circulate all over the galaxy. Photos of me, wild-eyed, trying to run away."

Lizzie laughed. "It's true. Your eyes are always wild."

"Exactly. So I zipped out last night and things got out of hand, I guess, and I woke up not remembering anything, and my father pretty much grounded me. Put an extra security team on me and everything. But, zaggit, I'm eighteen and—." He interrupted himself, looking sheepish. "Sorry. Poor me and my family drama."

Lizzie cocked her head. A few times lately, she'd over-heard her mom ranting to Mrs. Harader about the President's increasingly erratic behavior. As if that had any-thing to do with their insular life in Yorktown.

J.D. continued, "I know it's a lot to ask, but I wonder if you would help me stay incognito. Maybe just for a little while, I could feel, I don't know, normal."

"Well, life isn't exactly normal here," Lizzie said. She glanced at Cab, who shrugged. "But okay. Sounds like you could use some downtime, and we sure as hell could go for something new. But holy stars, hiding a famous guest has gotta be against Yorktown policy."

The snow had started falling again, already covering the glider's tracks. Lizzie looked back toward Main Street in the distance. Everyone still bustled about, in and out of shops. With the double blinders of nostalgia and consumerism, no one had noticed a thing.

The three teenagers spent the next twenty minutes dragging the tiny flightpod into the huge gray barn. The glider was surprisingly light—nothing but the latest technology for this guy. The hardest part was Lizzie and Cab tripping over their voluminous skirts.

After stowing the glider toward the back of the cavernous barn, they collapsed on hay bales lining the walls. Lizzie breathed in the warm air, sweet with the smell of leather and hay. All too soon, Cab opened the locket watch pinned to her sky blue gown.

"That's a zippin' little gizmo," J.D. said.

Cab sighed. "From my parents for my eighteenth birthday. I would have preferred something more 22nd century. But they are total Victoriana freaks."

"So you must have an old-fashioned name. Something like Cabrina?"

"It's Cab. Just Cab." With a flounce of her blond curls, she turned her back on him and faced Lizzie. "Break time's almost over."

Crap. Lizzie did not feel like going back out there to be merry and bright. She leaned toward J.D. "Our choir has one more performance tonight."

"Cool! I'll come watch. I'll blend in with the tourists."

Lizzie looked him up and down. His white pants and shirt were really nice, the latest in temp-controlled menswear. Not exactly ordinary. And definitely worthless in covering his oh-so-recognizable face and floppy brown hair.

She said, "Yeah, I don't think you'd last a minute without being spotted. And listen, this is serious. If any of the managers find out we hid a glider in the barn and are fraternizing with a guest, they could level some major fines at us. Could you just hang out here? We won't be too long."

Cab added, "After our last set, we have a short shift of historical improv and then we're done for the night."

J.D.'s crooked grin reappeared. "Wait, come again? Historical improv?"

Lizzie sighed. "Yeah. We pretend like we're shopping or chatting or whatever. When we're done, we'll come back and figure out what to do with you."

They closed up the barn with the President's son inside and raced back over the bridge, shrieking when they hit a couple of icy spots. When they reached Main Street, they slowed and fell into character.

Breathing hard, they sidled up to the rest of the carolers, already in quaint formation. Little Meghan flung Lizzie a look of disapproval before facing Mrs. Harader, lips in a perfect O, ready to sing.

With a swish of her red plaid dress, Mrs. Harader addressed the gathering crowd. "Good evening, ladies and gentlemen. Thank you for visiting Old Yorktown. We nineteenth-century citizens of Earth enjoy singing holiday carols, sometimes going door-to-door in a tradition called *wassailing*."

Mrs. Harader designed her little speeches to be mildly educational for visitors and to signal the set of songs for the choir. The choir leader flicked her hand three times and the young women started singing in perfect unison:

"Here we come a-wassailing
Among the leaves so green;
Here we come a-wand'ring
So fair to be seen."

Lizzie was about to stare off over the audience's heads when someone in the crowd caught her attention. An older woman with a shock of white hair. The white-haired tourist leaned forward, practically glaring at the carolers. Sheesh, Happy Holidays to you too, lady.

Lizzie glanced at Mrs. Harader, who had taken her usual position off to the side so she could observe both choir and audience. Mrs. Harader's gaze had also been caught by the white-haired visitor.

At the end of the song, Mrs. Harader cleared her throat and announced, "Our last carol of the evening will be *It Came Upon a Midnight Clear*."

Lizzie's eyebrows shot up and there was a rustle of skirts around her. Mrs. Harader had changed the line-up of songs, and she *never* changed the line-up of songs. But there she

was, round and plaid, flicking her hands three times for them
to begin. Right on cue, they began to sing.

"It came upon the midnight clear
That glorious song of old
From angels bending near the earth
To touch their harps of gold."

Now something else in the crowd caught Lizzie's
attention. A pair of dark eyes were fixed on her, eyes that
peered out from under the brim of an old-fashioned cap.
Unruly, dark hair escaped from the cap. J.D.

Half his face was covered with a red scarf, but he was
clearly pleased with himself. He gave them a little flourish, as
if to say, "Hey, check out my outfit." Simple brown over-
coat, rumpled vest, and too-short, tan trousers hovered
above rough black boots. He'd rummaged through the old
farmhouse.

Lizzie sighed. *Well, there's another rule broken.* All
costumes had to be assigned by unit leaders. Hopefully with
all the seasonal employees roaming around, no one would
notice an unfamiliar Victorian farmer. *Good thing her mom
was working in her office tonight instead of making the
rounds on Main Street. Harriet Braynor would spot him in
an instant.*

They finished their song, and as Mrs. Harader gave her
closing remarks to the tourists, Meghan rammed her elbow
into Lizzie's side.

"Dammit, Meghan, what the hell?"

Meghan's high-pitched voice was more annoying than
ever. "Language, Elizabeth. Who's that?" Meghan flicked her
head toward J.D.

"Looks like a farmer."

"Well, duh. I mean, what's his name? You guys were
ogling each other for like half of *Midnight Clear.*"

"I have no idea what you're talking about. But I'll go
find out." Lizzie spun away from the ash-haired girl, linked
arms with Cab, and marched up to J.D.

Meghan minced—oh so authentically—after them. Lizzie raised her voice and said, "Pardon my boldness, good sir, but are you visiting our fair town from the countryside?"

J.D. cocked his head. Cab leaned in and whispered, "There's someone behind us who will report us if we're not in character."

Cab gestured to the shops to the west along Main Street. "May we show you some of Old Yorktown's fine establishments?"

J.D. cleared his throat. "I thank thee, fair maidens."

Lizzie shook her head and whispered, "Too Medieval. Jump forward about five hundred years."

He whispered back, "I have no zaggin' idea what's thou speaketh of. I sound zippin' great."

"Maybe you should keep the improv to a minimum."

The girls each took one of his arms and whisked him down the street. Lizzie cast a quick look behind her. Sure enough, Meghan was fuming. There was no way she'd chase after them, demanding to be introduced—that would be way too modern.

For the next hour, they ducked in and out of shops, keeping two steps ahead of Meghan. Even though Lizzie dreaded the idea of J.D. being recognized or Cab getting into trouble, it was the most fun she'd had in a long time.

They took him to all their favorite spots: The Sweet Shoppe, with its syrupy aroma and overpriced penny candy. The dark and moody Apothecary, with its jars and bottles and packets of powders. All conveniently for sale, of course.

In The Millinery (with its oh-so-clever sign reading, "Put a Feather in Your Cap!"), J.D. tried to guess Cab's name while she trimmed a hat with ribbons. "Cabernet? Cabinetry? Cabbage?"

Fiercely ignoring him, Cab made a show of being delighted with her hat and sauntered to the counter to "buy" the hat. One of Lizzie's mom's strategies was "the suggestive purchase." All Yorktowners were given pocket money to spend on items that were immediately returned to the inventory.

31

As Lizzie waited, a tourist marched up to her, the woman with the shock of white hair. In a husky voice, she asked, "Where can I find this shop's manager?"

Lizzie smiled and pointed her toward Miss Catherine, the manager who was pushing fifty and single. Hence the "Miss."

Without a word of thanks, the white-haired woman made a beeline across the shop. Stars, what could possibly be so urgent in a fake Victorian hat shop? Lizzie couldn't help herself; she strolled a little closer to them. The tourist leaned toward Miss Catherine and asked in an artificially casual voice, "Do you have any additional hatbands? I'm looking for two in indigo."

Miss Catherine jerked a tiny bit. She cast a look around and said politely, "Oh, yes, we have some beautiful new bands in the back. Follow me, please."

That was odd. Miss Catherine was one of Yorktown's best employees; she must know it was against the rules to take customers into stockrooms.

At that moment, Meghan sashayed into the shop. She scanned the room while pretending to adjust her ash-colored hair under her gray bonnet. She locked eyes on J.D., who was playing with a pile of dyed ostrich plumes.

Lizzie grabbed J.D., then Cab, and said under her breath. "Come on. I know where we should go for the rest of our shift."

Back on the sidewalk, they dodged tourists until they reached the very end of Main Street. There was nothing beyond it but the shuttle busses that took tourists to and from the nearby flight station. In front of them was a large building with a brightly lit marquee that read, "Victorian Photos and Optical Illusions!"

Lizzie looked back along the busy sidewalk. No sign of Meghan. They stepped inside, into a wide exhibition hall featuring 19th century photographic equipment and optical toys. Guests milled around examining the display cases and playing with hands-on models. There were stereoscopes, zoe-tropes, and Lizzie's personal favorite, phenakistoscopes—

paper discs with images that when spun, blurred together like animation.

J.D. picked up a stereoscope and peered through the viewfinder at a double-imaged card of a woman on a bicycle. He said loudly, "Vintage tech! This is so zippin'!"

A few people turned his way, smiling at his enthusiasm. Lizzie whispered, "I'm beginning to understand why you always get recognized. You're not exactly discreet."

She led them to the far side of the room where two wide doorways boasted heavy red curtains. The sign next to the curtained doorway on the right announced, "Dress Up as a Victorian and Have your Photograph Taken!"

Lizzie nudged them on to the left. The next doorway was accompanied by a slightly desperate sign that read, "Magic Lantern Show—See Glass Slides of Earth's Wonders! (No Ticket Necessary—Come Right In!)"

Lizzie pushed one of the curtains aside and led J.D. and Cab into a small, dimly lit vestibule. On either side were curtained entrances to the theater and in between was a narrow wall with a single flickering sconce. An information plaque rambled on about the popularity of slide shows, "during a time before movies, television, and I.G. datapads!"

Well, they had all those things now, and no one wanted to see these old slide shows. The trio pushed through the curtained entryway and walked into the dark theater. Sure enough, the place was empty.

Cab flounced down in the middle of the back row and J.D. sat next to her, chuckling as he shoved her big skirt aside. Lizzie took the next seat and stripped off her gloves, bonnet, and mantle. Holy stars, it felt good to sit down.

The large screen lit up with hand-tinted photographs projected from a boxy wooden contraption behind them. A soundtrack of tinkling piano music emanated from carefully hidden speakers. There should be live pianists and "lanternists" who plugged each glass slide into the projector, but her mom had rigged up automatic systems. Harriet Braynor had busted out one of her awful business slogans saying, "A small sacrifice of authenticity for cost-saving efficiency."

One after another, the photographs faded on and off the screen, images of now long-gone places on Earth. The leaning Tower of Pisa. The Parthenon in Greece. The pyramids in Egypt.

The 19th century was—what—two hundred years before the Nuclear Fusion Incident? Those places on the screen were around then, but most Victorians would have seen them only in postcards (for sale in the display hall!) or during a show like this.

Still, it must have been nice to think they *could* have visited them. Everyone knew the story—ugh, those endless, repetitive Galactic History lessons back in school. Earthlings had destroyed their own planet with their Nuclear Fusion experiments.

In one of its "shining moments," the brand-new Inter-Galactic Government had swooped in to save a few billion people. It also managed to salvage this small area and designated it as one of the seven living history museums that were scattered across the galaxy.

For some reason, the I.G.G. had allowed those museum zones to be self-governing, which was why Old Yorktown could impose no-fly laws and other tech restrictions that would be unthinkable—undesirable, really—anywhere else in the Galaxy.

The slides flickered on and off the screen. Although it was hard to fully relax in her outfit, Lizzie's breathing slowed and her mind slipped sideways. She was pretty damned comfortable when an image caught her eye.

A woman stood in front of the gothic arches of the Brooklyn Bridge, pointing up at it with a serious expression. The woman's long, dark dress had two wide bands at the hem, tinted a purplish-blue. That dress looked familiar somehow.

At the top of the slide were two handwritten words: Independents Day.

Huh. Did that mean the old Earth holiday, the Fourth of July? But why was it spelled Independents instead of Independence?

A loud, jangling alarm split the air. Lizzie and Cab bolted upright.

"What's going on?" J.D. shouted.

Lizzie and Cab ignored him and stood up, tense and alert. The alarm stopped, and a voice came over a loudspeaker. Lizzie knew it well.

"Ladies and gentlemen, this is Harriet Braynor, manager of Old Yorktown. Please excuse the interruption. An urgent situation has been brought to our attention. Stay tuned for an urgent message from President Plisskin. Thank you."

J.D. was now standing, too.

Another voice came over the loudspeaker. A dramatic, masculine voice. "Fellow Galactans, I seek your assistance tonight. My son, J.D. Plisskin, is missing. My security forces believe he may have been kidnapped in your vicinity. We need your help. Harriet Braynor, manager of Old Yorktown, will inform you of the specific protocols you will follow as the town is searched and evacuated. I urge you to remain calm, be patient, and to consider whether you have seen my son—" The President's voice broke with emotion.

J.D. muttered, "Nice job, Dad. That sounded almost real."

"J.D. is eighteen years old, tall, with dark hair and brown eyes. I thank you for your cooperation and your support during this difficult time. Good Night, Galaxy," he signed off with one of his many catchphrases.

Lizzie and Cab turned to stare at J.D., who looked just as stunned as they did. Lizzie broke the silence. "Holy freakin' stars, J.D. He thinks you've been kidnapped."

Cab added, "And does he think *we* kidnapped you?"

"No. No way," J.D. said. "I mean, they would've put out an alert for you, right? But it is weird, isn't it? Someone must have figured out I was off-grid and taken credit for kidnapping me."

Lizzie asked, "Who in all the stars would want to do that?" J.D. grinned and raised his eyebrows.

"I mean," Lizzie continued, "You're *very* valuable and all, but the Galaxy has been peaceful since Reconstruction. Who would want to use you as a bargaining chip?"

J.D.'s grin disappeared. "A bargaining chip?" His hands flew up to his neck and felt around for a few seconds. Two fingers stopped just under his right ear. "Oh, my God. That zagging bastard."

"What, J.D.?" Lizzie asked.

"This may sound crazy. It is crazy. But I used to be—I guess I still am, zaggit—a sort of walking, talking safe."

"What?" Lizzie was dumbfounded.

He pulled up the sleeve of his simple white shirt to display a series of small, half-moon scars. "Um, yeah, my loving father used to implant digital chips in my arms."

Cab whispered, "Oh my stars."

"Yeah, I know. He's so paranoid, always talking about spies and Independent infiltrators. I guess he thought I was safe storage for top secret information. People used to think he was such a protective dad. Ha. I didn't even know until a few years ago, and I was so—" He stopped and took a breath. "Anyway, that's when I started bolting. I figured if I took off with his precious information, he'd stop putting it in me. And it worked. Or at least I thought it did. Last night when I was passed out, he must have done it again."

A wave of realization passed over his face. "So that's why he was so insistent that I didn't leave the grounds today. That's why he assigned extra security to me. He knows I'm not kidnapped. He's just trying to find the chip."

The loudspeaker interrupted.

"Ladies and gentlemen, this is Harriet Braynor. Inter-Galactic Government Security officers have arrived in Old Yorktown." Her mom's voice was professional but taut with —what?—annoyance? "Together, we have developed the following procedure that will ensure everyone's comfort as the I.G.G.S gathers information. Old Yorktown residents will escort all guests to the two large buildings at either end of Main Street, where you will be interviewed and released. If you are already in line with merchandise, please go ahead and complete your purchases."

Lizzie groaned. "Oh, God, Mom."

"After everyone has gathered in the two exhibition halls, you will be called—alphabetically by last name—to be questioned by I.G.G.S officers. Then please take our courtesy shuttle buses to the flight station for transport off Earth. We hope that you return to Old Yorktown for a more relaxed visit. Thank you."

Cab turned to Lizzie, "I hope you don't take this the wrong way, Lizzie, but this kind of organizational challenge is right up your mom's alley."

"Yeah, but she sounds pissed, doesn't she?" She glanced at J.D. "No offense. But my mom does not like your dad."

He shrugged. "Join the club. But I shouldn't get you maidens involved any further. I'm going to head back to the glider and take off."

Lizzie sighed, "We are not *maidens*, J.D., and we don't need protecting." Her stomach twisted. Why was she reluctant to let this guy go? She barely knew him. "But sure, if that's what you want to do."

Cab added, "With guests converging in the display hall, we probably don't have much time to get you outside."

They quickly picked up their outerwear and started wrapping themselves back up. J.D. shrugged into the farmer's brown coat and dug in the pockets for his gloves. He withdrew a piece of folded up paper. "Hey, what's this?"

Lizzie recognized the weekly events flyer. "Oh, nothing. It tells visitors about all the super fun and wholesome activities."

"Oh, yeah, these sound really zippin'. 'Make Your Own Victorian Christmas Ornament,' 'Wassail Punch Tasting.' Ooh, here's a good one. A lecture called 'Indigo: Jersey-Dyeing Pulp Extraction. And it's today!' No time listed, though."

"Wait, what did you say?" Lizzie asked. "Cab, have you heard anything about indigo pulp dyeing or something?"

Cab shrugged, "Sounds kinda random, but your mom does like her historical details."

"Yeah, I guess. It's weird, though. And nobody uses the barn or farmhouse this time of year, so why would that farmer's costume be in there with a schedule of events with tonight's date on it?" She reached for the flyer. "Can I see that?"

She muttered out loud, "Indigo. I heard that word earlier." She bent close to the flyer. Were those erasure marks? She pulled her datapad out of her muff and clicked on the light. The first letters of Jersey Dyeing and Pulp had been circled and erased. And there were some erased words in the margin. She tilted the pad light so it raked across the paper's surface. She read the tracings and her heart leapt into her throat.

"'J.D. Plisskin Extraction. Midnight.'"

She swallowed hard and looked at J.D. "I think you really have been kidnapped."

Somehow J.D.'s mad adventure and boring old Yorktown were linked. What the hell was going on?

Lizzie considered finding her mom and asking her. But somehow she felt they needed to protect J.D. from everyone. The best thing to do was to get him out of here.

They snuck into the vestibule and peeked through the curtains into the exhibition hall. A handful of gray-suited I.G.G.S. officers gathered around the exit. With a jolt, Lizzie realized how omnipresent those gray uniforms had been on Kepler, her old planet. On every planet she'd ever been to, actually. Here in the carpeted, wallpapered exhibition hall the officers were totally out of place with their slick uniforms and gray tubular guns.

Guests filed in from Main Street while officers set up an interview station, dragging over a vintage table and chairs. A tall officer who wore her dark hair in a severe bun surveyed the scene. When everyone was in place, she nodded and boomed across the hall, "Visitors with last names beginning with A or B."

A handful of guests made their way over to her at the exit. At the cash register, a line of people dutifully purchased vintage postcards, daguerreotypes, and stereoscopes. Everyone else stood around in groups, whispering. Lizzie could sense the growing tension. People were eyeing each other, as if J.D.—or the kidnappers—might be there among them.

J.D. gave a low whistle. "That doesn't look good. No going through the main door."

"We could go through the photography studio and out the employee entrance," Cab said.

Lizzie nodded. "Good idea. The only tricky part will be getting there without anyone noticing J.D."

"How about I go to the studio first and come back with a different costume for him?" She turned to J.D. with her gap-toothed smile. "We could dress you up like a Victorian lady."

Lizzie looked up at the tall young man. "Hmm, I don't know. He's not very girlish."

J.D. laughed under his breath and poked at Lizzie's big green skirt. "These dresses are so huge, people probably wouldn't even notice me under all the fabric." He paused. "Hmm. Maybe that's a better idea."

J.D. kept poking her skirt until it swayed back and forth like a bell. Lizzie swatted his hand away.

"No," she said. "No way. I am not hiding you under my hoop skirt."

Lizzie stepped into the exhibition hall with J.D. under her hoop skirt. He waddled next to her left side, his arm wrapped around her hips. They shuffled along the wall with Cab on their right side to block the gaze of curious guests.

J.D. pressed his cheek against her thigh. Thank God she'd worn black tights instead of the more authentic drawers they were supposed to wear. She didn't even want to think about the fact that the regulation drawers had no crotch.

A woman's voice called out, "Excuse me, girls?"

Crap. It was the harsh-looking I.G.G.S. officer. Cab and Lizzie froze. Too abruptly. J.D. lost his balance and grabbed onto the front straps of her hoop skirt to keep from falling over. Lizzie jerked forward and shot out a hand to steady herself against the damask-papered wall.

Aware that many eyes were on them, Cab gave a nervous giggle. "Dearest, are you all right? Is your corset too tight?"

Lizzie nodded demurely. "I'm perfectly well, thank you, but perhaps you could attend to the officer's request?"

Cab steadied Lizzie's wobbling skirt before she crossed the hall to the interview area. Cab smiled at tourists and shifted her sky blue dress to avoid bumping into the clumps of people starting to sit down on the carpeted floor. The I.G.G.S. officer leaned in to show her something on a datapad.

Lizzie felt a pat on her thigh. And then another one. She twitched her hip against J.D. Tap. Tap. Holy freakin' stars, what was he doing? She nudged him with her left knee. Tap tap tap. She brought her hand down quickly, as if smoothing her skirt, connecting firmly with the top of his head. The patting stopped.

Cab returned, and they resumed their awkward procession. Finally, they reached the photography studio, already closed up for the evening. Lizzie and Cab pushed through the red curtain and let it fall.

Immediately, Lizzie hoisted up her skirt with one hand and pushed J.D. over with the other. She hissed, "What the hell, J.D.?"

He sprawled out on the floor, cheeks flushed, and brown eyes twinkling. "Heh. I don't know. I just wanted you to know I was still around."

Lizzie spluttered, "You know, for someone who's supposed to be all intergalactic and 'zippin,' you sure are—"

Cab interrupted them. "Listen, guys. We've gotta get moving. The officer told me there's an I.G.G.S. team at each end of Main Street. After they get all the guests out, they're going to make their way toward the center to do a thorough sweep."

"Oh," Cab continued. "And she showed me a message from your mom. Not for you, specifically, just for any

Yorktowners who happened to be around. It said, 'Yorktown managers are to follow the evening's planned events.'"

"Okay. Whatever. Let's go," Lizzie said.

As they made their way to the back of the studio, Lizzie noticed that the sepia-toned photographs along the wall had been rearranged. One photograph stopped her in her tracks.

It showed Lizzie and her mom shortly after they'd arrived here. Everything had felt so new back then. How ironic. She remembered being excited to pose for the photograph, dressing up in a white lace pinafore. Her mom had worn an imposing, high-necked black dress. The black and white photo had just one area that was hand-tinted: the two wide bands on Harriet's skirt. And they were colored a purplish-blue.

A chill ran through her. Lizzie knew it wasn't a coincidence. It was the same dress as in the lantern show. With the same purplish-blue stripes. She whispered, "Indigo."

"What?" Cab asked.

It was time to tell them her suspicions. Even if they thought she was bonkers. It all came rushing out: her mom's dress, and the slideshow image with the word Independents, and the white-haired tourist asking for indigo hatbands.

She turned to J.D. "I think my mom may be an Independent. I think Yorktowners kidnapped you."

"That would explain why I lost control of my glider. But why didn't anyone nab me in the field?"

Lizzie shook her head. "And what the stars does the color indigo have to do with anything?"

J.D. rubbed a hand over his eyes. "I'm trying to remember something my dad said recently. Bear in mind, he's always saying crazy things, but I swear he said something like, 'Why can't those goddamned Independent Indigos let bygones be bygones?'"

Everyone was silent.

Cabbie cleared her throat. "Okay. So, indigo, whatever that is, and the Independents, and J.D. may all be connected. But how?"

J.D. touched his neck. In a hushed voice, he said, "It's gotta have something to do with the chip, right? Maybe I shouldn't leave yet. If you ladies can put up with me for a while longer, maybe we could find out something about the Independents, and I could figure out what's making my dad so paranoid."

Lizzie felt sick to her stomach, but she had to find out what was going on. She nodded slowly. "With all the Yorktowners busy, it's actually kind of a perfect time to snoop around. And I think I know where to start."

At the studio's employee exit, Lizzie warned J.D., "This door leads right into a corridor that runs behind Main Street. It's usually pretty busy with employees."

"But most people will probably be doing their jobs and staying put, unlike us," Cab said.

"True," Lizzie agreed. "Still. Keep your head down and let us do the talking."

J.D. nodded. "Got it. Head down, mouth shut."

They stepped through the door. The long white corridor, starkly lit by fluorescent rods along the ceiling, was a shock after all the plush carpets, dark wood, and warm lamplight.

J.D. whistled, a piercing sound that echoed against the concrete walls. "Kinda harsh."

They walked down the corridor, boots clacking against the floor. They passed shop door after shop door on their right. Finally, Lizzie stopped in front of one. "Here we are. Brooklyn's Bookstore and Stationery."

She grabbed the handle and pushed it open, peeking inside. The lights were on, but it was empty and silent. They crept inside the two-story store. Bookshelves lined the walls and stretched all the way up to the high ceiling.

J.D. broke the silence. "Zag! I've never seen so many books."

Lizzie chuckled. "I was all starry-eyed when I first saw this place, too."

"So, what are we doing here?" Cab asked.

"I don't know, exactly, but my mom is always going on about how important the bookstore is. 'It's not just retail. It's history.'"

"Spot-on imitation," Cab said.

Lizzie continued, "And that lady in the slide show, the one wearing the same dress as my mom? She was standing in front of the Brooklyn Bridge, so I figured maybe there was some clue here."

Lizzie scrunched up her mouth. The main floor alone must hold thousands of books. A cast-iron staircase led up to a catwalk that edged the walls and overlooked the main floor. Even more books up there. Running down the center of the main level were cases displaying old-fashioned inkpots and dip pens, vintage magazines and newspapers, and photos of Victorian printing presses.

"There's a lot of stuff to look at in here. Any clues?" Cab asked.

"I don't know, books with the title Indigo? Or those purply-blue bands on something?"

"Right," J.D. said with an air of both skepticism and eagerness. "Let's spread out and get to it." He hustled up the staircase while Cab wandered over to some nearby bookshelves.

Lizzie crossed to the opposite wall and started looking at book after book. The 19th century titles were mostly unfamiliar, but a few classics rang a bell: *A Tale of Two Cities* by Charles Dickens, *The Adventures of Sherlock Holmes* by Arthur Conan Doyle.

They were all alphabetical by author, of course. Hey, there couldn't be someone named Indigo, could there? She rushed over to the I's. Ibsen, Irving, Jasper. Dammit. Lizzie inspected the I's in the nonfiction sections, too. Nothing.

Maybe a periodical? She moved to the center of the room and examined the vintage magazines in the cases. She couldn't see the word indigo anywhere.

Upstairs, J.D. started whistling. He seemed like he was actually enjoying himself. Guess it was nice for him to have something to focus on other than his crazy father.

Lizzie's eyes fell on the staircase below J.D. The cast iron railings repeated a pattern: pointy gothic arches. Just like the Brooklyn Bridge.

Lizzie squinted, trying to remember the lantern show slide. The woman had been standing with her back to the bridge, pointing at it with her right hand. Lizzie moved to the foot of the stairs and called up, "Hey, J.D.? Could you do me a favor and check something out?"

"Sure thing."

Lizzie placed her back to the stairs, and extended her arm, pointing up and to the right. She felt ridiculous, but what the hell. "Could you look where I'm pointing?"

"Um, okay."

He crossed over to that side of the catwalk and looked back and forth between Lizzie's pointed finger and the books. "What am I looking for?"

"I have no zaggin' idea."

"Zaggin', huh? You're catching on. But I still don't see anything." He stood back a little and scanned the whole area.

Cab came over to join Lizzie. "What's going on?"

J.D. let out a whoop. "You're not going to believe this!" He held up a black book. "Ready? Here it comes."

Lizzie didn't have time to tell him not to throw the merchandise. The black book sailed over the railing. She caught it and read the title on the cover to Cab. "*Organization is Next to Cleanliness: The History and Practice of Modern Household Management.* I don't get it."

"No, not the cover," J.D. called down. "Look at the— what do you call it?—the narrow end."

She flipped the book so the spine faced up. Two bands of indigo bordered the title. A chill coursed through her.

"Ready for the next one?" J.D. asked. Down came another black book.

On its spine, indigo bands surrounded the title *Nations of Trade: Histories of Barter and Exchange.*

"Heads up!" J.D. called. Another book flew over. And another. Then three more. Squealing, Cab stepped in to catch some.

J.D. bolted down the staircase to join them. "Those are all the books with indigo stripes."

They sat on the bottom steps and stared at the seven books. J.D. shook them to see if anything would fall out. Nothing. Lizzie grabbed one titled, *Inter Thy Beloved: A History of Mourning and Funerary Practices.*

Umm, maybe she'd come back to that. She set it down and picked up another one: *Independent Scholars: The History of Autodidacticism.*

Independent Scholars! There must be something in that one. She flipped through the pages, hoping to find... something, but what? Highlighted passages or secret handwritten codes? Nothing.

She read the table of contents; nothing stood out. She sighed and started to read the incredibly long introduction to the incredibly, incredibly dry methods of research that the author used. Who would want to buy this?

She looked at Cab. "Anything?"

Cab shook her head. "Nope. You'll be shocked to learn that *Galactic Visions: The History of Spectroscopy and Telescopy* is really boring." She sat up straight. "Hey, are they all history books?"

"Probably," J.D. said. "That *is* the history section up there, Caberah."

"It's just Cab."

Lizzie tossed her books down. "This is ridiculous. I mean, do you think we'll have to read them cover to cover?"

"Hold up a sec," J.D. said. "When I was a kid, before my dad went all insane, he used to be into codes and stuff. He insisted that a lot of codes were obvious because they were meant to be read. But only by certain people. So, to crack a code, you just have to figure out who is being invited to access the information."

"That makes sense," Lizzie said. "But how does that help us?"

45

"Well, there are deliberate clues being left around Yorktown, right? For people who know how to spot them?"

He lined up the books on a stair step so their spines were showing. "Okay, so let's pretend that we've been invited to read the code. That the answer is obvious. Let's just name what we see."

"They're all history books, as I brilliantly deduced," Cab said. "And they're all the same size. All black with indigo stripes. They look the same, but the topics are totally different."

"Right!" Lizzie said, "It's like they're meant to be read as a set, but no one ever would unless they were looking for the indigo symbol." She paused, studying them. "Oh, my stars, what if we rearranged them?"

She moved the books around until she had six lined up in a neat row. She held the seventh in her hand. "I don't know what to do with this one, but look at those. Read the first word of each title."

J.D. read them aloud, "Independent Nations Defying Inter Galactic Organization." He looked at Lizzie. "Whoa."

Lizzie nodded. "And the initials spell INDIGO."

"What the stars is going on?" Cab whispered. "Is this a new thing? I've heard of Independents but not Independent Nations."

J.D. pointed to the book in Lizzie's hand. "What's that?"

"*Seven Seas and Sunken Ships. A History of Exotic Maritime Lore.* So, it's the number seven, I guess. Where should it go?" She put it at the front of the row. "Maybe here?"

"Seven Independent Nations...? Could be," J.D. said.

J.D.'s datapad buzzed loudly. It was rare to receive an I.G. text in Old Yorktown; someone would need a pretty powerful signal to get through the scrambled zone. J.D. fished his pad out from his pocket. He stared at the screen for a full minute before mumbling, "Looks like I can't ignore my neck anymore tonight."

He showed the girls his pad. On the glowing blue screen, neat white letters spelled out the eeriest I.G. message Lizzie had ever seen:

Son, this is URGENT. *Your life is in danger. Implanted chip has time-sensitive and site-resistant applications. Contact I.G.G.S. immediately for removal. Chip will detonate at midnight tonight, if still on Earth. I'm sorry.*

Lizzie couldn't move. Couldn't think of a thing to say.

J.D. touched his neck. "I've heard of this kind of thing, but never in a million light-years did I think he'd use it on me."

"I am so sorry, J.D.," Cab said, gently. "What does site-resistant mean?"

"A chip can be rigged so if it enters a set of coordinates, it triggers some kind of alarm or self-destruct device."

"I don't get it, though," Lizzie said. "Why didn't he send you that message earlier? Why send I.G.G.S.?"

J.D. replied, "He's probably covering his bases; he doesn't trust me to come home on my own. And he's right. I'm never setting foot on his planet ever again."

"But what about the chip?" Cab asked. She checked the locket watch pinned to her dress. "It's almost ten o'clock. We've got two hours."

J.D. pushed up his right sleeve. Instead of the neat, semicircular scars they'd seen on his other arm, this one had three jagged welts.

He cleared his throat. "Well, I happen to know that it's possible to remove the chips yourself."

Lizzie, Cab, and J.D. snuck back into the employee corridor. Still empty. They headed further east down the bright hallway. J.D. and Lizzie each carried a short stack of books, bundled together with old-fashioned book straps they'd borrowed from the store.

J.D. swung his books back and forth from the strap, but his head was low, and he kept his eyes on the concrete floor. Lizzie racked her brains for something to say. But stars, what do you say to a guy whose father planted a bomb in his neck?

They walked in silence until they arrived at the right door. Lizzie opened it a crack and peeked inside. The lights were out, and it was totally empty. Stepping inside, the employee door swung closed behind them, and they were left in total darkness.

In the dark, J.D.'s voice quivered a little. "Where are we exactly?"

"The barbershop," Lizzie said. "It's the nearest place I could think of to...to do what we need to do."

J.D. clicked on his datapad, illuminating the room in a cool glow. They were surrounded by black wood cabinets, display tables full of toiletries for sale, and against each wall, a row of black leather barber stools. The sharply sweet smell of shaving cream and cologne lingered in the air.

Cab fired up a lamp and rummaged around the barber supplies and toiletry products. "Pomade, no. Macassar Hair Oil, no," she muttered to herself. "Tooth-powders, definitely not. Ah-ha! Travel kit."

J.D. stood in the center of the room, his bravado almost visibly draining away. Lizzie motioned to one of the barber stools. "Okay, J.D., lie down. They recline for a close, old-fashioned shave."

Silently, J.D. took off his coat and sat down. He pulled a lever, lowering the seatback. Lizzie pulled up a stool next to him. He looked pale, even in the warm glow of the lamp. "You sure you want to do this?" she asked. "Maybe you're safer with the I.G.G.S."

"No way. My dad has totally lost it. He's sure as hell not getting this disc back. But I can't ask you to do this. I can do it. I've done it before."

"Stars, you are not cutting into your own neck. No. I'll do it."

He unbuttoned his shirt and pulled the collar away from his neck.

Cab placed the supplies on a cart, recounting, "Blade, rubbing alcohol, gauze, thread, needle."

While Cab swabbed J.D.'s neck, Lizzie wiped her own shaking fingers with alcohol. Her throat constricted, but she swallowed hard. She felt his neck under his ear. His skin was warm, smooth. There was no mistaking the chip. It was just under the surface, a disc about the size of an old Earth nickel.

She picked up the folded razor blade, opened it, and didn't stop to think. She pressed the front corner of the blade against his neck and felt it pierce his skin. J.D.'s hiss of pain went right into her ear. She blinked back tears.

Blood trickled out of the incision. Lizzie carved halfway around the disc. Then she put the razor down and smeared some of the blood away. She inhaled and reached into J.D.'s neck with her index finger and thumb. The chip was warm and slippery. She pinched it tightly and pulled. Out it came. She dropped it onto the cart.

Cab swooped in to press some gauze against J.D.'s neck. The tears finally ran down Lizzie's cheeks. Her fingers were bloody, so she pressed her velvet sleeve against her eyes.

After Cab got J.D. cleaned and bandaged, she wiped off the silver disc. She tilted her blonde head and examined it. "All right, so it's not going to explode inside J.D.'s neck. But it's still going to explode, right? What do we do with it?"

J.D. sat up and took the chip from Cab. "Huh. When I was younger, I'd never noticed...." He pulled out his I.G. pad. "Doesn't it kinda look like a datapad tab?" He removed the datatab from his pad and plugged the disc in. It fit perfectly. He pushed a few buttons. "Zaggit. It's not transferring the data. I guess that would be too easy."

He checked the time. "Ten-thirty. The detonation device probably isn't very big, but you never know. We've got to get it away from people." A hint of his mischievous grin flashed across his mouth. "You know what would be great? To let it blow up somewhere and record it to send to my father. Oh, yeah, I could pull a switcheroo and send him my own datatab. He'd play it, only to see the real chip go ka-boom."

Lizzie gave a wan smile, "Okay, evil genius, how about the village green? Where you crash-landed? There's something poetic about that."

"For you, too, Lizzie," Cab said. "I can't even count all the times you said you wanted to blow up this town."

"It would serve my mom right, I guess. What has she been keeping secret from me?"

While J.D. fiddled a little more with his pad, Cab and Lizzie crossed to the side of the store that faced Main Street and peered out the blinds. Lizzie could make out small figures moving past the theater. Guests on their way out of town.

As she turned to look the other way, a gray uniform filled her vision. Lizzie gasped and scrambled back. She whispered, "They're right outside! Let's go."

They scrambled across the room and slipped out the employee exit, just as the Main Street door creaked open. The brightness of the white corridor dazed them, but they ran as hard as they could, back the way they had come.

With one hand, Lizzie clutched a bundle of books. With the other, she gathered up her heavy skirts. She'd just settled into an awkward rhythm when doors started opening far down at the end of the corridor.

Crap! Who was coming into the hallway? Yorktowners who'd been questioned and released? I.G.G.S.?

Lizzie didn't wait to find out. "Come on," she hissed, and pushed open the nearest shop door.

They found themselves in Bell's Phonographic Studio. J.D. turned on the small white light on his I.G. pad. He whispered, "More Victorian tech! This stuff is right up my alley."

To their left, a large, glassed-in booth boasted a sign that read, "Create your own Phonographic Recording!"

Shelves displayed phonographic cylinders and discs. Behind the counter was a row of neatly wrapped albums in square, brown paper envelopes—the unclaimed recordings that visitors had made and neglected to buy.

In the center of the room was a display of antique record players. J.D. walked over to a Victrola with a large, funnel-shaped speaker blossoming out of its wooden box. "Zip, an old music machine, right?" He turned the crank a few times. A tinny, scratchy melody emerged.

Lizzie was about to shush him but stopped when his crooked grin emerged. He deserved a tiny bit of fun. He flipped through the nearby bins of recordings, reading out the old-fashioned titles, "'Sweet By and By.' 'The Laughing Song.'" He waved an album in the air. "Oh, girls, here's a good one: 'The Old Yorktown Carolers!'"

Lizzie groaned and tried to grab it from him. He laughed and said. "No way. I'm keeping this one. It's even got a photo of you." His smile faded. "Hold up. Check this out."

J.D. held out the album for Cab and Lizzie to see. Sure enough, the choir's authentically unsmiling faces graced the album cover. And on the top, bordering the title, were two indigo bands.

"What the zaggin' stars?" Lizzie breathed. "Can I see it?"

Lizzie flipped it over. Nothing surprising there, just a list of the song titles. But wait, at the bottom it read, "Epilogue by Harriet Braynor."

Lizzie strode over to the Victrola and put on the disc, placing the needle at the centermost groove in the record.

Her mom's voice was thin and echoey coming out of the speaker. "This is Harriet Braynor, Manager of Old Yorktown, one of the seven living history museums. These seven sites were established by the Inter-Galactic Government during its 'Shining Moments of the Reconstruction'..."

Huh. Her mom sounded almost sarcastic. Lizzie kept listening.

"...when the I.G.G. purportedly rescued the planets after a series of devastating events. We are committed to the preservation of fact and to the spirit of independent research. If you are like-minded, please visit Old Yorktown, or any of the seven history museums, and ask a shop manager for more information. Thank you."

Lizzie's head was spinning. "Did you hear that?"

"What, the way-too-serious marketing pitch?" J.D. asked.

"No. I mean, yeah, but also how the Government only 'purportedly rescued' the planets? And that thing about 'independent research'?"

"And she mentioned the number seven a few times."

Lizzie grabbed the two stacks of books and unbuckled the book straps. "Seven books. Seven history museums. There's got to be a connection, right?"

J.D. picked up the book *Seven Seas*. "A pretty standard cipher embeds information within non-information in a certain pattern."

Lizzie arced her eyebrows. "What?" he protested. "I just meant that we could try every seventh word. Here, listen, it might be nonsense, but what the hell?"

He opened up the book and started reading, shining his I.G. pad light across the page. The words came slowly, haltingly, as he picked them out. "'In the year... two thousand one hundred and one... most of planet Earth was decimated... not by its inhabitants... but by the Inter-Galactic Government.'"

An ice-cold tingle shot through Lizzie's body. They all looked at each other.

"Keep reading," Cab whispered.

"Seven planets had resisted the new Government's efforts to consolidate power...These independent nations were threatened by the Government...Crops were destroyed on Kepler... A mysterious disease struck Tau Boo... Each time, the new Government swooped in with a solution... food drops or a miraculous cure... Still, the Independent Nations resisted...So Earth was destroyed as the ultimate example... The rest of the planets fell in line... The Galaxy spent decades reconstructing planets... spreading propaganda... and wiping history clean... but the Independents preserve the truth."

J.D. stopped and shook his head. "Do you think they do? I mean, is it true?"

Lizzie looked at the other books on the floor. "Why else would the Independents take such care to write it like this, to have it available but also secret? My mom is apparently many things, but she's not crazy." She paused. "Um, sorry, J.D."

He shrugged one shoulder.

"So," Cab said slowly. "There are seven books that hold this alternate history. Or this real history or whatever. It would take way too long to read it all now. We've got to deal with the disc."

"Oh, zag, right." J.D. stood up and fished out the disc from his coat pocket. He paced around the room, staring at it in one hand and his datapad in the other. He mumbled, "I wish we could crack the code on this sucker."

Cab and Lizzie had almost finished bundling up the books when muffled voices came from the employee corridor. Lizzie froze. People were gathered on the other side of the exit.

The door opened an inch and stopped. A high-pitched voice wheedled into the shop. "Yes, officer, now I'm certain it was the President's son. He's dressed as a farmer. Tan pants, brown coat and cap." Ugh, no mistaking that sycophantic tone. Meghan.

Lizzie and Cab grabbed the books and bolted for the front door. Lizzie yanked it open and dashed out. The cold air hit her face and then her shins as she picked up her heavy skirts to run across the cobblestone street. She heard Cab panting right behind her.

They reached the wide, grassy riverbank that ran parallel to Main Street. Not much cover there. But up a hundred yards or so toward the bridge was the carriage shed. Part storage facility, part tourist attraction, the white, open-fronted building was the starting point for charming rides through the village.

Without looking back, they raced as fast as they could to the shed and ducked inside the open façade. In the quiet darkness, Lizzie and Cab turned to each other, smiling despite their heaving chests. Their smiles quickly faded.

Cab whipped her head around. "Where's J.D.?"

Lizzie's heart sank. She peeked out from the tall wooden frame of the carriage shed. The street was empty. She squinted toward the phonographic studio. It was dark inside, but she saw shadowy figures moving around. She squeezed Cab's arm. "Crap. I think they got him inside Bell's."

Cab whispered, "What do we do?"

Lizzie shook her head. "Just wait here, I guess. If he can get outside, we'll grab him. If he can't, he'll have to tell them about the disc. There isn't much time."

She leaned against the wide doorframe, staring at the phonograph shop. The minutes ticked by. Her breath misted into the air. The longer she stood still, the colder she got.

Behind her, the shed was dark and empty except for a wagon and a buggy parked for the night. Lizzie rummaged around the wagon's storage box and grabbed a couple of heavy blankets. She tucked one around Cab who nestled her head on Lizzie's shoulder.

All of a sudden, a dark figure emerged from Bell's. Lizzie stood upright, forcing Cab's head to slide off her shoulder. "Hey!" Cab said.

Lizzie shushed her. The figure looked up and down the street. It was tall and lanky and wearing a cap. J.D. Thank the stars. Palms tingling, Lizzie stepped out from the darkness of the shed and waved at him. Noticing her, he bolted across the street.

He dipped inside the wide doorway, a big grin on his face. "Hey, ladies. Zippin' hideout." He scanned the shed, eyes locking on an information plaque that read, *Fun Facts about Victorian Transportation!*

J.D. smiled even wider. "Hey! I just figured it out!"

Lizzie's heart was beating a mile a minute. She couldn't believe how happy she was to see someone she'd just met a few hours before.

"What?"

"Cab is short for Cabriolet." He turned to Cab. "You're named after a 19th century carriage!"

Lizzie had never seen Cab so mad and flustered. Her blond curls practically vibrated.

Lizzie threw off her blanket and shoved J.D. Hard. "What the hell happened to you? We were worried sick and then you show up, and—"

J.D. held his hands up in a conciliatory gesture. "Hey, hey. I'm sorry." He leaned toward Cab and pointed to the sign. "I saw that sign and got excited. I'm really sorry. I didn't know it was such a sore topic."

Cab's glare softened a little. "Whatever. Let's change the subject. What happened at Bell's? We were really worried."

"Oh, yeah, that was close. But I hid in the recording booth. I may be tall, but I'm bendy."

Lizzie couldn't help smiling a little. "Okay. Let's just get rid of the disc before we all blow up. How much time do we have?"

J.D. checked his pad. "Crap. Fifteen minutes."

They snuck to the open doorway and looked around. Officers were on the prowl, moving in and out of shops, methodically making their way toward the center of town.

Lizzie led J.D. and Cab past the vehicles to the back of the shed and out the back door. They stood high on the bank, looking down at the dark, wide river. J.D. grabbed the books from the girls so they could pick up their skirts. They all slid partway down the snow-covered slope of the riverbank so they wouldn't be seen and scrambled toward the bridge.

They clambered onto the wooden structure. Lizzie glanced toward Main Street. The wide façade of the General Store stared back at her.

The double doors flew open and out marched a small troop of officers, led by the severe woman with the too-tight hair bun.

The tall woman bellowed, "We see you. We know you have the President's son. Stop where you are." The officers ran toward them, aiming their wide-mouthed tube guns.

Cab's eyes were wide with fear. Under his breath, J.D. said, "They won't shoot me. Run!"

They bolted across the icy wooden bridge. Loud pops of tubular gunshots split the air and burst on the bridge around them, sending up chunks of gray wood and icy snow. J.D. yelled, "What the hell?!"

They kept running. More explosive gunshots struck the bridge. One tore past Lizzie's shoulder and landed in front of her. She screamed and covered her face as bits of timber pelted her.

J.D. grabbed Lizzie and covered her. He called out to Cab to stop. They huddled together, panting.

"Listen, you have to stay here," J.D. said. "I'm going to go for it." He thrust the books into Cab's arms and took off again.

The female officer yelled after him, "J.D. Plisskin. Stop. We have orders to take you back to the President."

He kept running. Another round of small explosions hit the bridge on either side of him. The booming vibrations ran all the way up Lizzie's legs. They wouldn't actually shoot him, would they? J.D. kept running.

On the far side of the bridge, another group gathered. It wasn't I.G.G.S. in their sleek gray uniforms, but a group of thirty or so Yorktowners. They stood at the end of the bridge, brandishing lanterns, rifles, and old-fashioned handguns. And at the front of the group was a woman in a black dress with wide bands of indigo at the hem. Harriet Braynor, Lizzie's mother.

Mrs. Braynor held out a black-gloved hand and trained a pistol right at J.D. He stumbled to a stop just a few feet away from her. He pivoted back to the center of the long bridge, searching for Lizzie.

Lizzie screamed, "Mom! What the hell are you doing?"

Harriet ignored her daughter and called out in a calm, authoritative voice, "Inter-Galactic Security, please hold your fire. We need to have a conversation."

Lizzie was frantic. J.D. was hemmed in, and no one understood what was going on. She yelled, "Mom! We don't have time to have a conversation!" She called out to J.D. "You can't get to the field in time. Just get rid of it; throw it in the river!"

She dashed toward him. From behind her, the lead I.G.G.S. officer yelled, "Halt!" Lizzie kept running.

J.D. reached into his coat pocket. Mrs. Braynor cocked her pistol. "Don't do it, J.D. Please stand perfectly still."

Lizzie ran toward them, out of breath but still yelling. "Mom, you don't understand, he has a chip with an explosive device. It's going to go off any minute!"

Without taking her eyes off J.D., Lizzie's mom called out to her daughter. "My dear. We know what J.D. has, and he needs to hand it over to us. Now."

"No! Mom, it's going to explode!"

"Do you really think his father would give his own son a device that would kill him?"

J.D. chuckled sadly. "Yes. Yes, he would."

"I disagree. Please give me the disc, J.D.," Harriet said.

He pulled a silver chip out of his coat pocket and held it out to Lizzie's mom.

Lizzie, choking back tears, gasped, "No. J.D., no! Mom, don't take it."

J.D. dropped the disc into Harriet Braynor's black-gloved hand.

Lizzie's heart sank. "J.D., what the stars are you doing?"

He flashed her a crooked grin, reached into his other pocket, and pulled out another silver disc. He flung it through the beams of the bridge, and into the dark river below.

A wave of relief and understanding washed over Lizzie. She didn't give a zaggin' crap about her mother's startled expression.

A guttural boom erupted from the river. Officers and Yorktowners ran to the side of the bridge to see the water boiling and spitting. A sickening, hissing gurgle filled the air.

"Oh, my God. It was true." Harriet Braynor's face was pale in the moonlight. "My dear young man, I am so sorry. That would have—" She looked at the silver disc in her hand. "Then what is this, may I ask?"

"It's my pad's datatab. Sorry about that, Mrs. Braynor, I just didn't want you to shoot me."

Harriet smiled faintly and sighed. "So the real disc is destroyed."

J.D. leaned in close. "Yeah, but hang onto that one. Just in case."

57

Harriet tilted her head toward Main Street. Something over there had caught her attention. Lizzie stared hard at the lamplit street. Figures were silently approaching the I.G.G.S. officers from behind. Cab's parents, Miss Catherine from The Millinery, Mrs. Harader, the white-haired tourist, and a dozen other tourists Lizzie didn't recognize. They all had rifles trained directly at the officers.

On the bridge, Yorktown employees had taken advantage of the confusion, fanning out around the rest of the I.G.G.S. They were surrounded.

Lizzie's mother turned to the female I.G.G.S. officer and called out, "Officer? We ask that you kindly remove yourselves from Old Yorktown."

The tall officer jerked her head around, assessing the situation. The antique weapons of Old Yorktown were clearly inferior to the tube guns, but they were deadly nonetheless. And at least one gun was aimed straight at every single officer.

The officer gripped her gun tightly. "Very well. But we are under orders to return J.D. to the President."

J.D. stood up straight. "Actually, my father didn't want me, he wanted the disc. And that's no longer an option."

The officer stepped toward J.D. "Regardless. Orders are to return you. And we all must follow the orders of our President."

Lizzie's mom took a step toward the I.G.G.S. officer. "I believe you know, or at least your superiors do, that Old Yorktown is *not* under the jurisdiction of the Inter-Galactic Government. And we are demanding that you leave."

The officer stood, eyes locked with Harriet Braynor's. Then the gray-suited woman turned to J.D. "J.D. Plisskin, are you stating that you refuse to come with us and are seeking asylum in Old Yorktown?"

J.D. shot a questioning look at Lizzie and her mom. They both nodded. He cleared his throat. "I am."

The stern security leader addressed J.D. "Best of luck to you, young man. Your father will not be pleased." She turned to her officers. "Fall out, back to the transport." They stomped off into the cold night.

A girlish figure minced across Main Street and onto the bridge. Meghan. Her tiny, gray-bonneted head swiveled from the retreating officers to the Old Yorktowners with their pistols and rifles. Her mouth opened and closed. Finally, in her high-pitched voice she called out, "May I be of assistance to anybody?"

Lizzie's mom sighed. "Mrs. Harader? Will you please escort Meghan back to employee housing and inform her that she is off-duty for the rest of the evening?"

Mrs. Harader nodded and swished her big red dress back toward Main Street. Meghan followed, protesting all the way.

Lizzie tried to process what had just happened. Her head was wooly with confusion and her stomach churned. She turned to her mom. "You mean the whole time we've been living in this boring backwater it's actually been some kind of rebel outpost?"

Harriet nodded. "I'm sorry I kept you in the dark. I was trying to protect you."

Lizzie pushed further. "And what's up with the asylum thing?"

"It's rare, but it does happen. The seven living history museums have always been Independent. It was part of our deal with the Government, way back in 2101. The Independents knew what had really caused the Nuclear Fusion Incident and the other planetary disasters. So the government made us an offer. The historical sites would be allowed self-governance or we would expose the truth as widely as we could."

"Why haven't you? I mean why keep the real history so secret?"

"The Government had so much support. We needed to grow our numbers and wait for the right time. I'm sorry to say it, J.D., but your father's mental instability may have given us our chance."

She raised her voice and called out to the fifty or so people gathered on the bridge. "Listen up, everyone. The evening did not go as planned, but we worked in solidarity and in the spirit of independence. Good work, Indigos!"

Applause and cheers filled the air. "Let's adjourn to the barn, warm up, and debrief."

The old wooden bridge vibrated as the crowd moved toward the barn. J.D. and Lizzie walked next to her mother. "Um, Mom? There's something in the barn you should know about."

"J.D.'s glider?"

Lizzie's eyebrows shot up.

"Lizzie, sweetheart, we brought J.D. here. We intercepted his glider."

"So," J.D. said. "I really was kidnapped?"

"Well, we prefer the word 'extraction.' But you have my deepest apologies. Our sources informed us that you had a chip and that you were on the move. We had no idea what your father had done. We had planned on keeping you safe as soon as you landed, but we lost track of you." She shook her head. "Our own scrambling technology worked against us. And you came early! We were planning on a midnight extraction."

"It Came Upon a Midnight Clear?" Lizzie asked.

"Exactly."

They reached the barn. Lizzie, her mother, and J.D. stopped just outside the wide doors as the rest of the crowd flowed inside and sat down on hay bales. Old Yorktowners in capes and overcoats talked excitedly with people in contemporary temp-controlled clothes. It felt like a reunion. Everyone ignored the little white glider at the back of the barn, as if it were nothing out of the ordinary. These folks had a much bigger perspective than Lizzie had ever suspected.

Cab marched up, carrying the two bundles of books. "Don't mind me, guys," she said with her gap-toothed grin. "I've got these." She entered the barn and plopped down on a hay bale next to her parents.

Harriet stared after Cab and the books. "You have been busy tonight! You must have a million questions. And I will answer every one. But, Lizzie, J.D., let me just say that while I hope you will join the cause, it's *your* choice."

Her mom gave her a quick hug, turned, and strode into the barn to address the crowd. Lizzie's head was swimming. It would take a while to piece together all the new information about her mom, their life, this town.

J.D. looked down at Lizzie with a hint of a grin. "I guess we both have secretive control-freaks for parents. But mine beats yours by a mile. I trust your mom, somehow."

"Yeah, I've always known she's a good person. But, stars, all the secrets." She paused. "Hey, what kind of secrets do you think were on that data chip?"

"Oh zag, I can't believe I forgot." He took off his farmer's cap in an overly formal gesture. "Miss Braynor, as a token of my appreciation for your protection and companionship—"

He reached inside his coat and pulled out a square, brown paper envelope. "I'd like to offer you this phonographic recording of what was on the disc."

'That's what took you so long in Bell's?"

He nodded. "While I was hiding, making sure the officers had left, I figured out how to play it on my pad. Just in case, I made a recording of it, too. 'Cause, you know, sometimes it's smart to record history in more than one way."

"So what's on it?"

"I guess you could call it a confession. It's like five minutes of my dad reciting a list of the things we read about—the famine, the mysterious disease, even Nuclear Fusion—all the terrible things that happened to the seven Independent planets. He rants about how genius the Government was back then. Causing the catastrophes, covering them up, making Reconstruction seem all heroic. And then he makes outrageous plots against the Independents, his staff, most of the planets."

J.D.'s face fell. "He sounds like a lunatic." J.D. touched his neck and winced. "Huh. You realize he turned me into a living history museum?"

Lizzie gently removed his fingers from his bandaged neck and held them between her gloved hands. "I'm so sorry, J.D."

"I think he'll be ousted. He's gotta be, right?" J.D. exhaled a steamy breath into the night. "Even though it's totally zagged how all of this played out, I feel like I've finally escaped."

"Escaping *to* Old Yorktown. Who would have thought?" Lizzie asked.

"What about you? What are you going to do?"

"I've wanted to get out of here for so long, to be part of the galaxy again. But there are so many lies out there." She smiled up at him. "I think I'll stick around here for a while. Figure some things out."

"Yeah," J.D. said, his crooked grin creeping back onto his face. "This just might be the most authentic place in the galaxy."

In the 1981 movie *Escape from New York*, Snake Plisskin (played by Kurt Russell) snarls, "I don't give a fuck about your war... or your president." There's less cursing in my story, but plenty of political corruption, along with riffs on the movie's plot—a glider crashing into an insular world, the deadly neck implant, a race across an exploding bridge. Rather than using a futuristic, anarchic New York City, I set my story within the anachronistic, highly ordered Old Yorktown.

Why this combination of Victoriana and cult movie classic? Well, *Escape from New York* is one of my husband's favorite movies. And as my design history students can attest, I've got a thing for 19th century culture. Secretly, I think I'd be an excellent employee at a living history museum. Although, from what I hear, it's really hard to run in a hoop skirt.

G. Clemans

ODYSSEUS FLAX & THE KRAMPUS

BY MAIA CHANCE

Christmas legends aren't all sugarplums and stuffed stockings. As with most myths, joyful rituals and promised gifts intermingle with sinister warnings and terrible fates. In "Odysseus Flax & the Krampus," Maia Chance invites us to a village celebration of the Krampus, a judgmental, devilish forbearer to today's jovial Santa Claus. Instead of a toy-laden sack, the Krampus carries an empty basket, on the hunt for misbehaving girls and boys. Chance tempers this menacing vision with her thrillingly charming style and a likable hero with his own moral complexities. At heart, it is a winter's tale, reminding us that darkness—at times—is more present than light.

–G. Clemans

Everyone has their own notion of Hell on earth, and for Odysseus Flax, Hell was traveling sickness.

The steam train snaked deeper and deeper into the Alps—what country was this? Odysseus didn't care—hugging mountainsides, plummeting in and out of tunnels, churning over precarious trestle bridges. In flashes he glimpsed ravines and outcroppings lit and shadowed in mysterious ways, and then they were gone.

He leaned his forehead on the velveteen seat in front of him, eyes squeezed shut, his spatial imagination in cartwheeling freefall inside his skull. Lord, he did not wish to vomit. He already had assessed his belongings as potential sick receptacles and had concluded that since his valise contained all of his earthly possessions, and he required his coat in December, his bowler hat must suffice. And he had only the one hat.

63

The track descended—or did it rise?—and then locked into a series of loops and—truly?—spirals. Odysseus began to perspire in odd places—the back of his hands, his chin. His jaws panged with saliva. Vomiting was inevitable; he fumbled for his hat.

Then, a chink of light in the black ceiling of Hell: the train screeched to a stop.

Odysseus lifted his head. Outside the window a snowy slope rose up, pillared with black wet trees. Wilderness out there, and a chamber in a baroness's castle waiting for him miles and miles down the track.

A few people were filing out of the train carriage, all bundled up. Through the opposite window Odysseus saw a neat little station with a sign that read KIEFERTAL. So, maybe not *total* wilderness, but close.

Nausea rocked him again, and suddenly a featherbed in a baroness's castle didn't sound half so tantalizing as a breath of fresh air. Odysseus clamped on his hat, grabbed his valise, and leapt off the train just as it was gearing up once more into infernal motion.

Well, Odysseus had, by the look of things, stopped at Kiefertal on the wrong day.

Sure, in the falling dusk, with those heavy-eaved wooden buildings and the stars twinkling above the snowy line of peaks, it could've been on a Merry Christmas card. But as Odysseus walked from the train station and onto the main street, he sensed that things weren't winding down for a snug winter evening. Women bustled behind lit-up windows. Children and dogs still romped in the icy streets. He passed three drunken men. What looked like two hairy costumes dangled on a clothesline. Was there to be a pantomime?

Why, precisely, had he gotten off the train?

At the station Odysseus had learned that the next train out wasn't for twenty-four hours. Tarnation! Three more hours on the train wouldn't have *killed* him, and now he'd be a day late to steal that painting from the baroness.

No use crying over spilled milk. Anyway, Odysseus knew that suffering could not quite be remembered, for if it could, well, all of life would be Hell, wouldn't it?

He found a tall wooden building with a sign that read *Hotel Baumberg*. He paid for a chamber, dumped his hat, coat, and valise in it, went back downstairs to the dining room, and seated himself. He was still a little queasy, but his chamber was lonely.

"Good evening, sir," the waitress said to Odysseus. Her plump blondeness glowed, holy, from inside her somewhere.

"Uh," Odysseus said, forgetting to blink. His pupils throbbed, attempting in vain to absorb her gorgeousness.

"You do not speak our local language?"

Odysseus woke up. "Yes, I do," he said, to prove it.

"All right then, what would you like? The sausage is nice, served with leeks and potatoes, and I could bring you first a plate of pickles and onions."

Odysseus's jaws twanged and he gulped back the thought: *vomit*. "Only a glass of water, please, and perhaps some wine, Miss—?"

"Anna." She retreated in a swish of blue skirts and white apron strings.

The dining room, pine-beamed and cozy with that blazing fire in the stone hearth, was near empty. A pale, thin-lipped gentleman all in black sat alone at the corner table reading a book. He wore blue-tinted glasses with steel bows. Such tinted glasses were designed to be sunshades, with lenses that could flip to the side for use on moving trains, like blinders. Why the gentleman wore them inside, Odysseus chalked up to eccentricity or an eye ailment.

Huh. Maybe Odysseus could have used some of those glasses on the train. Maybe they would've saved his equilibrium.

A family of three occupied the center table: mother, father, and a boy of perhaps twelve. Dishes and domes and bottles clogged their tabletop, as though they were sampling every dish on the bill of fare thrice over. They spoke in low, prickly tones. A burly young man slumped, bleary-eyed, over a glass of clear spirits at another table. The rest of the tables sat empty.

Anna returned and set glasses of water and white wine before Odysseus. "Are you British?" she asked.

"American."

"I should have known, you being such a tall and handsome young man. What are you doing here? Americans never come here."

"Traveling through."

"Not here for Krampusnacht, then?"

"What is that?"

"The night when the Krampus comes to scare all the naughty children into behaving themselves. You have never seen him, with his forked tongue and hooves and horns and all that hair?"

"Not in the flesh, no."

"I meant in storybooks and such," Anna said. "He will walk right out of Hell tonight with a basket strapped to his back and a birch switch for swatting the naughty ones."

"What is the basket for?"

"For carrying the really bad ones off to Hell."

Saint Nick truly was a goody-two-shoes, wasn't he? "I saw some hairy costumes hung out for an airing on my walk through town," Odysseus said. "I suppose they were Krampus costumes?"

Anna nodded. "Tonight, people will dress in disguises—Krampuses, witches, and wild-men. People drink a great deal and run through the streets. Remember" —she laughed— "if you have a run-in with one of the drunken Krampuses you must offer him schnapps, and he will let you be."

"Schnapps."

"The children fancy Krampusnacht is exciting, but they all get a good scare, too."

"I have noticed in my travels that every place has its own childrearing methods."

"What is that?" Anna asked, pointing to Odysseus's hip where his jacket had fallen open.

"Nothing." His hand flew to a leather pouch the size of a plum attached to his belt. He arranged his jacket to cover it.

"Looked like something to *me*. Allow me to see it—the beadwork is ever so fine. Is that from America?" Anna reached out.

Odysseus drew back. "No one might touch it but me." Panic washed over him, the boneless panic of a rodent in the jaws of a cat. Why hadn't he seen that sneaky spark in Anna's eyes before? Wait. No—it was gone. His muscles regained their vigor. "It is only a small token that is significant to me, yet with no value beyond that." He would never untie the pouch from his belt, and when he died it would be buried with him.

"It is something made by natives of America, perhaps?"

Odysseus drained his water glass. "From the far western territories. I worked out there as a gold miner and a tracker."

"Gold?" Anna's eyes flared.

"Never found much, sorry to say."

"What is a tracker?"

"I'm good at finding things, out in the woods, say, or in a city, too. There are little signs, see, that most folks don't notice."

"Such as footprints in the snow?"

"Sure. I can track anything in the snow. I could track a ghost in the snow."

The boy at the center table emitted a gooselike honk. He was ruddy and rotund, with a sullen brow and pooched lips. His father, also ruddy and rotund, reprimanded him in a booming voice. His mother, a fashion plate beauty in jewels and fur trim, scolded him in an acid undertone.

"If you do not eat your leeks, Fritz," she said, "Saint Nicholas will not bring you your gift, and it is an ever so beautiful gift—so he *told* me, of course."

Fritz crossed his arms. "There is no such thing as Saint Nicholas, and I have known that for years, and besides, I have already seen the silly set of toy soldiers hidden in your traveling trunk—"

"What were you doing in my traveling trunk?" his mother cried.

"—and I do not want them, anyway."

"Why not?" the father said. "They are solid gold!"

Gold. Odysseus's hand froze on his wine glass.

"Do not care," Fritz said, smashing something on his plate with a fork.

Odysseus said softly to Anna, "Solid gold toy soldiers?"

"Sounds mad, but I would wager it is true," Anna whispered, tidying the tablecloth. "Herr Metzger is as rich as an emperor and little Fritz is spoiled rotten. So is Frau Metzger, truth be told."

"From around here?"

"No, no. Travelers from far away. Still, working at a hotel like this, you hear the most peculiar things about the guests."

Odysseus hoped that wasn't *always* the case.

Anna looked straight into Odysseus's eyes. Things inside him popped and sizzled. "Herr Metzger made his fortune by stealing," she said.

"Stealing." *Stealing!* Odysseus was a thief, a thief by vocation at this point, really, but he only ever stole from other thieves. So....

"Well, after a fashion," Anna said. "Herr Metzger steals away the lives and the souls and the bread of his manufactory workers, they say—"

"*Who* says?"

"I do not know. People. He pays them with crumbs while he lives in a palace and can afford to buy things like golden toy soldiers. I am surprised they even stopped here, but then, this is the only hotel for miles around, and sometimes people become stranded." Anna smiled, flashing two bewitching dimples.

Bliss liquefied Odysseus. "Yes, folks get stranded, but that sometimes amounts to a stroke of luck, I believe."

"Miss!" the burly drunk called to Anna, holding up his glass. "More!"

"One moment," Anna called to him. She turned to Odysseus. "Poor Peter. He is not usually so miserable and drunk, like so. He is a good man. More wine?"

"Yes, please."

After two glasses of wine, Odysseus's bladder was full. He could not bear to ask the beautiful Anna if there were a water closet near the dining room, so he went up to use his private chamber pot. Going back down the twisty stairwell, men's voices just beyond the turn in the stairs below made him stop.

"I will pay you handsomely," a man—yes, Herr Metzger—said in a furtive tone.

Furtive tones usually signaled something noteworthy; Odysseus held his breath.

"Twenty-five," another man's rough voice said. Odysseus recognized it as that of the drunk who'd been in the dining room. Peter, Anna had called him.

"Twenty."

"Thirty."

"You do not even know how to bargain!"

"I am not in the mood for bargaining, *your highness*," Peter said in a churlish tone. "So I will just be going—"

"*No.* Halt. Thirty—but I will not pay you until you deliver him back here at the hotel safe and sound at nine o'clock *precisely*. I only wish to give the boy a scare, not to make him miss his sleep."

"I will scare him, all right," Peter said. "I will scare him silly. My sweetheart fancied up my mask this year. Patched up the missing fur and put on new horns—real goat's horns. Where should I steal the little blighter from?"

"Do not speak of your superiors in such a fashion," Herr Metzger said, "and do not err in supposing for a moment that my son is anything but your superior. He will be abed in our chamber—number two—by seven o'clock.

Frau Metzger and I will endeavor to be absent from the chamber at that time so that you may steal him without him crying for his mother—something he is wont to do—or anything of that sort. Enter at about ten minutes after seven. He will be asleep. I shall leave the door unlocked."

"Ten minutes after seven o'clock. Yes, sir."

"Do not make a muddle of it, or you will be sorry."

Boots clattered, and the men were gone.

Odysseus was not one to go interfering in other folks' childrearing. He himself had been reared by an exhausted maid-of-all-work mother and the birch switch of the schoolmaster in Littleton, New Hampshire. He had turned out all right. Well, he *was* a thief, but he was more or less a contented man, and he never wished anyone harm.

Herr Metzger's plot, however, beat all, even if rotten little Fritz had it coming to him in spades.

Also, Herr Metzger's plot presented Odysseus with two priceless things: a window of opportunity during which to steal those golden toy soldiers, and the assurance that Herr Metzger was enough of a thief—in a manner of speaking—to be stolen from.

Odysseus did not return to the dining room. The notion of Anna was at least temporarily eclipsed by the richer luster of golden toy soldiers. He awaited seven o'clock in his chamber, pacing. Now and then he peered through the window into the street below. Folks were gathering. Children and dogs darted amid shapes—odd shapes, fur-edged and hulking, carrying obscure things. Only a few drunken hoots cut the cold air, but it was early yet. Tension tightened on its crank.

A few minutes after seven, Odysseus went to guest chamber number two. He knocked softly. No reply. He opened the door a bit, wincing at the hinges' squeak. Fritz's sugar-loaf silhouette filled a small bed against the wall. The larger bed was unoccupied.

Odysseus heard footsteps behind him. He turned. No one. He slipped inside the chamber and gently shut the door. He tiptoed to a wardrobe and stuffed himself inside just as the door hinges squeaked again. Through a crack in the wardrobe doors, Odysseus saw a big, hairy shape creep toward Fritz: Peter the drunk, all togged up. Something made a sound like *crick-creak, crick-creak*. Peter was in need of a bath for he reeked like a wet dog. At Fritz's bedside, Peter stopped and unstrapped the large basket on his back. He set the basket on the floor and opened the lid.

Fritz popped up in bed. In the near-darkness, his face was but three black holes. He made a scrambled cry.

Peter scooped up Fritz with an elastic force startling in a drunk, stuffed him into the basket, shut the lid, and latched it. Fritz's cries were muffled.

Odysseus changed his mind. To tunkett with not meddling in other folks' childrearing; he could not allow a child to be kidnapped. His mind told his body, *Burst out of this wardrobe.*

Peter turned. Urine-yellow eyes beamed straight through the crack in the wardrobe door. Odysseus went limp with that boneless rodent lethargy again.

Peter slung the basket to his back by its straps, the wicker *crick-creak*ing, and strode out of the chamber.

Odysseus couldn't stir for maybe two minutes. Then with a shudder, he released a stale breath; he'd been holding it.

It had been an act, all a splendid act. Anna had said that Peter was a good man. Surely Fritz would be fine as frog hair.

Odysseus stumbled from the wardrobe. Well, as long as he was here, he may as well steal the golden toy soldiers.

Fritz had said the soldiers were in his mother's traveling trunk, and yes, there they were in a slender wooden box, hidden beneath a mound of finery.

Odysseus carried the box to his chamber and opened it. Six toy soldiers nestled in crimson silk. He lifted one, and its slick density told his practiced fingers that it was indeed solid gold. It ought to have made his muscles thrill, and he ought to have gone to find Peter and Fritz. Instead, Odysseus spread out on his bed and instantly fell into a shallow, sweaty sleep in which he dreamt of urine-yellow eyes.

Odysseus woke with a snort. The room temperature had dropped and his fingers and toes were near numb. He checked his pocket watch. Nine-thirty. Had Fritz returned? He put on his boots, tucked the box of golden soldiers into his inner jacket pocket, and went downstairs.

Shouts and weeping came from the dining room. Odysseus paused in the doorway. Frau Metzger sobbed, doubled-over in a chair before the fire. Herr Metzger bellowed orders at a clutch of shabby-looking policemen.

Holy Moses.

Odysseus made his way unnoticed to the bar. Anna was wiping pewter cups, her eyes on the others. Her gold-white aura seemed to vibrate as Odysseus drew closer. He smelled, faintly, sweet fresh pine sap.

Anna's eyes fell on him. Cold. She called to the police, "Here he is! Yes, I did not realize it till now, but *this* is the man I saw."

Herr Metzger's voice trickled off. All eyes fixed on Odysseus.

"What did you do with my child?" Frau Metzger shrieked.

Odysseus's mouth popped open. He could not speak.

"I saw this man creep into chamber number two," Anna said. "I believe you will find, too, the box of golden toy soldiers he stole inside his jacket."

How in tarnation had she known that?

"Arrest this man!" Herr Metzger shouted.

Three policemen rushed.

"Did you murder my boy?" Frau Metzger screamed. "Did you kill him because he witnessed your theft?"

Odysseus vaulted over the bar, almost knocking over a bottle of schnapps. "There is some mistake," he said. "I did nothing to the boy. His father—"

"Lies!" Herr Metzger shouted, purple-faced. "He lies. A criminal!"

The policemen were clambering onto the bar.

Odysseus grabbed the bottle of schnapps, spun around, and pushed through the curtain behind the bar.

He ran through a deserted kitchen to a door, shoved it open, and tripped into a drift of snow. His breath billowed into the slicing air. Shouting and pounding boots behind him. To the right, the side alley terminated in trees. To the left lay the swarming main street. Odysseus scrambled to his feet and bolted left.

Soon he was shouldering through the crowd. An accordion and a clarinet weaved squawking, buoyant music like a ribbon through the crowd's garbled voices. Hooked witch faces and too-smooth animal masks nodded. Everywhere were hairy backs and horned skulls and sloshing cups.

Odysseus backed into an alleyway to catch his breath and try to cogitate.

It was pretty clear that, there being no train out of Kiefertal till tomorrow, he must find Fritz and bring him back to his parents—and find Peter and make him confess to the police—or else be arrested.

A woolen-faced creature strode past, so tall the wearer was surely on stilts. Not real. Only a costume. And yet, winter.... The deep wildness of folks comes out in wintertime, Odysseus knew. The busyness of agriculture saved people in remote places from sinking back into the landscape. But in winter, with not enough work to do and snowdrifts piling at the door, wilderness crept through all the carefully sealed cracks. He'd seen it before in New England, when roof-high snow made that axe in the corner start looking like a fine way to silence a nettling spouse.

Odysseus wasn't traveling light, with the box of toy soldiers and the bottle of schnapps. He was unwilling to jettison the schnapps since it was the only weapon he had tonight. The soldiers must go.

He went down the alley and stopped at a glowing window. Inside, a horned Krampus embraced a bear. Odysseus's breath shallowed out. *Only costumes. Only costumes.*

At the next lit window, a bony woman sat at table with a litter of children in patched clothing, all eating soup from a single bowl. Odysseus rapped on the window.

The woman dropped her spoon. Her thin face lengthened in fright. She said something to her children—all staring at the window—and hurried over. She cracked the window. "We have no schnapps for you," she said. "Go away." She tried to shut the window, but Odysseus stopped it with his hand.

"Here," he said. "Here is a gift for you and your children." He pushed the box of soldiers through the window. "Hold onto these as long as you can, and then sell them, one by one, in different towns. They will fetch you enough to eat for years."

The woman stared.

Odysseus ducked out of sight. Down the alleyway, he paused to burrow the schnapps into his jacket. Good. Hands free.

The starting place was to check every drinking establishment in town. True, tonight the entire *town* was a drinking establishment, but aside from those moments in chamber number two, Peter had seemed a lackluster drunk. Even if he was still in costume, he was likely to be slumped over a table somewhere rather than dancing in the street.

Odysseus turned up his jacket collar for warmth and privacy and waded back out into the throng. Three witches in shriveled leather masks danced in a circle, giggling. A creature of woven rushes made Odysseus's heart stop. He could not rip his gaze away from the stagnant black slits of its eyes until the creature moved on. Furred Krampuses rattled chains and flicked birch branches. Children cowered on doorsteps in their nightclothes, mothers hovering behind them. Some of the smaller children were crying. A little boy shouted at a Krampus to go away, and a girl holding a rag doll wailed "I want Saint Nicholas!"

Odysseus found a drinking establishment. Inside, smoke and sour spirits hazed the air. A dozen bodies milled in licking firelight, most faces obscured by hairy or wooden or porcelain masks. Odysseus peered into every face and mask in turn. "Peter?" he shouted above the clamor. "Peter?"

No one responded.

The door whacked open and two policemen burst in.

Nutcake.

Odysseus dodged to the rear of the inn and slipped out the back way. He crunched through the icy alley to the main street.

He found another drinking establishment at the furthest reach of the street where it merged into dark, snowy under-growth. The Krampuses and wild-men inside sat rather than stood, and they spoke rather than roared.

Masks pivoted toward Odysseus when he entered. Conversations sputtered out.

"I am looking for a man called Peter," Odysseus said.

"Well, you have come to the right place," a man's voice replied, muffled by a mask like a gnarled tree trunk. He pointed to the chimney corner.

Peter was slumped against the stones, mouth hanging open, eyes drooped shut. No mask, no costume.

"Drunk as the devil," someone else said.

"And is there a child here?" Odysseus asked.

"Child? No children here."

The men turned back to their drink and conversations. Odysseus went to Peter and shook him. Peter's limbs felt like slabs of wet clay. He was utterly senseless. "How long has he been like this?" Odysseus asked the creatures at the nearest table.

"Oh, getting on about eight years," one of them said, and they all guffawed.

"How long this evening, I mean to say?"

"Oh, since about six thirty or thereabouts," a wolf with a creaky old-timer's voice said. "Came in boasting about an important job he had been hired to do. I suppose he was paid for the job in advance, for he drank up all the money. Then the innkeeper dragged him out of the way."

"Six-thirty?" Odysseus frowned. "Are you certain?"

The wolf pointed to a carved clock on the wall. "I keep track of the time because my old woman keeps track of me."

More guffaws.

If Peter had been here since six-thirty, then he couldn't have stolen Fritz from his bed. Someone *else* had stolen Fritz. What was more, Herr Metzger had told Peter that he would pay him only *after* Fritz was delivered back to the hotel, so someone must've paid off Peter early on, to get him out of the way.

Odysseus swallowed bile once, twice. Those urine-colored eyes....

"Looks like you need a drink, young fellow," the wolf said.

"I reckon that's the last thing I need."

"What did you want with Peter? He is a useless heap of nothing."

"The waitress at Hotel Baumberg told me otherwise. She said he was a good fellow and that he usually doesn't drink."

"Who told you that?"

"The waitress at Hotel Baumberg. Anna."

"There is no Anna working there. Only old Jacob."

"Anna must be his daughter, then."

"Jacob has no daughter, no wife—only a son two valleys away."

"But you *must* know Anna. She is very lovely."

"You have been tricked, young man. This is Krampusnacht. Trickery reigns. This Anna of yours could have been a witch."

"Humbug." Odysseus's belly squeezed. A *witch*? He bade good evening to the wolf and staggered out into the iced starry night. Woolly paranoia filled his head, and the cold was a relief.

Anna—whoever she was—had meant Odysseus to take the blame for kidnapping Fritz. Had she been the one dressed up as Krampus in chamber number two? What if... well, simply for the sake of argument, what if Anna *was* a witch? Witches in fairy stories stole children, particularly plump, naughty children like Fritz. To eat them.

He must return to Hotel Baumberg and demand answers from Anna, even if it meant being caught by the police. If Anna was a stranger to town only masquerading as a waitress, she had a bundle of explaining to do.

Odysseus took a few steps in the direction of the hotel, and froze. On the snow at his feet was a single drop of blood, bright in the inn's window-light.

Probably from a drunken man. Drunks were dealt gashes, they fell.

But.

But beside the drop of blood was a large cloven hoof print. And another and another at man-stride intervals, leading to the end of the main street and into the trees.

Odysseus followed the hoof prints.

The snow was deeper under the pine trees. Odysseus plowed through shin-deep. He picked out the hoof prints, faint in the starlight. The mountain sloped steeply, but the hoof prints took a diagonal course, wrapping around the mountain.

Odysseus swung his arms and grew wet with perspiration. The schnapps bottle bounced against his ribs. He would find that cloven-hoofed monster. He *would*. He had no time for the gut-twisting recollection that he had boasted to Anna how he could track anything in the snow....

Presently, the diagonal course opened out onto a ridge, below which were a bare snowy slope downward, another slope up, and then more trees. Odysseus paused, panting. A shape loped up the far side. A basket bulked its back, and a long tail swung behind. It merged into the trees.

It was true, then. Odysseus was tracking a devil. He touched the pouch at his belt, the contents of which he had killed and preserved at the base of a giant Redwood tree. Courage. Nimbleness. He ran down the slope, stumbled face-first into the snow, and rolled to a stop. He struggled upright, breathing hard, snow melting on his hot skin.

He got up, brushed himself off, and noticed for the first time a little cottage nestled in the valley's crook. Smoke undulated from the chimney and light shone in the windows. A shed leaned against the side. If there were a horse....

Odysseus slogged over. He opened the shed doors, blocked at first by snow, and peered in. No horse. Only a goat bedded down in straw with staring yellow eyes.

Wait.

Odysseus cracked the door wider to let in more light, and saw hanging skis and poles. He grabbed them, brought them out of the shed, and buckled the skis to his boots with leather straps. He took up the poles and launched himself across the fine powder.

This was less frantic, gliding rather than staggering. Odysseus's thoughts smoothed out, too. For the first time he could wonder, if Fritz had been stolen by, well, whatever that thing was, at seven o'clock, then why was he being carried off into the woods only *now*, hours later? Was Fritz even in that basket?

Odysseus slowed at the top of the slope and surveyed for hoof prints. There they went, a staggered track back into the forest. He skied after them. On and on the prints went, zigging and zagging through trees and mounded snow. Bare bushes grabbed and tore his clothing. Rocks jarred him. He was soaked to the skin, and he longed to unbutton his jacket, but he was unwilling to stop. He ascended gradually, digging the ski poles deep and hoisting himself up the steepest places.

The forest unfolded onto a moonsheened blue-black vista. He was at the top of a cliff. Below him, spiky treetops.

Where in Tartarus had that thing with the pack gone?

Wind wafted. Pine boughs whispered. Then, unmistakably, the *crick-creak* of wicker down below. Yes, there was a way down, a snowy swoop off to the side, precarious, dented with cloven hoof marks.

Odysseus angled the tips of his skis together and went haltingly, silently down. At the bottom, he glimpsed the thing disappearing into the trees, close enough now to catch a whiff of its wet-dog stink.

Crick-creak, crick-creak went the basket.

The thing didn't look over its shoulder, but it sped up. It knew Odysseus was coming.

Odysseus's limbs locked into fluid striding motions. The skis whistled faintly. Closer, closer. The wet-dog stink grew stronger, the *crick-creak* louder. Odysseus made out the repulsive back-bent knees of the thing, the way its goat-legs bobbled slightly with each step, not out of weakness but because of an alien way of moving that was unforgivable.

Odysseus was upon them. With one last muscle-burning heave he toppled himself, skis and all, onto the thing and its basket. The thing sprawled facedown in the snow. That wet-dog reek! Something inside the basket whimpered. The thing writhed, bandy-muscled, but it was caught beneath skis and poles and Odysseus's large body. Odysseus fumbled the basket lid open. Fritz crawled out, sobbing.

"Go," Odysseus told him, panting and grunting as the thing tried to rear up under him. He pointed to the cliff. "Climb up there—see the track? Follow the ski marks through the wood, and after that follow the footprints, and you will find the town and your mother and father."

Fritz shook and sobbed. He wore a nightshirt and nothing else.

"*Go!*"

Fritz staggered off toward the cliff track. Odysseus was left alone on top of the writhing, stinking thing. Without Fritz in its basket, the thing had more leeway. It dragged itself out from Odysseus, got up, and stole deeper into the trees. Odysseus hadn't seen its face.

"Nutcake!" Odysseus roared up to the pine boughs. The tangle of his own skis and poles and lanky limbs had trapped him.

The primordial hunter that lurks inside every man's blood screamed. His muscles would pop his clothing seams. The dark night was luminous not with light but with a pulsating *realness* that he had not noticed before. He unbuckled himself from the skis, tossed aside one of the poles, and tipped up the second pole like a spear. He went once more after the thing.

There it was, darting through the tree trunks. Odysseus ran, panting, his only thought the sensation the sharp ski pole would make when he speared it into that thing's back.

They were going down again, down, down, and then here was another little valley. What was that silvery double-curve over there? A train track. A station, too, and a short platform beside the track. The thing bobbed on its backward knees toward the platform. Odysseus ran after it. In the distance came the hollow *hoot-hooooooot* of a train.

This was not the train station at which he'd arrived. No sign announced the name of the stop. The windows and door handles gleamed, and a pearly-faced clock with missing hands hung under the gable.

The thing, its back to Odysseus, mounted the platform and stopped.

Odysseus slowed, spear still aloft His blood bubbled down to a simmer. The thing was waiting for him. This could be a trap. But it was an animal—wasn't it?—and so perhaps it was merely confused or exhausted.

Odysseus mounted the platform and stopped two paces off.

The thing turned. A familiar face, a man's face not a thing's, with pale knobs of cheekbone and narrow sculptured lips. The mysterious gentleman in black who had been at the corner dining table at Hotel Baumberg. He did not wear blue-tinted glasses now. His urine-yellow eyes looked straight into Odysseus and seemed to pull his essence out with some intricate hook. "Good evening, Mr. Flax," he said in the silken voice of a gentleman.

80

"Who are you?"

"Why, the Krampus, of course."

"But you don't have any fur up top. No horns." That train was rumbling closer.

"Fur and horns do not a Krampus make, dear boy. Devils keep abreast of the times, unlike country bumpkins."

"Why did you steal the boy?"

"He was but a pawn on the chessboard. It was *you* whom I wished to see."

"Me? I'm only passing through here." Odysseus re-gripped the spear.

"*Are* you, though?"

"That woman, Anna, in the hotel—"

"Bewitching, yes? Not for the likes of you, Mr. Flax, although I am well aware that one of your mortal torments is a weakness for pretty girls. I knew that long, long ago, you see, which is why I asked Anna for her assistance."

"That drop of blood in the snow—"

"Illusion."

"What do you desire? To tease me? To mock me? To exhaust me with this chase through the forest?"

"Those things do have their charms, but no. You are a naughty boy, Mr. Flax. Very, *very* naughty. A thief, a professional thief—"

"I steal only from thieves."

"Ah, but that is just it. That is the falsehood that consoles you to sleep. Your rocking cradle, the line that separates you—so you believe—from the more grasping, *common* sort of criminal. But do you know what I detest more than anything, Mr. Flax? No? I detest a self-deceiver. You are a thief, plain and simple, and what is more, you do not steal out of necessity. Oh, no, no. You steal for the thrill. More despicable still, you steal as a way to tamper with fate. That woman to whom you gave those golden toy soldiers? She was bound for pneumonia this winter, but *now*.... Naughty, naughty."

"Why the ruse?" Odysseus asked. The train was almost there, hissing and clattering just around the bend. "If it is your custom to stuff the naughty into your basket and carry them off to Hell, why steal poor Fritz? Why the chase?"

Here came the train.

"Fritz required a good scare." The Krampus almost yelled to be heard over the sounds of the train. "His father was correct. And you, Mr. Flax, well, you simply would not have fit into my basket. However, I *do* fancy you'll fit quite nicely through the gates of Hell."

The train screeched to a stop beside the platform, steam ballooning. A door fell open beside Odysseus.

"Go on, then," the Krampus said. "Step on like a good boy. We don't want a fuss, do we?"

"Step onto the train?"

"Everyone has their own notion of Hell on earth—I believe you agree with me on that point, Mr. Flax—and for you, Hell on Earth is suffering traveling sickness on a train. And so it is that Hell itself, for *you*, must be traveling sickness on a train that never, *ever* stops."

Odysseus tried to dodge past the Krampus, but the Krampus blocked his path with an oily sidestep. "All aboard, Mr. Flax. I should mention that this particular train will not leave without you."

Odysseus dodged to the other side, and again the Krampus blocked him. Odysseus became aware of the bottle of schnapps pressed against his ribs. Anna had said that one must offer the Krampus schnapps to appease him. She was a witch and could've been lying, but with that train fizzling and steaming behind him, what else could Odysseus do? He whipped out the bottle. "Schnapps, Mr. Krampus?"

The Krampus's shoulders sagged. The forked red tip of his tongue flicked out. "Perhaps a drop, yes, only a drop."

"Excellent." Odysseus uncorked the bottle and passed it over. The Krampus took it and drank greedily as if it were water. Odysseus darted past, bumping the Krampus as he went and feeling fur, frock coat, brass buttons, the inside of a woolen pocket. He sprinted along the platform with the dense black shape of the train in the corner of his eye. Past the station, down the platform steps, across the snow, into the woods. Only when he was safely behind a tree did he dare look back.

The Krampus stepped aboard the train, swaying on his bent-wrong legs, clutching the bottle. The door whapped shut and the train chuffed and wailed into motion. It slid like a black fish around a bend in the valley and was gone.

Odysseus looked at his fist, shaking a little, and opened it. The Krampus's blue-tinted glasses with steel bows glittered. Tomorrow on the train, he would learn whether or not they provided relief from traveling sickness. Of course, even Odysseus had enough money to purchase his *own* glasses, but despite everything, he still reckoned it was necessary to steal from thieves.

Steampunk fashion has fetishized Victorian flip-up glasses, but glasses with lenses that flip to the side, called "railroad spectacles," were around in the nineteenth century, too. Blue-tinted glasses with steel bows make a brief appearance in Nathaniel Hawthorne's 1849 sketch "Main-Street." They finagled their way into a chapter of my dissertation, and I knew they'd be back again someday in a story of my own.

Maia Chance

OL' ST. NICK

BY RAVEN OAK

You've heard of locked room mysteries, but how about a locked spaceship?
Raven Oak shows us how petty realities could extend into grand futures. She
gives us organized crime, a host of unreliable characters, derelict spaceships,
and the death of a Santa. What more could a space sorta-pirate ask for?

–Janine A. Southard

Jolly Old Saint Nicholas,
Lean your ear this way;
Don't you tell a single soul
What I'm going to say,
Christmas Eve is coming soon;
Now my dear old man,
Whisper what you'll bring to me;
Tell me if you can.
When the clock is striking twelve,
When I'm fast asleep,
Down the chimney broad and black
With your pack you'll creep;
All the stockings you will find
Hanging in a row;
Mine will be the shortest one;
You'll be sure to know.

Original lyrics as published in 1881

The hole-riddled ship reminded me of my Gran— broken and just a touch too old to remain in an ever-changing world. I'd seen many a battered ship, but standing on the bridge with nothing but a spacesuit between me and possible—scratch that, *probable*—death, set my stomach turning.

Two walls of the bridge were intact, though their computer displays—the undamaged ones, anyway—lay unresponsive. I floated near a hole as tall as me. Something had ripped its way through the transport ship's shields and into the hull.

Treaty negotiations between Earth and the New Jhovens left union crews unwilling to contract with freelancers like me. That left me with salvage work like this. The creepiest kind of work.

Creepy or not, this job was perfect. Honest theft as these folks had no need of their ship anymore. Besides, we needed this gig. If I had to eat another protein bar for dinner, I'd be tempted to abandon my *own* damned ship.

Maybe it was *too* perfect. A ship that size, you'd expect someone to miss her or at least miss her crew. If nothing else, word of the attack should have reached someone.

Yet the *Lucky Fish* stood empty—except my meager crew who floated about searching for anything worth selling or using to repair my ship, *The Perffaith*.

Jake's shadow darkened the computer display in front of me. "Fight like this, makes me wonder if there's injured on board."

Half-fix-this, half-carry-that, Jake was my go-to man, though currently he was my dig-for-parts man as we combed the bridge of the *Lucky Fish*.

"Body scans came up negative for life forms. If anyone's injured, they're long past needing our help, Jake."

"As we boarded, Lissa said she thought there might be unfriendlies on board. Maybe left over from the fight."

When I turned, his spacesuit's helmet light nailed me directly in the face. I winced, and he tapped a button at his wrist to dim it. "Sorry, Captain," he said.

"If you're that concerned, run another scan."

Jake passed me his handheld. "Can't. Scanner's dead again."

No heat sources registered, and I swore.

"There are all manner of species that don't read right on our scanners—*provided they work*—so no sense in being lax with security, sir."

I winced at his paraphrasing. "Remind me to give you the job if I ever need a new security officer. You nailed Lissa's deadpan perfectly." Her uptight personality used to be a boon. Now it was just a reminder of our past.

The thick, synthetic fibers of my suit protected my fingers from the jagged metal hole in front of me. Jake pulled himself closer until he reached my side, his blond dreads mashed up against his sweaty face inside his helmet. "This is one battle I'm sure glad we missed."

Despite the fresh shave, my black scalp itched as sweat trickled down my jaw. I glanced at Jake's dreads again.

"Itchy?" he asked.

"Yeah. Must be time to switch out the filters." Yet another thing to add to my growing list of repairs-to-make-whenever-we-have-money-again.

"Maybe the *Lucky Fish* will have the parts." Jake's breathing was loud in my helmet speakers. "I'm glad they ain't here. The stiffs, I mean. Hate when we hafta work around dead folks."

"Open channel two to *The Perffaith*," I spoke into my helmet, which buzzed in response. The channel light flipped to green, connecting me to my chief engineer. "Zac, any luck talking to the computer over here? Or getting her to power up?"

My helmet crackled, and when Zac answered, his voice was louder and clearer than before. "Nope. Something must've blown out the system. I'll need to hop on over to see what's the—"

"Negative, Zac. Remain on board *The Perffaith*. Close channel two." I flipped a power switch beside me several times with no response. "Gut what you can, Jake. The bridge is a loss. But keep a lookout for the black box."

He removed the protective glass from a panel and set to stripping the innards of wires and circuits that didn't show obvious char-marks.

If I could find the black box, maybe I could sort out her last moments...The panel's sliding door below me was fused together. I pushed away from it and floated across to the more intact portion of the bridge. One console bore a few scorch marks but little else. The cover almost fell off in my hands, but its insides were a mess of wires. No box.

"Open channel four." When the light lit, I asked, "Hey, Seb, how's it looking in the cargo hold?"

There was a delay in either the comm or his response. Maybe the *Lucky Fish* was bouncing the signal around. Or maybe our suits sucked. I resisted the urge to rip off my helmet as static crackled in my ears and set them ringing.

"...Salvaged one crate...moved onto...."

"Did you catch any of that, Jake?" I asked.

Shoulder deep in computer hardware, he mumbled, "Said something 'bout salvaging a crate."

How helpful.

"Captain, we have an issue." Seb's voice rang too sharp in my ears.

"Report!"

"There is someone unexpected on the ship. A survivor perhaps."

Either the scanners had gone belly up again, or I needed a new first mate. Sweat rolled down my back, and the suit adjusted its humidity levels to compensate. "Where?"

"Unknown, Captain. The heat signature is sporadic."

"Zac—" There was no response on channel two. "Locate Officer Zac Curtis."

A squeal let loose in my helmet. Channel five pulsed before autoconnecting. "Captain?"

"Why are you on a suit channel? Hurry up and shut the cargo doors on *The Perffaith*, Zac. I don't need anyone getting any ideas like making off with our ship."

"No-can-do, Captain. I just boarded the *Lucky Fish* to help track our mystery person."

Shit. No one could've survived on this ship full of holes. That left other salvagers. Folks likely to shoot first and ask questions later. I figured at most we might run across some space critter or another—usually did on a salvage trip—but nothing humanoid or weapon-carrying.

But then, derelicts and wounded ships attracted the most unsavory types, didn't they?

No misplaced shadows outside the bridge. I snatched a serrated hunk of metal debris floating in front of me and shielded myself as I pushed my way along the corridor. Zac, my chief engineer, met me and Jake at the junction between Hallway A and Corridor C.

Zac gripped a piece of a wooden crate. He'd come from the left instead of the right, and I frowned.

Besides being an excellent engineer, the goofy guy had been my best friend since childhood. He must have guessed my thoughts as he said, "I rechecked the cargo hold on my way to you."

The corridor to engineering was as empty as those to the bridge had been. Outside the engine room, Lissa stood guard. The spacesuit hid her muscular frame, but she was imposing enough with the chill across her face.

"Jake, is Seb showing up on the scanner?" I asked.

Jake slapped the device. "Is now."

"You and Zac intercept him. I don't want him tracking this heat source alone."

I didn't have to add, *too inexperienced*. Both pulled themselves down the corridor. I stuck my head inside the engine room. My other engineer was waist deep in engine parts. Too busy to notice anything but chipsets and circuitry.

I drifted back into the hall and asked Lissa, "Seen anything or anyone?"

"Nothing yet."

"Stay with the crew members here."

"But—"

I held up my hand and she *tsked*, something she did more often than I liked. Before she could voice her opinion, my speakers squawked in my ear. "Captain, we've got a problem."

"What is it, Zac?"

Silence made me hurry—as much as one could in a spacesuit.

More popping and sputtering from my speakers. Zac's voice returned, halting my forward propulsion. "We found Seb. Damned heat source vanished."

"Vanished? Equipment malfunction?"

I'd replaced all the handheld scanners' memory chips last month. Cheap New Jhovensian shit.

"Worse. Our heat source is freshly dead."

The room Seb had found was little more than a closet. Crates and sacks crowded it beyond cozy, and the dead body splayed through the center took up more than his fair share of space. His round belly floated over a thick, black belt cinching pants stained with grease and who knew what else. Then there was the garish red jacket. Ugly thing with too much fur for this century.

"He is freshly deceased, Captain. The body— " Seb's voice cracked, "—still bears warmth."

White whiskers were sprinkled across the dead man's broad chin, and his cheeks were round cherries. Those cheeks were rounder than I remembered. I forced my hand to relax around the hunk of debris I'd grabbed as a makeshift weapon.

Seb's white skin was near translucent as he hovered in the doorway. He was the only non-human on board, but with a pair of stylin' shades over his eyes and his orange afro wig, you could almost think him human. Right up 'til he opened his mouth and spewed something about the sins of freedom and enterprise in his near-perfect English.

He was the newest member of my crew—the most annoying member of my crew—but right now, I didn't blame him for getting a case of the wiggins.

Petrie, my medical officer, squeezed past him. Her hip brushed his leg, and Seb flinched. "Back away from the body, please," said Petrie.

She crouched beside the body with a grunt as the crew watched. The sour smell left my tongue too thick in my mouth.

"You good, Captain?" asked Zac.

I blinked several times to clear my head. "Unnecessary complications bug me is all."

"So what happened to him, Doc?"

Petrie glanced at Zac, then returned to the victim. "I'll need to do a full autopsy to be sure, but I suspect he asphyxiated," she said.

"What's the scanner say about that heat source now, Zac? If someone on board killed this man, it's not too far a stretch to think they might kill someone else," I said.

He held up his scanner. The blue grid held a dozen heat sources, every last one of them traceable to the trackers in our suits.

Seb glared at the functioning scanner. "I followed the foreign heat source here before it disappeared. This was the man who appeared as an additional heat source."

"Ya really think someone killed him, Mark? I mean, ship's pretty damaged—what's one more stiff on a ship like this?" Jake asked.

I didn't remember our dead man having a beard last time I saw him. I blinked away the memory and said, "There's something odd about this whole thing. Between the body, the sensors...this man was alive before we boarded. How? There isn't a spacesuit anywhere in this room."

"So how'd he breathe?" asked Zac.

"Murder or not, we'll make a full sweep of the *Lucky Fish*." I opened a channel to Lissa. "Get that engineer and whatever he salvaged over to *The Perffaith*, then join me in canvassing the bow. Keep your eyes open."

"Roger that."

"Zac and Seb, search the stern. I'll work from the bridge back."

Both frowned. "I would best seek with you, Captain."

"You're with Zac, Seb."

"But—"

Zac petted Seb on the shoulder. "Don't sweat it, Seb. Captain here works best *without* our advice. You'll get used to it."

I flicked Zac on the shoulder, though with my gloves it came out more of a tap and caught his grimace before he hid it with a gloved hand.

"I do not understand."

"Give it time. You'll learn to love this ship and its crazy crew once you've been here a while," I said. With a nod to Zac, we set out on our hunt for a possible survivor...or murderer. Between the debris and bulky spacesuits—I couldn't afford the good stuff—the search was slow going. Other than a few bodies that hadn't been wrenched into space during the fight, no original crewmen remained on the *Lucky Fish*. Our lone heat source was no more.

I set out for the crime scene with every intention of blowing the crime off. A quick search had turned up the body's ID, though I barely bothered to glance at it. It was probably fake. Five years and a funny outfit didn't hide those green eyes any more than they hid the scars along his face from one too many brawls.

I dimmed my helmet's visor, blocking out my father's face. It shouldn't have bothered me. We hadn't seen each other in years, and it wasn't like I gave two shits about him. Even worse, I couldn't afford the distraction. Nevertheless, my jaw ached as I guarded his body. Lissa found me a few minutes later.

"Mark, are you all right?"

"Open channel one—code private." When the green light inside my helmet flickered, I said to Lissa, "Check out the doorway."

"The door was pried open."

I pointed at a gouge mark. Paint chips were embedded in the metal.

"Blue paint," she said.

"*Our* blue paint."

She frowned. "You don't know that for a fact."

"Who else uses Cadmium Blue #20 to label their tools? That's not the norm. Freelancers Guild uses Cedar Green #8."

Her gloved fingers flicked a large paint chip from the gouge and sent it drifting. "It's a common paint color, Captain. For other things at least." She kept frowning.

Two channels lit amber in my helmet's display. "Release privacy status," I said and spotted Zac floating toward us with Seb a foot behind.

"Captain, ship's clear as clear can be," said Zac. Seb reported an all clear over the comm unit ten seconds later.

Lissa handed me the key card to the victim's room. Someone—probably me—was gonna get to dig through his belongings. "I know I asked before, but are you okay, Mark? You look...shaken," she said.

I turned from that look, a look that wasn't hers to give anymore. Text on the card said Room 5, Level 3. No power meant no lift, so I set out for the emergency stairs. I used the railing to pull myself up until my helmet lamp shined on the number three. When I paused in my ascent, I caught Lissa trailing behind me. "You didn't have to come along."

"You're searching the room."

"Someone has to."

"Is it his room?"

I shrugged. "Not sure, but if nothing else, I'd like to know why he had the key card on him." I cleared his face from my mind as we stopped outside room five. Like the closet-sized room we'd found him in, the door had been forced open. Pry marks made by something metal had left regular indentations on it. *Unlike* his final resting place, no blue paint chips marred these.

A fold-up cot took the majority of the room. Five wall-drawers shared space with a pull-out sink and toilet bowl.

Typical traveler's quarters. I almost laughed to think of someone as flamboyant and crass as Nick living out of a room like this.

I would've figured he'd opt for a suite.

My light reflected off something on the floor, and I rotated upside down to retrieve it. Glass. "Give me a hand," I muttered, and Lissa gave my legs a push 'til I got upright.

"What is it?"

I held it up to our eye level. "Looks like a snow globe. Used to have one of these as a kid." Small, white dust swirled around inside the glass dome and glittered in my light.

She held up an old paperback just as Zac and Seb crossed through the doorway.

"Is that an honest-to-god real book?" asked Zac.

I nodded and set the glass object on the cot. "Real paper, too. I take it your search is done?"

"Yep. Na-da-thing on board but us."

Lissa passed the book to Zac, and he gasped at the cover. "It's our victim!" A fat man in a red suit grinned at us. "The Tale of Jolly Ol' Saint Nicholas. Some old artifact from Earth, maybe?"

As much as I hated to admit it, the saint on the book did bear a certain resemblance to our victim. It was uncanny the way those same green eyes stared back at me, and for a moment, I was a child again and running.

Always running.

"Captain, look." Zac pointed to some text on the front page. "Says here this Saint Nicholas man was some special dignitary on Earth way back when."

There was a cough in my ears. Seb and Jake crowded around the door, hanging on every word Zac uttered. He rambled on about some long dead holiday where folks exchanged gifts and sang about happier times.

"That body isn't a saint. Certainly not some gift-giver," I muttered.

The chatter around me ceased. Zac cocked his head in his helmet. "How you figure? Looks like the real deal—the real Santa Claus—to me."

My brain caught up with my mouth. "Too many scars on him. That man's seen too many brawls to be some cheerful myth."

Seb asked, "But how would you explain his attire? It is identical to that on the book."

Damn him. The Alphan latched onto anything like it was gospel truth. A habit I'd have to break him of if he wished to remain first mate.

Seb continued, "He even possesses a—what did you call it, Zac? A traditional gift?"

"What gift?"

"The snow globe and book. A find like this might be worth some coin." Zac's eyes glittered.

"Should we not be worried about how this saint died?" Seb shook the snow globe I'd cast aside earlier, sending white flutters around the tiny city inside.

My stomach threatened to empty itself right there in all that junk. From simple salvage to a crime scene, this job was everything I'd hoped to avoid. Including seeing my father, Nick. Either way, I wasn't gonna be able to walk away without the answer to at least one question:

What the hell had Nick been doing on this ship?

"According to his identification, the victim's name is Nick Johnson."

Banes, not Johnson. My brain corrected the details. Why'd he choose Gran's maiden name for his false persona? I ground my teeth as the crew crowded around the body like voyeurs. Petrie, my chief medical officer, rattled more information from the display in *The Perffaith*'s infirmary.

Petrie continued, "Until we're able to access the derelict's computer, we won't be able to ascertain his purpose on the *Lucky Fish*. Maybe he's following the old Earth myth of Santa Claus." Eyes the color of weak tea twinkled, lending beauty to an otherwise plain face. "The team found a sack full of Earth artifacts stowed in a crate in the cargo hold."

Knowing Nick, the goods were probably stolen. I swallowed back bile.

"The identification plate on the crate's side matches that of our victim." Petrie pulled back the sheet to expose Nick's face. The swollen, red skin marred the sterile and clinical white room. Like someone had opened a can of animal innards and maraschino cherries, molded them Nick-shaped, and plopped them down on the table.

Lissa's muscles strained at the shoulders of her blue shirt as she leaned over the victim. She held back her long red braids with one hand and pointed at a pinprick in his neck. "Is this how he died?" she asked.

Petrie pointed at the large display panel. Scans of various organs scrolled by with a ton of numbers that meant nothing to me. "His toxicology screens show he suffered anoxia—"

At our blank stares, she added, "He asphyxiated as a result of exposure to carbon monoxide."

"When? Seb said we had a heat signature," I interrupted.

"The victim was alive when we hailed the *Lucky Fish* and found their computer unresponsive. He died within ten minutes of our coming aboard."

"What about this injection or pinprick cut?" asked Lissa.

"Coincidental. Something done prior to death."

I ran a finger over the tiny wound. "You sure, Petrie?"

"Yes, Captain. Cause of death is anoxia."

Behind me, Seb and Zac whispered over the death of *Santa Claus*. Speculation bred rumors, and I shushed them. "Can you tell me how he survived so long without a ship suit? Was there air in that room?" I asked.

"Oxygen was present and cycling after whatever fight left holes in the *Lucky Fish*." Petrie's eyes narrowed. "You look like you have another question."

"Yeah, which one of us killed him?" You'd have thought I'd sucked the air from our ship the way Seb gasped. "Do the math, Seb."

I couldn't see his eyes behind those enormous sunglasses he wore, nor did his mouth-flap tilt to indicate comprehension. Seb held up his hands. "There is no math to complete. I assume this is another idiom?"

The only non-Earthling on board, and he spoke better English than me. Toss him a saying, and he'd be chewing on it for the next hour. "Think about it. Victim died of...anoxia, but that room took no damage. Air was circulating. So how'd he die?"

Zac asked, "Airflow controller ain't on the fritz, is it?"

"Sensors would've picked up the increase throughout the ship."

"Not with all them holes, Captain." Zac frowned. "Wasn't any air to check. It'd all been sucked out."

Lissa leaned against the wall, arms crossed and eyes narrowed. "Airflow controller was one of the salvaged parts. Booted up just fine for Zac's lackey," she said.

Nick had been right. Damned fool had been destined to die in space. Not that he 'hadn't had it coming. He was an asshole at best and mobster at worst.

"I think the room was a safe room of some type. Pretty common on passenger ships, and it would explain why the room had its own circulation system," said Lissa.

"Maybe this Santa felt all dizzy or something from CO buildup. Messed up and took the wrong drugs? Maybe he went and shot himself up with something that later killed him? Something that interacted with the levels of CO?" Jake asked.

"Captain?"

I wrested my glance from the stiff.

"Mr. Johnson received a dose of adrenaline sometime before death. If it had been fatal, his heart muscles would display signs of stress, of pumping harder," Petrie explained. "His blood work would show the increase of adrenaline or the chemicals found in whatever drug he could've taken, but nothing showed up in my preliminary tests. The dose he received was too small to do much of anything. Certainly not kill him."

I tapped my gold sliver of a wristband. "Bridge." Once connected I asked, "Did our sensors pick up any trace signatures when we approached the *Lucky Fish*? Like someone leaving as we arrived?"

The crewmember on duty answered in the negative, then asked, "Would you like me to run a second analysis of the scans to be sure?"

"Yes, and send the report to my inbox."

Lissa's fists rested on her hips as she eyed everyone huddled in the infirmary. They stared at each other, each taking turns to weigh suspicions and prejudices. It was comical in a way, made more so by the stripes of pungent cinnamon paste under their noses.

The wall display read 21:04. A long day that would only get longer if I was gonna figure out who knocked off Nick. "Zac and Seb, I want a complete report on the airflow controller and any other parts on the *Lucky Fish* that might explain this. Petrie, run your tests, and Lissa, start looking into what crew may or may not have had ties with our victim. We'll meet at 02:00 in the common area."

Five people I trusted stood around a dead myth until Petrie zipped the mesh bag closed, covering up Nick. My crew left the room individually. Not one of them wanted to turn their back on another.

Not that I blamed them.

Alone with the doc, I asked, "Petrie-Dish, I don't want to jump to any conclusions, but do you really believe someone from my crew killed him?"

With a glance at the emptying hallway, she leaned close to my ear. "Don't tell a single one of them what I'm going to say, but yes I do. You were on the *Lucky Fish* for twenty minutes before we found Mr. Johnson. Based on the body's lack of lividity, Mr. Johnson was deceased for approximately ten minutes when Seb found him. He died right under our noses."

"The room was sealed, Petrie. It had its own air circulation."

She wrinkled her nose but didn't smile. "And no damage inside the room?"

"Nope. None immediately outside either."

Petrie said, "Then we're all suspects at this point. Someone did something to cause the buildup of carbon monoxide, possibly intentionally. I'll run more tests."

She slid the metal tray bearing Nick into the wall and closed the door. The unit locked with a beep after she pressed her hand to the frontal display screen. "Captain, don't take this the wrong way, but something odd did show up in my autopsy."

I tilted my head but said nothing.

"I ran a print scan, and this Nick Johnson, he doesn't exist. There is no record on file."

I allowed the breath I'd been holding to seep out in a slow exhale. "He must be a criminal then. Any record of such things?"

"Captain, when I say there's no record, I mean it. He's a ghost." The stringent odor of antiseptics hit me as she lathered her arms up to the elbow. "I'll run DNA, but that will take time."

My insides trembled. "Keep digging," I said and fled the infirmary.

Once in my quarters, I leaned against the door as my body shook. I wasn't certain why I was hiding Nick's identity; whether it was for his good or my own, I couldn't be sure, but they couldn't know.

They didn't need to know because *I* didn't kill my father.

I dug through a wall-drawer for a tattered box hidden in the back. I wrestled it from beneath an old pair of boots and set it on my desk. At first, I merely stared at it, but as the silence settled around me, I lifted the lid off the memories.

Nick's face stared at me from the digital photo, his cheeks pink from the mountain's snow. What began as a sigh left me curled in a ball like a child.

I didn't love him—hell, I didn't know him—but now I never would.

I hadn't meant to doze.

The report on the *Lucky Fish*'s circulation system confirmed that the air system was fully operational at the time of death. Someone had to have tampered with it.

It was the latter part that bugged me as it pointed all sorts of fingers at my crew. After zipping through Zac and Seb's report, I'd dozed until something woke me.

A door rattle wasn't the type of noise I'd notice, but my sleep had been uneasy and light. Dreams about the day Nick had left, Gran shouting at him and cursing his name. Seeing her again, even in dreams, left me brittle.

The bleary-looking wall-clock struck midnight, and thumping footfalls paused outside then continued on.

The door panel glowed blue at my approach. "Display heat sources in corridor A," I whispered. One figure moved toward the common area. It wasn't unusual to see folks moving about, but something in my gut told me to follow. The door hissed open as I left my quarters in pursuit.

The creeping figure wore all black and carried a sack tossed over his shoulder. The overhead lights, dimmed for nighttime, cast jagged shadows, and I cursed the lack of foresight that left me weaponless. A door ten feet ahead opened and closed in rapid succession.

When I approached, the door slid open a second time, bathing me in light. Too much light for the common area. Rather than their normal white, the overhead lights twinkled in reds and golds to the rhythm of an odd thump, and I held up a hand to block the glare. "What in all hells—"

"My apologies, Captain. I was testing their luminosity. Allow me to decrease the illumination." Seb's hairless eyebrows danced above heavily darkened lenses the size of my fist. He dropped the bag on the table before he set about adjusting the lights on a handheld control screen.

"Seb, I don't mean you any insult, but what in the world are you doing in here carrying—" I riffled through the bag. "—A bag of socks?"

He slid a sealed box of thumbtacks across the table. "Once I completed my report on the airflow controller, I researched the mythos of Santa Claus. With one of his servants on board, I thought it might help us through our turmoil if we carried on with our own good cheer."

"What are you talking about, Seb? That man isn't Santa—"

He shook out the lengthier socks before tacking them to the wall above the baseboard ventilation shaft. "Captain, I am aware of these facts, but we have a murderer among us. That is not something I wish to dwell on. Instead, I will hang these stockings by the chimney with care—"

"Stop." Another sock dangled between his fingers, this one bearing blue and green stripes, and I asked, "Why are you nailing socks to my ship's walls?"

"In the mythos of Earth's Christmas, Earthlings suspended stockings from chimneys in order to summon the great Saint Nicholas."

He hung two more socks on the wall, and I shook my head. "You realize he's a myth, right? Santa Claus isn't real."

Seb continued his "decorating" until ten socks hung from the wall—one for each of my crew—though one sock dangled half the length of the others.

"What's with the short one?" I asked.

"Have you ever heard of *gherblins*?" I shook my head. "Sometimes *gherblins* creep onto the ship at night and steal the socks my mother knits. When my socks no longer possess a mate, I stow them in a box to send home."

"So what? You shrank one?"

Seb shook his head. "Someone left the miniature stocking in the cargo bay last year after we ferried a group from Yabanc. I suspect one of their offspring may have mislaid it."

He slung the empty bag across his shoulder. His mouth-flap split, both top lips forming a half-grin. Coupled with his sunglasses and unusually pale skin, it painted a grotesque picture. My skin crawled like I'd walked through a cobweb.

"Is there anything else you require, Captain?" Seb asked.

I wanted to tell him, explain why I was bothering with Nick. I mean, he was my first mate. I should've been able to trust him. Instead, I shrugged it off. "I hate complications."

"That is completely understandable."

"Seb?" He turned away from the door frame. "Someone killed that man, and I gotta ask, why do this in the middle of the night? Did it ever occur to you that I might've thought you the murderer? Might still?"

His bushy orange wig escaped his hood when he laughed. "Me? Kill Santa? I am not the one experienced in dead bodies."

"Petrie? Why suspect her?"

"Why not? We are all capable of horrible deeds, are we not? Even you are, I suspect."

Yes, I am.

He mistook my silence and said, "No offense intended, Captain." He sauntered from the room, fro first. I was alone with blinking lights and empty stockings, both of which chased my thoughts in circles. Petrie had been on my ship during the murder, or so I'd thought. Besides, no way a woman like her would know a crook like Nick, much less kill him.

As much as I didn't want to think it, Petrie *did* have access to all manner of medicines and the knowledge to cover up the crime. It wouldn't be the first time Nick had steered a new crewmember my way in order to set me up. It was time to find out what Ol' Nick had been up to in the years since I'd last seen him.

I swore as I trudged back to my quarters. Nothing good would come of this business with Ol' Saint Nick.

But then, nothing ever had.

The trace report on the sector had noted no fewer than five ships in the area before our arrival, but none of them during Nick's murder. Just my ship, *The Perffaith*.

Without access to the *Lucky Fish*'s computer, a spacewalk in a black hole would've been easier than tracing Nick's movements. Zac could've helped, being my local computer expert, but at this point, I couldn't trust anyone.

Sad truth was, I wanted to trust them all.

The last time I'd seen Nick, he'd been on Europa running "errands" for Junto, the father of Europa's crime family. I pecked at the handheld screen, which glared in the darkness until I swiped a finger down the side to dim it. A search of his name pulled up a list of warrants, arrest records, and bounties. His current address showed up as unknown. Not exactly surprising, especially if he were still working for Junto.

We'd last met on Europa in a shack that reeked of sweat and mold. Too much condensation and not enough filtration had left the walls a pattern of black and green splotches. The business card he'd given me that day—*Raymond Royant, Antiquities Dealer*—had a relay code I keyed in. Error messages scrolled across the screen. "*No such contact. Would you like to execute a last known trace-run?*"

I hit the "no" button and leaned my head against the wall. How do you find a guy who lives off the grid? A green light blinked. "Incoming Call—Unknown Number."

"Accept call," I said. No picture appeared—just an empty, black screen.

"Whosit?" a gruff voice asked.

"You tell me since *you* called. Is this Raymond—"

"And I asked you a question, boy. Whosit?"

I cleared my throat. "Um, this is Mark Banes. If this is Raymond, I met you once with Nick—"

The black screen fizzled a moment until Raymond's grumpy face appeared. If I hadn't known any better, I'd have sworn he'd been wearing that same flannel shirt when I'd met him a few years' back. Bloodshot eyes glared at me above a week's worth of stubble. He sat cross-legged in some shack whose walls were lined with cardboard, and he smacked his screen when it grew fuzzy. "I get ya. Yer that turd who left yer dad when he's all sick and shit. Rat bastard's who ya are."

I rolled my eyes visibly, even for a bad connection. Fool had to know he'd been played. But then, Nick played everybody. "Nick wasn't sick. It was his usual spiel. Look, I'm not here to argue the merits or lack of them with you. I just wanna know where he is."

"He left."

"When?"

"I dunno. Do I look like his secretary? Damn bitch was hot, too. Hotter than me." Raymond took a swig from a bottle he'd been storing between his knees. "Yer hair's shorter than that time you visited Nick."

I ran a hand over my brown head. "He still working for Junto?"

Raymond flinched but nodded. The screen flickered then went dark, and the dissonant tritone of a disconnect assaulted my ears.

The last time I'd seen my father, he'd given me some song and dance about being terminal. It wasn't the first time I'd heard that line of bull. Nick's one skill was looking out for number one—that was him. Whether he'd owed Junto's boys money or had bought into some get-rich-quick-scheme, he'd come running to Gran and me when he was low on cash. Or booze. Or both.

And I'd run just a little bit further into space and away from him.

I thought I'd run far enough. Seems as though he'd found a way to run to me.

Nick's death and my lack of sleep left me with visions of drunken bums dancing in my head like a bad 3D flick while I contemplated calling Junto. I had a good hour before the 02:00 meeting with the crew. I sighed and put in a call to the Callisto Space Station.

I'd repeated my request to five lackeys before I reached someone physically stationed on Europa, then to another lackey before reaching the Family proper. "I know you don't wanna tick off your boss, but see, he owes me one," I said to the funny little man on my screen. His mustache—if one could call a pencil-thin line above one's upper lip an actual mustache—twitched. "Tell him Captain Mark Banes would like to call in a favor."

The screen went a hazy, snowy gray for another minute or two before the man himself appeared. He'd lost a good fifty pounds since I'd last seen him, and his comb-over was more wilt than comb. I grinned like we were old friends. "How's life in the Family, Junto? You're looking good."

He didn't return my smile but wagged a thin finger at me. "Where is he?"

"Where's who?"

Junto leaned so close to his screen that his nose near bumped against it. "Your father, who do ya think? Sonofabitch stole some priceless antiquities from....a client. He was s'posed to deliver them to me, but he got all chicky. Took off with the goods."

"Nick's anything but a coward," I said.

My left eye twitched. I tried to ignore it.

"There's somethin' you ain't tellin' me. Now I know I owe you a favor, which I'm willing to make good on, but I can't help you if you're lyin' to me."

"Let me guess. This is what he stole." I held up the snow globe. This time, his nose touched his screen, and I got a shot of more nose hairs than I needed.

"Where is he? Don't make me—"

"He's dead."

Junto's lips tilted up at the corners. So he already knew that, did he?

I continued fishing. "Found him dead on a beat-up ship out here in the Theros cluster. What was Nick doing on the *Lucky Fish*?"

"I assume hidin' from me."

"And it's just a coincidence that I happened upon him?"

Junto leaned away from the screen for a moment of whispering with some shadow in the background before he returned. "Look Mark, I'll tell you what I know, because we're...friends, but after this we're square. I won't owe you shit. Got it?"

It wasn't a fair trade, and the rat bastard knew it. "Fine. Tell me everything."

"Normally Nick made good on his deals, one way or another, but sometimes he gots to thinkin' he could skip the middle man. Took off with that globe-thingy you got, some honest-to-god books—"

I cut him off. "I mean no offense, Junto, but I already know what he took. Get to the bit about him being all corpsified on the *Lucky Fish*."

Junto's eyes narrowed. "My sources say he'd fooled that captain into thinkin' he was more than some two-credit con artist." He waited for me to react, and when I merely shrugged, he asked, "What? No love for *honest* Nick?"

"Say what you want. He *was* a con man. I've got no warm fuzzies for him."

"Raymond's right. You're quite the bastard. I like it!" Junto laughed with his arms wrapped around a much smaller gut. "Once I found his hidin' spot, I sent some of my boys to recover the goods."

"You sure that was all they were there to do?"

"If I wanted Nick dead, there's all manner of folks I coulda sent. I wanted the loot. That's it."

I shook the snow globe before the screen. "I assume the goods are valuable. Why'd your boys leave without them?"

"Fool captain of the *Lucky Fish* believed Nick. Can you imagine? Thought your old man was some freakin' saint or some shit. Captain refused to give me what I was owed, so my boys got...messy. Ship was in pieces when they boarded. Weren't any trace of Nick or the goods."

"You didn't look very hard."

Junto smiled into the screen. "You know everything I do."

He was lying. If he'd wanted the goods, he'd have taken them. Or asked me to fetch them seeing how I was holding them. I wouldn't push a man like Junto too hard—doing so would only result in my death if I were lucky, and the deaths of my entire crew if I were not—but I could certainly play a little.

"Seeing as how you've gone and lost your goods, what's in it for me to return them? I could part—"

Junto severed the connection before I'd finished. While I had the *why* to Nick's appearance on the *Lucky Fish*, it didn't tell me who had killed him or their reasoning. Junto's boys had been long gone by the time Nick had asphyxiated.

I swiped a hand across my screen to lock it. I'd hoped it would be unnecessary, but maybe the search among my crew would yield more answers.

Before I could shadow my eyes from the twinkling lights, Lissa's pile of braids blocked the brightness. "Morning, Captain." Rather than return to her seat, my security officer paced.

The rest of my crew straddled benches along either side of the table. Bags drooped beneath most eyes, and no one paid any mind to the socks tacked to the back wall.

"It's not even 02:00 yet," I muttered and hooked a stool leg with my foot. When it scraped across the floor, Seb flinched and sent a splash of some red sludge over the rim of his mug. "Everyone's a mite jumpy this early morning."

Lissa cleared her throat. "Not surprising given the circumstances and lack of sleep."

"Fair enough. I did a little digging about our corpse. Seems he had a run in with Junto and the Family."

"Our stiff was a mobster? Cool." Jake threw up his hands at my glare. "Or not cool. Shame on him. Bad Mr. Mobster."

I rapped my knuckles on the table. "Enough. Junto's boys were long gone when we arrived, so they weren't the killers. Someone on *my* ship murdered Sant—I mean, Mr. Johnson. Maybe it was self-defense. Maybe it was spur of the moment. Either way, we got a corpse on our hands and not a whole lotta answers."

"Are we sure it was one of us?" Lissa asked, and I nodded.

"Analysis says we were the only ship within three hours of the *Lucky Fish* at the time of death. Someone on *The Perffaith* killed him. I want everyone interviewed, Lissa. Where they were, what they were doing—report to me by noon."

"There is not any need, Captain." When Seb stood, his eyes hiding behind oval frames, my gut played a round of slug-it-out with my esophagus. "I think we know who our killer is."

Many feet shuffled beneath the table. "Considering we don't have much more than a mob connection and an autopsy, I find that surprising, Seb."

Zac whispered, "The autopsy. It would be easy to—"

"To what? Lie? Break my oath? Is that what you're suggesting?" asked Petrie. Her end of the bench slid sideways as she rose to her feet. When she leaned across the table toward Zac, Lissa's hand on my arm stopped my own forward motion.

"Might as well see what shakes loose. This has been brewing all morning," Lissa said.

Without so much as a glance in our direction, Seb said, "Peter, I—"

"It's pronounced Pe-tree, not Pe-ter."

"Petrie then. You cannot deny how easy it would be for you to doctor an autopsy. You have access to needles and medicines we do not, and—"

For all her plain looks, Petrie's body size made for an imposing figure as she leaned close enough to kiss Seb. The tips of her shoulder length hair hit his chin, and he flushed to match the blinking lights. "Why would I risk my career to kill a stranger?"

"It is not my business to say."

"Don't think I don't know, Seb."

She broke eye contact when I knocked my fist on the table. "Enough double-speak. If you know something, either of you, get to it. Otherwise, sit down and shut up. We've got better ways to spend our time."

"Seb's been spying on me. Late at night when he thinks no one's watching," said Petrie, and Seb hissed.

"Why would he do that?" I asked.

Lissa, who had been calm a moment before, paled. Petrie gripped Lissa's shoulder. "Lissa and I are lovers. Alphans are not known for their tolerance of...well...."

I closed my eyes. Onboard relationships—damned things never ended well. At best they fizzled out, and at worst, they burned a hole through the ship. A picture of the *Lucky Fish*'s bridge came to mind.

Beside me, Lissa was a confident woman who wore her strength physically as well as mentally. My chief medical officer—Petrie-Dish Extraordinaire as I called her—was an old friend but the complete antithesis of Lissa. Petrie embraced her curves like she had middle age, with shy apologies. The idea of Lissa hooking up with someone suffering under insecurities made little sense to me.

But then, nothing about the past twelve hours made any sense.

Petrie bit her lip as she awaited my response.

"As a general rule, I dislike onboard relationships. However, I see no reason for concern here. What Petrie and Lissa do in their spare time is their own business," I said.

Seb's shoulders slumped forward as Petrie turned away from him. If his mouth-flap could've frowned, I'd bet it would've. Lissa kept herself angled between him and Petrie, and her finger brushed the taser clipped to her belt.

"Lissa will interview folks, then I'll interview her. She'll send me the reports by noon."

"I'd suggest we search rooms as well," said Lissa.

I waved a hand at her. We weren't there—*yet*. There had to be an easier explanation to this than murder.

"And who gets to interview you, Mark?" asked Zac.

Lissa said, "I will."

"But what if you two are in cahoots? I hate to suggest it, but if we're all suspects, we're all suspects. And you two have a somewhat colorful past."

Zac was right. I hated when he was right. I rubbed my temples and answered, "You can all interview me. Fair?"

"Whatever you say, Captain."

The edge to his voice confused me. I glanced around the table only to be met by furrowed brows and deep frowns. Trouble was brewing like a solar flare. I was gonna have to deal with this quickly.

The Perffaith's sensors showed the majority of my crew on the *Lucky Fish* as they should've been, the exceptions being Zac and Petrie. Sensors indicated both had left *The Perffaith* when Seb had spotted the heat source.

Another blip—this one from Petrie—pinged my inbox before noon. I don't know what I'd expected the medical report to tell me beyond what I already knew—carbon monoxide poisoning, adrenaline injection, blah-blah medical jargon—but her write-up gave an alarmingly accurate portrayal of Nick's life. I reread the last paragraph twice to be sure I'd gotten it right.

> *Liver cirrhosis indicates a heavy drinker. Scarring of the lungs and esophageal tissue indicates heavy tobacco use. No indications of drug use in the blood or tissue. Five cysts 2 cm. in size were removed from the lungs, and two 1 cm cysts were removed left of the trachea. Tests revealed these cysts to be malignant in nature. Patient suffered from Stage IV lung cancer at the time of death. No evidence of standard cancer treatment was found.*

Damn. My old man hadn't been lying after all. I closed the report and put in a call to Zac.

He stood beside a pile of scanners, their motherboards spread out across the table. "Whatcha need, Captain?" asked Zac.

"Meet me in the captain's station in five minutes."

As I walked to the bridge I passed Jake, who stared at his shoes. No one on the bridge paid me any mind. Once the door to the captain's station slid shut, I settled in behind my desk and pulled up my recent research. "Officer Zac Curtis requests entry," the computer announced a few moments later.

"Approve."

The door slid open, and Zac stepped inside. "I figured you'd call me down sooner or later." When I cocked an eyebrow, he added, "I've done all I can to try and salvage the *Lucky Fish*'s computer, but the data's too dang damaged—"

"That's not why I called you here."

I tapped the screen beside me and angled it to give him a better view. The picture of Nick and me was old, but it didn't take Zac longer than a minute or two to make the connection. He opened his mouth, then closed it, and then opened it again. "I assume you plan on telling me why you went and took a picture with Santa."

I nodded. "You remember a few years back when my old man sent me a message saying he was dying?"

"Yeah, but—wait, *that* Nick is *this* Nick?" He squinted at the screen. "Whoa. Last time I saw his raggedy ass we were both still kids and your Gran was tossing him out for drinking again. When'd he get so old?"

I closed the image with a shrug. "Years bouncing from place to place, doing odd jobs for Junto and his boys will age someone quick enough." I pulled up Petrie's autopsy report. "Petrie says he was dying. Cancer."

Zac let out a low whistle. "So he wasn't scamming you last time, huh?"

"Apparently not. Though it doesn't explain who killed him now."

"Or why you're keeping this info secret from everyone," said Zac.

"What happened between me and Nick...it's personal, and you'll keep this information to yourself for the time being. It'll only make waves, and the last thing we need is more tension."

Zac nodded, but his fingers toyed with the buttons on his shirt. "You know they'll think it's you. Especially if they knew the damage between you two."

I pulled up the last email I'd received from Nick. "I can't help that. It wasn't me—I've got no reason to kill him."

"Except that he abandoned you and your ma, and later your Gran. Hell, left your Gran with quite the debt if I recall. Then he left you with nothing more than a dream of what a dad's s'posed to be. Sounds like a pretty damned good reason to me."

Zac scanned the email on the screen. "You went to see him?" When I nodded, Zac asked, "Why?"

"Curiosity mainly. You know me well enough to know that I wouldn't kill him, no matter how much I hated him. The others don't. Especially Seb. He's new to the crew and wouldn't understand."

I didn't imagine the scowl on Zac's face, but like a flickering screen it blinked away a second later. "Why'd you go and pick him up, anyway? Nothing against his people, but it's uncanny the way he looks at us. Like we're dinner."

Another report scrolled across my screen. This one an addendum from Lissa on which crew had kin ties to the Europan Family. Only one name popped up, an engineer in Zac's department whose great-great-great grandmother married an ex-mobster. The details blurred before my eyes. "Junto."

"You took on that freak for your first mate for Junto?" Rather than his usual laughter, Zac's nostrils flared slightly.

"He arranged for some of the more...lucrative jobs to come our way in exchange for my accepting Seb on board as first mate. It's complicated, and we needed the cash. What can you tell me about Jelgins?" I asked.

"Engineer?" Zac rubbed his jaw. "Seems stable enough. Why? Peg him for the murderer or something?"

"Lissa found a tie with the Family—"

"His great-something-or-other, right?" Zac snorted. "He's no more a mobster than I am."

I closed the report for the time being. "I need you to hack into Nick's email account."

Zac leaned closer to the screen. "He uses mnet. Shouldn't be too hard."

My best friend clicked the login button and typed a long word into the password field. One keystroke later, Nick's email scrolled across the screen.

"Easy password."

"That *was* easy. What was it?"

He rolled his eyes. "Your full name."

Zac left me alone with the emails and my thoughts, neither of which were any good. The man had barely said more than a dozen words to me (when he wasn't asking for money that was), but had used my name for his password. It left me unsettled as I crawled through messages from Junto and his boys. The majority were little more than an address and a date and time. Damned fool didn't delete anything, which must've driven Junto crazy with all his rules on security and traceability.

Three screens in had gotten me nowhere. Rather than spin my wheels on mob business, I pulled up the search screen to compare Nick's account with the names or email addresses of my crew. It took time to type in all the data, but once I had, the computer made short work of my search.

It wasn't the name I'd expected to see.

Over a dozen messages between Lissa and my father, the earliest made two years prior. The first message from Lissa inquired about the murder of Melinda Mathis-Kerric. I made a note to look into it and kept reading. Her emails to my father grew more insistent, first a short inquiry and when Nick revealed his usual non-caring self, she pointed fingers at Junto, the mob, and finally Nick.

The last message asked to meet, and the date lined up with some vacation time Lissa had taken a few months back. Nothing further appeared in the search, and I typed in a request for emails to Junto on the same date. One result appeared.

Received: by 10.93.34.126.43.122 with SSIMTP id
3927be492;

Saturday, February 8, 2106 03:45:21 (-7 Standard Time)
Content-Transfer-Encoding: ProxyBit.

TO: J3984@i.mw.mail.com
FROM: NickyYB@e.mw.mnet
SUB: Melinda
MESSAGE: Just so we're crystal, I don't plan to tell her
nothing about the hit. Ain't like she's Family. So get your
head out of your ass about this. I got it.

My search on Melinda turned up dozens of articles. The
laser gun used and the way her body had been tossed into the
black to drift pointed to a mob hit, but police found little to
link her to the Family. She'd once dated one of Junto's boys,
but when she'd discovered his ties, she'd broken it off. The
obituary had been brief and lacking emotion, and I skimmed
through it until I reached the final line:

> *Melinda Mathis-Kerric is survived by her husband, Clay; her
> sister-in-law, Lissa Kerric; and her two children.*

I tagged the pages and saved them in a folder. Not only
did Lissa have the ability to take out someone like Nick, she
had motive as well.

Dammit, Lissa. Why'd she always have to complicate
everything?

When the door slid open to the common area, my crew
awaited their turn with a galaxy between each of them. No
one talked. No one shared stories about Lissa kicking the ass
of some thief or Zac getting *The Perffaith* to limp along on
half-baked goods 'til we hit a repair station. The only people
touching were Lissa and Petrie, who held hands under the
table.

"I ran a search on everyone's email accounts." Minor
reactions to my statement: Lissa's jaw clenched, Zac nodded
to himself, and Seb's shoulders slumped. But it was Petrie
who surprised me as she bit her lip. "I know where everyone
was supposed to be when we searched the *Lucky Fish* and

where they said they were, but I want to hear it for myself. We'll start with Jake."

He answered as soon as I finished his name. "Was on the bridge with you, Captain."

"The entire time?" asked Lissa.

"I followed the Captain to the engine room once Zac let up a shout. Never left the Captain's side."

Zac held up a finger. "Wait, aren't you gonna tell us what you found in your search? I mean, you—"

He stopped when I gave the slight shake of my head. The fewer who knew about my crawling into Nick's past the better. Besides, everyone but Lissa had come up clean. She was no Petrie, no jumpy woman who hid behind frumpy clothing and a microscope. She didn't use her physical appearance as some women might either.

Lissa's cargo pants weren't too tight, nor was her button-up shirt undone in some lame attempt to sway opinion. Nor did she lean across the table in my direction. Instead, she leveled her gaze on me—relaxation to a T. Had she been this calm when meeting with Nick over her sister-in-law's murder?

"The data search didn't pay off. Nothing beyond the typical came up: porn, family correspondence, the regular. Lissa, retrace your steps for me," I said. A small lie but a necessary one.

"Until Seb spoke of trouble, I was standing guard outside the engine room as requested. No crew left until I escorted them back to *The Perffaith* on your orders."

"You stood outside the doors, not inside?"

"Yes, Captain."

Did you ever leave your post? Did anyone else see you there?

She must've followed along the same trail as she shook her head. "No one passed by until you arrived, so no one can verify my whereabouts."

A red light dangling from the ceiling blinked once more before going dark, and my officers glanced up at the sudden shift. "Okay, what the hell is all this crap?" Zac asked as he pointed at the stained child's sock on the wall.

"I had attempted to encourage cheer through the use of items from the mythos of Saint Nicholas," whispered Seb.

Zac held the short sock by its end. "Yeah, but what's up with the midget stocking?"

His laughter pulled up short as Lissa spoke. "That must be yours, Zac. See? It's short like your...temper."

Zac's face froze as he clenched his jaw. Something had broken in our group, and a few minutes' laughter wasn't gonna heal it.

To distract him, I asked, "Zac, why were you coming from the cargo hold when Seb mentioned trouble?"

"I wanted to check on little Seb first. Make sure he wasn't in any trouble, being new and all and most likely to get killed walking up the stairs." Zac slapped Seb on the back. Seb's sunglasses slid down his nose, and he winced from the lights before shoving the thick glasses back into place.

I would've said he met my gaze, but with his eyes hiding behind his sunglasses, I would've never known. He didn't flinch or scowl like I would've at Zac's ribbing. Calm as I'd never been—not since before we'd found Nick's corpse.

"He would not have discovered me in the cargo hold as I was already seeking our heat source. The cargo bay bore an enormous hole in its hull. A single crate remained, anchored to the wall. After the scanners began working, I followed the blip."

"Did anyone see you?" asked Petrie.

He shook his head. "Not until I encountered Jake and Zac."

"And you, Zac?" I asked. "Seems to me I ordered you to remain on board *The Perffaith*."

"Ain't no way I did it. By the time I got on the *Lucky Fish* and got the heat source all sorted out, I would've had no time to reach our vic," said Zac.

I shrugged. "That leaves you, Petrie-Dish."

"I was on board *The Perffaith* until Seb mentioned the corpse."

"Where on *The Perffaith*?" asked Seb. He was standing again, his mouth-flap curled back and open. "Can anyone confirm your precise location?"

"The computer can," answered Zac. "The logs show the correct time stamp for when she left Lissa's room for the *Lucky Fish*."

Interesting. She hadn't been in the infirmary, and Zac had known it. Why'd he been digging through the logs? Seb halted his pacing to glare at Petrie.

Lissa rose when Seb stepped in Petrie's direction—a swift motion I caught out of the corner of my eye. She placed both hands on Seb's shoulders. Lissa towered over Seb and glanced down her nose to see past his shades. "If you've got a problem with Petrie's personal life, get over it. Look at her or anyone else on this ship like that again, and it won't matter that you're first mate. I'll pitch you out the ship myself," she said.

He wriggled in her grasp, but she held him firmly in place. "If you would let me go."

"Apologize."

Seb shot me a plea for help, and I shrugged. He got himself into this; he could get himself out of it.

"My apologies, Petrie. Everyone."

He stumbled back when Lissa released him. "Captain, I think it's time for that room search. It's too easy for us to cover for one another," said Lissa.

I nodded. Maybe in our search, we'd find something tying someone to Nick, or maybe I'd figure out what had happened when Lissa had met with him.

Or maybe I'd figure out why it rattled me so much to see her kicking sideways with Petrie.

Petrie's room was first on our list, if for no other reason than to shut Seb up. Everything tucked into place, her room was nearly unlived in. Dust gathered in the bottom of a laundry hamper and across the food dispenser. Everything in its place, unused.

She stood, arms across her chest, as Zac and I dug through what few belongings remained in the room. At the door, Seb and Lissa watched.

It didn't feel right to be combing through her belongings like I was, but my hands busied themselves as my mind wandered.

I almost didn't catch it, so buried was it in a wadded up shirt shoved into an otherwise empty drawer. When my fingers closed around the hard object, I sighed. "What is it?" Zac whispered, and I opened my palm to display a capped needle.

"Safety ring's missing. I assume it's used, though it's hard to say if it was used on Santa."

In a room the size of a small shuttle, whispers carried like a baby crying. By the look on Petrie's face, she'd heard it all.

"The needle is mine, though it wasn't used on our Santa." Petrie pulled out a vial from a drawer and held it up. "Allergen serum," she said.

"For...?" I asked.

"I'm allergic to Lissa's cat."

Seb muttered something in Alphan as he fled the doorway.

"Run it for DNA...On second thought," I turned and handed the needle to Jake, "have her assistant run it. Send the results to me direct."

Jake left, and Petrie followed closely behind. Lissa stepped on my boot heels as she followed me toward Seb's room. When I reached the door panel, the door read *unlocked* and the room occupied. Lissa stood opposite me, her hand on her taser.

"Be careful, Mark," she whispered, and I arched one eyebrow. "He's been...Petrie wasn't lying when she said he's been following us. Something's off about him."

"Don't tell me you believe all that prejudicial horseshit about Alphans?"

"I know you don't want to hear this, but it's true. Seb believes...." She trailed off and stared at the taser in her hands. "He believes that Petrie and I are *taurists*. Evil."

I scanned the band on my wrist to announce us. "You're right, I don't want to hear about your paranoia." The same old shit as before, only it was Seb this time instead of Zac. And here I'd thought she'd changed in the past few years. "I expect you to do your job without prejudice, Lissa."

The door slid open with a faint chime. The musty odor itched my nose something fierce as I stepped inside the dark room. Seb's faint shape sat across from the door, his hand shading his exposed eyes from the hallway light. "If you do not mind, please close the door until I have my sunglasses," he said.

At my nod, Lissa stepped inside and allowed the door to slide shut. We stood in near pitch darkness as Seb rummaged around to my right. A slight hiss closed a metal drawer. When the lights rose, Seb leaned against the wall donning his shades, arms crossed over his chest. "Please feel free to search my personal belongings. There is nothing here I wish to hide."

As I approached the wall-drawers, my nose flared at the pungent odor—like sweaty socks in a microwave. No stains along the walls, so he hadn't set any biohazard growing in my ship. The odor was definitely inside a drawer.

I tugged one open at random, and the stench of sweat and something sour bowled over me. Lissa passed me a pair of rubber gloves, and I nodded my thanks.

Nothing hid within the "clean" laundry, but nestled inside the corner desk were three journals, each held together with a sinew-type thread down the middle. "Please do be careful with those." His voice cracked as he spoke.

"Is that leather? Or...something else?" asked Lissa.

Touching their covers was not in my plan. No telling what skin they came from. Lissa picked one up at random, and I muttered, "I didn't know anyone still wrote on paper. If that's even paper."

Seb bobbed his head up and down. "My mother bound these journals from the hide of a *whonta* on the day of my birth. Their pages are from the mighty *rew* tree, which stands thirty meters in height. These books will tell my life story to my offspring and their offspring."

118

After a few page turns, Lissa handed me a book and pointed.

03/1/2108 21:54 PM

She has remained another evening with the security officer. They carry on, right under the captain's nose, as if it would not hurt him to see his *amhon* with another. To be *taurists* is unforgiveable, but how can I see her as such?

Is she unaware that I stood outside for ten minutes? Did I perhaps misjudge her invitation to stop by and discuss current medicinal treatments for the itching of the scalp? Perhaps she meant another time.

03/2/2108 09:20 AM

I cannot sleep. What am I to do? How can I love something so vile? My mother would be ashamed.

The surveillance dated back months, though his feelings were a more recent development. I snagged the other journals. Looks like I had a little light reading to do tonight.

"Will those be returned?" he asked.

"Once I've taken a look at them."

"Captain," he said, and his shades slid down his nose an inch to expose damp, dark eyes near the size of my fist. "Those—those are personal."

"So was this murder."

My wristband beeped. The DNA results were back on Nick and the needle. I swallowed hard.

"Something up?" Lissa asked.

"Later."

Other than the journals, our search of Seb's room came up empty. The Alphan lived an odorous and bizarre life but had nothing connecting him to Nick. Lissa's jaw clenched as we left Seb's room.

"What is it?" I asked.

"I didn't realize...I thought—"

"You thought it was something else, not a crush that had him stalking Petrie."

She nodded. "Not that stalking isn't an issue, but oddly enough, I don't think he's our murderer. He's too much of a chicken shit. Though I suppose he could've planted that needle on Petrie."

"Nope. Tests came back. Only Petrie's DNA on the needle. It was used for her allergy shots."

"Doesn't that mean Petrie's innocent?"

I leaned against the wall with a sigh. "Not necessarily. She could've tampered with her assistant's results or even those of the autopsy. Seb's not wrong on that point."

When she shook her head, the silver beads in her braids glittered in the overhead light. It was good to see her hair long again rather than the short rainfall she'd sported before. "Maybe Seb did a botched frame job? No, it has to be someone else. Why frame someone you love?"

"Maybe because you can't have them?" I asked. The door panel outside Seb's room changed to the locked signal, and I pulled Lissa away from the door. "I tend to agree with you that he's not our guy, but I can't rule him out just yet. No more than anyone else."

She must have caught the unspoken implication as she pointed in the direction of her quarters. "Let's get this over with."

"Lissa—" I followed her down the corridor. As my security officer, her quarters were next door to mine: something that had once been convenient. I bit back my question.

Her room was as I remembered it—simple and without decoration. The occasional book out of place gave the room a lived in appearance but other than that, her room was as clinical and cold as Petrie's had been. The exception was the cot, which lay in a mess of tussled blankets. "Tell me, Lissa. Did you kill Santa?"

"No." The light-brown hand on my forearm was pale against my dark skin. "I thought you knew me better than that, Captain."

"Why Petrie?" I cursed the wrong question that had escaped me. "Never mind, I'm not sure I care to know."

She shrugged and pulled open the wall-drawers for my perusal. I dug through her belongings and swallowed back more emotion than I cared to admit when I encountered one of Petrie's polka-dotted cardigans. "Why'd you meet with our victim, Nick?"

"What?" she asked, her hand in midair.

Lissa's desk drawer was mostly empty—save for a small book on hand-to-hand combat—and I moved to the single shelf above her cot, which was full of trophies and awards. "You met with Nick concerning the murder of your sister-in-law, Melinda. I'm asking you why."

She folded her tall frame into the padded chair in the corner with a long sigh. "Melinda's murder was a mob hit. I knew you had a contact to Junto, to the Family. Zac gave me the email address for a Nick Melorrey. I thought if I talked to him, he'd be able to tell me why Junto called in a hit on her. But I never met with him, not in person."

I was gonna kill Zac for tangling her up with the Family. To Lissa, I said, "That last job with Junto went way south of normal, Lissa. You almost died. In fact, you left me after that job. What in the world would possess you to get mixed up with the Family?"

"I had to know!"

The shout caught me off guard, and I shoved a wobbling trophy back onto the shelf. Her cheeks were flushed and her eyes wide.

"The police knew it was a hit, but they refused to do anything, Mark. They said Junto was untouchable. What would you have done...if it had been me? Would you've let it go?"

No. I would've buried him with my bare hands.

"Did you kill Nick?" I asked.

"No, though it wouldn't have mattered. Nick wouldn't tell my anything. He wouldn't meet with me. Just sent me useless emails full of nothing. Hell, I didn't even know our victim was *that* Nick until you mentioned the mob connection earlier."

It would've been easier if I could've believed her. "So you didn't recognize him?"

"I never saw him in person. He wouldn't accept video calls. It seems our victim has many names."

I closed the last of the wall-drawers. "Room's clear."

"You believe me then?"

I spun to find her all too close. She smelled like strawberries, and I leaned forward until my nose nearly touched hers.

"Is this what you came here for, Captain?" she asked, voice colder than the *Lucky Fish.*

I flinched at the door's hiss behind me, and my nose bumped hers.

"Sorry, Captain. Didn't mean to interrupt—" I winced at Zac's words.

Behind him stood a surprised Jake and confused Seb. Petrie bumped into Jake's shoulder when he stopped. "Why the—" Her face crumpled.

"I apologize for suggesting it, Captain, but is it possible you have a conflict of interest?" asked Seb as he brushed past Zac. He opened the wall-drawers with less care than I'd taken. With a shrug, Zac joined him while I stood there looking the idiot. Her room turned up nothing again. Seb stepped back, stray hairs from his wig sticking to his sweaty face.

"Satisfied?" asked Lissa.

Seb stumbled away from her and tripped over a chair leg.

"Since you're convinced there's something going on, we'll do the Captain's quarters next," she said.

They expected me to lead the way. I'm not sure why I didn't, only that my brain was still arguing with my heart over what the hell had just happened. Zac led the short procession ten feet over with me trailing behind like a guilty party.

Except I wasn't.

My officers watched as Zac and Seb searched my quarters. While they searched, I stuffed Seb's journals into a wall-drawer for later reading.

When Zac and Seb reached my desk, Seb's jaw pulsed. He held up a picture frame I recognized all too well. "Why do you have a photo with Santa?" he asked, and my tongue rolled across the dry roof of my mouth. The old school digital frame was passed around the crew.

Nick had said he wanted to connect, to make up for lost time while we still had it. Rather than swallow my pride and the past, I'd shut him down.

And he'd given up.

I might as well have killed him myself.

"Mark?"

Damn Lissa's eyes. If they could've bored black holes through me, they would've.

"I don't know why I didn't see it before." Lissa handed Petrie the wooden frame. "Look at the nose."

"Dominant arch, flared nostrils," Petrie said. "I ran DNA on our victim, Mark. I thought it a mistake, but seeing this picture...."

Zac glanced between the digital photo and me as he shifted his weight from one foot to the other. He tried to hide his *I-told-you-so* expression behind a fake sneeze and failed.

"You know, don't you?" Lissa asked, and Zac studied the dirt beneath his fingernails.

I said, "Leave Zac out of this. He was following orders."

"Captain, if you have a connection to the deceased, it would be best to reveal that now." Lissa paled at Petrie's comment.

I took the photo from the doctor. "His name's not Nick Johnson. It's Nick Banes, and he's my father."

Saying the words made them real.

Feet shuffled in the room, but no one spoke. When Lissa's hand touched my shoulder, I flinched. "Mark, your father was an asshole. He abandoned you. I think we'd all understand if—"

"If what?" Voice too sharp, I bit my tongue. "If I snapped and killed him? I know what this looks like, but I didn't do it. Much as I would've liked to years back, this wasn't me."

"How'd your father end up dead on the *Lucky Fish*?" asked Jake.

123

"And why were you hiding this photo?" Petrie pointed at the false bottom in my desk drawer. "No offense, but this isn't adding up."

There wasn't any way I was walking out of this without being gutted. The story tumbled out too fast, too raw: his scamming first my mother, then Gran; his need for money and booze; the jobs he had done for Junto; and finally, his attempt to reconnect. "He came crawling out of the meteor field to give me some line about dying or some shit. Wanted to get all enlightened with forgiveness at the mountain. That's when that photo was taken."

"And you decided to keep this hidden because?" asked Petrie.

"I wasn't hiding it. It's private and not relevant."

"Not relevant, my ass." Zac flushed. "Forgive me, Captain, but that's what we'd call a motive right there."

Swallowing proved difficult, yet I managed.

Petrie said, "But our victim *was* sick. The autopsy determined that."

"He was, but by the time he'd reached out to me, he'd told so many lies, killed so many...it didn't matter if he was being truthful. Either way, I didn't kill him. Jake was with me during the time of death. Are we done here?"

Zac nodded to Lissa, who announced, "Room's clean."

"Jake could be protecting you, Captain. It wouldn't be the first time someone from your crew kept you from the noose. That last job from Junto...," said Zac, and I could've strangled him. Zac threw up both hands. "Just laying out the facts...Captain."

His jaw clenched as he turned away from me.

"I didn't kill him," I said, but no one was listening.

The crew followed me from my quarters with mumbles and whispers, and my stomach churned. My crew'd gone from family to a maelstrom of accusations in less than forty-eight hours. A sweep of Jake's quarters turned up nothing more than the typical array of dirty laundry.

Lissa turned to Zac. "Where'd you get the idea to run salvage on this particular ship?" she asked.

His smile tightened at the edges. "We haven't had decent work in months. Not since...not since we took Seb on board. No one wants to deal with a vessel with an Alphan. Add in all that union crap—"

She waved her hand in the air. "Yes, yes, but how'd you find *this* job?"

"If we don't get more memory for the food replicators, we're gonna be eating like the junkies on Europa. When I saw this job come up on that board for folks looking for side-work, I figured it was a good fit. Ran it by Mark and off we went."

"Which board?" I asked.

I thought his lips would split, the painful way he over-grinned. "Side-Slide."

"Dammit, Zac. That site's quasi-legal at best."

"Yeah, well, it ain't like you've never taken the odd job to keep *The Perffaith* running."

Lissa sighed. "Did you know the site is backed by Junto?"

"Yes."

The answer was too fast in coming, too confident. Lissa and Zac. Both with motive. Both my friends.

"You just happened upon a salvage job within hours of a fight?" asked Lissa.

"Well, yeah."

I stared at Zac. Every lie he told poked a hole in the façade of calm demeanor. I was drowning in lies.

"While we're speaking of weirdness," said Zac as the crew walked to his room. "Lissa, how'd the meeting go with Nick?"

The procession halted. "Ya knew our stiff?" asked Jake.

Lissa sighed. "Not really. I was investigating a murder—"

"So you've done this before then?" Zac smirked.

"Dammit, shut up and let me finish. I was investigating a mob hit and needed info from someone within the Family. *Zac*—" she stressed his name, "—gave me the email address for Mark's contact, a Nick Melorrey. I didn't know it was the same man, because I never met him in person. Never even had a video chat. Just emails."

"I'm sure that's all it was," said Zac.

When this was dealt with, I was gonna have a little chat with Zac. I didn't need more shit stirred on my ship.

Petrie stepped away from Lissa's outstretched hand as the group began walking. The rest of the trip to the bow was an unusually silent one.

Zac pressed his hand to his door's panel, and the lock released. "After you, Captain," he said.

Here was another room I'd visited many a time, though usually while piss-drunk. It was the only time he'd sucker me into playing a round of poker or jack. The walls held holographic images of a dozen starships, each more decadent and expensive than *The Perffaith*. Like Petrie's room, his was neat leaning on not lived in.

I'd already skimmed each crew member's log, but I pulled up Zac's for another look while Lissa rifled through the wall-drawers. Each log noted his entrance and exit from his room, none of which were particularly suspicious until the day of Nick's murder. At 08:00, he'd left his quarters for the morning. We'd all left the infirmary at 21:04, but the computer never logged Zac as returned to his room.

All of us were desperate for sleep, and knowing Zac, he'd have caught some zee-time when he could. I scrolled down and caught this morning's log. He'd left his room at 07:30.

Zac's shadow across the screen grew in size, and I closed the file. A few clicks later had me scanning his browsing history, emails, and calls.

"Feel free to enjoy my porn collection," he said and laughed. Gaps appeared in his history—moments where he'd logged into the system and done nothing. When I didn't laugh, his reflection on the screen frowned, and I forced a grin.

Something about the lack of computer data turned my stomach something fierce. In my study of the crew's logs, dozens of lines showed their movements and computer conversations in the past two days. Zac's were mostly the same except for the holes. "Zac, when did you come back to your room last night?" I asked.

"It must have been about 23:00 or so. Just after finishing my report. Actually, make that 23:15 since Lissa interviewed me toward the tail end of things."

He'd taken the bait. Now to drag the fish along until it stopped flopping. "Something odd's going on with the computer. Between this and the scanners, I wonder...."

Zac cocked his head. "Think we've been hacked or something?"

"Interesting choice of words coming from a former hacker," said Lissa. When I turned away from the computer, Lissa held Zac's scanner before her. Six heat sources read in his room. "I thought you said the scanner wasn't reading right," she said.

He shrugged. "It wasn't, but I replaced the memory this morning. Been reading just fine since then."

Lissa closed her mouth at my look. Last job we'd run had left our scanners blipping when they oughtta have been blooping. Damned planetary moisture had done quite a number on their innards. I'd placed the order for new parts myself, only they hadn't arrived yet.

I didn't know why, but this was a bet I'd make sober.

Zac was lying to me.

"Seems convenient," muttered Petrie from the doorway.

"What does?" Zac's voice was level, but he curled one hand into a half-fist.

"Your missing the heat source like that."

"Look, Petrie. I get that you're pretty gung-ho to find who killed Santa, especially if it takes the heat off of your girlfriend, but this don't mean shit. So I missed the heat source. With people blathering in their speakers at me, it's an easy mistake. Besides, Mark's dad died from CO poisoning. I still think he coulda jabbed himself with something when he felt himself go all woozy."

Seb brushed past Petrie. "Or maybe you are attempting to frame everyone for your own actions. You possess the needed knowledge to render the *Lucky Fish*'s computer silent."

"Maybe," said Zac, and he leaned nose-to-nose with Seb. "Or maybe you want it to sound that way. Since the murder, everyone's been hell-bent on accusing one another, but maybe it's just as I said. Here we are spinning our wheels over solving an accident when we could be selling our salvage. I don't know about you, Seb, but I'd like to eat something not replicated from protein sometime this year."

Stress and lack of sleep had rendered them useless to me. I moved to step between the two, but Lissa beat me to it. "Enough," she shouted.

Before accusations started flying again, I said, "Every-one to their quarters. Let the skele-crew handle *The Perffaith*. And when I say your quarters, I mean your *own* quarters."

Petrie frowned but nodded.

"I've got to make sure the rest of the scanners are—"

I interrupted Zac with an upright hand. "I have a few leads to follow up before we finish grabbing salvage off the *Lucky Fish*. Stay in your room. Don't make me lock everyone inside."

My crew muttered as they spread out toward their quarters. Zac flopped into an empty chair, his fingers already running across the screen beside him.

"When this is all done, we're gonna have a talk, Zac."

"I'm sure," he muttered.

I followed Lissa outside and sighed when Zac's door shut behind me. "You know something," she said.

"Possibly. Feel like helping?"

Lissa grinned and led the way to my quarters. Outside my door, she turned about-face. "I'm sorry. I should've told you about Melinda—"

"Don't," I said as I opened the door with a handprint. I locked the door to my quarters behind us.

On the wall screen, I put in a call to Junto.

Another hold as I waited for my message to reach the proper person, and Lissa fiddled with her sealed braid tips. "Why are you calling him?" she whispered.

The screen twitched before Junto's mug popped up. "I thought I made it clear I don't owe you."

"You did, but I needed some information."

He furrowed his brows, then a slow smile spread across his face as he glanced over my shoulder at Lissa. "I see you two have worked things out."

I dismissed his attempts to push my buttons with a shrug. "Last time we had a chat, you said your boys were here to get the goods, yet they didn't. You and I both know you sent them to knock off Nick, but you had to ensure Nick was dead in the debris. Who'd you call on my ship to be sure?"

Junto's smile didn't falter as he wrested his attention from Lissa. "What makes ya think I did any such thing?"

"No games, Junto. If you had a mole in the fam, you'd flush him out faster than I could toss the *Lucky Fish*. Allow me to do the same."

"What will you give me for such intel?"

It was my turn to smile. "I won't mention to the authorities where to find Melinda's killer."

"You won't, anyway. You got nothin'."

I pressed a button on my screen to forward a message his way. "In a few minutes, or maybe an hour with the way relays have been delayed, you'll get an email from Nick's email account—one where he makes very sure to state that he won't meet with Lissa here or tell her what happened to Melinda. I'm sure it could link Nick and you to her, which may open more doors than you want blown open at this point. Hell, they may find the clues in their own search of your computers there on Europa." I shrugged. "But hey, if you wanna take that risk, be my guest."

Junto's left eye twitched, but he gave the slightest nod. My account pinged. Guess he had faster mail relays than me. "Don't call again."

"I don't intend to."

The screen darkened, and I pulled up the message he'd sent. The decrypted file contained a series of video messages. Whoever our killer was had disconnected the video feed and fed the voice through the computer. A robotic voice read off the details of the hit—where, when, who—not much else. "Dammit," I muttered.

"Open another one."

Confirmation that Junto had told someone on board about the salvage and hired them to kill Nick *(if found)*, but nothing more. Another file, this one giving details of a meeting between Nick and Lissa. A meeting that never happened. At least according to her.

"That...that never happened. I didn't meet with him." She curled her fingers into fists. "You have to believe me."

"I can't."

"What are you going to do?"

"Find the proof I need. One way or another." My door slid open at my approach, and I gave her a brief nudge in its direction. "Look, just head back to your room. Stay put until I figure this out."

Lissa rested her hand against my chest—a moment's warmth in the situation's chill. "Mark—"

"Don't say it. We both know you wouldn't mean it in the morning," I said. The words were harsh, but I couldn't trust her. Not yet. I'd ask her forgiveness later, assuming I was alive to do it.

Assuming she wasn't the murderer.

My gut clenched as she left, and I pulled up the ship's map on the door panel. Heat sensors showed the two-member skeleton crew in place while the rest were in their rooms.

My body sank into my cot, and I pressed the button to my right. A screen slid out, and I pulled up the logs from before.

The hole from last night was gone. Zac had altered his coming and goings again. The question now was why. What was he hiding now? What had I missed? I pulled up the logs from the last twenty-four hours for Lissa's rooms, but they'd been cleared as well. He'd muddied the waters.

130

Maybe he was protecting Lissa. Maybe they were working together.

I scrolled away from the logs and into the command panel. The computer's line to the derelict rang true enough, but the damaged ship wasn't singing back. The *Lucky Fish* ignored my request to power up. Her computer was as lifeless as my father's corpse, which shouldn't have been the case. If nothing else, she could've piggybacked off our power. The ship's black box was intact and should've been singing one last serenade.

Maybe if I brought the black box over to *The Perffaith*, I could get it talking. I grinned at my reflection in the screen.

But first, I needed to know if Lissa had met with my father. The audio mentioned a meeting at a swank hotel in Garthus. Being all hoity-toity, maybe they'd have a record.

If I'd had to pinpoint the moment when the screen grew fuzzy, I wouldn't have been able. Only that as I stared at the small screen beside me, my vision rolled with my stomach. I blinked my way through the rocking long enough to pull up the article on carbon monoxide poisoning.

Damn.

So this was how it'd been done.

The room spun as I staggered to the door. The killer couldn't poison the entire ship without going down with us. If I could get to the hall.... The door ignored my presence when I reached it, and I pushed on the hand plate, which read:

LOCKED. OVERRIDE? Y/N

My finger slid across the Y, and the screen chirped a refusal. I tried to speak and couldn't. When birthdates and the names of family members didn't remove the lock, I blinked a few times while staring at the yellow glare. By the time I finished typing the L in Rachel, the world was a mix of gray haze and jagged edges. The door slid open and fresh air smacked me in the face. As I fell to my knees in the hall, I made a mental note to send the ex-girlfriend a gift of some sort. Coughs flooded the hallway as crewmembers escaped their rooms.

Jake crawled his way over to me from his room next door. "Need to make...sure everyone...escaped."

I nodded, but my legs refused to lift me from the floor. Weak and quivering, I reached up and slapped my hand on a nearby panel. "Head count, please," I croaked.

Eight heat sources on board *The Perffaith*. "We're missing two."

Jake said, "The murderer. And his or her accomplice?"

"It appears to be the case." This time when I tried my legs, they held, though my stomach churned. "Check that everyone's okay. I need to get to the *Lucky Fish*."

Jake took the left corridor while I went right. Coughs covered what little could be said as I passed by my crewmembers. The stairwell's door shut behind me, and I took the stairs two at a time. Two flights down, salvage from the *Lucky Fish* scattered across the cargo bay. In the airlock chamber, two spacesuits were missing.

Dammit. The killer was going for the black box. The remaining evidence.

My legs quivered as I pushed one foot and then the other through the legs of a spacesuit, and my fingers trembled against the zipper pull. Part of me wished I had help—Lissa's help, to be honest—but for all I knew, she'd kill me rather than help.

The zipper moved easier than I did. Fitting the helmet in place was a relief as cleaner oxygen swept through it, and I inhaled deeply a few times before sealing off the chamber for depressurization.

Two seconds into the derelict, goosebumps crept across my skin. Wasn't much reason for it—my lone light split across her darkness as expected—but a slim one foot of metal between me and the dark embrace of space set my wiggins-radar to off the charts, especially being alone with one, possibly two killers.

If the killer were smart, he—or *she*—would be hiding in a twist of metal wreckage. Maybe both of them were stupid, hiding out in the bridge. The idea made my steps achingly slow as I shined my flashlight's beam into every shadow between me and the evidence I needed.

Dead ahead, the sliding doors to the bridge remained pried open from our previous excursion. The knife in my hand wobbled as I leaned my head around the doorway.

Nothing. The bridge was empty.

One floating lap around the bridge confirmed what my eyes told my brain. The main panel lay open, and I used the lip to pull myself beneath it. Its innards were an enigma to me, but I had a hunch the dead panel wasn't from damage. Not directly. I reached behind a mess of wires until I brushed up against the manual power switch. It was switched on.

Beside it lay the reset button. Once flipped, the black box's display lit up. Lights blinked and error codes scrolled across the three inch screen for a full minute before the command prompt blinked twice. Waiting.

I noted the killer's entrance by the pop of my speaker and gripped my knife. I couldn't ignore the cold sweat inside my suit.

Zac held one hand behind his back. A weapon of some kind? I used the panel for leverage as I faced him. "Was it you?"

He didn't answer—his eyes focused on the black box.

"Why?" I asked, and he pushed himself through the doorway and into the bridge.

Zac held an old-fashioned gun in his hand. "Money." He jerked the weapon to the right, and the speaker in my helmet crackled. "Get away from the box."

"Or what? You'll shoot me?" My breath came too fast. If he destroyed the black box, all evidence would die with me. "You're my best friend, Zac. I can't believe you'd kill me for money."

"Quit stalling. I saw you come alone. No one's coming to save you."

A bead of sweat crawled its way across my chin. Where was Lissa?

"How do you know that thing will even work?" I nodded at his gun. "No oxygen on the ship."

He rolled his eyes. "See? This is why. This!" The gun jumped with his gestures. "You don't have the brains to climb out of a paper bag, yet you're the mighty captain of his own ship. How many times have I pulled your ass from the proverbial fire?"

"More times than I can count. Which is why you've got me wondering what this is all about."

My helmet's speaker crackled again with his answer. "You. Here I've gone and done everything you've ever asked of me, saved your life any number of times, nursed your broken heart after that bitch dumped you, and how do you repay me? Hmmm? By making some bigoted Alphan your first officer!"

He wasn't working with Lissa? My breath caught in my throat. Then where was she? I coughed in my helmet. Oh gods. Was she dead?

"Seb was an accident. I should've never accepted him from Junto."

Zac floated within a few feet of me. Spittle decorated the interior of his helmet, and his eyes were too large for sanity. I held the knife uselessly at my side.

"If you had a problem with me, why go after my father?"

Over his shoulder, a light flashed once in the corridor before fading. "I told you!" he shouted, and the gun jumped closer to my faceplate. "The money. Junto was willing to pay shiploads to make sure Nick was good and dead. You weren't going to miss him and with all that money, I'd be free of *The Perffaith*."

I tried to focus on his face rather than the new shadow in the hall, but the gun sent a new round of shakes through me. For whatever reason, Zac was convinced it would fire.

I held up my hands. "You were never a prisoner here, Zac. Take your money and go."

The grin that split his thin lips was full of malice. "Can't. You know too much. How'd you figure out it was me, anyway?"

A booted foot stopped within the emergency doorway behind Zac. The silver strip across the helmet matched those across our feet. One of my crew was here. I sighed with relief, but Zac misread my reaction.

"That's it? This is all I get from the mighty captain of *The Perffaith*? So much for being perfect. What would your precious Gran think of you now?"

Anger flushed my face. Despite the lack of gravity, my arms and legs moved too fast through the dimly lit bridge. I reached for Zac as the pistol's muzzle flashed. Something hit me and pain erupted across my ribcage.

I flipped the latches of Zac's helmet, releasing the pressure seal. His mouth opened but whatever he said was lost with the lack of oxygen.

Lissa brushed past him. When she reached me, she slapped a glob of sealant across the hole in my suit. "Can you breathe? Did the bullet penetrate?"

My helmet occluded my view of my middle. "I don't think it penetrated completely. Suit's too thick. Though I think I bruised a rib or three."

As I spoke, she held up my arm to check gauges and sensor readings. "The sealant should hold long enough to get you back on the ship, but we need to leave now."

"What about him?"

I didn't want to look at Zac. I stared at the floor while my ribcage throbbed.

"Don't look," she whispered.

"We need the black box."

Lissa tugged at my arm to get me moving. "Can you access it from *The Perffaith*?"

Zac's feet drifted past my view of the floor. "Yes, now that its power is on."

We drifted through the *Lucky Fish*'s dark corridors in silence. My face grew warm as fog coated the interior of my helmet. The airlock chamber stood ten feet at most, and my arm trembled as I pushed away from the wall.

"Liss...."

Her open mouth swam in the red tint of my vision, and I closed my eyes.

The overhead light doubled in brightness, and I winced. "Somebody do something about that light," I said, or I tried to say, but the first few words were more a croak than actual speech.

"Sit tight, Captain. Sip this." Petrie placed a straw against my cracked lips. The water burned going down, yet soothed the back of my throat. This time when I opened my eyes, the light was less harsh, though my tear ducts worked overtime.

"What happened?" I asked. "Lissa—"

A hand squeezed mine, and when I turned my head, she sat beside me in the infirmary. Too many wrinkles lined her frown. "The bullet didn't reach you, but it tore enough of a hole to cause problems."

"You patched it."

"Not enough. There was a pressure loss, enough that—" Her voice cracked, and she paused. "We almost lost you."

Several crewmembers waved at me from the view screen to my left. Petrie swiped them away and pulled up a list of numbers and diagrams. "Your blood was trying to boil its way out of your body," Petrie said and injected something into the IV in my arm. "While the bullet didn't tear through the entire suit, you still bruised your ribs. You'll need to stay here overnight for observation. You're dehydrated and need the increased oxygen. "

"How long was I out?"

"A few hours. You came out of the hyperbaric tube half an hour ago."

Whatever she'd stuck in the line made the world prettier than I remembered, and I smiled at the fuzzy warmth.

"That's my Petrie-Dish." I tilted my head toward my security officer. "And my Lissa. Always looking out for me."

The former smirked while the latter frowned.

I didn't care so long as they were both beside me.

"Careful now," Petrie said.

I waved her away. "Doc, I'm fine. All patched up. Walking and talking even." I allowed my legs to wobble, and a dozen arms reached out to catch me.

When I laughed at my crew, Lissa lobbed a punch at my shoulder. "That's not funny, Captain."

I chuckled harder as they escorted me to the common area. Everyone stopped outside the door, and Lissa waved her hand. "Captain's first."

The door slid open, and when I stepped into the room, my eyes watered at the assault of lights. Greens and reds and whites twinkled, and a potted ivy sat in the corner. Someone, or perhaps several someones, had perched a flameless candle in the pot. Some damned fool had painted the thing a merry set of red and green stripes. The socks hung across the wall were full of lumps and bumps, and a small box sat at the ivy's base.

"What's all this now?" I asked, and Seb grinned.

"Christmas!"

There was a hole in the wall where the shortest sock had been. Zac's. Lissa caught my frown and said, "We burned it, along with his body. While you were recovering, we blew up what remained of the *Lucky Fish*."

My strength left me, and I stumbled. Jake shoved a chair under me, and I fell into it. "But—"

"Don't worry, we stripped her bare first. We got the black box data, too," she said and patted my arm. "It was a good haul all things considered. We should even be able to get some fresh food at the next fueling station."

Seb picked up the small box and handed it to me. "Happy Christmas!"

Someone, probably Seb, had bundled the box with a shirt and tied a silly knot at the top. My fingers fumbled with the thin rope until Lissa took pity on me and cut the fool thing.

"It is not fresh food, but perhaps you will find it equally enjoyable," said Seb.

Inside the box was the snow globe.

The twinkling lights overhead reflected off the flakes inside making them dance. I stared at it while my vision did a little dance of its own. "Damn dust on this ship. Time to cycle the air again," I said as I wiped my eyes with the back of my hand.

Lissa handed me a tissue. "We found it in...in Zac's quarters. We figured you'd want it, seeing how it was your father's."

"Thanks. What'd you find on the black box?"

The crew, who'd been digging through their "stockings" full of vitamin-candy, ceased moving at my question. Lissa took a deep breath and answered. "Junto admitted to paying Zac 500,000 credits to kill your father, though Junto wasn't the only one looking for him. He was wanted by the Family of Europa as well as crime syndicates in three other systems. Looks like this Santa thing was one of his covers. When Junto put out his request, Zac promised the Family he'd take care of him in exchange for the cash and a ship of his own."

"How'd you pull that info out of Junto?"

Lissa glanced at Petrie. "I made a deal," said Lissa.

I tried to stand and failed.

"I never said *I* wouldn't alert the authorities," she said while I laughed. "The black box contained brief notes from the captain of the *Lucky Fish*. It seems he bought Nick's cover story and tried to protect him from Junto's boys. The captain hid him in that closet. Some protective shelter, I guess. It had its own oxygen system, which is how Nick survived post-battle. Gave him a shot of adrenaline to keep him going in the cold when the heat went out on the *Lucky*

Fish. Junto's boys couldn't find him because their ship was too damaged in the fight."

I asked, "How'd Zac know about the request?"

"He's been on Junto's radar for a while. Managed to snake a long list of jobs out of Junto that were shunted our way so Zac could perform side-jobs for the Family. When we arrived at the *Lucky Fish*, he found a single life source on board. The one Junto said might be there. We had the new scanners, so we picked up what 'the boys' had not. Zac hacked the *Lucky Fish*'s computer and flooded the safe room with carbon monoxide."

Seb curled his hands into fists around his empty sock. "And while we were chasing salvage, he set the controller back to confuse the investigation. He may have succeeded had I not found the body."

"Junto knew we were in the sector, so it was the perfect opportunity to do what his boys had failed to do," said Lissa.

I swallowed the lump in my throat. "All this because he wanted to be First Officer. Felt like I'd slighted him."

"Is that what he told you?" Lissa asked. I nodded.

"How did you deduce he was the murderer?" asked Seb.

"Little things weren't adding up. The scanner that suddenly didn't work when it did, the logs that were too perfect, the salvage job when we needed it most. The helmets crackling and such. We'd just replaced them—seemed weird to have them malfunctioning only when we needed to communicate most. I'm embarrassed to say this, but the black box of the *Lucky Fish* should have been a red flag. Even in a damaged ship, we should've been able to pull something from it, yet we got no response. Zac had cut all reserve power to it. I had to hit the manual reset button to restore it. All the info from Junto helped point me in the right direction. Suppose I owe him for that."

I flicked a peppermint across the table where it glanced off Petrie's arm. She stared at the cellophane wrapper a moment too long before she met my gaze. "He reproduced the methods and tried to kill us all in our rooms. Only two people on the ship could do that—the captain and—"

"—Someone able to hack the computer. Our killer," I said. Little piles of candy were strewn across the table, but we sat silently while the red and green lights made pretty patterns on the wall.

I stood up in a rush and clapped my hands together. "Look, Zac was bitter and angry about change. I don't know about you, but I can't spend my time looking over my shoulder for the what if's and why's."

Jake grinned and held up a small flask. "I agree, Captain. I say we celebrate the holiday with a quart of my uncle's finest."

"Finest what?" Petrie asked as she sniffed the proffered container. "Is that intended to be drinkable?"

Jake set glasses on the table, and my medic poured a splash or two into each one.

"I propose a toast," said Seb, and he held up his glass. "That is what you do on Earth, is it not?"

The crew laughed as five glasses glittered, though from the overhead lights or the uncle's alcohol, I couldn't say.

"A toast then," said Lissa. Several glasses clanked too early, and Jake held his side with one hand as he laughed. Desperation might have driven us to it, but under the programmed Christmas lights, we were alive and grateful. "To our captain, who brought us all together."

"And to Father Christmas!" Seb shouted.

"To Father Christmas," they echoed.

"Here's to you, Dad," I whispered.

The booze burned like three suns going down, and Lissa hooted. "Happy Christmas indeed! You got any more of that stuff, Jake?"

"I do! My Christmas present to each of you, I guess."

"Did I ever tell you about how I met our great captain?" Lissa said.

I groaned. There wasn't enough hooch in the galaxy to keep my ears from burning through this story, but I grinned, anyway and took another drink.

I was with the only family that mattered, and it was a happy Christmas indeed.

I've always had a fascination with the absurd, which is probably why I enjoy British TV so much. When trying to think of an idea for this collection, I thought, what's more absurd than Santa being part of the Mob? Mob-Santa being murdered in space!

I wrote this after reading *And Then There Were None* by Agatha Christie. I loved the idea of an enclosed space mystery, especially since they devolve into everyone pointing the finger at one another. It's similar to "The Monsters are Due on Maple Street" by Rod Serling in that regard. And what can I say? I've always enjoyed a good episode of *The Twilight Zone*.

Raven Oak

BEVEL & TURN

BY G. CLEMANS

Family curses are hardest on the young—not always so in this folktale inspired piece! A high school loner's survival depends on competence and riddles, and she has that same old-fashioned competence her ancestors did: crafting with her hands. G. Clemans explores compulsions, and her genre combination of YA with Germanic folk-telling blends to make the perfect backdrop. What compulsories of genre must she work within, and which does she ignore?　　　　　　　　　　　　　　　　　—Janine A. Southard

The chisel bucked and shimmied in Georgia's hand, but she held it tight against the block. As the chunk of wood spun around the mechanical lathe, chips flicked away from the bit, releasing an earthy, bitter smell.

Georgia turned off the lathe, pushed the oh-so-fashionable safety goggles on top of her head, and glanced at the clock on the other side of the cavernous classroom. Crap. The bell was going to ring soon for lunch. If Mr. Peterson would only leave the shop open, she could stay and work. She was running out of time before winter break and she really, really wanted to finish this project. No. She *needed* to finish. Every bone in her body told her to keep carving.

Besides, working through lunch would be better than sitting by herself in the cafeteria. Even if she wanted to hang out with the stinky stoners and arts slackers who took wood-shop, *they* didn't want to hang

142

out with her. Somehow, over the last three years, the kids in her high school had decided she was a weird loner, the only girl who took woodshop for every elective, every semester.

They were right, of course. Her aunt had said it was hereditary—a family tree of obsessive craftspeople and unlucky misfits. At least five of her ancestors had lost limbs or digits in accidents that were never quite explained.

Apparently, her parents were the most well-adjusted of the bunch. They were pulled-together, successful, ambitious. They had all their fingers and toes. They claimed Georgia was just like them—reasonably smart and relatively good-looking. Just that morning, her mom had said again, "Georgie, maybe if you styled that brown mane and tried *a little*, you'd have more friends."

But she didn't want to try. Didn't feel capable of wanting to try. Never really had. And it had been even worse since Auntie Ash had vanished during Georgia's freshman year. No one had gotten her like her aunt.

Georgia tightened the elastic band that valiantly held her thick dark hair in a ponytail. A ponytail was a hairstyle, right? She abandoned the electric lathe and walked over to the worktable she shared with the sandy-haired new guy.

After lining up the freshly carved spindle next to the other finished pieces, she checked everything against her plans. She breathed out, "Crap."

The new guy lifted his head. "Wassup?"

His question jolted her. She was used to being ignored. His dark blue eyes sent a tingle through her. Her eyes slammed down to her sketches. She murmured, "Oh, I screwed something up. No big deal." There. She'd offered an explanation and a closure to the exchange. Done.

But he slid off his stool, ambled to her side of the table, and leaned over to see her notebook, which was filled with sketches and loose sheets of instructions she'd printed off the Internet.

He said, "I'm new to woodshop, but who knows, maybe I can help. Wassup?"

What was up with this guy and his "Wassups"?

The other day she'd been vaguely intrigued that a new kid had joined woodshop at the very end of the semester, but mostly she was perturbed that she had to share a worktable. Now, here he was, standing so close that his arm brushed against her baggy gray sweatshirt.

She jabbed a finger at a sketch of a Christmas whirligig composed of a simple A-frame with a propeller on top. If all went well—which it wasn't—heat from candles around the base would turn the propeller, and a little scene of carved figurines would spin around.

"Um, you see this propeller? I've already shaped the blades and this center hub that they attach to, but I cut the notches at the wrong angle so the whole thing is backwards."

He picked up the wooden hub. A prick of annoyance went through her. He was touching her stuff.

"Can't you just flip it over?" he asked.

"No, I've already carved the finial on top and a hole at the base for the spindle, see? It looks simple, but it took forever. Dammit. And now I have to make another one."

Now there was no way she'd finish before winter break. Her parents would never let her work on it at home, and Georgia had decided that she absolutely had to have a Christmas whirligig of her own. She couldn't explain it; she just kept brooding about her missing aunt and the now-in-storage family heirloom—an elaborate three-tiered Christmas tower. She had decided to make one of her own, as a kind of modest, really modest, homage.

The boy picked up a blade and inserted it into a notch in the hub. Just like that, he was fiddling with her project. She blurted out, "Hey!"

His eyebrows shot up and he put the pieces down. "Oh, sorry, did I break woodshop protocol? I change schools a lot, and I never know what the unspoken rules are."

Her cheeks were warm. "Oh, I don't think it's a rule or anything. It's just me—I'm kind of obsessed with this."

"Well, the apology still stands." His fingers hovered near the pieces. "I was just trying to wrap my head around your problem."

"Which one?" Whoa, she'd attempted to make a joke. A surprised smile played on her lips.

He returned the smile. "Let's stick with the propeller problem for now."

He swiveled his gaze between the blade jutting out of the hub and her drawing. "Okay, this might be a dumb question, but if you still used this hub and stuck all the blades in, then the whole thing would still work right?"

She nodded. "But it would go the wrong direction."

"Well, what makes it the wrong direction?"

Now her cheeks got really hot. Her aunt had always insisted that their family whirligig must turn clockwise, which made sense because that's the direction that the little characters were facing. She managed to speak. "Well, every Christmas whirligig I've ever seen goes clockwise. But I guess I could glue the figurines onto the platform facing the other direction."

"Exactly." He grinned. "And what did you call it? A whirligig? Aren't they usually called Christmas pyramids?"

"You've seen these things before?"

"Yeah, they're big in Germany. We lived there for years. Mom's in the service. They're called Weihnachtspyramide."

She tried to pronounce it, "Vy-nox-peer-uh-mee-duh?"

"Close enough."

Georgia tilted her head to consider this wavy-haired boy who had every appearance of a skater dude. "Huh."

"Huh, what?"

Dammit, she was blushing again. "Oh, nothing. It's just, um, interesting that you lived in Europe. I haven't been anywhere."

"So, if you could go anywhere, where would you want to go?"

What was happening? This was veering away from woodshop problem-solving into what, a conversation? She didn't know what to answer or how to answer, and he was looking at her with those damned blue eyes.

The bell rang. Thank God.

Mr. Peterson made his usual announcement. "Okay, people. Turn 'em off, clean 'em up, and get the heck out."

Georgia placed the whirligig parts in her cubby below the worktable, shoved her sketchbook into her backpack, and bolted for the door.

It was the last day before winter break and Georgia was freaking out.

The sandy-haired boy wasn't in shop. Hadn't been all week, but that wasn't the problem. She didn't need the distraction. Her stomach clenched. There was no way she was going to finish. She could manage to sneak in some balancing and gluing at home, but she needed the shop equipment for some things. Dammit, dammit, dammit.

Why was she killing herself over this? Mr. Peterson didn't care if she finished now or after break. Her parents sure as hell didn't care. They didn't even want her to take woodshop. She could picture her dad, with his trim salt-and-pepper beard, saying again, "We know you're creative, sweetheart, but woodworking has brought our family nothing but trouble. How about a class in digital design?"

But Georgia had always been drawn to woodcraft. Like it was unavoidable or something. Auntie Ash had understood. She'd told her it was in her blood and that her great, great, great grandfather had been a carver in Germany. He was the one, in fact, who had created the family heirloom—the three-tiered whirligig—that Georgia had helped her aunt set up every Christmas.

It had been like a ritual. It *was* a ritual, joyful and solemn. They'd chat all the way through the unpacking and assembling. Her aunt would scold her if the pieces were out of order. Then, in silence they'd light the candles and watch the three scenes spin around.

It had been three years, almost to the day, since she'd seen her aunt. And that tower, come to think of it. Her parents had cleaned out her aunt's house after she'd disappeared. All of her belongings were sitting in their garage, but no one thought to bring out the Christmas tower. Or maybe, like Georgia, they couldn't bear to see it without Auntie Ash there to boss them around.

Was that why she felt compelled to make this god-damned sad excuse for a whirligig? She missed her aunt all the time but even more so at Christmas. This year, it was intense. Thoughts about her aunt, the beautiful family heirloom, and her own unfinished whirligig swirled through her head day and night.

Georgia's chest tightened. She couldn't move. She just sat there, wasting precious minutes.

The door opened, and the boy loped in. Her heart lifted despite herself.

He crossed the big room, strolling through the clear, wintry sunlight to Mr. Peterson's desk. He handed the teacher a note and then slid up to Georgia's side of the worktable with a grin. "Wassup?"

She managed a half-smile. "Where have you been?"

"Oh, man, my schedule has been so messed up, I was pulled out of woodshop to make up some reqs, but I wanted back in. So, here I am. How's the pyramid coming along?"

Dammit, tears of frustration tingled at the edges of her eyes. His grin disappeared. "Oh, man, is there another problem?"

She shook her head. "I don't think I'm going to be able to finish it."

"Look. I am not a great woodshopper or anything, but let me be your assistant today."

She couldn't help smiling. "Even if you helped me, there's no way we could finish in —," she glanced at the clock, "forty-five minutes."

"Hmm." He leaned in closer. "Well, what if I told you I was skilled at taking advantage of school facilities after hours?"

"So, in addition to assisting with my shop project, you're offering to help me break and enter?"

He nodded, settling his blue eyes on her hazel ones.

She glanced down to her whirligig. "Why?"

"I'm used to being the new guy, walking into different social situations. Sometimes people are dicks. Sometimes they fall all over me. I've learned to choose where I want to go, who I want to hang out with. Usually the most interesting people are on the perimeters."

Her cheeks grew hot. She stared at her whirligig and managed to mutter, "Okay. Thank you."

"No problem. If we're going to be partners in crime and woodcraft, I guess we should know each other's names. I'm Caleb."

"Georgia. Nice to meet you."

That night Georgia picked him up at eight after shamelessly lying to her parents, saying she and a friend were going to see a movie.

They would have bought any story, really, they were so thrilled that she was going out. Her mom got particularly ridiculous when she heard it was a boy. Georgia must have said "It's not a date" fifty times.

Outside the school, Caleb strode to the bathroom window he'd left open. "The trick is to leave it open just a crack so no one notices." He pushed it up and they wriggled in, one at a time. Georgia was not impressed by the boys' bathroom. But the hallways were nice and empty—dark but peaceful. Less lonely than usual.

The shop seemed endless in the cool glow of Caleb's flashlight. Georgia reached to turn on the lights, but he stopped her, nodding at the windows. "Probably against Peterson's safety policies, but we're going to have to do this without the overheads."

For the next three nights, they carved and drilled. Well, the first night, Caleb mostly held the flashlight. The second night, Georgia brought a camp lantern and gave Caleb little jobs to do: sanding, assembling, testing the balance.

Every once in a while, they'd hear some thud or clang within the building. They'd snap off their lights and crouch behind a workbench, waiting, listening. But that had been it. No one had busted them.

And then it was finished. The pyramid wasn't perfect, by any means, and it would make a sad contrast to her family's three-tiered tower. But the single round platform was level and it held four tiny, lathe-turned musicians. The propeller's blades were perfectly balanced. The whole thing just might work.

Georgia placed four candles around the base and lit a match. Caleb snapped off the flashlight and lantern. As soon as Georgia lit the first candle, the propeller glided into motion. With all four candles lit, the round platform spun at a pretty good clip. The little trumpeter, drummer, cymbalist, and singer raced around in a circle.

Georgia and Caleb grinned at each other.

"You did it, Georgia."

"Couldn't have done it without you. Thank you."

"Yeah, my mad woodworking skills really came in handy."

"Hey, you did some first rate sanding and gluing," she said.

"So. What are you going to do with it? Is it a Christmas present for someone?"

"Um, no."

He waited. She swallowed and said, "It's kind of for my aunt, even though she's...she's not around anymore. She was amazing. She called herself the world's best whittling attorney at law."

Caleb asked softly, "What happened to her?"

Georgia gave a tight shrug. "She disappeared three years ago. We lived nearby, and she and I talked almost every day. She'd been acting weird. Not crazy weird, just distracted and serious. Well, she was whittling like crazy." Georgia paused. "Anyway, when I didn't hear from her for a few days, my folks contacted the police. They couldn't find any trace of a sudden trip or of anything more...serious. The only things missing from her house were some strange bone ornaments she always brought out at Christmastime. They totally freaked me out when I was a kid, but they were kind of beautiful. Other than that, her place was totally untouched. Freshly decorated for Christmas, complete with the three-tiered tower we had set up on her living room table. My aunt was just...gone."

"Oh, man, Georgia, I'm sorry."

Georgia stared at the whirligig zipping along. She blew out one candle and the spinning slowed. She murmured, "That's better. Less manic."

"Maybe shorter candles next time?"

"Next time?"

He cleared his throat. "Well, yeah, I was thinking maybe we could start a new project or something."

Jesus, she'd been so self-absorbed, but now it hit her like a ton of bricks. He came off all casual and confident, but he was just a new kid in a new school in a new town. He was lonely, too.

And besides, an ache kept whispering deep within her. Something still needed to be done.

She smiled. "Yeah, let's come again tomorrow night. I have an idea."

The next night, Caleb went through the bathroom window first. One at a time, Georgia handed him three old hatboxes and a heavy backpack. In the woodshop, she carefully set the boxes on the floor and unzipped the backpack at their worktable.

He nodded to the machinery on the side of the room. "What, no lathing tonight?"

"Ooh, using lathe as a verb. Nice. But no. Tonight we're going to celebrate. Have a seat."

Caleb pulled up a battered metal stool and watched as she whipped out a lace tablecloth and covered the grungy work surface. Then she set out plates, napkins, a thermos, and a couple of mugs.

Caleb laughed when she unwrapped a loaf of frosted bread. "You're kidding me. Is that Christstollen?"

"Yep. I looked up German Christmas food and found a recipe. It's got raisins and nuts and sounds kind of disgusting, actually."

"Oh, totally. The stollen I had in Germany was awful."

"But at least we've got booze." She opened up the thermos and wine-scented steam wafted out. "This is—oh God, I'm going to butcher the pronunciation—Glühwein."

Caleb chuckled. "Gloo-vine. My mom let me have some last year. It was pretty damn tasty."

"But it sounds weird, right? I mean, hot, spiced red wine? I'm just hoping my parents don't miss the bottle."

Georgia set their whirligig in the center and replaced the tall candles with four stubby ones.

In the candlelight, they tried the fruit bread, which was in fact pretty awful. They sipped the mulled wine, which was weird but tasty. After two mugs of wine, they decided the stollen wasn't that bad. They watched the pyramid whirl about.

Georgia was warm and loose. She was finally ready. She hopped off her stool and lifted the three boxes onto the worktable. Her heart thumped. She opened up all the lids, revealing bundles of bubble wrap. Inside the layers of clear plastic were wood spindles and discs and figurines.

In a quiet voice, Caleb asked, "Your aunt's pyramid?"

Georgia nodded and started unwrapping. She pictured her aunt with her brown-gray hair swept up in a wiry bun, laughing as she told stories about each of the pieces.

Caleb reached for a round, flat bundle. "May I?"

She nodded. He revealed a small, circular platform with two standing figures and a cradle, complete with a tiny swaddled baby. "A nativity scene?"

Georgia nodded again. "But it also could be about my family's history. My great, great, great grandfather carved this when his first child was born."

"Oh, that's cool. Multiple narratives."

"You like that, huh? Well, then you would have loved my aunt. I could never get a straight answer out of her. She was a civil rights lawyer and was always questioning the obvious answers, the stories we get handed."

When all the pieces were laid out on the lace tablecloth, Georgia fit the spindle onto the ceramic disc in the center of the base and slid the first platform all the way down the spindle. Then she added the base level's outer structure, a little gazebo with delicate columns. Then another platform and another gazebo for the center tier. And another set for the upper tier. Finally, on top she attached the wooden fan.

Caleb said, "Wunderschön. Wonderfully beautiful."

Georgia just nodded. The silence grew thick. She poured out the last drops of the mulled wine and then slowly lit the candles.

Georgia held her breath as the discs started spinning. She tried not to think about the last time she'd seen the Christmas tower in motion, standing next to her aunt in her cozy living room.

She half-laughed, half-choked. "Oh, no! It's going the wrong way."

Sure enough, Mary and Joseph were gliding backward on the top tier. On the middle disc, a toy train led a reverse chase toward backward-facing children who held other wooden toys. On the bottom, the largest platform, a parade of candle-bearing villagers circled in the wrong direction.

"I never knew this propeller could go either way." She reached out a hand to flip it over. The tower jumped into high speed and she snatched her hand back.

The whirring propeller grew louder and louder until a gale whipped around them. Far from sputtering out, the candles glowed brighter against the wind, casting bursts of light across the woodshop. The room spun as though *she* were the one standing on the plates. Round and round, the worktables, machines, and exit signs flashed by. Pain ripped through her stomach. Desperate, she clutched for Caleb's hand. His eyes were wide with panic.

On the tower's top tier, the tiny man, woman, and baby swirled backward. And then everything went black.

152

When she opened her eyes again, it was quiet and dark as pitch. Her head was stuffy and her mouth was dry.

Oh my God, was this what a hangover felt like? Maybe she'd passed out. She'd never be able to face Caleb again. She sat up and groped around. Her fingertips touched—what—a hardwood floor? She definitely wasn't sitting on the concrete floor of the woodshop.

Caleb's muted voice asked, "Georgia?" Why did he sound so near but so far?

Her voice came out muted and echoey, too. "Caleb? Where are you? Where are we?"

His fingers grasped her leg just above the knee. She reached out and clumsily bumped her hand against his face. "Oh, my God, you're right here. I'm so sorry!"

His breath came close to her ear, but he still sounded far away. "What the hell's going on?"

A high-pitched wail filled the air. A baby crying.

A door whooshed open and warm light flooded the room. A plump woman swept through the door and past them. Her brown skirt brushed over Georgia's legs. At the far side of the room, the woman picked up a swaddled baby from a simple cradle.

In a sing-song voice, the woman murmured to the baby. Georgia couldn't understand a word she was saying. Where were they? The wide-planked floor was scrubbed clean and the whitewashed ceiling was pitched at a steep angle. Somehow, some way, they had ended up in someone's attic apartment.

She turned to Caleb and inhaled sharply.

The candlelight glinted right through his sandy hair, which was usually thick and wavy, but was now slightly transparent and delineated with golden squiggles. His face was translucent and flattened out. She couldn't see straight through him, necessarily, he just seemed not fully there. What the hell?!

She stared at her hands. Same thing. Georgia and Caleb met each other's eyes, seeking answers. The plump woman, now holding the baby, walked toward the door, not seeming to notice them at all.

Georgia struggled to her feet, "Um, hello, ma'am." The woman tilted her head slightly but didn't stop. Georgia turned to Caleb. "She has no idea we're here. Are we ghosts?"

Caleb shook his head and forced a smile. "If we're dead, my mom is going to kill me."

They crept after the woman into a sparely furnished, pitch-roofed room. A modest fire glowed in a stone fireplace on the opposite wall. At a wooden table, a bearded man played with the baby who was now tucked into his lap.

The curvy woman bustled around the room, taking dishes from the table to a kitchen area next to the fireplace. The kitchen had only a single counter with a few shelves above it.

The woman took down pewter mugs from the shelves, carefully removed a small pot from a grate in the fireplace, and poured two steaming drinks. Smiling, she handed one to her husband, saying, "Fröhliche Weihnachten"

Georgia turned to Caleb, who translated, "*Merry Christmas.*" At the sound of his voice, the young mother and father glanced at each other, as if questioning whether the other had heard something. They both laughed.

The man handed the baby back to the woman, then walked to a large cupboard and pulled out a three-foot tall package wrapped in brown paper and a green ribbon. Georgia's heart quickened. The man set the gift down on the table and murmured something to his wife. With one hand, she removed the ribbon, letting the paper fall away.

It was the three-tiered Christmas pyramid.

They were in the home of her great, great, great grandfather and grandmother. Georgia racked her brain for their names. Fromm, that was their last name for sure. And the woman's name also started with an F—Fergie? Frida? Fredda! Yes, Fredda Fromm, a name that had always stood out to her.

The woman dabbed at her eyes and beamed at her husband. "Wunderschön, Birk." That was it, Birk. Her great, great, great grandfather was Birk Fromm.

He set four candles around the base, lit them, and the pyramid slid into motion. He raised his mug to his wife and then to the baby. "Zu ehren unser ersten Kind, unser kleines Wunder."

Caleb murmured in Georgia's ear, "He said something like, *In honor of our first child, our little wonder.* Or maybe not '*wonder,*' maybe '*miracle*?'"

The young mother smiled and glanced down at her ring finger that bore no ring. The family simply sat and watched the whirligig for a while until Birk took out ink, pen, and paper and began drawing.

A jolt of recognition flashed through Georgia. She knew exactly what he was putting down: diagrams and instructions. She'd seen that piece of paper before.

While her husband drew, Fredda walked over to the large cupboard with the baby on her hip. She reached into a drawer and pulled out a slender white ornament, dangling from a red velvet ribbon. Georgia inhaled sharply. It was a bone ornament just like the ones missing from Auntie Ash's house.

Fredda studied the bone with an expression Georgia couldn't quite place—a kind of awe, maybe. When the baby reached for it, Fredda yanked it out of reach and dropped it back in the drawer.

She next withdrew a small, folded piece of paper. She read it slowly, then crossed to the fireplace and tossed it in the fire.

At that moment, the fire began to vibrate and the room began to spin. Pain and dizziness swept through Georgia. Static ate away at her vision. Caleb fumbled for her hand just as everything went black.

The sharp scent of wood chips came to her first. And then the woodshop's cold concrete floor beneath her. Georgia reached up to massage her thrumming head.

"Georgia?" Caleb's voice was clear.

She opened her eyes to the darkness but quickly shut them again when Caleb clicked on the camp lantern. What the hell had just happened? And then it hit her. "I think I know what happened to my aunt."

"What do you mean?"

"She must have done the same thing we did, only maybe, I don't know, she got stuck or something. How did we get back here?"

"You are asking the wrong guy. I mean where was 'there'? Back in time? An alternate universe? A shared hallucination? What the hell was in that wine?"

Snippets swirled through her head: the candle-lit attic apartment, Fredda's bone charm, Birk's paper with diagrams. They were like fragmented images rather than full memories. And already they faded.

Georgia tried to ignore her pounding head as she rose to her feet. She rummaged through the boxes that stored the Christmas pyramid. Sure enough, at the bottom of a box was a brittle envelope, so old it looked tea-stained rather than merely yellowed.

She carefully retrieved the sheet of paper inside. She remembered it clearly. About five years ago, her Auntie Ash had smoothed it out on her dining room table where they always set up the tower.

Georgia had been skeptical. They'd always assembled the pyramid in exactly the same way, in the same order. Every year, with no instructions. But that year, her aunt brought out the paper for the first time. Georgia had looked at the diagrams and exclaimed, "We don't need those."

But her aunt had insisted that she examine the page. "Yes, Georgie, these are instructions, but look carefully; there's more going on here. More than even I know, and I've studied this a thousand times. What else do you see?"

Georgia had perused the drawings of the whirligig parts and the numbered diagrams for assembly. Nothing too exciting there. She moved to a long passage of text written in a different hand. The writing was elegant, more feminine, but also severe.

She shook her head. "This is beautiful, but I can't read German."

Her aunt had chuckled. "It's okay, that's just a poem that I'll translate for you sometime. Look over here instead." Her aunt pointed at a list that ran down one side of the paper. "Here is the mystery. What do you notice?"

Georgia looked at the list. "Names and dates." She squinted. "And each line is in different handwriting." The names and writing styles suggested personas. Günther Baumgardner was announced in bold, fat letters. Wilhemena Zink was stuttered in a spidery cursive. The names became more modern and Americanized as she moved down the list.

Georgia reached the last name. "Bernard Ash. Grandpa."

Grandpa Bernie had been a boisterous man—an accountant by day and a woodworker on the weekends. He would unabashedly show Georgia the stump of his index finger whenever he caught her staring at it. But he never explained how it had happened, saying, "It's all a blur, actually. A small sacrifice to pay for a happy, healthy life."

"Grandpa's is the last name on this list, which is— what—a list of the whirligig's owners?"

Auntie Ash's brown and gray bun bobbed as she nodded. "Yes, that's my best guess. But I don't understand all the dates next to the names. Some names have several dates listed."

Georgia studied the multiple dates after Grandpa Bernie's name. 2000, 2003, 2006, 2009—the year he had died. "They're all three years apart."

"Yes. And I've never understood why the tower moved around the family so much. Why it didn't stay in one home for decades, like other heirlooms."

"Auntie Ash? Why isn't your name on it?"

Her aunt traced her finger over the list of names. "I don't know. It hasn't felt like the right time, I guess."

And that had been the end of it.

Caleb's gentle voice interrupted her reverie. "Georgia? Wassup with all of this? I already feel like it never even happened."

The memories of their time in the attic apartment were slipping away. She turned the paper over and grabbed a pen. "We need to record what happened."

They spent the next few minutes writing down everything they could remember, building on each other's partial recollections.

And then Georgia flipped the paper back over and showed Caleb the old instructions, list, and poem. She relayed what her aunt had told her about them. "Maybe these dates are when these people went back in time? I don't understand any of it, Caleb. And now I really wish I'd taken German instead of French."

"You know I'm pretty fluent, right? Want me to take it home and write it out for you?"

Georgia nodded her aching head. She was bone-tired and afraid to say what was on her mind. Her aunt was back there, wherever—or whenever—that was. She felt it in her bones. "I hate to ask. You don't have to, you know. But I'm going try to go back. Tomorrow night."

Caleb was silent for a moment. "Okay. I'm going with you."

The next night, as Georgia set up the tower, Caleb read their notes from the night before to remind them that it had really happened. It all seemed like a swirling dream.

Georgia put the propeller on upside down. Would it happen again?

Heart racing, wanting it to happen but dreading it, too, Georgia lit the candles. The three tiers of the tower shifted into motion, circling backwards. She didn't have to wait long. The whirring sound grew louder and the candles burned brighter.

Georgia tried to focus on the top tier, but her gaze was pulled to the middle where the tiny toy train zoomed along backwards, following backward-facing children holding other wooden toys. Her stomach jerked sharply, and she reached out to Caleb before everything went dark.

Georgia awoke with the same befuddled head and dry mouth, but in an entirely different place. She and Caleb were sprawled on the floor of a large, brightly lit room. Just as before, her hands were slightly flat and translucent.

Children of various ages scampered about, almost ploughing right through Georgia and Caleb. The ghostly pair quickly scooted backward into a quiet corner of the shop. At the end of a nearby counter, a stocky, middle-aged man half-scowled, half-smiled at the rambunctious kids.

A little boy marched by pulling a wooden train behind him. He was neatly dressed in a blue suit and seemed to belong to a wealthy couple who stood by watching him. A little girl in a thin gray dress sat on the floor trying out a wooden top.

They were in a toyshop. No, wait. A cluster of Christmas pyramids caught her eye. And on the wall behind the shopkeeper, intricately carved clocks ticked away. It was a woodworker's shop.

And then she saw it. On a shelf underneath the clocks stood her family's Christmas tower. What was it doing there? Had her relatives brought it in for repairs? That didn't make sense. Birk Fromm had made it; surely he could fix it. Georgia's insides tightened with anxiety.

The door opened, letting in a blast of frigid air. A man limped through with one hand on a wooden crutch. Birk Fromm. He nodded to the shopkeeper but didn't smile. He looked...not older but worn down. One of his pant legs dangled below the knee.

He hobbled toward the counter and began an earnest conversation with the stocky woodcarver. Birk gestured toward the tower he had created. The shopkeeper nodded, but then shook his head. Had Birk pawned it and now wanted it back? Was pawning even a thing in 19th century Germany?

The shop owner's expression was sympathetic. Sad, even. He turned and gently picked up the tower from the counter. A burgundy dress flashed within the back room, catching his eye. He tensed, then turned back to Birk, placing the tower in front of him on the counter. He spoke kindly but forcefully.

Caleb leaned toward Georgia's ear. "He's saying something like, *It's beautiful. I'm sorry that you've been unable to find work since your accident.*" Caleb paused and listened. "*But my wife will not —. No. Never mind that. I cannot sell it, and I cannot offer you a job.*"

A gust of cold air signaled the arrival of someone else. A woman, holding the hand of a little boy about six years old. Georgia realized with a start that it was Fredda and her son. She was barely recognizable. Her pleasant curves were gone and her face sagged. She met Birk's gaze. He simply shook his head.

Despair flashed across the woman's face, but then it was gone. She let go of the boy's hand and nudged him toward his father. Head held high, she walked to the counter and picked up the Christmas tower.

Fredda addressed the stocky shopkeeper but looked past him into the backroom. "*Herr Holzheim, is your wife available?*" Without waiting for an answer, she swept past the shop owner into the room beyond. The two men exchanged a nervous glance.

What was going on? Georgia needed to know. She mumbled to Caleb, "I'm going to follow her."

They stole behind the counter and into the workroom. It was tidy and bright and empty, except for wood projects in various states of completion. Women's voices raised in heated debate reached Georgia. The argument was coming from behind a closed door at the back of the workroom. The door was painted a deep, blood red.

What the hell was back there? Georgia placed a hand against the red door and gave a push. It creaked open a few inches. She pushed again, harder, and entered a cluttered room dimly lit with candles.

In the center of the room, a striking middle-aged woman in a long burgundy dress stood with Fredda, who seemed small and shabby in comparison. The tall, dark-haired woman nodded at the open door and commanded, "Schliessen Sie die Tür." Fredda sighed and closed the door just as Caleb slipped through it.

What was this place? A workroom behind the workroom? Along each wall was a counter littered with feathers, herbs, ribbons, and some off-white knobby things that looked like animal bones. Georgia's scalp tingled. This was where the ornaments were made.

The elegant woman began speaking again, her voice dripping with disdain. Caleb translated into Georgia's ear, pausing and correcting himself at times.

"*I do not know what you expect from me, Frau Fromm. When I was married —.*" Caleb interrupted himself, "No, not married. Engaged. *When I was engaged to Herr Kaut, I could have helped you, perhaps found office work at the mine for your injured husband.*"

The woman in burgundy folded her long arms across her chest, silver rings flashing on every finger of her right hand. On her left hand, a single silver ring encased her pinky finger—the only finger remaining on a mutilated hand.

Georgia knew the difference between the smooth joinery of a birth deformity and the scarred results of an accident. Something terrible had happened to this woman.

Frau Holzheim continued her mock-humble speech. "*But in the end, I married a woodworker. I have no power.*"

Fredda Fromm replied, her voice simmering with barely contained frustration. "*Frau Holzheim, you have enormous power. Six years ago, I came to ask for your...good wishes...as my husband and I struggled to have a child. So many people have offered you gifts in exchange for your charms.*"

The older woman flicked her mangled hand at Fredda. "*Bah. People bring me mere trinkets.*"

Fredda's eyes flashed. "*My wedding ring was not a trinket.*"

Frau Holzheim strode over to a counter, and with her good hand, knocked over a wooden box, spilling its contents. Rings and necklaces and brooches. "*You want it back? It must be here somewhere. Take it!*" She considered the stumps on her hand. *"I once wore a diamond and ruby engagement ring. And now, the woman who almost owned a silver mine has nothing. Nothing to amuse her, nothing to look forward to."*

Fredda swallowed, as if trying to keep calm. *"But you have a good husband and comfortable house. You help others with your charms. I only want some help."*

"And yet all you offer is a Weihnachtspyramide? I am so bored with woodcraft!"

"I have nothing left to give. What is it that you want?"

Frau Holzheim tilted her head, considering Fredda and the Christmas tower. She reached out her pinky finger and spun the whirligig. The gashed stumps from her missing digits were all the more gruesome next to the only remaining finger with its ornate silver ring. *"Hmmm. There is something I would like. Something from the past. And I crave something new. New blood. Life in this small village is so tiresome. The same small people, the same small problems. They know nothing of true tragedy."*

Frau Holzheim abruptly stopped the spinning with her pinky and pushed the tower in the opposite direction. The tiered figurines raced backwards. She leveled her dark, glinting eyes at Fredda. *"Past and future. I can make them meet, I think. But it will take sacrifice from your family. If you are willing, I will help you. I will give you some of my jewelry, and I will permit my husband to offer your husband work. Do we have a deal?"*

Georgia's great, great, great grandmother hung her head. *"But what is it, exactly, that you are asking in return, Frau Holzheim?"*

A searing pain erupted in Georgia's stomach and the cluttered room slid into motion. Caleb's hand plopped onto hers just as everything faded to black.

They awoke again in the high school woodshop. The candles from the Christmas tower were snuffed out, but they had left the camp lantern on. Georgia's head pounded. She was more confused than ever.

"We went back in time again, right? The little boy was probably around six. A lot happened since our first visit."

Caleb nodded and moaned. "Oh, man, remind me not to move my head." He massaged his temples. "Georgia? I can already feel the memories slipping away."

She hauled herself to her feet and removed the old envelope from its box. "Let's write it down. I guess we just witnessed the enchanting of the tower."

They talked it out, taking turns writing down what they remembered. Then Caleb was silent for a moment.

"Something that psycho Frau said reminded me of the poem." He turned the piece of paper over. "Some of the poem is kind of, you know, poetic, like 'Leben-Kreise um sich selbst.' *Life circles round itself.* But a few lines down, listen to this:

> *Three tiers, three years,*
> *A familial form appears,*
> *To uncover a gift,*
> *Or leave one behind.*

> *Love and loss are bone-deep,*
> *In a ring where past and future meet.*
> *Fortune is taken by the hand,*
> *That gives even as it moves away.*

Caleb paused. "I'm not entirely sure of my translation. But the original is beautiful—it rhymes better in German."

Georgia smiled a little. "Oh, good, I can't stand it when German poetry about a cursed, time-travelling whirligig doesn't rhyme."

He chuckled and pointed to the lilting handwriting of the poem. "Someone must have added this to Birk's diagrams after the witch enchanted the Christmas tower."

"You think that's what she was? A witch?"

"I don't know how else to explain it."

Georgia stared at the pyramid on the table. What was this thing? Some monstrous combination of woodcraft and witchcraft?

On the topmost tier, which had once seemed like a simple nativity scene, she now saw her relatives—new parents, a loving family, in a simple, attic apartment. The middle scene of children and toys now held all kinds of dark mysteries: play and poverty, gifts and sacrifices.

The bottom tier held eight tiny villagers, holding lanterns in their knob-hands and wearing yellow-tipped candles on bands encircling their foreheads.

Georgia cleared her throat. "I guess our next stop is the village square. Or rather, my next stop. I feel like I'll forget everything if I wait. I need to go back tonight. Right now. But I can't ask you to keep doing this with me."

Caleb ran his fingers through his wavy hair, then carefully folded the paper and put it in his pocket. "I'm in this, too. Let's do it."

They came to in a dark craggy mine. Even in her numb state, Georgia could feel the pressure of the surrounding mountain. Dusty, oily vapors hit her nose. This was a black, dank place. Shadows flickered crazily, cast by the candles on the headlamps of miners who moved in and out of adjoining tunnels.

They were in a cavern, bolstered all around by thick wooden beams. They lay dangerously close to a large drilling device that spun steadily in the center. Its shaft continued down through the rocky floor.

Georgia tried to see down the hole, but there was nothing but darkness and a rumbling, crunching sound. She followed the drill upward and saw a circle of dusky light far above. Caleb batted at her arm and led them away from the drill, over to the cavern wall where a long, rough-hewn bench had been carved out of the rock.

Three miners trudged into the cave, their faces caked with rock dust and streaked with white where they'd wiped a brow or cheek. They sat down on the craggy bench, not far from Caleb and Georgia, and pulled things out of their pockets. One man wiped his face with a handkerchief. Another—a boy, really—unwrapped a roll of bread. The third—furthest away from Georgia—pulled out a knife and a piece of wood to whittle.

Georgia didn't recognize any of them. She turned to Caleb. "I don't get why we're here. I mean, my aunt said something about how miners started the woodworking tradition in this part of Germany. Something to pass the time, I guess, when they couldn't go up to the surface. But why are we here?"

An echoing chant filled the cavern. The miners paused, listening. Georgia felt the woman's voice deep in her body. The intonation was eerie but intimate, as if it were meant for her. It was gone as quickly as it had come, lost in the rumbling sound of the drill.

The boy turned wide eyes toward the older men. The whittler laughed and leaned in toward the boy. "*Nothing to worry about, kid.*"

Caleb's breath was hot against Georgia's ear as he translated. "*That's just the Fraulein of the mine. She used to be engaged to the mine owner, you know. One day, years ago, around this time of year, she surprised him at work, came down to bring him and the workers Christmas treats. But she was a vain one, she was. All dressed up in her finery.*"

The miner nodded his grimy face toward the drill. "*Her fancy sleeve got caught on that very machine, almost dragged her under.*"

The boy's mouth dropped open.

"*Don't worry, she didn't die here. She just left behind a few fingers and her ruby engagement ring. They say that the mine owner broke off their engagement after that.*"

The drill emitted a particularly loud crunch. The other man laughed. "*Ah, hear that? That's her fingers being ground up beneath the drill.*"

The chanting returned. This time Georgia felt it deep in her bones, rhythmic and alluring, like siren song.

Georgia rose and drifted around the cavern, trying to locate the sound as it bounced around the rocky walls. Caleb called after her, but she barely noticed. As she neared the drill shaft, the voice reverberated within her. It was echoing up from below.

She had to go deeper. Whatever—whoever—was down there was waiting for her. It was her turn.

Georgia rushed away from the drill room into another lamp-lit cavern. Caleb followed behind. "Georgia?" he called, in a voice tinged with fear. "What's going on?"

Ahead of them was a pulley-system elevator; on either side, two narrow passageways shot off into the dark. The tunnel on the right sloped steeply downward. That had to be the one.

She grabbed a lantern and raced down the narrow tunnel. The chanting voice lured her down a rocky path that spiraled to the right, going deeper and deeper into the mountain. The craggy floor bit at her shoes and the walls reached out to scrape her arms, but she stumbled forward.

The chanting stopped, and with it the bone-deep certainty that she had to find the voice. Georgia stopped running—breathing hard, head spinning. Caleb took the lantern from her and held it up so he could see her face.

"Georgia? What are you doing? Why are you chasing the poem?"

"It's the poem?" She shook her head, trying to clear it. "I...I don't know what's happening. I thought it was a message for me or something."

They were only steps away from the bottom of the path, which opened into a large rough-hewn cavity. They walked inside. The drill spun steadily in the center, just like in the cavern far above them. But this space was different. It was smaller and craggier and barely tall enough for Caleb to stand. The drill chewed into the rocky floor, creating a pit of churning rock and dust. The only sound was a constant, sickening crunch.

Caleb raised the lantern to scan the room. Along the wall closest to them were mining tools and wooden bins on wheels, partially filled with rock debris. Georgia moved past them and around the drill. And there she saw it. A crumpled body lying against the craggy wall. It was Auntie Ash.

"Oh, God. Oh, my God, no!" Georgia knelt by her aunt and looked at her gray, decomposing face. Her eyes were glassy, unseeing. She was dead, Georgia knew she was dead, but she had to be sure. She gently prodded her aunt's shoulder. The stiff, lifeless arm shifted, and her aunt's hand, encrusted with dried blood, hit the floor.

Georgia whipped her head away and squeezed her eyes closed. She couldn't look. There must be missing fingers.

Caleb brought the lamp and crouched beside her. "I am so sorry, Georgia."

The drill continued its horrific grinding sound. And then the eerie voice, chanting in German, filled the room. "Leben-Kreise um sich selbst." Georgia recognized it this time. It was Frau Holzheim, the witch, reading the first line of the poem.

A pervasive, inevitable desire swelled within her, as if every muscle, every bone of her body needed to find something. She turned toward the center of the room where the drill churned through rock debris. That was where she needed to look.

The chanting voice continued. "Drei Ebenen, drei Jahre, Eine familiäre Form erscheint."

A sense of determined calm settled through Georgia. "It's my turn." She walked toward the center of the room.

Caleb yelled over the voice, over the grinding drill. "Georgia! What the hell are you doing?"

But Caleb was insignificant to the task at hand. She would be the one to find it. She reached the edge of the pit, where chunks of rock boiled up and away from the drill. It was down there, wasn't it? She dropped to her knees and reached out her hand.

Suddenly, Caleb was there. He grabbed her arm away from the drill and held it tight. "Georgia? Georgia! Listen to me."

Georgia managed to fix her eyes on Caleb's for a second before they slid back to the drill. She murmured a line from the poem, *"To uncover a gift. Or leave one behind."*

It was the way it should be. She would sacrifice her body to find the ring. She twisted against Caleb's firm grip.

Caleb yelled, "Christ! Okay, Georgia, if you can't listen to me, listen to the poem. Listen carefully to the words."

Georgia nodded. That made sense. She needed to have all the information before she completed her duty. Her muscles relaxed a little.

The witch's voice kept reciting the poem. Caleb translated into her ear. When he reached the line *Love and loss are bone-deep*, a jolt ran through her. She forced herself to look at her aunt's mangled hand, her left hand. On her ring finger, the flesh had been peeled away, revealing the bloody bone.

A flicker of sad understanding ran through her. But she couldn't concentrate. Her body kept yearning to search for the ring. Caleb kept a tight grip on her, whispering the poem into her ear, "*In a ring where past and future meet.*"

That was the witch's ring, right? The pit continued to churn with rubble. She tore her gaze away and glanced around the circular cave. Or was there another way of thinking about it? Was the ring an arena? This room?

And then the poem was over. The voice stopped. And the deep longing within her body subsided. She looked up at Caleb, her eyes filling with hot tears.

In a quivering voice, Caleb said, "It's going to be okay, Georgia."

But Georgia didn't see how it could.

At that very moment, as if a switch had been flipped high above them, the mechanical whir from the drill went quiet and the shaft slowed to a standstill.

"Must be quitting time," Caleb said. "I've got to get you out of this mine, away from that voice."

She nodded, but she was not convinced. It was her responsibility to find the ring. Caleb loosened his grip on her and stood, swinging the lantern with him. The light hit the rocky wall behind Auntie Ash. They both inhaled.

Across the wall were carvings of words and phrases. It was the poem repeated over and over, with words scratched out and underlined. More words, in English and German, were carved next to the poem, in different styles.

One phrase caught her eye: *Fortune is taken by the hand.* Someone had crossed out the "by" and carved the word "from." A chill ran through her. *Fortune is taken* from *the hand.*

And at the very bottom, near her aunt's body, was a different sentence, written in dark blood. *The poem is a contract. Break it.*

Understanding flooded her.

Her aunt had figured out a loophole that might fulfill the contract or break it. And she had died trying. Georgia would finish what her aunt had started.

Her eyes fell upon the mining tools neatly lined up along the wall: pickaxes, sledgehammers, handheld drills, other metal tools she couldn't begin to identify. They'd have to do.

Georgia whispered, "Thank you, Auntie Ash. And I'm so sorry."

Caleb squeezed her hand. "Whatever you're about to do, Georgia, you have to hurry. Before the poem starts again. Please."

Minutes later, they raced up the tunnel and reached the main intersection where the last miners were packing up for the day.

Caleb and Georgia squeezed into the rickety elevator alongside the workers and emerged from the mine into the freezing night air. A tall wooden tower rose over the mineshaft. The drill machinery that it housed was silent and still. Georgia gazed at the shaft that led down into the caverns below. The lump in her throat made it hard to breathe.

Swinging their lanterns, the miners trudged down the dark road into the village. Georgia and Caleb followed.

He asked, "You okay?"

She nodded, but then shook her head. "No."

Caleb took her cold hand.

She said, "I just hope this works. It has to work. Then my aunt will have broken the curse." Georgia wiped away tears at the edges of her eyes. "She won't have died for nothing."

The village windows glowed yellow in the night. Georgia was relieved to walk onto the main street and approach the woodworker's shop. As terrified as she was, she needed to get out of the dark and the cold. She needed this to be over with. One way or another.

Georgia and Caleb stepped inside and pushed the door closed. A few heads turned their way, wondering, perhaps, how the wind had blown the door open and shut. Fredda Fromm, now even rounder than before, stood behind the counter talking with her husband. They were both quite a bit older than the last time Georgia had seen them. Birk's full beard was now mostly gray.

Georgia looked at Caleb quizzically, then led the way to the back of the shop, around the counter, and into the neat workroom beyond.

She stopped and asked Caleb, "Will you be my assistant one more time?"

An hour later, they were finished in the workroom. They turned to face the blood-red door, the door into the witch's room. Georgia pushed it open and entered the cluttered workshop. Frau Holzheim was still elegantly dressed and regally handsome. Her dark hair was now shot with white, and she sat slightly hunched at a counter, tying a ribbon onto a charm with her one good hand and the pinky finger of the other.

As the door creaked open, she turned to look at it, narrowing her eyes. "Wilkommen?"

Georgia swept her hand across the counter, brushing aside herbs, feathers, and bones.

Frau Holzheim stared at the work surface, a smile playing on her lips. "Ach ja, ich habe einen Besucher." As she spoke, Caleb translated in Georgia's ear. *"Ah, yes, I do have a guest. I thought I heard noises in the next room. But this is so unexpected. Usually, I need to visit the mines to find traces of my visitors—relics, so to speak."* She shuffled her pinky finger through a pile of slender bones.

When Georgia began to speak, the old woman sat up, listening intently to the foreign words. "Happy Holidays, Frau Holzheim. We have brought a gift to you this time."

Caleb translated Georgia's words, speaking up so the witch could hear. Confusion flashed across her face. *"There are two of you here? I have never had two visitors at once."*

Georgia replied, "Three, actually. We just left someone down in the mines. We have brought you something from her."

Georgia placed a tiny, bone-white ring on the counter.

The witch sat still, staring at the ring. Then she swiveled toward Georgia and Caleb, looking wildly for them in the empty air. Her voice was shrill. *"What is the meaning of this? This is not my engagement ring!"*

"No, but it satisfies the contract. It is carved from the ring finger of the Fromms' great, great granddaughter. It is our family's final gift to you."

Caleb took the piece of paper from his pocket. He read the poem aloud in German and then in English.

> *Three tiers, three years,*
> *A familial form appears,*
> *To uncover a gift,*
> *Or leave one behind.*

> *Love and loss are bone-deep,*
> *In a ring where past and future meet,*
> *Fortune is taken from the hand,*
> *That gives even as it moves away.*

The old woman simmered silently. *"...taken from the hand. A ring where past and future meet.' Clever interpretation."* She picked up the tiny ring in her good hand. Finally, she said, "*It is far too small.*"

Georgia felt vomit rise to her throat. Her aunt had died trying to release her family from the curse. Georgia had chopped a finger from her aunt's hand to carve that ring. And this witch might not accept it?

The elegant woman turned the ring back and forth in the candlelight. "*But it is well-crafted. And just for me, you say?*" She unfastened a long silver chain around her neck and slipped the ring onto it.

She gazed toward Georgia and Caleb. "*Very well. This game was growing tiresome, anyway. Every Christmas, I go down the mine and find bones but no ring. Disappointing.*" Dangling the bone ring from her necklace, she murmured, "*From now on the past shall remain in the past.*"

She picked up the Fromm's contract and placed a corner to the candle. As it went up in flames, there was a sharp pull in Georgia's gut and the room started to spin. Georgia reached for Caleb's hand.

They woke in the school's woodshop in the cool glow of the camp lantern. Tears pooled in Georgia's eyes.

Caleb shuffled closer and put his arms around her. They stayed like that, not moving, not speaking, for a long time. Finally, Georgia pulled away, just a little, and wiped her eyes. "Thank you, Caleb. I couldn't have done any of this without you."

"I am so sorry about your aunt, Georgia."

Georgia just nodded. Visions of her aunt's stiff body, the dank mine, and the witch's woodshop were etched in her mind. "It feels different this time, doesn't it? Returning, I mean? I can remember everything clearly. Too clearly."

"Me, too. I guess the spell really is broken." He helped her up and they stood at the lace-covered worktable, looking at the Fromms' three-tiered tower.

"What are you going to do with these now?" Caleb asked.

She flipped the propeller over and spun the tower in the right direction. "Well, I'm fixing the propeller so it can only go one direction, that's for damn sure." She laughed quietly, sadly. "But I feel like it's safe now. And mine somehow. Is it weird that I don't want to just smash it or set it on fire or something?"

Caleb shook his head. "It's always going to connect you to your aunt and your family's history. Just, you know, not in a literal, time-travelling way."

Georgia reached under the worktable for her simple A-frame whirligig. "Do you remember when we finished this thing, asking me if this was a present for someone?

Caleb nodded.

Georgia smiled. "I've decided it's for you."

I've always wanted one of those multi-tiered Christmas whirligigs. Writing is a way of conjuring something up, seeing it in your mind, owning it. In my story, the young heroine creates her own tower, a feat inspired by my creative, feminist daughters. Carving my own whirligig is probably beyond me, although I have watched every video I could find of them being made. God bless YouTube.

My research also turned up some fascinating history—the Christmas tower's origins in German mining towns and the tradition of creating one for a firstborn child. These facts spun my fiction in directions I hadn't predicted. Research and writing generate each other in amazing ways—almost like magic.

G. Clemans

DEATH NODE

BY JANINE A. SOUTHARD

Time travel is a well-worn path in literature. And for good reason—we delight in being transported to places forbidden to us by the laws of physics. In "Death Node," Janine A. Southard plays with the possibilities, creating a mysterious past from which multiple futures grow—futures that are, in fact, the protagonist's present. Theorist Christoph Bode calls these possibilities "future narratives," not because they all exist in the future, but because variable stories unfold from a single "node" in a nonlinear way. Southard's deliciously ominous "Death Node" spins time backward, forward, and upon itself, compelling us to think about alternate realities, fate, and the possibility—and impact—of free will.   -G. Clemans

Williamsburg, VA – 2525 – 09:57:33am

Detective Marie Postrel is going back in time today. She's studied her twenty-first century slang and grown her hair long. She's been briefed on the tech. She and her partner, Ryan Chu, have taken all the intertemporal trainings. She has memorized the dossier on Richard B. Miller, unresolved death victim and the First Senator's publicly mourned brother.

Her mission is to find out what really happened while keeping the timeline pure. There can be no paradoxes.

As her soon-to-be contemporaries might say: screw that.

With all the glories of time travel, they still haven't fixed the dystopian present, but maybe it won't stay dystopian for long. After ten years with the Williamsburg Protectorate Division, it's finally her turn to go back and right a wrong. Her turn to fix up society.

Even if that's not her official mission.

The captain calls the detectives into his office, voice cutting through the clatter of disgruntled informants and trilling communication chimes. "Postrel and Chu," he says, "We've got a *special treat* for you today." He says it like he knows just how much she's gonna hate it. "Now, word came down from the top that we had to send you back. You two aren't the best or the most senior, so I hope you're going because someone noticed you. You don't let politics stand in the way of your investigations, and that's something special down here."

Just *mentioning* politics is the closest they get to treason in Williamsburg. Everyone who works on the city's south side is a fanatical separatist, but you can't say that out loud. Just in case. So why is the captain bringing it up today?

Postrel can't ask, of course. "Yes, sir," she says instead.

She *does* try to be fair above all things. Without the rule of law, all would be lost. Humans live in society, thus they need a systematic way to make it better. A way to make more people happy and healthy.

A way like time travel, though it didn't seem like anyone had used it for such a purpose. Or maybe they had, and the unaltered timeline had something *worse* than the First Senator, overlord-extraordinaire for almost five hundred years. Damn, that'd be depressing.

Chu, for his part, just stares straight ahead. His body slumps with boredom, but his eyes betray his excitement about joining the ranks of TimeCrime-certified detectives. Chu hasn't shut up about joining the TimeCrime Bureau in Tampa since their second week of intertemporal training.

Like it's a pep talk, the captain says, "I know you're thinking about the way we lost the last pair of time-trained detectives from this division. They've left a hole and we'll all miss them, but we'll find out what happened to them soon. Don't worry about them. Just do your job. Sampson and

Rodriguez made a mistake somewhere is all. You two know what you're doing. You'll be fine."

If Sampson and Rodriguez stay missing much longer, they'll have to hold a funeral. It isn't fair to their families otherwise. Postrel hasn't seen any news about Sampson and Rodriguez—Men Missing in Time!—anywhere. What other time machine malfunctions hasn't she heard about?

The boss says, "Now for the honor. The First Senator himself is coming to give your final briefing before you go through."

"When, sir?" Maybe she can leave before he gets here.

He tips back in his chair. "Ten o'clock." Two minutes from now. "I expect you to be polite."

He means he expects her to refrain from killing the maniac. She's never been close to the First Senator, and she has plans for just how to cut him down in case it ever happens, like any good separatist would. And now it's happening, and there's nothing she can do. She's talented, probably deadly, but even she doesn't want to take on the First Senator with only her bare hands. No one knows how he's stayed alive so long; normal people die at sixty.

The First Senator, the only senator she's ever lived under, strides through the Protectorate Division's front doors. Framed by the boss's office window, he looks like a movie star with a tightly trimmed beard that can't hide his chin's pointiness. All his hair is halfway white. Thin lines drag from his deep brown eyes, and he wears the same flowing red silk outfit seen in every photo ever taken, like it's attached somehow.

Her own brown wool uniform is a lot more practical. Still, she's looking forward to the time machine changing up her clothes to match 21st century fashions. She could strangle him with a historically-accurate spaghetti-strap if he comes close enough...and if no one stops her.

Four newsmakers follow the First Senator. They take close ups of depression-enhancing blue walls that someone once thought would be soothing. They make rude faces when they wander too close to detectives who are questioning people who should've bathed days ago.

Postrel never makes faces.

Like a bloody scarlet phoenix, the First Senator is in the captain's office, and then it's just the three of them. Postrel and Chu and *him*. The captain was smart enough to get out of there. "It's an honor to meet you, Detectives," he says. His vowels are longer than hers, drawn out. Could it be old age is catching up to the cruel oppressor at last?

She replies, "You're too kind." There's a framed photo on the boss's desk. She could slam a corner into his eye socket, stir his brain a bit before Chu could stop her. If Chu would stop her. The First Senator is not innocent of any-thing...except of finding a jury and executioner able to stand against him.

The First Senator smirks like he knows her thoughts. Maybe he does. "Thank you for your willingness to risk the technology and discover what exactly happened the night of my brother's murder. Richard was very important to me."

So important that he's sending somewhat expendable detectives to find out. Postrel understands why he wouldn't send more lauded ones: the technology is still shaky and no future-based technicians have come back to help out. How messed up does your present have to be for potential future friends to decide not to render assistance?

Chu leans in like a mischievous child hoping to learn a secret. "Can you tell us anything that might be missing from the files?" He even winks.

Chu is such a fool. Even if the files are sparse after an unfortunate data purge three hundred years back, the First Senator clearly has a vested interest in this case. He's gone so far as to see them off. He's not going to have left anything out of a file he probably wrote himself. At the very least, the First Senator personally approved all the information they have.

The First Senator leans in to match Chu's confidential posture. They're a study of opposites: whitening hair to black, red silk to functional brown drab, ageless elegance to energetic use. "You'll be at a party," he says. "There'll be plenty of suspects. I wasn't there, so I don't know much about it. You've got photos of the family house where Richard lived at the time and where the party went down."

He lowers his voice, and Chu practically tips into him with his eagerness to attach an ear to the First Senator's mouth. Chu may not be trustworthy. "Remember that you can't change anything. I miss my brother, but I would never have become First Senator if he'd lived. It would destabilize our great society."

Postrel stares into those deep dark eyes that have no fear of the abyss. "I'll do my best." If saving the brother means an end to tyranny, then all hail the bloodless revolution.

The First Senator clasps their shoulders, and her insides shrivel. She stays utterly still and resolves to wash that arm twenty times after he's gone. "Let's go meet your team."

He pushes her ahead of him, and the detectives meet one last science consultant at the time machine's plastic doorframe. It'll glow green, and they'll walk through. Then, instead of being next to the senior vice cop's desk, they'll be in the 21st century. Whenever she uses her recall button, they can return through whichever doorway they walk out of in the past.

Chu is all smiles, and he bounces like a puppy. "I'm so excited to be on this case, and I *love* your beard, sir," he gushes at the First Senator. Chu's own mustache looks like uneven dirt smudges on his upper lip.

The First Senator gives them both a benevolent nod, somewhat marred by his never-ending smirking. "Good luck, Detectives," he says, "and don't forget what I said in the office."

"I'll interrogate the suspects, sir." Postrel can't say more than that.

She can't say: *I'll try to save your brother, sir. I'll remember all my duties, sir. I'll do my best to erase your existence, sir.*

The time machine trills its readiness, and she steps through the doorway. The station is gone. The crowded space and blue walls transform into a narrow hallway with red and gold carpets, wallpaper with diddly little flowers, and a ridiculous amount of real wood for baseboards and wainscoting. It smells like floral perfume.

Chu stumbles behind her. "Whoa," he says. He's been practicing his local slang too.

She smooths her hands over her skirt. Her palms skid out to the sides, and the skirt's hem twitches in a circle inches away from her ankles. That doesn't seem right for ladies' 21st century American fashion. It should be more streamlined, and probably slinkier, for party attire.

There's a mirror above a pointlessly tiny table only a few feet down the hall, and she swishes forward on the plush rug. Her hair is arrayed in a circular poof, like a caramel-colored halo with ringlets dripping down. A cobalt silk corset confines her ribs. Postrel turns, and yes, it laces downward in the back over a puffy skirt in the same color. "What on earth?"

Either the machine's clothing camouflage function is broken, or this isn't the 21st century.

The Past

Marie checked out the portal through which they'd come. What had once been the year 2525 was now a closet bunched full of black wool pea coats with the odd regimental cape poking out on a hanger.

It smelled of wet sheep.

Chu, for his part, was decked out in a black and white suit complete with white bowtie. The garments forced his posture straight. In the time period they'd intended to reach, his outfit would have been overwhelmingly formal.

He giggled and pointed a shiny-shod foot out to the side. "Check out these *shoes!*"

Clearly, her partner was a complete moron.

Her chest throbbed against the bones in her corset and the blood had nowhere to go but up, flushing her skin. What color had the lights around the time machine archway been when she'd come through? She couldn't remember. Had she even checked? She'd heard the trill and just *assumed...*

"This can*not* be the twenty-first century," declared Postrel. This wasn't what she'd studied for the trip. "This is all wrong. When are we?"

God, they could be anywhere and anywhen!

They'd been blown off course, and now they ought to go home before they couldn't anymore. Before they were forever lost like Sampson and Rodriguez.

Postrel reached into her pocket for the return device, only to find that her giant dress had no pockets. A frustrated hum built in her throat, and she pushed at her skirt with gloved hands, only succeeding in moving the hoop from side to side like a ringing bell. Sweat drops rolled from her hairline and into her eyebrows. What was the point of this huge amount of fabric if you couldn't hide things in it?

Chu had a completely inappropriate grin on his mustachioed face. "You all right there, Postrel?"

Did she *look* all right? She raised an arm to reach out and slap the idiot's shoulder, which was when she noticed the emerald green velvet sack attached to her wrist. Postrel tore into the cords that held the bag closed. Who cared about Chu? She'd found a pocket!

"Marie?"

She held the recall device aloft and beamed at him. The exertion brought a heated glow to her exposed shoulders.

Chu slumped as far as he could in his restrictive get-up. "Do we have to go just yet?"

He sounded like a whiny child, but...they *should* confirm that they hadn't gotten to Richard B. Miller's death scene. Besides, wherever this was, it had to be better than home.

Postrel returned the device to her wrist-bag. "Let's go see where we are," she said. Picking a direction, she led him down the hallway. The walls bore portraits of Caucasian men in various uniforms, all painted against backgrounds that said nothing about when or where they might be. Dim uplights in crackled glass sconces kept the art viewable.

Ahead on the left a door opened, flooding the hall with soft light. Carolers harmonized "Deck the Halls" in five parts, but they were barely louder than the crashing whispers of competing conversations.

The man who stepped into Postrel's way squinted at her through wire-framed glasses. Nose to throat, he was taller and darker than she, balding on top from advancing age, and wearing a crisp, slate-blue uniform with a pistol on each hip. "Who are you?" His breath smelled of cinnamon bread and liquor.

Without context, anything she said could be the clue that got her discovered. Or thrown out of the house and her only way home. "Who are *you*?" she challenged.

Behind her, Chu gasped, probably in admiration of her clever avoidance tactic.

The man puffed his chest out, the better to show off the shiny bobs on his chest. "I am Lieutenant Pankaj Goswami. I was at Gettysburg this morning and plan to practice at Appomattox next weekend. I've been a member of this society for longer than you've been alive, young lady."

If this were an army man, and he spoke of Gettysburg and Appomattox, then she had to have landed in the American Civil War. She and Chu had traveled to the 1860s. That was a bit before their intended target but close enough that she understood the language at least.

Postrel dared to bend her knees in an awkward curtsy, pleased her hoop skirt stayed relatively in place. "It's a pleasure to meet you, Lieutenant." She hadn't known men of his age could still be part of the active military forces during this time, but at least she could now put together some names and dates.

Lieutenant Goswami ran contemptuous eyes over Chu's costume and sniffed. "Is that a *zipper*?" He sounded utterly offended.

Postrel's eyes widened, but Goswami wasn't looking at her. She could only make excuses. "My companion and I are newly arrived to, ah, this society." Though she was unsure why zippers should be so awful, ignorance of local customs should serve as explanation enough for this misstep on the time machine's behalf. Perhaps the zipper company was owned by someone on the other side of the war, or they'd stumbled across Civil War reenactors, or the lieutenant was just severely old-fashioned. He was quite old, after all.

"Yes, well." Goswami passed her and paused in front of Chu, looking down into her partner's eyes in a manner she often used on young suspects. They found it impossible to look away and tended to internalize everything she said. "Next time leave the Yankee contraptions at home."

Ah, so the problem was the industrialized North. All right. This was a Southern party. She could handle that.

"Yes, sir," squeaked Chu.

"Now if you'll excuse me, dear lady"—he made a brief bow in Postrel's direction—"I left my phone in the coat room."

Postrel let him go and sailed through the door Lt. Goswami had come through. She had no goal, no mission, no need to sully her hands with the First Senator's brother's innocent blood. Because there was no brother. No murder. It was far too early for all that. Her lips stretched; she was free.

The room smelled of pine, nearly overwhelming the floral perfume and the eggnog in a punch bowl. A once-living evergreen tree dominated the room. Its emerald pins stood at attention, though a few had dripped to the silk skirt at its base. The tree was decked out in sparkling silver and light.

Chu abandoned her and rushed to the tree's stand to circle around it. "Look!" His whisper sounded loud in her ears, much louder than the caroling choir performing "Joy to the World." He'd activated his earworm transmitter, then. "They look like little candles, but they're actually electric. How clever!"

"I'm sure only the wealthy have them at this point in time." She may have been free of the First Senator's mission, but she was still duty-bound to help Ryan Chu with whatever he wanted to further his application to TimeCrime. And then she could send him back all on his own and stay here. The 19th century was just civilized enough for her taste. "Would a local person be so excited about the lights? At a historical scene, we can learn only so much from object observation. We don't have enough context for this. So we go with what we *do* know. People."

Taking her own advice, she looked over the room. Beside her—at a food table laden with breads, wrapped sweets, and baby carrots with hummus dip—a gorgeous woman whose black hair fell in loose layers to her scapulae was adding a full bottle of brandy to the punch. As soon as she finished, three men flocked to the sideboard with mugs at the ready.

In the far corner, a man in regimental gray posed next to a globe. He was handsome at first glance, with wide shoulders and suntanned skin that set off his uniform, complete with a sword at his side. A thicket of dark locks grew shorter, neater from his crown until they clipped at his ears. His eyeglasses' thick black frames didn't even try to hide their presence. Postrel might have classed them as *hipster* if she'd successfully traveled to a later date, but she knew the term too modern for this party.

What set the man apart, however, was not his solitary posture. Not the way everyone side-eyed him as if debating the approach. No, it was his uncanny resemblance to the First Senator.

Oh, they didn't look exactly alike. The First Senator had more lines on his face, different glasses, and a penchant for red silk. The First Senator had more than a little white in his hair and pale on his cheeks. But the both of them had broad shoulders, aging movie-star looks, and the same pointed chin. The same piercing eyes. The same height. The same build, the same posture, the same noncommittal smile that inspired both confidence and fear.

Her ears roared with blood and shock and a Turkish-inspired version of "Drummer Boy." The time machine had sent her to one of the First Senator's kin, even if she was too far in the past for her original mission. Even if her *intended* mark had never worn glasses.

She could find the vile overlord's ancestors, killing him before he rose to power, before he was ever born. It was so obvious that it had to have been tried, but somehow it hadn't yet.

All sorts of temporal ethics said she shouldn't, but every separatist ever born would say that she should.

Postrel's hands trembled, and she contemplated a cup of the spiked punch to steady them. She'd never killed an innocent person. She'd come back expecting to *save* a life. What kind of protector would she be if she went around destroying everyone she didn't like?

A corrupt one, that's what kind.

Her heart fluttered under her corset, but she set her shoulders. She was going to do this. She could find out if this were one of the First Senator's progenitors or simply an unfortunate uncle. All she had to do was ask. In this time, no one would find her questioning too terribly odd. Seditious. And she was going to do it now. Before she lost her nerve.

She got two steps away from the tree before another party guest cornered her quarry. She'd missed her first chance to get him. But she had all the time in the world.

"Postrel?" Chu's plaintive voice edged out the nerves and the blood and the carols. "I'm going to explore the house. You good here on your own?"

She inhaled so deeply that her nose made sniffling noises. Cinnamon, brandy, pine, apple, amber. "Keep me apprised," she said.

"Yay!" The tree shivered with his excitement. He cleared his throat and lowered his pitch. "I mean, see you around, Marie."

During the course of this short conversation, the First Senator's kinsman had changed partners twice more. That was...an unlikely amount of activity. Something about this man made him different from the other party guests. And Postrel knew just how to find out what.

People were always the most talkative when eating and drinking.

Though it put her on the opposite end of the room from her quarry, Postrel joined the black-haired brandy-spiker who had yet to abandon the food table. "Hello," Postrel said as she pretended to evaluate the offerings.

The woman's wide lips parted in a smile so enthusiastic it wouldn't have been out of place on Chu. "Let me get you a drink!" Her mascara-clumped eyelashes fluttered, and her golden ear hoops swayed. "What's your poison?"

"Anything is fine," said Postrel, somewhat wrong-footed by this show of zeal. Flattery was the easy way to recover from that. "I like your dress."

The woman turned in a circle, showing off her tall, slender figure. She belonged in a health food advertisement, maybe for yogurt. "And no zippers. I know the drill." She reached under the table and sloshed something brown into a punch cup that she shoved into Postrel's waiting hand. "Here."

The fumes rising off the liquid would intoxicate anyone. "A friend of mine got in trouble over zippers earlier."

"Hah! I learned my lesson ages ago." Her shoulders hunched. "I used to come to these parties by choice, you know, but now...Well, *he's* not getting out easy. We're going to stay and party all night. Drink up!"

Postrel sipped the tongue-cauterizing mystery and coughed. "Can you tell me about the man over there?" She gestured with the cup, "accidentally" splashing liquid onto the golden rug. "He seems very popular."

The woman snorted. "Bear? I can tell you more than you'll ever want to know. I used to be married to him."

Postrel's facial muscles went slack and her eyes went so dry that she knew they'd widened to an alarming height. *This* was possibly the First Senator's foremother? She knew the family tree: Richard and First Senator Joshua, sons of Andrew son of Bear son of Joshua son of Bear.

"Yep," the woman confirmed the unspoken question. "That was me. Shanna Young Miller. Now just Shanna Young. Bear's hosting this party tonight, which is why everyone wants to talk to him. Talk *at* him really. He hates these parties."

"And you hate him?" It was a likely conclusion.

Shanna Young poured herself a glass of punch and slammed it back. Her voice came out in a hiss that was half emotion and half alcohol scratchings. "Hells yes I hate him. He's a cheating dickwad. And a cheapskate besides. I bet he's going to stiff the carolers." She looked up and to the side as if thinking deeply, no longer mired in her anger. "I heard the lead caroler at a fair last weekend, saw her sword dancing too. That woman is wasting her talent on parties like this."

The First Senator's ancient kinsman sounded lovely. Given what Postrel had learned, this Bear had to be the First Senator's direct ancestor. She just had to make sure the next ancestor in line, an Andrew or a Joshua, hadn't been born yet.

But how could she ask without stepping on local notions of propriety? While she figured that out, she had to keep the conversation going. "Why does Bear host if he doesn't enjoy these events?" Postrel nudged her still-full cup behind the baby carrots where no one would find it.

Over Postrel's earworm, Chu raved, "A power outlet with two holes! I've heard about these. I'm going to follow it."

"He has to host these parties to keep the house. It's in his parents' will." Shanna shrugged, jiggling her décolletage. The action summoned two men with empty cups that she happily filled with her spiked punch. "You boys having fun?"

They answered in the affirmative.

Postrel injected a gossipy incredulity into her voice, "And will his kids have to do the same?"

Shanna growled low, her face still bearing a smile for the men accepting their doctored drinks. "Oh, he doesn't have kids. Prophylactics are the only thing that man is faithful to."

If Shanna Young had no children with him, his death would end the line. And the ex-wife wouldn't be upset if Postrel truncated the Miller family. This time period would be better off, and the future would be different. Children would grow up free from fear and with all their parents and grandparents alive and well. No one would lie or cheat or steal or kill because everyone would have everything they needed. Trees would grow in parks on every corner. Medical researchers would devote time to curing every disease that plagued humanity and its friends.

In a world with no First Senator...

Shanna told her captive drinkers, "I'll be hosting some games later when everyone is drunk enough to appreciate them." The men snorted more than laughed, and she followed up with: "So tell all your friends."

They saluted and returned to their previous station next to the fireplace, dismissed.

Postrel tilted her head until ringlets brushed her right shoulder. "Games?"

Teeth bared, Shanna declared, "This party is going to last as long as I can possibly make it."

Another Williamsburg (Williamsburg Prime) – 2525 – 09:57:33am

Chief Detective Marie Postrel's cell leader has wiggled onto the TimeCrime Oversight and Assignments Board (TCOAB). Madam Casswerla has made sure to get Postrel this particular assignment, but she couldn't stop them from thrusting a trainee upon her. Ryan Chu: young, enthusiastic, an albatross.

Still, she's going back. After twenty years with the Williamsburg Protectorate Division, it's finally her turn to right a historical wrong. Her turn to fix society. *With all the glories of time travel, we still live in the dystopian future.* But that won't be true for long.

Postrel's only worry is whatever happened during Sampson and Rodriguez's disastrous trip to the past. There hadn't been much to research. The detectives had been there one moment and not there the next. They're permanently on the missing lists. There's nothing conclusive in their notes from before the trip or from the scientists' diagnostic tests afterward.

Every time the time machine whines, the whole division stops to stare at it. Everyone holds a breath, waiting, hoping, not quite believing that *this time* the missing men will step through.

Postrel wants to believe they chose to stay in a simpler time, a happier one. Sampson and Rodriguez come from a district even more disaffected than her own.

She wonders what *exactly* kept them from returning.

. The boss calls her into his office, voice cutting through the never-ending click-clack of personnel writing up citizens for infractions. Real or imaginary. Postrel doesn't work that kind of sniveling beat anymore. "Chief Detective," he says, "Remember that you're being sent because you're the best. You don't let politics stand in the way of your investigations, and that's something special down here."

Just mentioning politics is the closest they get to treason on the south side. Sure, the locals are all fanatical separatists, but you can't say that out loud.

The boss says, "It's an honor, Postrel. The First Senator himself is coming to give you your final briefing before you go through."

"When, sir?" Maybe she can leave before he gets here.

He tips back in his chair, "Ten o'clock." In two minutes. "I expect you to be polite."

That gives her no time to sneak out before the First Senator—Joshua Miller, son of Andrew son of Bear son of Joshua son of Bear—strides through the front doors. Framed by the boss's office window, he looks like a movie star wearing flowing blue silk like angry water.

His attendant newsmakers take close ups of the historical brick walls—the original building materials, though mightily shored up. They make rude faces when they wander into the scent cloud of people who should've bathed days ago. Postrel never makes faces.

Like a vicious ocean wave, the First Senator is in the boss's office, and then it's just the two of them: Postrel and the First Senator. "It's an honor to meet you, Chief Detective," he says. "I've been following your career since your first major case. I take a personal interest in the detectives working my capital city."

Postrel is pretty sure that's creepy. "You're too kind."

He nods like she's accepted a great honor, then leans closer to tell her a secret. "I have a special request," he says. "I want you to save my brother if you can. Even if it means changing the course of history."

Postrel stares into those deep dark eyes that have no need to fear the abyss. "I'll do my best." If saving the brother means an end to tyranny, then all hail the bloodless revolution. "The reports mention a woman crouching over the body with a blade," she says, taking advantage of the First Senator's insider knowledge. "No one at the party recognized her. I know it's been a long time, but do you know who she might be?"

He shakes his head, and his movie-star hair moves like a helmet. "Her DNA couldn't be conclusively matched." The First Senator clasps her shoulder, and her insides shrivel. "Let's go meet your team."

He pushes her ahead of him, and they meet Ryan Chu, her trainee, as well as Senior Vice Detective Casswerla at the time machine's doorframe. It's next to Casswerla's desk, and he's been complaining about its intermittent whining all week. That hasn't stopped him from looking up whenever it happens, searching for Sampson and Rodriguez with everybody else.

Casswerla bows deeply before the First Senator like the toadying lapdog he is. He's never met the First Senator before either, as far as Postrel knows. "All my loyalty," he says without even a hint of sarcasm.

Chu's mouth is a gaping grin, and he bounces like a puppy. "I'm so excited to be working with you, Chief Detective Postrel," he gushes. He's not intimidated by the First Senator at her side, but that may be because he hasn't yet recognized the man.

The First Senator gives us both a benevolent nod, somewhat marred by his never-ending smirk. "Good luck, Detectives," he says, "and don't forget what I said in the office."

The Past

Postrel strained to hear Bear's voice from across the room. "Oh my god!" His cry rose above the general melee. "I don't owe you money. I'm just borrowing these clothes from the guy who does."

His companion replied, "They fit you very well for being someone else's."

Bear growled. "Which is why I borrowed them. Excuse me." And Bear stalked out of the room through a doorway to his right.

Postrel didn't want to lose him. "I'll be sure to send other guests your way," she assured Shanna Young, Minister of Booze and Games.

Postrel's shoes clunked over the hardwood boards in the middle of the floor, then clicked onto thin laminate when she entered the next room. Thankfully, Bear hadn't gotten any further ahead than that.

She'd followed him into the house's kitchen. A large refrigerator-freezer combination presided from a corner. There were two islands with marble tops and one long bar where gingersnap cookies sat half-wrapped in plastic bags labeled "Food Lion."

Comparatively, it was much quieter. This room was less densely packed with only a few wine drinkers snacking on the gingersnaps. Why, Postrel could barely hear the carolers' rendition of "O Come, All Ye Faithful."

Still, Bear had been waylaid. Postrel plucked a ginger-snap from its container to look like she belonged, and then stared unabashedly at Lieutenant Goswami as he tried to browbeat Bear into lending him a cannon.

Bear shook his head so hard that his hipster glasses rattled. "I don't *have* a cannon!" Bear's voice rose into ever-louder shrieks, and the wine-drinkers in the kitchen focused on the arguing pair. Good. That meant Postrel's interest wouldn't be unseemly.

The lieutenant's own spectacles stayed firmly in place when he echoed the maneuver. "I can see it through this very window." He laid hands on Bear's shoulders and forcibly turned the host to face the outside where the dark and a blanket of snow conspired to make everything invisible. "You've already said you'll do this for the community."

"I can't have said that! I don't even have a cannon! What are you looking at?"

Here was Postrel's chance to earn her quarry's trust. She sashayed forward in a waft of cinnamon scent. "Darling," she crowed as she reached out for Bear, "I've found you." She insinuated herself into his arms and he let her, utterly without reservation. Good, now she only had to get him alone. "Oh!" she pretended to notice Lieutenant Goswami for the first time since joining their conversation. "Hello again."

He grunted.

"You remember," said Postrel, all sweet innocence, "we met in the hallway?" She didn't give him time to respond. "Well, I need some time with my darling man here. Would you mind giving us a moment?" When the lieutenant made no move to leave, she suggested, "I hear there will be games in the other room soon."

In her ear, Chu gushed, "Ooooh! Games!" He clicked the speaker off and on again with his tongue. "But I've found a bunch of doodles in the study. All this white-and-blue lined paper is just too cute!"

Lieutenant Goswami did not take her proposal nearly as well. He stomped to the kitchen door and turned back dramatically when he came to it. "I'll see you with pistols at dawn, sir. And the winner will keep the cannon."

Bear slumped against an island. "Sheesh."

And there was another person who'd be happy to see the First Senator's ancestor dead. Now Postrel only had to get him alone to make it so. First, she needed to establish a deeper rapport. As she'd done earlier with Shanna, she began by complimenting his outfit. "Wow. Is that a real sword?"

In the background, the carolers came to an abrupt halt in the middle of "The Holly and the Ivy."

"Why, yes. It came with the house." Bear straightened and tugged his uniform belt until he could pose heroically.

"Do you have any others?"

He favored her with a lopsided grin and leaned down until their faces were close enough for kissing. His liquored breath tingled in her nose, and Postrel let herself sway into him. "Lots. How about I show you?" Let him think she could be conned into going somewhere more private. Let it be his idea. "We could take a private tour."

A wine drinker in the kitchen scoffed and followed the lieutenant back into the main room, and Postrel kept a firm grip on Bear's intentions. She angled her head to show off her vulnerable neck, the only part of her that was naked in this ridiculously old-fashioned outfit. Removing her gloves and laying them on a countertop added a bit more seductive skin.

He stroked her nape. The warmth from his fingers seared her.

In Postrel's ear, Ryan Chu asked, "Do you know whose house this is exactly? Because I'm looking over a bunch of letters in a glass topped cabinet, and everyone in the family has the same names. Like, those portraits on the wall were of three Joshuas, two Annabelles, and four Bears. Bear! What kind of name is that?"

But of course Postrel was in no situation to reply, not that it would have helped Chu. Her current companion was in the most statistically large subgroup he'd mentioned.

Bear leaned in to bring their noses almost flush, and Postrel reached one hand up to hold his face close. If she brought up the other, she ought to be able to snap his neck... though the angle had gotten a bit awkward now that he'd pressed their bodies together so strongly that her hoop skirt flipped back to push against the counter.

Williamsburg C – 2525 – 09:57:33am

Marie Postrel is underground—literally and figuratively. The uncovered lights stab her eyes with yellow white whenever she messes up and looks at them. Everything smells like mold, even her hair. She got in the previous night, and the rest of the team trickled in slowly.

Postrel's cell leader has organized the place for super quick set up and tear down. She and Chu will suit up, go back, and stay in the past while the rest of their group get the hell out of here.

The time machine is in a shadowy corner. Postrel doesn't know how her cell leader managed to steal it and relocate it. Its plastic arch seems out of place between the dirt floor and damp stone walls.

"Don't fuck this up," Cell Leader Casswerla says. "We won't get a second chance at this."

Chu and Postrel have been chosen for this mission because they're replaceable. The technology is dicey, and the cell leader's son has told them terrible tales of lost detectives. *Trained* detectives who went through and went missing.

Someone mumbles, "Good luck."

They'll need it. Postrel and Chu haven't been trained. They're not detectives either. All they know is they're going back to the day the Over-President's brother died in some horrible accident. With all the glories of time travel, someone should have done this before. Then no one would have to live in someone else's dystopian future.

Tromping boots echo in the stone stairwell. They sound like a herd of stupid kids, but no street kid would be stupid enough to come down here. Not when Madam Casswerla has posted guards and laid rumors on the street.

"Fuck," Chu breathes into the heavy, mold-spore-laden air.

Everyone scrambles. The time machine plastic hums and lights up a glowing green. Casswerla and the others form a barrier three people deep. Their shoes scuff on cobbles and concrete. There's a moment of silence—all breathing stopped, all rustling paused.

Then the cellar door splinters under an axe.

Protectorate officers stream through the new gap. Their faces are covered so no one can see their eyes or features. They swipe with clubs, and light up the dark corners with laser-red gun sights.

Grunting bodies already litter the ground.

"Nobody move!" the protectorate leader yells. Postrel recognizes the voice of Leader Casswerla's son.

Postrel and Chu leap through the doorway. They can stop this before it begins.

The Past

Postrel adjusted her grip on Bear's jaw. There. One hand on his chin, disguised as scratching his evening scruff. The other hand above his nape. A shriek startled her, just as his lips met hers. She opened her mouth wider to keep from biting off his loathsome tongue. That would get messy.

Bear pulled back. "What was that?"

Postrel had lost her chance.

With an apologetic wince, the First Senator's ancestor flung himself back into the party. Postrel followed.

The main room looked much as she'd left it. The pine tree stood tall and besparkled. The sideboard had more crumbs than before, and the carrots lent a splash of orange to the otherwise dark tones. The punch bowl had been refilled with something less creamy than eggnog. Possibly straight up whiskey if Postrel had been reading Shanna correctly.

The carolers were hooting and trilling, not singing, in breathless excitement. Because right next to the tree, the lead caroler was demonstrating her sword dancing skills. She twirled and swished under Shanna's watchful eye, surrounded by drunkards. Lieutenant Goswami's mouth was open wide enough to fit an ornamental bulb.

The sword glinted in the dim, ancient lights, and Postrel's lungs squeezed in on her heart. *Swords.* Swords were blades, and women with blades were dangerous in this house.

Shanna was laughing, perfect red lips stretched in hypnotic contortions. And Bear was looking straight at his ex-wife like he was going to start a fight. Maybe because he hadn't paid for this or because it was keeping his guests engaged and excited longer, who knew?

But the lead caroler's eyes were closed as she concentrated on the feel of the sword that now balanced on the crown of her head. The dancer spun in circles, faster and faster. The sword wobbled.

Postrel sidled over to a caroler who still clutched a song book. "Shouldn't she have her eyes open?" Someone needed to clear an area before the partiers got hurt. Clear the area of everyone but Bear, that was. A simple slip and the lead caroler would do Postrel's work for her. Free of guilt.

"Kay Amber is so amazing," gushed the caroler. "On top of leading our group, she has ten years' experience with belly dancing. She knows what she's doing."

The rest of the troupe made general noises of agreement. Postrel wasn't so sure. That blade looked awfully light at the speeds it was spinning. Why, it could fly off at any moment.

Williamsburg 4 – 2525 – 09:57:33am

Marie vibrates with excitement. After six weeks of intense work, she gets to see the past. Ryan, her favorite study buddy, grips her hand beneath their shared desk. He's got tremors too. She hopes they get to go together.

"For your final project," says the training leader, "we'll be sending you on a short jaunt into the past. You're going to go in pairs. First up, Sampson and Rodriguez!"

The student pair approaches the machine's arch. Rodriguez is doing that stretch-and-dance thing like a professional athlete. Sampson cracks his neck.

Almost too quiet to be heard by the rest of the students, the training leader gives out final reminders. "You can only go to a place we know you've been, otherwise you cease to be. There can be no paradoxes, so if you're somewhere unknown, get out immediately. Be sure to check in or leave some evidence while you're there so that we know to send you now."

Sampson nods, but it could be just another neck crack.

And then the pair is gone. Straight through the green glow.

The training leader calls up three more pairs before getting to, "Chu and Postrel!"

Suddenly aware they've been *holding hands* all this time, the pair detach from one another and head to the front of the classroom. They can't help the grins on their faces, the fast beating in their chests.

Their trainer reassures them, "Marie, Ryan, we know you go to this party. We've known it ever since your DNA first entered the citizen tracking system. You have nothing to worry about. Just leave some evidence, okay?"

They nod and go through.

The Past

Postrel's vision went completely dark. She couldn't see the tree wrapped in fairy lights, nor Kay Amber's sword dancing. Could remember only where she'd left Bear.

Ladies' gasps and men's cursing filled the blackness.

Bear muttered, "I know we have candles somewhere."

In Postrel's earworm, Chu swore. "Ack! Sorry, Marie. I flipped a switch, and the lights went off. Just give me a second, and I'll fix it."

This would be the perfect moment to have Kay run Bear through, or to take the sword and do it herself, if only she'd prepared for it! Bear Miller's death would be the First Senator's and, with him, his entire oppressive regime. Future generations could not countenance his continued existence.

Ryan Chu's voice came back in, muted in her skull. "There's this beeping noise in here, lemme find it. Oh, hey. This cord's attached to a box about knee height. It's got flashing blue lights on the front and says, ah, HP on it. Do you think that stands for *Harry Potter*?"

A flashing box with HP on it? Hewlett-Packard. A computer! This wasn't the Civil War.

Postrel understood, then. They'd arrived as they were supposed to, but during a living history party. All of the little anachronisms that *could* have been in period but were more popular in later years—electricity for the rich, stainless steel refrigerators, Richard's middle initial, even the language that she'd been able to understand all too well—they all tumbled through her with a kind of clarity.

The lights came back on with a hum that she hadn't noticed before. The refrigerator kicked back in. And the sword's tip was sliding from Kay Amber's head to angle down straight toward where Bear—the First Senator's dear brother whom she'd determined to protect!—stood in an angry loom over his ex-wife.

Postrel swept forward into the dancer's space. Kay Amber's eyes were miraculously still shut, too caught up in concentration to notice the things around her. Postrel couldn't stop the blade's uncontrolled descent, but she could displace it.

She knocked into the caroler's shoulder just as the sword's hilt descended from her head and brushed against fingers. They were off course, just slightly. Just enough.

Kay Amber fumbled the grip. "What are you doing?" she cried. "Everyone look out!"

And the sword rammed through the air with all the centrifugal force she'd built up.

Straight into Bear's stomach.

He toppled, and Postrel dropped to her knees on the wood floor beside his convulsing body. Her ears buzzed. No, no, no. She had to save him. This was the First Senator's brother. *This* was the moment that had created her hellish childhood. Postrel put pressure on the wound, just as she'd practiced for years.

The sword's hilt stuck straight up toward the ceiling, point thrust into his gut with her own hand leaking sweaty DNA all over the murder weapon. The wound seeped with septic stink. Bear's blood crusted inside Postrel's palm lines. His last gasps ghosted alcohol fumes across her face.

Chu, recently arrived, joined her on the floor. She couldn't make out any words he was saying over the rushing blood tide in her ears and over her hands.

As if through layers of fabric, she made out Shanna's screams. "Oh my god. Bear? Bear!"

Bear wasn't in any shape to answer.

Chu shook her, ruining her seal on the streaming wound. Her focus leapt from his mouth to his shoulders to the wall and back to the body under her touch. She'd just been kissing Bear in the kitchen. "The police are on their way."

Postrel and Chu had to get out of there. The moment someone asked for their papers or took their fingerprints, she'd be discovered. She didn't want to spend her life in a primitive jail or let these people know about time travel. Did nonentities get sent to torture prisons or medical labs at this point in time?

There was no other choice. She couldn't stay now. Postrel tossed her wrist bag to Chu.

It flew through the air and cut the emotional barrier that had been holding the guests outside her circle of utter failure.

"You killed him," Shanna screamed. She lunged, whether for Postrel or for the body, and Postrel leapt to her feet, skirt clutched in her hands.

Postrel dashed into the hallway, palms sticky and calling to Chu with what little breath she had. "Go, go, go!"

Williamsburg Blue – 2525 – 10:10:00am

They dash through the coat closet's doorframe and back into the twenty-sixth century. Postrel's dress disappears, and she stumbles on the lack of hoop skirt. Sweat blurs her eyes, and an ocean hammers her ears.

She brushes her eyes with the backs of her wrists, keeping the blood from spreading too far. The Williamsburg Protectorate Division is not like they left it. The walls are all made of windows that look over a moat. Why on earth would they have a *moat*? And how did they get it put in so quickly? The time machine technician said they'd only be gone for ten minutes.

Some things are the same though. There is a news crew in sensible brown wool milling around the goldenrod-silk clad First Senator. Wasn't he wearing red when they left? He always wears red.

He does, however, wear the same movie-star beard, the same I-know-everything-peon smirk. Her knees lock and her molars clench. He may still exist, but he will not see her crumble.

Chu shrieks and runs past her to a person in the crowd. She squints to see where he's gone. Is that—

"Rodriguez!" Chu leaps the final few feet and wraps the bewildered detective up in a hug. "They got you back! You're alive!" He doesn't ask where Sampson is.

"Uh, yeah?" says Rodriguez, obviously unsure why he's getting such a welcome.

Even in the face of the fucking First Senator's continued existence, even against the blood drying under her fingernails, Postrel grins. Rodriguez is back! Something has gone right.

Stabbing needles pierce her brain, but she stays upright. The training advisors had warned them about the reentry period, and no migraine is getting the better of Detective Marie Postrel. No, of Investigator Marie Postrel. Right, Investigator.

"Welcome back, Investigators," says the First Senator. Every syllable is a shrieking knife made of frozen sewage. It accuses, it taunts, it torments. It stinks.

Her boss edges in before either investigator can say a word. "It's a *special honor* that the senator stayed with us until your return." He means that they shouldn't mess this up and say something impolitic.

Postrel doesn't have to worry about that anymore, though. What does she care if unwise words send her to prison? She's guilty, guilty, guilty. The rusty cakes under her nails prove it. She killed an innocent man, one whom she'd wanted to save. Her brain beats against her skull, and it's all she can do to keep upright. To get through this last debriefing with her enemy before she can go home and sleep. Maybe forever.

Chu rushes forward as though he's going to pump the boss's hands. "Postrel was *amazing*, sir. She almost saved that man's life. When can we go back?"

Chu is a total moron for calling attention to himself like this in front of the First Senator. And for spilling her secrets. Wasn't she supposed to let the brother die in order to preserve the timeline? Or was she supposed to save him in order to make the First Senator's life a happier one?

The First Senator nods so deeply his facial hair scrapes his silk shirt. It doesn't make any permanent dents. "I know exactly what she did," he tells Chu, but he looks directly at Postrel while he talks. His voice and stance give no clues to his meaning. "Ever since I learned about time travel, I've matched every newborn's DNA to the mystery sample found at my brother's death scene."

Of course he has. He knew before he sent them that Postrel would be his brother's demise. Except.... "It was the caroler, sir. I think."

He laughs and it shimmies the silk he wears. The fabric dances and dances and dances until he tires. "I knew you were clever enough to figure it out, Investigator Postrel." He is mocking her. She has to let him.

If only they hadn't been at a living history party! She should have known sooner, would have saved her world. She'd been so sure. But while she knows plenty about the 21st century, she's less an expert on earlier periods in comparison.

The First Senator dangles his hand for her to shake, and their skin connects through a coating of his brother's dried life-blood. "You are a true hero of our nation," he says. "Through ensuring my brother's demise, you have maintained our timeline. Because of you, our way of life has been preserved."

He smiles into the distance, and...no. Just no. His newsmakers are *filming* this. He's guaranteeing that no separatist will ever trust her again. And he's making sure everyone understands.

"Investigator Marie Postrel of the Williamsburg Protectorate Division," he enunciates her name precisely and slowly, "I would trust you with my life. Thanks to you, our society will continue."

Postrel will be remembered as the most devoted Loyalist. As the dog who cemented the First Senator's rule.

He raises their clasped hands in a victory pose. "Citizens! We must hold a festival in Investigator Postrel's honor so that everyone will know of her deeds."

People are clapping, but it's pure politeness. Vice Investigator Casswerla is the only one smiling. The rest glare at Postrel like she's destroyed them.

With all the glories of time travel, she still lives in the dystopian future. And now she is all alone. Only her enemies will act her friends.

It sounds funny, right? Time traveling assassins end up at a Civil War reenactment and stumble through mistaken identity issues. But it turns out that you can't put a dark frame around a funny story. Is the farce more important, or the creepy futures? You have to pick one or the other, as I learned when revising this story (when my steadfast early readers weren't sure how to feel). Hopefully, you enjoyed the dark version that found its way into print... in this universe.

Janine A. Southard

THE RINGERS

BY RAVEN OAK

Raven's moody, numbingly creepy "The Ringers" takes its place with underbelly-of-Yule stories like Charles Dickens' *A Christmas Carol* and Susan Cooper's *The Dark is Rising*. The bold young heroine Elise fights for open information in a way that strikes a chord in our own WikiLeaks world, while Dekwood's woolen mill suggests the sweatshop drudgery that lurks in the heart of contemporary American Christmases. Magic and free thinking may be victorious in the end, but jingle bells in the snow never inspired dread in my belly until now.   —Maia Chance

I t was an eerie fog if ever there was one.

If fog could envelop every pore of every creature, even then it could not be as dense and adhering as it was that night.

Far outside the grand city of Veleden cowered a village of silence. Whereas you or I might expect sugarplums and mirth in the early days of winter, the village of Dekwood embraced grays and blacks as evening fell, and its people secured their windows against the creeping fog.

Children buried themselves beneath well-worn quilts, but they didn't clamp their eyes shut. No, they slapped tiny hands over their ears to ward off the jingle-jangle of horses' reins as the Ringers approached.

A guardsman leaned across the jingle-jangle bridle of his perfectly normal-looking horse as it crossed the threshold into town. Snowflakes sprinkled across his red suit and blended in with his white sash. The four men in his brigade, if they could be called men, pulled up alongside him.

Five muzzles puffed frost into the air.

Five men, skin haggard as it draped skeletal frames, sat astride the white beasts.

Five days they would ride and rid Dekwood of those unneeded, those too bold for purpose.

A lone child coughed as he huddled against a tree. Tears mingled with snot as he muffled his cries with a ragged scarf. The bells jangled, the eerie sound carrying through the eve like a death keen. The child froze like the snow beneath him, and five faces grinned.

Two weeks until Winter Solstice

The day we sought refuge in Dekwood held no special purpose. Two seasons without work and my papa devised our bold plan. We would load up our belongings in a simple carriage and head north for better fortune.

I was fourteen, convinced I understood everything while understanding very little. It was a dark time to travel, but my mother's womb thickened with my brother and food grew scarce when the grand forests shriveled and died.

How does a forest die? Perhaps it was nothing more than a lack of rain or some magician's grim spell that shriveled the leaves mid-summer and rotted the bark 'til the logs fell without the help of a woodsman's axe. If logging was no longer lucrative, perhaps the more industrialized work of Dekwood could line my papa's pockets.

Five days' travel had left me without purpose. I taxed my mother's patience as I spoke of a spell to change rain into snow or the logic behind the life-giving elements that connected all living creatures and powered the magics of our world. When my feeble attempts to bring about snow froze my mother's morning tea, she hid my magical texts in a locked trunk. Their absence didn't stop me from walking beside the carriage to draw upon the soil's power. Every few hours' travel, I tugged the gloves from my fingers and spread them across the hard earth to feel the thrum of magic beneath me.

And when my mother wasn't watching, I'd whisper the words to call forth a slight dusting of snow across my brow. If she wondered why my red hair bore crystalline flecks, she remained as silent as our days on the road.

On the sixth day of travel, heavy snowflakes tickled my nose. They spread themselves across the hardened dirt road which snaked north to Veleden and south to the City of Escen. I'd never set foot in either, but I'd heard Tellers talk of the great magistrates who managed the towns of the North.

Rumors traveled about the Magistrate of Dekwood, an ageless and grim man who ruled from a hillside mansion. People said he mourned the loss of his sons. Whether from a factory accident or illness, I refrained from asking. Such tales were for *children*.

I was no mere child. I couldn't be if I wished to study magic. One day I would be a magician—capable of powerful magics to bring the trees to bloom and the rivers to flow.

And force the clouds to snow.

I opened my mouth to inquire after Dekwood, but my mother's pursed lips left me silent. My feet ached, but watching my mother struggle to maintain her posture on the bumpy trail made me glad to be walking alongside the carriage. Papa grinned down at me from the coachman's seat.

No manor homes or farms dotted the countryside nor any indication that we grew closer to our destination. I wrinkled my nose when a snowflake graced it, and my mother sighed. "Elise, if you continue to make such expressions, you'll gain wrinkles before you're wed."

Before my soon-to-be brother, an accident that puzzled the Physics aplenty, my mother had spent her days raveling yarn at the seamstress's shop. Like a skein of yarn, wrinkles twined their way across her forehead, and I grinned. "Yours are what I love best about you."

My brashness earned me another scowl before she busied herself with her knitting.

I tried to follow the air across my mother's belly to hear the whispers of my brother—as the Physics had done when my mother had taken ill—but it was only wind to me, the magic far beyond my abilities.

"Papa," I said, and his wood-warped hands tightened on the reins. "Will Dekwood have a school? Something beyond the elementary standard? Perhaps someone with magical knowledge to prepare me for the entrance exams?"

Firm fingers loosened their grip. "Any place that close to the City of Veleden is bound to have something. You'll be back to your preparations in no time."

Day ten brought us over yet another hill. A gritty forest loomed ahead like something out of a nightmare, and I shivered beneath my woolen cloak. "Are we to travel through there?" I asked.

His skin paled as we observed the swaying tree-corpses that cast long shadows across the trail. "Don't tell your mother. Go distract her while we pass."

I peeked in the carriage's window. My mother lay across the crunchy, thin-padded seat, eyes closed and breath slow. Her pale hair was messed against a pillow. "She's sleeping." I glanced at the trees and whispered, "But let's hurry."

The whites of his eyes reflected his fear, an odd emotion in a man who scaled great heights for his trade, and I shivered.

"Agreed. Last we need is your mother carrying on about evil curses cast upon our future." My papa laid a superstitious hand upon his heart.

Winter tightened its grip on the dead oak, and their bones shivered. Even barren, the trees' branches stretched across the sky and blotted out all light. Like the shriveled fingers of the dead they drooped down and reached for us, stealing our warmth and joy before we were more than a foot into the woods.

Nothing lived in these trees.

No sound besides the muffled hoof beats in frozen snow. No smell beyond the burn of cold air in the nostrils. Branches snagged along my cloak, and I pulled it tighter across my shoulders.

I held my breath 'til I thought I might burst. When I glanced at the spot beside me, my papa did the same and I laughed. The glee bounced beyond us and reverberated back, amplified and shrill.

"Hush," he whispered.

Every now and again, the marks of a woodsmith scored the narrow tree trunks, and a hollow log lay beside our path, a fallen soldier in the battle of survival. And so we traveled for nigh two candlemarks.

Just as we broke free of the forest, my mother sneezed and startled a shrill cry from my lips. "Control yourself, Elise," she said through the carriage's open front window. "A young lady need not give in to such whimsies."

She met my gaze but her death grip on her shawl relayed how long she had been awake.

Papa tapped my shoulder.

Nestled among the countryside's hills, homes rose from the hard earth, their rooftops covered in winter and chimneys smoking with warmth. A great warehouse marred the image, as did the grim mansion on a hill. Dekwood.

Papa grinned. "Welcome home."

3 Days until the Solstice

No one greeted us. No children scattered snow in the streets or chased a dog into alley carts. A few faces peered out dirty windows the size of dinner plates before fading into darkness.

At the village's center stood a grotesque statue of a man too tall, with a grin too wide that stretched his mouth past redemption. His horse-like teeth were carved of marble, and his hands held a skein of wool.

"Who's that?" I asked.

"The magistrate maybe?" guessed Papa. "Can't think who else would get a statue made of polished stone."

My mother tapped on the glass. "We've a place to go tonight, don't we?"

"From the magistrate. Said so in his letter."

The horses slowed before a brick monstrosity two stories high with edges of cast iron beams and cobbled bricks and stone. Not a brick out of place, and yet the dingy gray embraced the building and marred its appearance.

My mother alighted from the carriage with Papa's assistance. "What is this place?"

"Welcome to the inn," Papa said. He tied the reins to the post out front with a clove hitch.

"Surely we're not staying *here*, are we? Where will the horses be stabled? And the carriage?" My mother pouted at the imposing building, not at all to her customary taste. Inside, loosely grouped chairs and tables gathered dust. A single patron sat at the bar, completely ignoring us.

The woman behind the counter gave Papa a light smile. "You must be Erol Jankin. We've been wonderin' when you'd get here." She squeezed wide hips through the bar opening and ambled over to us, thick pink skirt ruffles dusting the floor as she moved. "The name's Beatrice."

My mother ignored the woman's offered hand, but Papa seized it with exaggerated enthusiasm. "Thanks for the welcome. Noticed quite an oddity on the trip here— that...forest...."

Beatrice gave him a curt nod. "You're welcome to two rooms upstairs 'til you can get somethin' of your own. The carriage and horses outside?"

Papa nodded. "In his letter, the magistrate said he'd board the horses—sell the carriage to cover room and board."

"For you and the missus, maybe, but the rooms're too small for the three of you. You'll need another room."

My mother's mouth popped open. "We'd be indebted to this magistrate."

Beatrice's soot-colored eyes settled on the heap of books in my arms. The woman paled at the infinity symbol on the cover, and said, "Shouldn't be long before something comes available, I wager."

The patron excused himself as my mother voiced her complaints. Papa forced a smile as Beatrice handed him two keys. "Ain't a kitchen or anything in the rooms, but there's a restaurant 'cross the way that serves meals. I've got the usual helpin's of meat and potatoes in the evenin'. Bread and cheese in the mornin'. I lock up at midnight. If you aren't inside by then, you'll be locked out."

Papa pocketed both keys, ignoring my outstretched hand. "Thank you."

"Won't I need my key?" I asked, and my mother shushed me. "Mother, I'm fourteen. If I am old enough to attend the Academe, surely I could be trusted with my key?"

"No, ma'am." Beatrice wagged a plump finger at me. "You listen to your folks. Stay in your rooms at night, no matter what you...hear."

"What would we hear?" I asked.

"Bells."

My mother tugged me toward the stairs. "Bells?" I asked.

"I'll send Vincent to help you unload your belongin's," said Beatrice, and Papa nodded his thanks.

Three steps from the top, I turned to face my mother. "The bells of the spirits? Is that what she meant?"

My mother pressed a finger to my lips. "Don't make trouble."

When I opened my mouth, Papa shook his head. "Listen to your mother."

I didn't know what shocked me more—that there were spirits in town or that Papa agreed with my mother. Either way, I was determined to remain awake and listen for the bells.

2 Days until the Solstice

Morning brought a misty rain to Dekwood. We stood in the town square, woolen jackets doing little to keep the chill off our shoulders. Either the bells had never sounded, or I'd fallen asleep.

A little slip of a man rushed over to us. Raindrops dripped off his umbrella and splashed upon my plaits.

"Are you Erol Jankin?" he asked, and Papa nodded. "I'm Magistrate du Leunt's assistant. The magistrate sends his most profound apologies."

"Erol, you said—"

Papa patted my mother's gloved hands, tightly knotted over her thickened waist. "I understand, Mr...?"

"Nicolas Ashton. The magistrate can hardly meet everyone who stumbles into town, no matter how...desperate their letters may appear. I'm sure you understand, Mrs. Jankin." He tipped his hat in my mother's direction.

To my father, he said, "I understand your former occupation was a logger in Devlon. I'm afraid we don't have a need for such work. If you wish to pay back your debt to the magistrate—"

"I was given to believe our carriage would cover our time at the inn," said my mother.

"Your carriage was hardly fit to cover your stay for a day, let alone a lengthier time." My mother glared at Papa.

Whatever the magistrate had arranged, our plans had changed. My mother squared her shoulders before she spoke. "Then I'm afraid we must take our leave of Dekwood."

Papa whispered something in her ear. Her face paled before her cheeks flushed like a ripe strawberry.

"As I was saying, men work in the leather mill or out in the fields with the sheep." Mr. Ashton frowned as he noted Papa's lanky figure. "I suppose you'll do with the tanner. Little old for apprenticing but work hard, and you could clear your sizeable debt in perhaps a year's time."

Sizeable? We had slumbered here one evening yet our debt was sizeable? Tuition for the Academe would stretch us beyond our means with my mother's need for society life, but surely a few seasons missed work had not brought us to such dire straits? Papa's hand rested on my shoulder, and I bit my tongue.

"Women and those not able-bodied work in the textile factory. Everyone pulls their share in Dekwood," continued Mr. Ashton.

"I'll admit to never having worked with leather before, but I figure can't be much harder than climbing trees in the nippy winter. Say, I was going to ask the magistrate about schools."

"School?"

"Yes, for Elise. Back in Devlon, she was readying for entrance into the—"

The man's nose twitched with impatience as he waved a hand at Papa. "She's too old for school here. As long as she's got the basics, she has all she needs. Doesn't take much by way of brains to work in the factory, now does it?"

"The factory? But sir, I'm to study magic at the—"

Like a striped tomcat of Devlon, the man hissed as he stepped back. "Magic isn't tolerated or needed in Dekwood. You'll be working in the factory or none at all."

"Then I'll take none, sir, as I have studies to attend to." Papa's fingers pinched my shoulder, and I winced.

"If you know what's good for you, you'll nip that in the bloom now," Mr. Ashton said to Papa with the wag of his finger. "If you want to stay in Dekwood, these are your options." Papa nodded and Mr. Ashton continued. "Work begins an hour after sunrise. Report to the tanner's at noon, and he'll fill you in on the rest. It's just down the street a few buildings and on the right."

"What about housing?"

His eyes, thin charcoal slits at the bottom of too large a forehead, rested on me, and that grin returned. "You shouldn't be too long in the inn."

He'd made it three steps toward the mansion in the distance when Papa called out, "We'll be in contact if we need something. Thank you, and thank the magistrate."

My mother elbowed him in the ribs. "When were you going to tell me of our debt? Had I realized we'd amassed so much in Devlon—" Her cheeks flushed as she turned her eyes on me. Unusually frizzy hair popped out from beneath her wide-brimmed hat, whose red poinsettias clashed with the rich plum of her scarf. She tucked the escapee behind her ear. "Dally about in the rain if you wish, but I've no purpose in this...mess."

We trailed behind her to the inn. A wide road such as this should have played host to many, yet it remained empty. My mother tugged on the doorknob of the inn's solitary door, but the swollen wood stuck.

Papa gave it a good tug and when it released its grip, my mother had an additional reason to scowl so early in the day. The door banged shut behind her. "She'll find reason enough to smile once our situation's settled," said Papa. I only half heard him as I studied the rain.

Like the town, winter lacked its usual patterns.

As if he'd followed my thoughts, Papa said, "I suspect everyone's at the leather mill or the textile factory. Odd little town this is."

"Am I to join everyone in the factory?"

He sighed. "You've heard more than you should, but your papa's gone and gotten himself into... a delicate situation. It's just 'til we can afford to send you to the Academe."

I frowned.

Something about this town didn't feel temporary—the way people's drooping shoulders matched their mouths, the way buildings held a hint of desperation with their creaks and wobbles. This town didn't release folks to bigger and better things. It kept them tight within its clutches.

Forever.

A shiver pricked goose pimples along my arms, and something deep within the earth made my nose itch. "What is it?" Papa asked, and I shook my head.

There was no reason to be suspicious of someone using magic, but after Mr. Ashton's reaction to the word, I tucked away the reminder to investigate further. Something just wasn't right in this town.

1 Day until the Solstice

My disappointment by the lack of bells warred with curiosity the next morning. The factory doors towered far above my red head. Moss grew between the doorframe bricks, and rust stained the mortar. When I stepped through the doorway and didn't feel magic's touch at my feet, I sighed. A shove from behind sent me sprawling face-first along the floor's dead planks.

"You're blocking the door. Get a move on." The gruff voice's owner shuffled past me, leaving me a spectacular view of worn boot-heels and coarse gray cloak. My mother's frizzy hair blocked my view of the factory as she knelt, her hand thrust out to take mine. If my mother had been a magic user, the owner of the worn boots would have needed a new pair. Instead, she helped me to my feet and glared as others passed.

From the disabled who hobbled in with canes clutched in knobbed fingers, to the mother with a baby strapped to her hip, women and children of all ages and sizes filed into the factory.

Large looms stretched nigh the full length of the floor, crammed against each other. Wedged in each corner rose four staircases. Women settled into their weaving with a simple rhythm while the children lined up against the front wall.

"You must be the new ones," said a man with a scruffy beard tucked into the collar of his shirt. My gaze landed on the top of his balding head, and I hid my grin. "You—" He jabbed his finger at me. "Join the other children."

My mother inclined her head, and I trudged over to stand behind a girl shaking rain out of her cloak. The man with the long beard led my mother toward the building's rear, and I shivered in the damp chill. "Who was that?" I asked the girl before me.

"That's the Tackler."

"The what?"

She tilted her head toward the looms. "Looms are in-intra-inter—"

"Intricate?"

"Intricate machines. When they aren't behaving, the Tackler fixes them to work so them on the looms can weave. You're the new one, aren't you?"

A girl older than my fourteen years shushed us as the Tackler approached.

"Good—you've already met Charlene," the Tackler said.

The blonde folded her cloak and set it on the floor without response.

I pulled mine tighter about my shoulders. "Yes, sir—" His thin nostrils flared, and I ceased speaking and joined the others in a rigid line that snaked around the interior walls.

We followed him silently—not that it would have mattered much with the looms' racket. The queue stopped beside a woman who pumped a foot treadle as her deft hands spun wool through the loom's grid. The Tackler gestured to a girl at the front of the line. "You turned sixteen yesterday, correct?" The girl who had silenced me earlier nodded. "You'll be working with Rebecca to learn the loom until you've developed the skill to weave on your own."

The girl's cheeks flushed at what obviously was intended to be praise, and I bit my tongue. Nothing about this job piqued my interest. A hundred or so women sat on hard stools in silence as they worked with hand and foot in a loud, drafty room. My mind itched for my books, but I followed along wordlessly as the line resumed its movement toward the rear of the building. The Tackler opened two doors and ushered us into a room the size of our old home in Devlon.

I followed Charlene to two stools against the wall. "I'm Elise."

She nodded and pulled two stiff-bristled brushes from a nearby basket. Charlene handed them to me and asked, "Ever carded wool before?"

"Never in my life."

She raised a brow and shoved a small basket of wool into my lap. Her demonstration with the carders proved thorough, but when I tried my hand at it, the wool caught in the spines of the brush. "You're pulling too hard. Be gentle," she said. She stretched the wool until it formed a uniform swath moving in a single direction. Thirty strokes later, mine remained a mass of fibers moving at odds with each other.

"It takes practice?" I asked. While Charlene shrugged, several children hid laughs behind oily hands.

"My ma says your ma used to sew for fancy ladies in Devlon. Is that true?" asked Charlene, and I nodded. "Then how'd you end up so...unskilled?"

I smiled. "My gran says I was destined for greater things."

213

It had been a point of contention between my mother and my paternal grandmother—right up until she had passed the year before. My gran had studied magic until she had married at her parent's insistence. It was her wrinkled fingers that had first touched mine to the soil and taught me of power.

The gentle lull of brushing the wool relaxed my shoulders, and my head dipped toward my chest until Charlene kicked my ankle. I jerked my head upright to find a woman old enough to be my grandmother in the doorway. I squirmed beneath her gaze until a few giggles caught her attention. "Remove your cloak," she barked.

"I'll catch a chill. Please, I'm not used to...such conditions."

More giggles, which she silenced with a look. Despite her bony frame, strong fingers tugged at my cloak and forced me to my feet. Both carders clattered against the wood floor. I towered over her and with the hunch in her back, she struggled to look me in the face. I straightened my cloak.

The others stared at their wool with rapt fascination. "You're new, so I'll forgive your insolence today. But tomorrow, I expect better. You aren't well-to-do no more, so don't be expecting no favors. Tomorrow, you'll leave your cloak with the rest."

When the doors closed, Charlene released the breath she'd been holding. "Is that woman normally so cross?" I asked, but she rotated her stool until her back was to me.

To keep myself awake, I sketched incantations in my head and wordlessly recited formulas until my hands were stiff and my stomach threatened to pierce my backbone with hunger. When two o'clock arrived, the other children pulled lunches from their satchels. Their meal was punctuated by brief whispers. My feet were nearly numb after half a day on a wooden stool, and I bent over to touch my hands to the floor before rolling up to a standing position. My hand was on the chilly doorknob when someone touched my shoulder.

"Where're you going?"

A boy stood behind me, a roll of bread between his fingers. "To find my mother," I said.

"Can't." His hand against the door kept it firmly shut.

"But my mother has my meal."

"She'll be working now. Her lunch brief was at one," he said.

"I promise I won't bother her. I just wish to fetch my lunch from her bag."

An old puffy scar beneath his eye twitched. "You'll have to eat later. Can't interrupt the weavers."

"But—"

He pried my fingers from the doorknob and once free, pressed one of them against the puffy scar beneath his right eye. "If you interrupt the work, we all suffer, see?" I jerked my finger away and returned to my stool, though my stomach grumbled audibly. Charlene handed me a wedge of cheese and some dried apple bits.

"Thank you," I said.

"No, thank you."

I got the feeling she was thanking me for remaining in the room, and I asked, "Is it like this every day?"

"Like what?" she whispered.

"Silent. Dejected."

The boy with the scar pressed his lips together, but otherwise ignored us. "There's too much to do for idle chat," she mumbled as she nibbled on a hunk of bread.

"I've never worked before, but surely you could talk while carding—at least as good as you are."

Someone shuffled by the closed doors. Once the person passed, Charlene asked, "You've never worked?"

"No."

"Then whatcha do before?"

"I went to school."

Scar boy laughed. "We've all been to school. What did you do after that?"

"I'm not referring to the elementary standard. I was studying for entrance into the Academe." When Charlene cocked her head, I added, "The Arcane Academe of Veleden."

Two dozen children edged their stools away from me. Those still seated on the ground drew their feet under themselves. "Don't tell," said Charlene. "Magic isn't allowed here."

"Why?"

The boy with the scar strode over and stopped an inch from my face. Mutton and the hint of apple soured my nose. "If you want to survive, stop drawing attention to yourself. Stop asking questions."

"Questions are how one learns—"

"Not in Dekwood."

This time, when the shuffle returned to the door, it didn't pass. The old woman stepped inside, a brown satchel in her hands. "Your mother made quite the fuss 'bout you gettin' this." She thrust the patchwork bag in my direction.

No one in the room glanced at the old woman, but they were aware of her every movement. Even the seven-year-old in the corner watched from the corner of her eyes. I took my meal, but I was no longer hungry. How could I survive this town? How could my parents?

Charlene would accept none of my lunch, not that there was any time. We returned to our labors after little more than three bites. The older children shifted from carding to spinning the wool into long threads on spindles. By the time work ended, my arms and back ached. No one complained, nor did they limp or tremble as I did.

My mother's pale head bobbed in the mass outside the room but quickly disappeared as bodies shuffled toward the drafty building's exit. My shoulders brushed against silent townies, and I'd nearly reached the front door when something tugged on my cloak. I had neared the doorframe when I felt another tug.

"Elise," someone whispered, and rough hands propelled me through the door. The bright sun made my eyes water until Charlene's gray form blocked the setting sun. "Elise, I needed to warn you to be careful."

"What reason would I need to be cautious?"

Charlene bit the edge of her lip. "Stop asking questions."

Before I could pry further, she vanished into the throng of workers. Someone tapped me upon the shoulder—my mother. Her shoulders drooped like decayed flesh. "I used to enjoy weaving." She rubbed her expanding middle and frowned. "I hope your father doesn't mind another round of the restaurant's corned beef."

Dinner bearing the consistency of an eraser didn't rest easy with my mind or my stomach, but my muscles screamed for sustenance and rest. It would have to suffice.

Like toy soldiers we formed a line that marched from the factory into the center of town, and from there, bodies separated to their homes without chatter or smiles. As my mother and I trudged toward the inn that served as our temporary home, snowflakes began to fall.

The Solstice

Papa might have possessed the patience for corned beef, but little else that evening had given him pleasure. My questions about the oddness of such a town had fallen by the wayside, as had my complaints about working in the factory rather than preparing for the Academe. His words were placations for ears too young to comprehend their warning.

My ability to attend the bells that evening had waned as exhaustion had set in. My eyes had closed the moment I had tucked myself beneath the scratchy woolen blanket.

When sleep released me the next morning, the inn retained its usual silence and my parents' room lay empty. On the table rested a scribbled note bearing Papa's scrawl.

If you felt like I did yesterday, I figured you deserved the day off. Use it for study, eh? Your mother will tell the factory you've caught a chill. I'll be at work if you need something. There is some bread and cheese in the breadbox.

The cheese was a touch too sharp and the bread just this side of stale, but they numbed my hunger. Outside, snow coated the cobblestone road and dotted the rooftops white against the gray sky. Tempted as I was to stroll past the factory and stick my tongue out at its closed door, the opportunity for a "holiday" pushed sense into my head. Besides, the crudeness of such a gesture would have set my mother to vapors.

The streets were as devoid of children and merchants as the day we had arrived. The town held its breath as its people worked—though for what purpose, I couldn't see. I tucked myself between two buildings and pressed my hand to the cobble, but the crumbling stone blocked any tingle of magic.

The door to the factory protested as it opened and closed, and I tried to sink into the cobble behind me. Charlene frowned at me from the alleyway's end, and I relaxed.

She said, "I thought you were sick."

"I caught a chill but upon waking, felt the air calling to me. Perhaps it might lend health to my lungs."

"Is that magic talk?" she asked, and I inclined my head. "See, that's the very thing that won't sit well with the magistrate."

"What would I care if the magistrate takes pleasure in my speech?"

She leaned against the building and closed her eyes. For all her youth, her frustration aged her and the eyes she turned on me could have been my mother's. "Take care, Elise. People who don't know their place tend to disappear."

"Disappear how?"

"I shouldn't say, but...it's only fair that you know, being new. Have you heard the bells?"

I shivered. "I tried to listen for them our first evening here, but they never came."

Charlene's eyes widened. "Be glad they never came, Elise. Be glad! What do you know of them?"

"Nothing much. Everyone in Dekwood fears them, which makes little sense. Yule approaches. We should be ringing the bells to welcome the coming of a new year and the gifts of our health and fortunes. To remember the dead and celebrate the future." Her eyes darted to the road as if she expected something, and I tilted my head. "Charlene, why do you dally with me? Shouldn't you be at the factory?"

"I was sent by the Tackler to search for you."

"For what purpose?"

She glanced a third time at the snow-covered street. "To make sure you were being truthful when it was said you'd taken ill." My snickering carried, and Charlene reached up to clap a hand over my mouth. "Shhh, they'll hear you."

"Who? The factory workers? Drafty though the walls may be, they would hear naught over the loom's thrum."

"No, not the workers. The Ringers."

"Beatrice, the innkeeper spoke of something unnatural in the bells. I've heard talk of spells that can commune with our ancestors, but never with foul intentions. Are these Ringers spirits then?"

"They aren't living. I don't know what they are."

The alleyway dimmed, and I flattened myself against the wall with Charlene. Our movements hid little as the innkeeper glared at us. "I knew you were up to no good. And Charlene—" She jabbed a finger at the girl, whose bottom lip trembled. "—what would your father say to hear you've been talkin' about things better left unsaid? Do you wish to court trouble this close to Yule?"

The girl squeezed past the innkeeper. I placed a gloved hand on my hip—a gesture my mother would have abhorred—and nodded in the direction Charlene had darted. "I do not see what business it is of yours what Charlene and I discuss."

"Charlene should be at work in the factory, as should you." The innkeeper stopped my sideways motion with a firm grip on my elbow. "Your family's new here, so you don't understand our town and our ways. But the Ringers aren't nothin' to laugh at, and if you know what's good for you, you'll leave it well enough alone."

She didn't stop me as I brushed by, but my insides quaked. I expected a child to fear the boogieman looming in the shadows, but for an adult to fear one so, lent credence to the idea that it was more than a mere spirit or specter— possibly something magical in origin.

Possibly something more dangerous than I was prepared for.

I could have returned to the factory like the young woman my mother wished I was, but I could not. Magical study drew rule breakers and thinkers—who wanted to make order of magic's chaotic nature. If I were to understand these Ringers, I needed information.

And for that, I was going to need my books.

My library rested soundly inside the worn leather chest in my room. The dull buckle remained latched, though the chest had been pushed away from the door. The basin held fresh water from the innkeeper's visit to my room, which was perhaps when she had discovered my escape.

Papa's employ had provided us a certain level of influence in our previous home of Devlon, though not as much as my mother had wished. Despite our more affluent standing, we were held in little regard by those with true wealth. We had ignored my mother's ostentatious nature while saving up for my first year texts at the Academe. My fingers remained gloved as I removed both from the chest.

The *Livre de Cantus* held the basic foundation for magical studies, and I set it aside. *The Histoires de Créabet Magia*, though, bore the history of magics and creatures of the known world.

I was convinced the answer lay within its pages, but several hours passed, leaving me with nothing more than a stiff neck and aching shoulders. A two-sentence paragraph on the probable existence of ghosts was the only reference to the undead in the entire tome. Nothing on bells or creatures with bells that caused people to disappear.

Information on the undead required a library—specifically, a library with the books of the grand arcanum. A town this small wouldn't have one...or would it? The first day we had arrived, I had felt the thrum of magic.

Downstairs, the innkeeper's fingers were lost to a pile of yarn and knitting needles. She ignored me until I stood beside her, then she glanced up from her needles with a cocked brow. "Do you need somethin'?" she asked, needles still clicking.

"Does this town have a library?"

The yarn wrapped around her index finger stilled. "Do you need a book to keep you company during your...illness?" I nodded, and she fetched a hardbound book from beneath the bar. "This here's a new mystery. Just finished it last week."

"I was hoping to choose my own reading material—" Her scowl deepened, and I retrieved the book from her waiting hand. "Thank you. But if I finish this and wish to read more, is there a library in town?"

"Not enough folks in town read for a library to be necessary. Ol' Henry does us right enough."

"Ol' Henry?" I asked.

"Local trader. Comes by once a month with whatever he picks up out in the world. A few books, some fabrics and yarns, random bits and things. You make sure that book takes no harm. Cost me a scarf and a good bottle of wine."

If someone possessed the books I needed, they weren't sharing. But then, most of the town kept tight lipped. The needles resumed their clicking as I left the inn. Only one person had opened up to me, and she was at the factory.

The factory's front door loomed like the coming snow, and as I crept through, I waited for the Tackler to pounce. His shiny head never made an appearance, though one elder worker nearby thwacked her knuckles on a loom's wooden frame as she worked. No one glanced up, but they shivered in the cold wind that accompanied me through the entryway. The looms' humming drowned out the closing door's snap and those of my footsteps as I sought the rear carding room.

One left turn too many had me lost.

In front of me stood a woman whose wrinkles carried wrinkles. Rather than throwing a wooden shuttle through the floor to ceiling loom, the woman used a metal rod to weave bright colored wool by hand. She hunched over her weaving, her nose nearly touching the wool, and added tiny starburst patterns to a bright blue sky.

"I'm sorry to interrupt, but..." If she heard me, she made no indication, and I stepped closer to the loom. "I said I'm sorry—"

The old woman set the rod aside and cocked her head. I tried again. "I'm Elise, and I appear to be lost." Her mouth moved with slow, exaggerated movements but without sound. "I don't understand—"

"You'll get nothing out of her," said a rough voice. The boy with the scar stood behind me, a basket full of washed wool in his hands. "So many years in the factory, everyone goes deaf."

"She tried to say something. Or at least I thought she did," I said and followed when he gestured for me to do so.

"She was just mee-mawing at you. You'll need to work here a span longer than a day to understand all that nonsense. Besides, I thought you were sick."

My cheeks grew warm despite the chill of the building. "The illness passed, so I decided to return to work." His basket full of wool bounced, and he pursed already-too-thin lips together. His expression read, *you'd-have-to-be-insane-to-come-back*, but I shrugged it off. "I became lost and decided to ask directions. What is mee-mawing?"

"The loomers talk without sound, through lip-reading and miming, though I suspect sometimes they just make it up." We turned right where I had turned left and ten feet later, we stood before the double doors to the carding room.

Charlene dropped her carder when I entered, and one of the older girls behind her said, "I thought you said she's sick."

I ignored the jibe and took my place beside Charlene. While yesterday had proven a quiet affair, the youngest children chattered in the corner while those older and nearing apprenticeship gossiped in whispers. I leaned closer to Charlene. "Is it true there is no library in Dekwood?"

"I think there's one in Magistrate Leunt's mansion. My dad mentioned it once. Why?"

"My books lacked the details on a particular research, but if I could perhaps look it up, that may give me answers. How do you function without a library or proper schooling?"

Charlene glanced up from her wool, but no one paid any attention to us in the hum of conversation. "Magistrate Leunt says there's no need for school beyond the basics. What use would we have for such knowledge working here?"

"But haven't you ever wondered why the sky is blue? Or why the snow only falls in the winter?" Charlene shrugged, but her eyes lit up like buds on spring trees. I asked, "Or why the trees outside this town have died?"

Several voices paused, awaiting Charlene's answer. "I..." She glared at the boy with the scar—who shared the same pointed chin and green eyes. Only a sibling could level such a look that flushed her skin, but Charlene was daring and she answered me in a quaverless voice. "I asked my dad once why other towns live with joy and food and warmth while ours shrivels like the forest outside. He wouldn't answer."

Air whistled between clenched teeth, and the boy with the scar crossed the room with a dozen steps. He leaned over and whispered something in Charlene's ear.

"No, Matthew, I won't be quiet," said Charlene. "Elise's right. Why don't we have a school anymore? Why is magic forbidden if it's a gift from the gods?"

She rattled off a litany of questions, but my brain latched onto one in particular. *Magic? Forbidden?* I'd never encountered such a rule or law, but the idea made sense when added to people's reactions. Lost in thought, I missed the door opening and the hush that draped across the room. Something rough slapped my motionless hand, and I tumbled back into the real world.

"—Asleep again? Why aren't you working?" The woman before me lacked an arm, yet her single hand was rough, her fingers bearing the same calluses of the other weavers.

She raised her hand to slap mine again, and I shook my head. "My apologies," I muttered as I dragged the carder across the wool in my other hand. The woman nodded, but her narrowed eyes followed me as she paced. For ten minutes the room held its breath and worked, and only when the disfigured woman departed did the group return to a hesitant chatter.

Charlene's breath tickled my ear as she leaned close. "My father has a few books. I...I might be able to get them for you."

"Thanks, but I'm looking for something in particular."

"I know, that's what I mean. I've seen them—they have special covers and—"

I clapped my hands over hers to still them. "Wait, your father owns books on magic? Why would your father have those?"

"You met him the other day at the statue. He works for Magistrate Leunt."

Matthew cast aside his work and returned to Charlene's side. He hauled her up by her bony wrists and dragged her into the corner where the youngest children worked. "You'll sit here until you can learn your place," he said and glared at me as he fetched her carders.

My fingers tingled in the cold room. The wooden floor kept me from the earth's soil, but moisture licked the air and brushed my cheek with the echo of magic. Air was trickier—thinner and more temperamental—but I set aside the carders and splayed my fingers across the surface of the air.

At first, my fingers remained chilled as I whispered the word for warmth, but after a few minutes, my fingertips flashed with sudden warmth. Sweat broke out across my forehead and trickled down my chin.

The air rose a degree at most before the energy fizzled. I slumped over, my breath haggard. Children stared and whispered. Across the room, Charlene's mouth hung open.

"Get back to work," snapped Matthew.

He did not look in my direction, but the edges of his shoulders and chin left me trembling. Rather than thanks for a warmer room, the children left me in frigid silence. At day's end, Matthew whisked his sister away before I could inquire further about the books. My mother frowned to see me, but must have noted the tension in my shoulders as we left. The walk home remained as silent as my afternoon had been.

I pled out of another corned beef dinner, instead choosing to curl up with the book the innkeeper had loaned me. My eyelids drooped as I turned the pages of yet another boring text that lacked the magic and adventure of the real world. The light peal of jingling bells reached my ears as the book fell against my nose, but when I opened my eyes, the sound was gone. Morning had come.

3 Days until Yule

I'd grown accustomed to the hum of the looms and the hiss of their whispers. When they vanished, my ears grew acutely aware of the bitter silence in the factory. Before, villagers had offered brief smiles and nods to each other on their way through the front door. Today, no one made motion to do more than shuffle in and stand. Waiting.

But waiting for what?

My mother squeezed my collarbone too tightly, and I squirmed until I tumbled free to skid to a halt before the Tackler. Whereas he normally tucked his lengthy beard beneath his shirt, it rested atop it this morning. His collar was buttoned too tight against slight jowls as he cleared his throat. "Today serves as a warning to us all," he said as he flicked his gaze in my direction. "Everyone plays a role in Dekwood, and when someone doesn't know their place or steps out of it, they're a danger to our way of life. A danger to us all."

A dozen workers over, a woman stifled her sob. The Tackler' sought out the source and finding nothing, continued. "Don't let loose the grieving thoughts that plague you, but instead, put your mind toward the task at hand. The Yule approaches."

The voices that recited his words lacked enthusiasm. "The Yule approaches."

The phrase transformed their faces. Where there had rested sorrow and fear, grim determination lit a fire in their eyes as they departed for their workspaces. My mother shrugged as the masses carried her away from me.

"No trouble today," the Tackler barked at me, and I frowned.

I remained silent until I spotted the empty stool in the carding room. "Where's Charlene?"

Matthew's lip welled with blood where he'd bitten it too hard. I repeated the question, this time while staring directly at him, and the carding brush in his hand snapped in half. "Let it go," he muttered.

"Where is she? And why did the Tackler profess such warnings?"

Like yesterday, they were destined to ignore me. I scooted my stool beside a little one stuffing hunks of wool into a basket. "I don't think we've met. My name is Elise. What's yours?"

"Belinda."

"Don't speak, Belinda. The bells will come." At Matthew's sharp warning, the child wrapped her arms about her legs, her eyes wide.

In the back of my mind, the bells jingled as the moon rose, and I dropped my carding brush. "Matthew, the bells did come. Last night—did they not? Tell me, where is your sister?"

He closed his eyes. "The bells shook the air last night, and the Ringers walked among us. I thought they'd come for you—" he said, stopping to look on me with tearful eyes, "—but they'd come for C-Charlene."

This was my fault. I'd encouraged Charlene to talk against her better judgment, and because of it, she was gone. "I-I'm sorry, I did not mean—"

"Didn't mean what? To talk Charlene into her death? Because of your talk of schools and magics—as if such things were possible in Dekwood—she went home and begged to be sent away. Can you imagine? She asked *our* father to be sent away so she could learn!"

Anger flushed my cheeks. "Matthew, I never intended for your sister to be taken, but asking to learn should not be a crime. Where exactly has she been taken? By whom? What are Ringers?"

"The Ringers ensure the peace and prosperity in this town. They make sure everyone serves their purpose. When they...they—when they take you, you're dead, Elise. Gone."

I did not recall when I stood, much less when I fled that room, but my running ceased when I reached the smallest building near the center of town: a lone house befitting someone who served Magistrate Revoir de Leunt. Its bricks crumbled a little less, were a little less faded than those around it, and instead of a single-floor dwelling, the house was its own two-story abode. The wailing from inside—a harsh, keening of pain that carried on with few gaps for breath—confirmed my suspicions.

The front step creaked beneath my foot when a shadow moved behind the window, and the same slip of a man from our second day in town leaned out the open doorway to wave an empty fist at me. "Go away! Haven't you done enough to this town?"

"I'm sorry—"

When he laughed, the wailing inside grew louder. "You watch it, girl. They'll be coming for you next!"

His words should have scared me, but the fluttering inside my stomach ceased as the earth beneath me hummed. Somewhere out there, someone called on the magics deep within the soil. Someone out there was not as backward thinking as the villagers. Someone out there was educated.

But not Nicolas. For all Charlene's belief that her father owned magical texts, not a single drop sang in his blood or whispered in his breath.

To him, I said, "I am quite sure they will seek me out, sir, and when they do, I have questions for them."

"You won't be able to ask."

"Why?" I asked, and the crying inside paused.

"Because when they come, they suck out your soul." He retreated and slammed the door behind him, but not even solid oak could drown out the cries inside.

Death magic. It had to be.

If the Ringers took ownership of people's souls, then for what purpose? Fuel? Something to power the dark magics required for the undead to walk the earth? Who would do such a thing? Who could?

I stared at the shadowed mansion that hovered in the distance. The only person people feared outside the Ringers was the magistrate. He possessed power and money enough to control an entire town. And if the rumors were true, he was ancient and learned—learned enough to make my knowledge of magic a mere thimbleful.

The thought filled me with dread.

No matter what words were uttered, Papa stood firm. "Their ways aren't ours, but we're here now. Keep your head down until we send you to the Academe. "

"But Charlene is missing." My mother's chair scraped across the floor as she excused herself, and I asked, "What reason do we have to remain in this town?"

"Just a smidgen longer, Elise."

"Papa—"

He closed his eyes a moment. "We owe the magistrate for putting us up here. To leave would be a mark against us."

"Do we need his favor so much then?"

Papa sighed. "A man like that—he'd keep you from school with only a frown. Don't court trouble. By mid-spring, summer at the latest, we should have the means to leave."

I fled, crossing the hall to my room. He had never been a man of excuses before, any more than my mother had allowed her appearance to falter or her tongue to still. Sleep avoided me as I stared, opened eyed, at the cracks in the ceiling until long after the hum of my parents' conversation changed to snores. When snowflakes tapped against my room's tiny window, I rubbed the sleeve of my nightshirt against the pane to stare out across the town below.

The street should have been bare this late hour, but diminutive twinkles danced in the air, cast off from the shimmer below. Rather than look away, I gaped as five white horses took form beneath my window. Five muzzles snuffed the falling snowflakes. One shook his head and sent up an eerie peal as the bells on his harness jingled—less a jingle and more like the scream of cold air across one's skin.

These weren't mere horses, and the five men astride them weren't mere men.

Red coats clung to gray flesh that stretched too taut over skeletal frames, and the mouth that grinned at me tugged at the corners until it might have split the near-translucent skin. This Ringer—his blue eyes ghostly and glowing—bore a sash across his red jacket, decorated with symbols burned black into the fabric.

Even from the inn's second floor, far from the touch of the earth, the thrum of magic in the air seeped into my feet. The bells rattled my ears as the horses stepped forward.

I flung my heavy jacket over my nightshirt and stuffed my socked feet in my boots. I threw open the door. Halfway down the stairs, I recalled the hour and slowed my steps to a creep.

The bolt was thrown over the inn's entrance; I shoved it upright with a grunt.

By the time the bitter chill outside blustered my face and threatened to rip the air from my lungs, the Ringers were gone.

Snow filled in the edges of the hoof prints. I followed them down the main street and around the corner toward the edge of town. In the distance, the forest darkened an already dark night, and I closed my eyes before I stepped across the town's threshold.

If they'd crossed into the forest, I'd never find them. Something...or someone whined to my left, and I followed the sound into a partially fenced yard. Tucked back against the trees lay a house made of lean-to boards and half-rotted wooden planks. A sagging roof groaned under the snow's weight and out front stood five white horses. I hurried my steps.

Inside the house, another whine, then a cry, and the air outside warmed. The snow stopped, and my feet sweated inside my leather boots. Magic. *Dangerous* magic.

I didn't know what kind, but the power of it made my vision swim. I stepped sideways to avoid the horse droppings. Horse droppings? Where they real beasts then? One of the horses shoved his muzzle into my shoulder blade, and I flinched.

The horses were living creatures. But what about the Ringers themselves?

My hand paused on the curtain that served as a door to the house. When a child screamed, I stumbled over my boots as I pushed my way through thick wool. Five beings who had once been men shimmered in the main room. One stood over a child no older than four, who cowered in his mother's arms. Tears stained the child's reddened cheeks and snot gummed up his nose, but no sound or breath escaped his blue lips.

His mother screamed at the Ringer, and when he touched his knotted hand to her flesh, her lips parted round.

I snapped my eyes shut, and inside my boots the soles of my feet burned.

Outside the air split with a cacophony of jingling bells, and when I pried open my eyes, two corpses lay in the corner, their hands tangled in one another's.

They weren't vanished or disappeared as Charlene had implied. They were dead.

2 Days until Yule

"What did you do?" Papa's voice carried more than a warning with the question, and I winced.

"There was magic; I could feel it! I needed to see what these Ringers were about," I said. My mother tore apart the roll in her hands, leaving little breadcrumbs scattered across the table's edge. Preoccupied with watching her, I failed to see Papa move until his hands seized mine in too tight a grip as he stood beside my chair.

"Don't follow them again. Leave it alone. Promise me now."

"But—"

"Do as you're told!" he snapped, and I tugged my hands away. "I'm-I'm sorry I snapped, Elise, but this is dangerous. This isn't growing a tree in the backyard or blossoming a flower in a vase. It's dangerous magic—the kind that comes with decades of learning and leads to evil beings and death. A-and I can't lose you." His voice caught, and what was left of my mother's bread fell to her plate with a thud.

"I need more time to clear our debt to the magistrate. Please mind me," he begged, and I nodded. After that, neither of my parents ate.

When my mother and I walked to the factory that morning, we passed the coroner's carriage. A trio of men moved two bodies wrapped in blankets—one child-sized and both bundled with care.

"Is that...?" my mother asked.

"Yes."

She wrapped an arm across my shoulder and squeezed. "Listen to your father, Elise. Please."

Up ahead, Papa spoke to Mr. Ashton. Whatever words Mr. Ashton spoke caused Papa's face to pale.

"We'll be late, Elise."

"I'll catch up," I said to my mother, who placed a hand over her swelling middle as she clambered through the snow without me. Papa furrowed his brows when he spotted me, but I hid in the shadow of the coroner's carriage until Mr. Ashton retreated.

"Why aren't you with your mother?" Papa asked when I finally approached.

"I forgot something. Was that Charlene's father?"

Papa nodded. "We're moving out of the inn in a few days' time. Probably after Yule. Magistrate Leunt has found us a place."

My stomach sank. "Where?"

"Just at the edge of town. It's in rough shape, little more than a lean-to at the moment, but they're going to repair it for us. Can't have your mother expecting in a place as drafty as that. Now hurry along to work."

If the cold air hadn't made my teeth chatter, the news would have done so. The home that would be ours had belonged to the two victims, and the thought of dwelling in such a place sickened me. Would our taking such a home further indebt us to this magistrate?

Papa watched me until I had turned the corner, but I waited twenty heartbeats—long enough for him to leave—before I returned to the statue at the town's center. There was something about this mysterious magistrate we never glimpsed—this magistrate in charge of a town of fear and death.

Animating the dead wasn't impossible, but it was forbidden for a reason.

I glanced into the statue's face. *Are you behind this?*

The stone eyes blinked.

I tumbled backward to land on my rear in the snow.

"It's how he knows." The voice belonged to a man buried in rags reeking of body odor. He ran a hand through graying, oily hair that hung a few inches past the tips of his ears.

"Who? The magistrate?"

"Who else? The man in control. He watches. He listens. And when you ain't right, the red men come."

"The red men? You mean the Rin—"

The hand he clamped over my mouth soured my stomach; it stank of blood and earth. I wriggled, and he pulled his hands away. "Don' say their name. Gives them power."

"What are they? Are they reanimated corpses or something more?"

He shrugged. "Does it matter? Until Yule passes, no one is safe."

"I know things, sir. Magics. Basic practice, but I could—"

The man shrank back at the word. The coroner's carriage stopped beside us, and a gentleman in a crisp, black suit approached. "Mr. Henry, come with me. It's time to see to Elizabeth and the boy."

The man's face crumpled at the name, and he allowed himself to be ushered into the carriage and away from the watching eyes of the statue.

The carriage set off in the direction of the mansion. If there were answers to be had, they would be there.

No magician worth his salt worked without a library. No one. It was long past the hour to discover what this magistrate was hiding, though it would have to wait. Another day's work missed would be noticed.

The hours dragged along as I carded wool in silence. Everyone gave me wide berth, and for once I did not mind. Papa spent dinner alternating between peering at me from behind his soup spoon and pausing with his mouth open, though he said nothing at all.

That evening, when I watched behind the frosted glass of my window, the Ringers and their horses materialized directly below me. The shortest one, with green eyes of a color that could melt hearts, peered at me beneath his red cap. When he hooked a finger and beckoned to me, I threw the shutters closed with a snap and fell beneath my covers until the jingling bells faded, and the sun crept over the horizon.

Yule's eve had begun.

I abandoned the inn before the town awoke and sought the lone path to the mansion. While I thought myself alone, red weaved itself against the drift covered trees and cobble. In the light of my oil lantern, I thought the trees painted with blood until the red moved. A person perhaps?

The figure ahead turned his green eyes on me.

He was alone, Ringer though he was, and when he beckoned for me to follow, my boots crunched in the fresh snow as we approached the mansion.

A grand porch of white stone led to wooden doors bearing stained glass depictions of angelic figures. Circular turrets framed the house on either side, topped by clay-tile spires and iron finials. When the Ringer's boot heel touched the first of twelve steps, the stone didn't shift, nor did the snow depress under his weight.

"Wait!" I whispered, but he gestured at the darkened porch. "I know, you want me to follow, but...are you real?"

His deep green irises marked his sorrow, and he inclined his head once. I reached out a trembling hand to touch his coat's fabric, but he leaned away from my grasp. His breath came in little puffs as he pointed again to the front door.

He did not progress beyond the first step, though his muscles strained and tugged as if he wished nothing more than to proceed. A small eight-pointed star was burned into the left side of the door frame, and when I touched it, it burned my thumb through my gloves.

"You can't pass...because whatever ties you to this world is here? In this mansion?"

His direct look intensified the burn that coursed through my thumb. "S-s...." He grimaced as his tongue hung from the side of his mouth. "S-s-sa-save...."

"Save? Or safe?"

"S-save us. All." The bells called out in the distance, and he clenched his hands at his side. "Save."

His figure wavered before it disappeared, and the snow fell in earnest. The doorknob turned beneath my hand, and the door swung open to an entryway of shadows and silence.

Was I expected? Or had the Ringer opened the door?

I muffled a cough in my sleeve as my dry mouth choked on the dust floating through the air. The steps of a grand staircase were draped in rugs long since faded and crushed. When nothing beyond the dust moved, I released my breath in little puffs that danced before me in the chill.

Melting snow left droplets along the wooden floor as I approached the first door on my right. A seating area, followed by a dining room with a table long enough to fit our family, cousins included. Beyond that lay the kitchens and pantry, a smaller eating area, a second living area, and a music room. My fingers lingered on the grand piano, leaving dust trails across the black and yellowed keys.

My breathing quickened, and the wind creaked through invisible gaps in the walls as I approached the grand staircase. The old rugs muffled most of my footfalls as I ascended to the second floor, and once there, I paused outside a room whose open door left a sliver of light in the hallway.

I nudged the door an inch, and when no one shouted or leapt at me, I opened it to a room clear of dust and loneliness.

The library.

Shelf-lined walls held books with gilded covers and lettering in more languages than I had ever seen. In the center of the room, a single desk rested, its velvet-lined top devoid of stationery or ink. The first bookshelf held histories of one kind or another, and I had almost skipped it when I spotted the eight-pointed star near the top: a heavy volume whose cracked spine read *The Accountes & Affairs of the Famile Revoir du Leunt.*

Once I had coaxed the book from its shelf, I settled into the corner with an unobstructed view of the doorway. Not that there was anywhere to hide, but it might have been possible to tuck myself underneath the desk. I squinted at the cramped handwriting on the first dozen pages. Mostly accounts of births and property acquisition, I skimmed first paragraphs until I spotted the pattern of dots in the top right corner of each page.

16: 05, 06, 07...the counting of years or months? The code was familiar to me from my studies. The halfway point of the book held the date of 1693, so supposing the dots' arrangement meant years.... I flipped to the last page, which was blank.

Was the magistrate adding to this book? I backtracked until I reached pages bearing a style of loose-flowing handwriting that was lengthy in stroke. The last entry was dated almost a century ago in the year of 1743. Blotch marks sprinkled their way across the yellowed page, and the hand-writing shifted as his emotions overwhelmed him:

> *My boys—all dead—Nothing good and pure and wholesome comes from a woman, this one more than most as her wyld and evyl ways brought my young Eli to ruin. There is naught more foolish than a young boy in love, and doubly so when in love with a sorceress. She thrice scoffed him before the town and his brothers rose to his aide, as brothers should. For nigh two hours they battled this sorceress and sought to drive off her evyl spells from this village, but ne'er had they fought with such a foul creature.*
>
> *I came upon their bare bodies in the centre of town, my sons' corpses drained of life and warped by magics far darker than taught by decent sorcerers. And she stood above them, her smile as grim as the winter's new sun. I will remember her words until my death.*
>
> *"Your sons thought to best me, Magistrate Revoir du Leunt. I merely wished to walk alone, but Eli would have none of it. Obsessed he was. An unhealthy and unholy sickness was upon him."*
>
> *Sorceress she may be, but my family's history she knew not, and I smote her where she stood. The ground reached up and buried her in its gaping jaws, but still my sons were dead. Still their bodies lay tossed like stones across the river top.*
>
> *Tonight, they will wander the land of the dead no more. Tonight, the earth will return to me what was lost, and this town will harbor sorceresses no longer.*

The writing ceased, the following pages blank. Not that it mattered. An event over a century ago involving our magistrate—the same magistrate, if the names were to be believed, had cast his sons into the realm of living dead. The skill required to create such beings...

I slid the book back into place. Three more bookcases held a variety of stories and treatises but nothing continuing the family story. Certainly nothing magical. On the last bookcase, I spied a collection of magical texts. Rather than focus on their concealed titles, I shut my eyes and whispered my fingers across their spines. Power ebbed and flowed from them, but my fingertips did not tingle until my hand rested on a slim book wedged between a behemoth of a text and the edge of shelf.

There was more than power to this book. There was hatred and envy and sorrow.

A well-worn yet simple cover—nothing to call attention in a grand library such as this—yet when its pages fell open at my touch, spells of death and life were sketched in grand detail. I shoved the book into my pocket, though it was not far enough away from my heart for comfort.

My lantern flickered as its oil burned low, and I crept away and down the stairs. As I tiptoed with aching, cold feet, I spotted a lengthy picture on the wall whose frame hovered an inch or two above the carpeted floor. An ugly beast all claws and teeth gnashed his way toward the edge of the canvas. In the opposite corner, a woman cloaked in red velvet crouched, her hands glowing as she fought the beast. I removed one hand from a glove and touched the painting.

Nothing. No response.

But it had to be here! Wherever his workroom lay, it would be on the ground floor. Somewhere that would touch the soil of the earth and open to the air and water of the sky. I set my lantern on the floor and, gripping the painting by its frame, tilted it. Behind the painting, the wall was missing.

The weight of the painting near tipped me on my side, yet I heaved it from the wall above to expose the open archway. As I leaned it against the wall, I prayed no one would awaken to notice the painting's misplacement. I brought my lantern into a narrow stairwell that smelled heavily of iron. A dozen steps down brought me to a metal door, which was unlocked.

The bottom corner dragged across the floor with a cry, and I winced as I wrenched it open. Nothing moved above or below, and I stepped across the threshold into an almost empty room: four bare walls, one archway walled off, and one wobbly-looking chair in the corner. The lone window near the ceiling confirmed I was in a basement. The perfect sorcerer's workroom.

Yet no sigils decorated the sparse room—not even the eight-pointed star that had burned my thumb.

A shift in weight caused the stairs outside to groan. Someone stood outside. I dragged the chair to the window. Even on my tiptoes, I struggled to push the window up and open as its jambs stuck. Outside, bells jingled and a set of hooves stopped before the window.

The Ringer with the green eyes touched the glass, which dissolved with a gust of snow and wind. I pulled my upper half through the window frame and received a face full of snow. More of the powder wiggled its way into my coat as I shimmied through. My jacket caught on the latch, and I gave it a firm tug before tumbling outside.

Something old and angry mumbled inside the room I'd vacated, and the ground beneath me trembled. With no care for the tracks left behind, I tossed up snow as I bolted toward town. Halfway to the inn, the bells ceased, and the earth shook no more.

My breath struggled in my chest until I crawled into my bed, and even then, my thumb throbbed with warmth.

I slumbered long past the rising sun and woke to shoulder shakes. When I opened my eyes, the shaking relented, though my mother sat on the mattress's edge as worry lines traversed her forehead. "What time is it?" I asked.

"Long past when young ladies should still be lying about. It's near noon."

Her words brought me upright in bed, and I cast aside my blankets in a rush. I crawled over the footboard and around my mother. "Why aren't you at work?" I asked as I dug through the bedside chest.

"I was. I came to check on you. You aren't ill again, are you?" She pressed a cool hand against my forehead, which I shrugged aside in order to pull on a pair of stiff pants. My mother scowled but said nothing about my choice of attire. Tufts of wool clung to her shawl, which she pulled closer about slumped shoulders. I glanced one-too-many times at my bed, and my mother crouched with a groan. Her round belly brushed against the mattress as she tucked her hand between it and the wooden frame. She would have liked to have been up to her shoulder in her search, but my soon-to-be brother didn't allow for it. Either way, she rooted around quite unladylike and undignified.

The woman who'd always taken such care with her appearance resembled the rest of the town—shoddy, rumpled, and tired. Her pointed shoes were faded and scuffed, wisps of pale-blonde hair had escaped her bun, and the bottom of her gray skirt was torn. Whatever nonsense the magistrate used to hold this town in disarray had to be stopped.

My mother's hand came back empty, but I held my breath rather than allow the sigh to escape. She reached for my arm to pull herself upright. I frowned, and she waved her hand in the air. "I thought—never mind. I need to get back to the factory."

Her heavy steps lumbered down each stair step and once she had arrived at the bottom, I retrieved the book I'd "borrowed" from the very back corner of the mattress. Simple bound, black leather with only the title etched in silver lettering: *Mort de Vie*.

Cold as it would be outside, I could not be caught reading this. My boots went on first, followed by my heavy wool coat, then a cream-colored scarf that reeked of mothballs, and matching woolen gloves. Lastly, I tucked the small book into my coat pocket and set out for somewhere quiet.

Despite the pallor over Dekwood, the sun glinted off the snow, nearly blinding me as I headed for the edge of town. No one would think to seek me out at the house that eventually would be ours, especially not with repairs set to begin after Yule.

The heavy curtain was missing from the doorframe, making me glad for my coat's warmth. I avoided the living area where the mother and child had been killed. The sun trickling through a wedge of window cast shadows where they'd lain, and I hurried my steps into the next room. The stove held no warmth, but I drew my own as I noticed a child's letters scribbled across scattered paper on the table. My smile faltered when I studied the page.

The little boy had sketched images of the Ringers.

I leaned on the chair, and when it didn't break, I took my seat and retrieved the book. Its innards lacked the printed text of most books on magic. This one held an older, shakier handwriting. Assuming *The Accountes & Affairs of the Famile Revoir du Leunt* had been penned by the magistrate and his predecessors, this work was by someone—or *something*—else entirely.

Most of the pages held spells—not just incantations or minor cantrips to light a candle or put a hound to sleep—but spells with real power: the kind I'd never see in school, the kind I wouldn't discover until long after I'd grown gray and crooked after the magic corrupted me.

One spell cast the soul of another into that of a beast, while another claimed to keep all ills at bay. When I turned the page, I dropped the book on the table where its spine splintered. *Clochen Mort de Noël.*

Death bells.

It was more than the cold that chilled me as I read. The half I comprehended was enough.

> *Upon the evenfall of Solstice, submit five upon the land. In the holy circle of Elshirei, draw forth the innocent and pierce the air with peals of five:*
>
> > *Thy will it be, five blind will see,*
> > *A year unmade, until the spade*

> *Doth break this circle of Yule that's made*
> *And set the risen free.*

The circle was easy. Every spell tied into the earth, into the land, but to create a circle of blood to honor Elshirei the Betrayed was an unclean deed. To raise the dead—

A hand touched my shoulder, and I screamed.

"Please, I didn't mean to frighten you." Mr. Henry hovered beside me. The rags he wore stank of booze, but he turned alert eyes on me in that moment. "I knew I felt something—"

He pressed a finger to my thumb, and the burning pulsed. "You've been to the house," he said.

I nodded. "How—"

Mr. Henry rolled down the collar of his scarf to display the *viziol* branded into the bluish skin on his neck. The protruding *V*, which rose from the top of two nested triangles left me slack with relief, and he shook his head. "I know that look. You think I'm here to save you, save this town, but I'm not."

"But you are a sorcerer, trained in the arts of high magic and served with protecting..."

Tears welled up as he cast a glance over his shoulder. "I've done my duty to this world and look where it got me. Elizabeth and Peter dead—their souls used to keep that filth alive for another year. When tomorrow passes, I'll be one more among the many and gladly so."

"Please," I said as he turned to pass, "Tell me what this is. I don't understand this spell or how to stop it."

He laughed a rich, belly laugh. "If I can't stop it, what makes you think a mere whip of a girl like you can? You've not even earned entrance to an Academe, much less gained an apprenticeship."

"I-I...may not be able to cease this spell's grip, but I must try, Mr. Henry. Please tell me what this spell means." I pointed at the paragraph in the book and the drawing beside it of the reanimated corpse with dull eyes and bells tied at its belt loops.

"I can't work the magic anymore, not for a long while. Something the magistrate's doing, I suppose."

"Were you sent here to stop him?"

He shook his head. "Not me, but my grandpa. He gave his life failing, as did my pa. That madman stripped the magic out of folks after that, but there's something...something deep down. A rumbling perhaps. I can feel it in the earth." His breath smelled of rot, and I took short breaths through my mouth. "He's losing control of his boys."

Outside the wind gusted, and the planks rattled around us. Mr. Henry didn't notice the goosebumps that decorated his bare arms. "His boys?" I asked.

"Them horsemen—the bell ringers. Those are his sons he's brought back."

"The story then, it is true? About the sorceress killing his sons?"

Mr. Henry nodded. "Rumors are that his sons deserved it. Either way, that spell's how he did it. At first, the mighty Magistrate Leunt did the killing. He slaughtered four women in their sleep that morning—all of them sorceresses—and used the blood to draw his circle. Did it at the Solstice's dawn, the day after his boys died. He anointed silver bells—it must be pure silver mind you—with the same blood and spoke the words. It near killed him from what I've heard, but then, he'd already had spells in place to protect against that."

"How...how old is he? The magistrate?"

"Older than this town. Or maybe not old enough. It doesn't matter." I closed the book, and Mr. Henry nodded. "Good, get your folks out of this town and away from this madness."

I slipped the book in my coat pocket. "I am not leaving. I am going to break the spell." His laughter drove icy air into my resolve, but I stood straight. "A Ringer asked me to try, so I must."

"Now I know you're nothing but silly. The Ringers can't speak."

"But he did—the one with the green eyes—he asked me to save them."

Mr. Henry tilted his head. "Huh. Maybe the magistrate is ready after all. Too many centuries passed him by in his sorrow. Look, if you're determined to do this, it must be tomorrow."

"On the Yule?"

"On the Yule."

"Why?" I asked.

"The Ringers feed to replenish the circle's seal between Solstice, when they rise, and Yule, when they sleep. Look again at the spell."

I retrieved the book and turned to the proper page. Mr. Henry pointed to tiny scribblings near the edge of the page. "The blood cord protect for five full days," I read, then shook my head. "I don't understand."

"To renew the seal, he must remove his protections."

"...And the circle will be vulnerable!"

He nodded. "But you still have to get to it. He'll see you coming. He has his eye on you yet, I'd wager."

"I'm counting on it."

"Mother?"

She laid aside her knitting and waited. How she found the energy after a long day working the factory loom was beyond my comprehension, but every evening since we had arrived, she prepared for my brother's birth. "Hmmm?"

"I need you and Papa to do me a favor." Papa, who'd been stretched out across the bed, sat up, eyes open, and I swallowed hard. "In the morning, I need you to gather the folks in town at the statue. Get everyone to bring all the bells they can—silver bells—"

"Is this about those funny fellas in the red coats? Didn't I tell you to stay away from that evilness?"

My toes curled in my stockings at Papa's questions. "How'd you know about their red coats?"

"Saw them just last night."

"If you see them again, flee. They are killers."

"That's what Frederick at work said. I know I told you to keep your head down, but something wasn't right with how they looked. I couldn't get warm after seeing them." He stared at his knees.

"They are the magistrate's sons, Papa. They died over a hundred years ago, but he brought them back from beyond. He uses the town to keep them alive." The entire story poured forth and by the time I'd finished, my mother was tossing her belongings in a chest. "What are you doing?" I asked.

"Packing. We're not staying here," she muttered.

"That's not a bad idea. Papa, you two should leave. At least until Yule passes."

"And what makes you think you aren't coming with us? Debt be damned," he said.

I left their room and crossed into mine where I retrieved the book from its hiding place. When I returned, I closed their door behind me and set it on the table. "What is that?" Papa asked.

"It is a book on dark magics. Foul spells that call for the murder of innocent people. I found it in the magistrate's house."

My mother hissed, "You trespassed?"

"I had to know what purpose he served in—"

"And now that you do, you'll what? Use that book against him? If he's really as old as you say, you won't touch him with the little tricks you know. Besides, no daughter of mine will commit such...ungodly acts!" Papa had found his feet halfway through the tumble of words, and the door slammed as he left.

My mother's knitting needles remained untouched on the table beside the book. "What will you do...if I gather the townspeople?"

"The Ringers will seek out the statue—imagine, a town full of unwillful people— and when I hear the bells, I will know he is vulnerable. I will break the circle with a single smudge. The spell will be broken."

"Surely it can't be that easy."

"Magic is organic. It comes from the earth and the air, the beings around us, and our will. If you remove any of those components, magic dissipates and returns to its natural state. The circle can't be protected if he means to renew it."

I withheld the mention that I'd be trespassing...again, not to mention the danger of crossing a magical circle, vulnerable or not.

She shook her head, and a gray curl fell across her cheekbone. "I'm not sure I understand it, but if you say you can do this, I believe you. Everyone will be at the statue on Yule if I have to drag them there at needlepoint."

I snatched the book from the table and turned away so she wouldn't see the tears in my eyes.

The crisp morning of Yule dawned across Dekwood—the one day of the year no one worked. Families would gather to eat and celebrate the coming of a new year, of new opportunities, and new beginnings. Sometime after sunrise, Papa would rise as usual and give thanks to *Wothan* for the sacrifices made in our honor. The town, assuming they followed tradition, would sacrifice five cattle—cows if they had it, though sheep would also honor the all-father. While children dreamed of the gift giving to come, I crept from my bed and into the falling snow in the pre-dawn.

Five horses stood in the field nearby, their bells removed as they pawed through the snow for whatever grasses lay underneath. The magistrate's mansion felt hollow to the touch, but where else would a mourning father be but here with his sons?

He would expect me through the front door—that plan would fail. I backed down the steps until my boots touched soil, then I slid first one foot and then the other from my boots. My stockings came next until I shivered barefooted in the snow.

While my feet froze, my skin hummed with the power beneath me. Around the mansion's side, the basement's window waited as paneless as I had left it. The room stood empty, but the chair had been returned to the corner. I drew a circle in the snow with an ungloved finger and picked up a pinch, which melted in my hands. The water droplets returned to the snow as I whispered.

Inside the room, the chair wobbled.

Sweat broke out across my brow, and I removed my wool hat, which I stuffed into my coat pocket. Nothing could leave the circle, not even to join the pile my boots and stockings made nearby. I dug my fingernails into my palms and focused.

Move the chair. Move the chair.

Still the chair wobbled.

The barest hints of sun peeked over the horizon, and I closed my eyes to the distraction. The chair trembled. A light scratching as it then slid an inch and another. I panted as drips of sweat sprinkled to land inside my circle. A thud of wood against stone rang out, and I opened my eyes.

Without breaking the circle, I leaned forward and peered down. The chair rested against the wall a few inches to the left of the window. The power drained from me in a rush, and I broke the circle with my chilled finger.

Despite the ache in my toes, my boots remained outside as I slid feet first through the window. I landed too hard on the chair, which fell over and toppled me on my side. Inside the empty room, I sighed and rubbed my hip where I had landed.

Nothing led to the location of his circle. The floor was cold stone, smooth and polished and completely unyielding to my probe for a power source.

I took out the silver ring in my pocket. It had been a gift from my parents, the single piece of silver to serve as the root. If I wished to study at the Academe, this ring was required to cast the compulsory entry spell. An expensive cost for our family but worth the price.

If I used it now, I might never set foot in the Academe.

Two bodies haunted me, and I whispered. The power inside the ring hummed and warmed my fingers. I allowed the warmth to wash over me, and when I brushed my fingers along the wall, a bell on the other side cried out in pain.

"Open," I whispered, and the silver ring dissolved into vapor. The air around me sizzled, and the stone wall wavered five heartbeats before disappearing to reveal a workroom. The walls remained of gray-slab stone, but the floor was compacted dirt and lacked the typical smells of manure and greenery. I poked a single finger in it and listened.

The soil was dead.

A circular rut formed the circle, its insides rimmed with fresh blood. At its center lay a single bell. Simple and plain, with no ornamentation and a single dent. The bell's original bloody baptism had long since faded. I couldn't cross the circle, not yet. Not if I wished to remain living.

Again a squeak on the steps alerted me to a guest, and I leaned against the wall and breathed while my muscles screamed to flee. My feet burned as someone halted outside the visible doorway.

"It's been far too long since there's been a touch on the soil other than my own." The voice was rich and deep and reminded me of my late grandfather. Far too kind a voice for someone exercising such atrocities. The man who stepped inside lacked the wrinkles his retreating hairline professed he should have. When he glanced at me, his eyes lacked his voice's humor. They carried the empty framing of winter, cold and dead.

I stepped away from him, careful not to touch the circle. The magistrate followed me, and I edged as close to the circle as I could. When he touched the top of my head, my vision swam. "So like her you are," he whispered. "And like her, you've stolen away Eli."

"Eli?"

"My son. He should ride the town with his brothers, yet he hovers behind to watch you. He always carried a heart sickness within him. Horsewhipped by the mere sight of a woman."

I melted under the layers of clothing: rugged pants tucked into men's boots; a plain, button-up shirt; and a coat hanging past my knees. No curves, nothing pink, and certainly nothing womanly about me. "I'm more likely to be mistaken for a boy than a woman. I've not distracted your son, sir. He wishes to die."

"He's already dead."

"Not completely. The bell ties him to this world. He wishes to rest."

The magistrate stepped across the circle. "Simpering fool was always the weak one. Maybe it's time to replace him." He reached for the bell.

"Wait!" I shouted, and his gnarled hand stopped mid-reach. "Why do you keep them animated like this? To serve what purpose?"

"To serve life! My sons were unfairly and untimely ripped from me at the prime of their youth. Why ask such questions though, when you already know this having been in my library."

His thumb smudged a blood droplet as he retrieved the bell. It sounded once, and Eli materialized before us. I scooted closer to the door until my back leaned against a workbench. Now that he was within the circle, I could not break it.

Eli's green eyes glowed in the room's dimness. "Kill me," he whispered, and the magistrate clenched his fist around the bell.

"After all I've done for you and your brothers, you truly beg for death?"

I glanced over my shoulder. A lantern flickered on the table.

While Magistrate Leunt argued with his son, I reached back and grasped the lantern by its base. Its heat burned my fingers for a moment before I tossed it across the circle's threshold. Its glass casing shattered, and the spilled oil caught in a bright flash of flame.

"Dammit," the magistrate muttered and shoved the bell into his pants' pocket. He removed his jacket and used it to beat the flames. Eli swiveled and nodded once in my direction. My thoughts were correct.

Arrogant as the day, the magistrate had failed to protect against non-human physical intrusions.

While he danced with the flames, I smeared my bare foot across the dirt and broke the physical circle. The shock drove the magistrate to his knees as the circle howled, and I retrieved the bell from his pocket.

I had but a minute before he would recover, so I made the only choice available to someone as thoroughly outclassed as I was—I ran.

Boots abandoned, I pounded up the stairs in quite the unladylike fashion. The bell in my hands rang louder than my footfalls, and I burst through the front door as I struggled to listen over the sounds of my haggard breath. Halfway to the statue, I heard them.

Bells.

Hundreds of bells rattling and clanging and jingling as the sun blessed the Yule day. Behind me, hoof beats on the road approached.

Mr. Henry had clambered up to the statue's arms, where he beckoned for me to hurry.

Between gasps, I shouted at him, "The horse's bells...are ringing! Why...Why haven't they...stopped?"

"We need a circle!" called Mr. Henry.

My feet were nearly numb, but the snow's sting sharpened my focus. There was no time to draw a circle this large. "Quick, make a circle! Shoulder to shoulder, and ring the bells!" I shouted.

Some villagers stopped ringing their bells when they spotted me; none of them made an effort to form a circle beyond my parents, and even they cocked their heads at the request.

The Ringers stopped before the group, and several villagers dropped their bells. A child cried—a whimpering hiccup that awoke the town to the danger before them. Several stepped back while others made motion to leave.

Mr. Henry stopped their flight by clapping his hands together. "Here's your chance. You can fall prey to the Ringers, or you can do what she says. Make a circle and keep ringing those bells! For Elizabeth and Peter and Charlene and countless others we've lost to the bells."

Like a well-manned loom, they circled around the statue with each person's shoulder pressed up against the next as they rang the bells of Yule. I stood in the middle and called out to Mr. Henry. "Now what?"

"Destroy the bell."

"What? How? The power—"

"Is broken. It's just a bell."

One Ringer reached for the woman in front of him. I held the bell in both hands and snapped its wooden handle. Both pieces tumbled to the ground. Blood coursed off the silver to pool in the snow. The Ringers shrieked—ungodly sounds of torture and joy—yet one set of green eyes found mine. Tears pooled in Eli's eyes as he smiled.

A few villagers paused in their ringing, and Mr. Henry cried out, "Keep ringing those bells."

I fished the bell out from the bloody pool and wiped off the remaining droplets with the corner of my jacket. Once clean, I held the bell by its crown and gave it five chimes.

Five brothers faded from the world. Five sets of bells fell tarnished to the snow below.

And in the distance, a disheveled man rode toward us. I pushed my way through the villagers until I stood as a shield before them.

They filed in behind me, a united wall as the magistrate approached. His years weighed on him like sand; his skin sagged as he dismounted. Each step grayed his hair until it flashed white, and his shoulders curled in on his frame until he hunched over—one lone man before the people of Dekwood.

"Magistrate?" a woman whispered, and he cupped a hand to his ear.

"Say again?"

"Do you know where you are, Magistrate?"

He frowned at her. "No, where am I?" His eyes blinked. When he met my gaze, recognition lit them. He raised a finger in my direction, but Mr. Henry placed himself before me. The *viziol* on his neck pulsed.

"Your magic has returned?" I asked.

He nodded, and the magistrate flinched. Mr. Henry touched his thumb to the old man's forehead. Five counts before the magistrate cackled and tumbled away. His feet carried him to his horse. The effort would cost him, but he mounted swiftly with another cackle. His horse's bells released a sour note as he galloped for the forest of the dead.

"Should we pursue him?" I asked, and Mr. Henry shrugged.

"The spells he used have warped him. Hard to say whether he has any real magic left."

"Good riddance," someone cried, and others muttered similar statements.

My mother draped an arm around my shoulder and pressed her lips to my head. I shivered in the Yule sun. "Can somebody fetch me some shoes? I seem to have left mine behind."

Laughter draped the village in a glow, and behind me, someone said, "Dearie, you can have whatever you want."

Spring brought life to the village. My mother gave birth to my brother, Saul, and the village of Dekwood established Mr. Henry as the town sorcerer. They bestowed the magistrate's mansion on him, though he never set foot inside. Rather than linger with the illness such dark magics cast upon a place, he rebuilt his home at the edge of town and set about restoring the success of its people.

The magistrate never returned to Dekwood.

Some believed he could be heard cackling madly in the forest of the dead, which never grew again, while others said he blew away in the wind that swept over the village in the coming days. Others still told tales of his voice ringing out in the highest pitches of the jingling bells deep in winter.

The bells returned no one, but their jingle held a bitter sweetness for the people of Dekwood until such a time as they forgot the Ringers. When the villagers kept their fear no longer, the forest returned and the looms sang songs of the bravery of the people. They smiled to think of the magic that had saved them.

And the red-headed girl behind the magic.

I can't take all the credit for this one as the baseline idea for this came from my husband. We were driving around Seattle when he said, "What if jingle bells were the bringers of evil? The sound summoned something from our nightmares?" His questions spun other questions in me. All of our fairytales and mythos have fragments of truth to them. What if Christmas did as well?

My brain envisioned undead creatures in red riding white horses through the snow as they traveled to a Victorian town straight out of a Dickens novel. Once there, they would feed on the souls of the outspoken and the misbehaved. The town knew they were coming by the jingling of bells. Just think of how well the lyrics to *Santa Claus is Coming to Town* fit with this picture? And thus, the Ringers were born.

Raven Oak

MR. AND MRS. MISTLETOE

BY MAIA CHANCE

Welcome to the retro-future, something different than the fairytale land in which Maia Chance usually resides. This is easily my favorite work of Maia's as it both pokes fun at several local neighborhoods while serving as cheeky social commentary on both gender roles and classism. Toss in the 1950's setting and you have a fabulous story reminiscent of *The Stepford Wives* and *Fallout*. Spinsters always get a bad rap—or they did until Miss Pynn!

–Raven Oak

Spinsters always wear glasses—at least they do in the movies. As though eye-slackening bookishness were the outcome of a life without manly kisses.

I myself am a spinster, living out my days as Mistlehurst's town librarian in pilled wool and bunion-provoking shoes. And yes, I wear glasses. A cat eye pair, if you must know, my lone tribute to fashion. To all appearances I have nothing better to do on long winter evenings than curl up with my robotic cat—purr switch set to Hearthside Rumble—in front of my Nuclear Flame and knit booties for other ladies' babies.

And yet, with my glasses, I am able to *see*.

Paradoxically, at the moment my observational faculties were being recruited, Dr. Cornelius's examination room was a blur of steel and creamy green. I'd removed my glasses at the good doctor's request. They sat on a cart across the room.

"Your appetite, Miss Pynne, you say it has diminished?"

"Well, it has never been good." *You look like a washboard and a couple of broomsticks*, Mother tells me. "Lately, however, I find myself forgetting meals entirely."

"I see." Dr. Cornelius looked into one of my ears through a probe. His bushy white beard brushed my cheek; I held my breath. He checked the other ear. Then he pushed his probe into the breast pocket of his white coat. "You may sit up," he said, rolling away on his stool to the desk.

I clutched the examination gown to my chest as I struggled upright. For the first time, I noticed the mistletoe ball—blurry, of course—dangling by a red ribbon, well, not *quite* over the examination table, but close. How festive.

Dr. Cornelius's back was to me as he scribbled something on a pad. "You have come down with female prohenteriariosis," he said without turning.

"I have? What...what is that?"

"The Victorians termed it hysteria" —Dr. Cornelius chuckled— "but of course they were mistaken about many things, foremost that it is not a disease of the womb but of the brain."

"I am not *hysterical*, Doctor. I have frequently heard the complaint, indeed, that I am *too* stable. Even when little boys run in the library, I do not—"

"Female prohenteriariosis takes many forms, although its root cause is always the same." He swiveled to face me.

"It is?" Why didn't these medical gowns cover you up properly?

"Oh-ho, yes." Dr. Cornelius pointed at the mistletoe. "The cause of your disease, Miss Pynne, is that you're not a *Mrs.*"

"What is the cure?"

Dr. Cornelius ripped the prescription from his pad and passed it over. I couldn't read it without my glasses. "Three pills daily—you may cut them into quarters, as some find them difficult to swallow. Do not be alarmed by their pink hue. I should add that it is perhaps not too late, Miss Pynne, to harvest some of your ova and preserve them. Tremendous scientific discoveries have been made."

"I am quite, *quite* happy as an unmarried lady, Dr. Cornelius."

"Your health suggests otherwise. Miss Pynne—if I may—it would be wise to engage in pastimes outside of the confines of the library and the home—I understand you live with your mother?"

"Yes."

"The Mr. and Mrs. Mistletoe Pageant is tonight—"

"I have plans." A lie, but I'd rather stick a pickle fork in my cornea than attend *that* tribute to dental hygiene.

"I did not mean to suggest that you should *view* the pageant—I suppose you wouldn't have anything to wear—it's a formal event, you understand."

"No...."

"However—well, as you know, I am a judge of the pageant each year—the people of this town seem to believe I have good judgment."

"You're a pillar of the community, Doctor. How many babies did you deliver in the past year?"

"Forty-two."

"Goodness gracious, we'll have to build a new school."

"A small matter has come up that, perhaps, you would find diverting to assist me with. Will you assist me, Miss Pynne?"

"Well...."

"It is for your own good."

"What is the task?" I could already taste the sour rubtex balloons and smell the atomo-perc coffee.

"The pageant scepter has been stolen."

"Oh, dear me. Was it valuable?"

"What sort of question is *that*, Miss Pynne?" Dr. Cornelius's cheeks turned a blurred cherry-red.

"Oh, I did not mean—"

"That scepter sits at the very center of everything Mistlehurst stands for—the New American Territories Dream! Prosperity, tradition, Christmas, *home*. At the end of each year, Mr. and Mrs. Mistletoe, a handsome, prosperous man and his beautiful wife, stand hand in hand together at the helm of Mistlehurst's bright future. A future filled, not with subpars and limp morals and filth but with intelligent, well-proportioned families, all with beautifully-formed work ethics." Dr. Cornelius was breathless. I dared not wipe away the fleck of his spittle that had landed on my cheek. "You do not talk much with the townspeople, do you, Miss Pynne?"

"In the library, we *whisper*—"

"You are too meek. Too eager to obey instructions. You keep quiet as a mouse, don't you?"

I pictured the pot roast-shaped silhouette of my mother before the light of the megavision screen. *She* said I was too meek, too obedient, mousy.

"I do have Tykes' Story Hour at three o'clock," I said to Dr. Cornelius, "and I simply couldn't miss *that*, but Mrs. Orville comes in to volunteer at the library this morning. She could surely look after things for a few hours, couldn't she?"

"How seriously you take your little job at the library, Miss Pynne."

"I will find your scepter, Doctor."

"I hope you will. We cannot complete the pageant tonight without it." Dr. Cornelius described how the six-year reigning Mrs. Mistletoe, Mary Chadwick of 151 Montcrest Avenue, had talkaphoned him just before my appointment that morning to report that the scepter had been stolen from her home. "I am extremely busy, Miss Pynne, and today no fewer than five women are due to give birth, so you finding the scepter, well, it will not only be helping *you*, it will be helping me, too."

"One-fifty-one Montcrest Avenue," I said. "Should I begin there?"

"Miss Pynne, I did not like to say it, but female prohenteriariosis is a...well, it is a degenerative condition. If you are to slow its terrible tide, you must take charge of matters. Talkaphone me the moment you locate the scepter, please." Dr. Cornelius left.

I wiped the spittle fleck from my cheek, hurried back into my glasses, dressed, and tidied my hair. I went out to the waiting room with its tank of rubtex Reel-Fish and walls thick with photographs of babies Dr. Cornelius had delivered. Newborn babies all look the same, don't they?

At the desk, Miss Gint was occupied on the talkaphone. I waited patiently. I am an excessively patient lady. A red-ribboned ball of mistletoe dangled even here, as though poor Miss Gint would like to kiss every rashy, feverish, or decaying person who stopped at her desk.

I settled my bill and went outside onto Main Street.

Such a discomfiting sensation, walking *west* along Main Street at this hour rather than east toward the library. A bubbling of glee coursed through me like champagne. I ignored it, as I am strictly a tap water lady. This wasn't playing hooky; this was for my health.

Salt gritted the sidewalks. Shop windows unfurled blankets of Kyndlyke-Snow, twinkling atomic lights, and shiny gifts. A big band "Jingle Bells" leaked out the post office doors. Women in coats and hats steered prams and led cherubic children by the hand and HooverPets by their leashes. Most of the women's husbands were miles away in the Suspended City office estate, which is treeless, bleak, and infested—so I have heard—with subpar encampments.

I left the prescription for my pills at Huxley Pharmacy and continued on. Soon I was walking up the gentle slope of Montcrest Avenue. Lawn ornaments—tasteful yet exorbitant, installed by workers, not husbands—cluttered every mock Tudor's yard. Reindeer, Santa Clauses, elves, candy canes, and angels, all glowing and pulsating in the wintry light. The Moores' yard boasted a red-and-white striped hot air balloon with Mrs. Claus in the basket. Slowly it floated up to rooftop height and down again.

Every thirty seconds or so a gleaming hovermobile whooshed past me, hover pads skimming the street, chrome mirroring bare trees and gray sky. Behind windshields I glimpsed frozen hairdos, mostly blond.

I hadn't mentioned to Dr. Cornelius that I knew what the six-year reigning Mrs. Mistletoe, Mary Chadwick, looked like. I knew what her husband, Merton Chadwick—a.k.a. Mr. Mistletoe—looked like, too. I had seen their blinding smiles on the front page of the *Mistlehurst Gazette* year after year. Their eyes seemed empty until one realized that they were simply trying not to crinkle their crow's feet.

The Chadwick house was a bloated mock Tudor with latticed windows, one turret, and a two-hovermobile garage. A pearly Hover-Benz floated in the driveway. A Helper Hack with rubtex tires, not hover pads, was parked behind it.

I heard whooshing behind me and turned to see another Hover-Benz, this one fleshy pink, jolt to a stop. A mound of a woman in a white fur coat, scarlet lipstick, and pillbox hat got out. A clipboard protruded from her large handbag.

"You're the librarian, aren't you?" she said, marching over. "Miss Din? Why are you gawking at the Chadwicks' house?"

"I am Miss Pynne. And you are?"

"Why, Mrs. Glover—Betty Glover. Is Mrs. Chadwick delinquent on a library fine? Is that why you're here?" It sounded like a joke, but Betty's baby-blues were guileless, crisped at the edges with black mascara.

"I am here to look into a...matter."

"A matter?" The mascara crisps quivered. "What matter?"

"It is to do with the pageant—"

"*What?*" Betty's voice dropped an octave and she grabbed my arm.

"The Mr. and Mrs. Mistletoe Pageant. Dr. Cornelius asked me to help find—"

"The scepter."

"You know?"

"Of *course* I know. I am the pageant committee chairlady. Mrs. Chadwick talkaphoned me the very *minute* she learned it was gone." Betty dropped my arm and wobbled to the front door in her high heels.

I contemplated going back to the library. It was very nearly time for my hot water with lemon, you see, and Mrs. Orville, well, once I saw her *dog-ear a library book*. Yet there was something infuriatingly officious about this Betty person. I joined her on the front porch.

A holly wreath decorated the door. The holly was rubtex, not real, and at four-second intervals it released a *pssssssssst* of woodsy perfume.

"Isn't that simply *lovely*," Betty said, her voice regaining a non-demonic register. "Makes me want to sing 'Joy to the World.'"

I hoped she would not.

The door swung open and Mary Chadwick appeared, blond-helmeted, almost-movie-star beautiful, in a white chiffon robe fluffed with marabou feathers. "Yes?" Mary made the same baby-doll blink that Betty had, and it was difficult to say who had executed it best. Mary's was prettier, but Betty's had been dumber.

"Mrs. Chadwick, it is I, Betty Glover—the chairlady of the pageant—you talkaphoned me earlier this morning?"

"Oh! How silly of me! I almost didn't recognize you. You were here only a few weeks ago at our little cocktail do."

"That's right. My husband, Mr. Glover—Bert—mixed you a pink squirrel, and both you and Mr. Chadwick said you'd never drunk one before and it was marvelous."

"Yes. Pink stains on the sofa cushions even now." Mary's white teeth glinted. "What can I do for you? I'm *terribly* busy with last-minute preparations for the pageant tonight."

Mary had yet to acknowledge my presence, probably assuming I was some sort of drab clerical assistant. But Dr. Cornelius had asked *me* to look into the disappearance of the scepter. Not Betty. I said, "Mrs. Chadwick, I am here about the stolen pageant scepter."

"*We* are here for—ah—*that*," Betty said.

"Oh. I see. Who are you?"

"Miss Pynne."

"Come in, then. I'll show you where we kept it."

Mary led us into the entry hall. A HooverPet buzzed toward us, yapping. It was a Corg-eez model, surprisingly, not a Dober-mince. Mary went up a curved staircase and Betty and I followed. Thankfully, the Corg-eez could not surmount the first step. Upstairs, everything was spic and span. The Chadwicks didn't have children, according to the *Mistlehurst Gazette*.

We entered a bedroom. Pink and orange roses bloomed on the drapes and the coverlets of two narrow beds. Betty gawked at the separate beds; I pretended not to see them.

"We kept it here," Mary said, stopping at the cluttered vanity table. A rectangular glass box sat on a green velvet cushion. "Under there."

"Not locked up?" I asked.

"No. Why would we? It isn't even made of metal, let alone gold. It's only rubtex."

I nodded. The scepter always figured prominently in the *Mistlehurst Gazette* photographs: a gold-tone staff topped with a red bow and a ball of faux mistletoe.

"Why does the glass box have little holes in it?" I asked. You could have kept a hamster alive under there.

"I don't know, honestly," Mary said. "To keep the rubtex from going soft?"

"Why don't we discuss this downstairs?" Betty said with another anxious glance at the beds.

"Wait," I said. "Isn't there anything else you can tell me, Mrs. Chadwick?" I tried to recall the detective novels I'd read at the library. *Only*, mind you, to ensure that smut is kept out of my library. "When was the last time you saw the scepter?"

"Last night, when I was cold-creaming my face. I always look at the scepter while I'm preparing for bed. It soothes me. Why don't we go downstairs?" Mary led the way out. Betty and I followed.

Downstairs, Mary billowed over in her robe to a drinks table in the living room. "What would you like?" she called.

Betty and I sat on a long, low white sofa.

"Nothing for me," I said. Even fruitcake fumes are too much for me.

Betty eyed the pink stain on the cushion next to her. "Nor I," she said.

Mary spun around and posed in front of the picture window, a clear drink in her hand. "All right. What else would you like to know? Be quick about it. I must hook myself up to the exercise machine soon, and then I must rest."

"Do you believe the scepter was stolen during the night, or in the morning?" I asked.

Mary sipped her drink. "I swallow two Snorils every night, put on my eye mask, and pop in my ear plugs. I have no idea. We *do* keep the house locked tight, of course."

Betty said, "The obvious culprit is the help, naturally."

"That's what *I* thought," Mary said, "but I gave Dolores—my housekeeper—the morning off since I cannot *abide* the sound of her suction cleaner, and anyway, I never eat a bite on pageant day."

"No one else entered the house?" I asked, staring past Mary. A man in blue coveralls was leaning a ladder against the house, just outside the windows.

"No."

"What about that man outside?"

"The what?" Mary said, tipping at the waist like an inquisitive bird.

"The man." Although I am aware that it is rude, I pointed.

The three of us looked at the man. He was headed up the ladder with wired Christmas lights looped around his shoulder. Young, black-haired, brown-skinned, with the taut efficiency of the very fit.

"His hands look *ever* so strong," Betty said, stroking her fur sleeve.

"Mmm," Mary said, sipping her drink without unhitching her eyes from the man.

"How long has he been here?" I asked.

"Oh, Wen has worked for us for *years*. Does the Christmas decorations, of course, and the hedges and lawn the rest of the year. We found him at the country club. Such a hard worker. His parents were subpars, *so* sad, but I think we can all agree that Wen is moving in the correct direction."

"I meant to say, how long has—ah—Mr. Wen been present *today*?" I said. "Could he have stolen the scepter?"

"He *looks* as though he would steal a scepter," Betty said, still watching Wen, still stroking her sleeve. "Simply *wrench* it from its cushion—"

"Yes, Wen could have stolen it." Mary drained her glass. "Through the window, with his ladder. I keep the bedroom window open. Is that all?"

Betty and I were somehow being herded out of the room.

"Might I speak to your husband, Mr. Chadwick?" I asked in the entry hall. I heard the Corg-eez yip in the distance.

"Merton really isn't one for ladies' conversation, but you will likely find him at Rodney's Steak Cave just about now. He takes two hour lunches. Goodbye."

Betty and I were outside. The door thudded.

"I will just go around and speak with the gardener," I said, going down the front steps. Perhaps I could lose Betty if I dilly-dallied.

"I'll catch up with you, Miss Vrynne."

"Miss Pynne. No need to join me." I kept walking, but when I rounded the house, I peeked back around the corner. Betty was sipping from a silver flask, lips goldfished around the spout. A tippler. Why had she refused a drink from Mary?

I approached the ladder and called, "Yoo-hoo. Mr. Wen?"

Wen looked down in surprise and then climbed to the bottom rung. "Yes?" His accent was thick with sweaty breezes and tangy fruits. His eyes were a becoming almond shape.

"Did you steal Mr. and Mrs. Chadwick's scepter?" I asked.

"Yes?"

"You did? But why?"

"Yes?"

"Mr. Wen does not speak English," I told Betty when I joined her at the front of the house.

"Oh." Betty stuffed the flask into her handbag. "Pity."

"I intend to speak to Mr. Chadwick at the—ah—the steak house."

"I do, too. I'll give you a lift."

Would Dr. Cornelius consider this endeavor a prohenteriariosis cure if Betty Glover tagged along everywhere? Come to think of it, Betty seemed like *she* might be afflicted with prohenteriariosis as well, even though she had a husband. She'd seemed so *appalled* by those separate beds.

On the way to Betty's Hover-Benz, I peered through the window of Wen's Helper Hack parked in the driveway. No scepter, unless it was buried beneath atomo-power packs and wires and colored lightbulbs.

In the Hover-Benz, Betty jerked into gear and we hummed down Montcrest Avenue. My side mirror whacked a life-sized twinkling angel that was too close to the curb.

"If the scepter is only made of rubtex," I said, "there does not seem to be a motive for stealing it."

"Unless whoever stole it didn't *know* it was only rubtex," Betty said.

"Perhaps it would be advisable to slow down," I said, covertly gripping both sides of my seat. "Oh look, there is young Mrs. Pitridge with her quintuplets. Aren't they sweet? I knitted ten booties in three days for that family. What a nice pram they have, too, with those white tires." Mistlehurst babies ride only in the cushiest prams, and when they become last year's model, they are promptly donated to less fortunate babies in Suspended City.

Betty pulsed on the brakes so we could look at the babies. Blonde Mrs. Pitridge waved. "So many triplets and quadruplets nowadays," Betty said. "When I was a girl, I didn't even know a single pair of *twins*. My, don't those little ones look *dusky*."

"Mrs. Glover!" I exclaimed. I stole a parting glance at the quintuplets. Betty was very coarse to mention it, and yet...how *had* fair Mrs. Pitridge and her ginger-haired husband produced those almond-eyed children?

Betty revved her reactor, and we zipped out of Main Street and onto the winding, wooded highway.

"Isn't Mrs. Chadwick *delightful?*" Betty asked. The speedometer crept upward.

"The very definition of it."

"She and her husband have won the pageant six years in a row, you know. No one is able to compete! Their turnout in the bathing suit segment last year was astonishing. Of course, *I* have never entered the pageant, but that's because my Bert is not pageant material, and let us be frank, neither are you and I, Miss Pynne. Ladies like us must content ourselves to be the little tugboats that keep these things running, you know, rather than the glamorous sleek yachts that steal the limelight." Betty sent me a desperate-eyed smile. "Toot-toot!"

I must make it perfectly clear that I have never, *ever* set foot in Rodney's Steak Cave. I *do* hover past it every Saturday afternoon when Grace from Mother's krochet klatch drives us to the extramarket for our week's shopping. Rodney's Steak Cave is what the architects probably term "daring," with its low rooflines and jutting angles. The rear overlooks the Mistlehurst Golf Green.

The reception foyer was dim. As soon as Betty and I stopped in front of the podium, a Robarmaid rolled up and said, "Take. Your. Coats." It was one of the swanky models that I'd only ever seen before on the megavision, with a metal dress made to look like a French maid's uniform. We handed over our hats and coats, and the Robarmaid rolled away.

An identical Robarmaid rolled up behind the podium. "Reservation. Please," it said.

"We don't have a reservation," I said. "We are here to meet Mr. Merton Chadwick."

A faint whirring from inside the Robarmaid. "Please. Come. This. Way."

Betty and I followed it into the smoky gloom of the restaurant.

Merton Chadwick lounged like a cigarette advertisement in a round leather booth. Alone. Trim gray suit, blond hair slicked and gleaming, pink cocktail. He took a pull of his cigarette, eyes narrowed, as he watched us approach.

"Mr. Chadwick?" I said. My voice sounded so tinny and *small* in here. Was it the piano jazz, or all the murmuring conversations, or this thick green carpet?

"That's me," Merton said. He looked at Betty. "Hi there, Betty. Almost didn't recognize you in that gorgeous fur—thought you were a movie star or something." He beamed and Betty simpered. We scooted into the booth. "How's the new Hover-Benz working out for you, Mrs. Glover?"

"It's peachy, Mr. Chadwick," Betty said. She turned to me. "Mr. Chadwick sold me my new hovermobile."

I was familiar with Chadwick's Fine Hovermobiles, although of course my style of living does not require such luxury.

"Drinks, ladies?" Merton asked.

"Yes, please," Betty said. "I see you're having a pink squirrel, Mr. Chadwick—I'll have one of those, too."

Merton signaled the Robarmaid. "And you, Miss—?"

How did he know I was a *Miss*? Was my prohenteriariosis visible to the naked eye? "Miss Pynne. Water, please," I said.

Merton winked, and I fumbled open my handbag just to give myself something to do.

Merton gave our order to the Robarmaid, and as it turned to wheel away, Merton smacked its bottom. It made a metallic clang.

"Oooo!" Betty cried, jumping as though it had been *her* derriere.

"You. Are. So. Naughty," the Robarmaid said, and buzzed away.

Betty was giggling and pawing Merton's arm. "You *are* naughty, Mr. Chadwick."

Merton settled back, smug.

"I *so* adore pink squirrels," Betty said. "You do remember that it was Bert and me who first introduced them to you, at your cocktail party a few weeks back?"

"Bert?" Merton said. "Oh, yeah. Bert. Had a real nice time playing squish with him at the racquet club on Wednesday."

"Squish?" Betty said. "No. Bert went out in *golf* clothes. He told me all about your golf game."

"It *was* golf, wasn't it?" Merton's face lit with a slow smile, but his eyes flashed a cornered-animal look.

Betty was frozen, her cheeks gone gray beneath her rouge crème. "Golf."

Merton said, "Now then. What can I help you two with? Let me guess: it's that scepter business, right?"

"Yes," I said. "Dr. Cornelius has entrusted me to find it."

"You? Say, where have I seen you before?"

"I am the librarian of the Mistlehurst Public Library."

"Welp, wouldn't have seen you *there*, then, seeing as I haven't cracked a book since high school." Merton chuckled. "Say, why did Dr. Cornelius ask *you* to look into it, when Betty here is the pageant chairwoman?"

"Chair*lady*," Betty said in a faraway voice.

"Because Dr. Cornelius believes that I am a competent and observant lady," I said. Did prohenteriariosis give one a neck rash? My neck felt rashy.

"Okay then, and why are you talking to me? I didn't steal the scepter. For crying out loud, it was stolen out of my own bedroom."

"I do not believe you stole it," I said, "but I hoped that you might be able to provide some sort of, well, that you might be able to fill in the blanks, as it were, about the...."

My words dribbled off. Merton wasn't listening; his eyes were caught on something across the restaurant.

Thick glasses do not permit discretion. I leaned out of the booth and craned my neck. Merton was watching a handsome young man in animated conversation with a group of diners.

Merton snapped back to attention. "Thought I knew that fella but maybe not. What were you saying, Miss Frinne?"

I leaned back into the booth. "Miss Pynne."

"Something about the scepter?"

"Yes. Do you have any idea who stole it?"

"None, except that I picked up the talkaphone at work yesterday morning to hear the wife squealing and crying about how it had gone missing. It happened *after* I went to work, you see. I figured the housekeeper took it. Dolores. She's a subpar, even though Mary insists she isn't." Merton sipped his pink squirrel.

"*Yesterday* morning?" I asked.

"You betcha."

Mary or Merton was lying about when the scepter was stolen. *Both* of them could be lying, in fact, and had neglected to iron out their story.

"I gotta tell you," Merton said, "Mary's going to be sore because the pageant bylaws state that if you don't take care of the scepter, you'll be disqualified from all future pageants. Not that I care much—hell, isn't winning six times enough?—but Mary's real upset. Gives her something to do I guess. She always wanted kids."

Mary hadn't seemed upset in the least.

"Just a moment," I said. "Are you suggesting that if the scepter isn't recovered today, then you and Mrs. Chadwick will be disqualified from competing in tonight's pageant?"

"Afraid so." A Robarmaid placed a steak reverently before Merton. Merton dug in.

My, my. *There* was a motive for stealing the scepter: disqualifying the unbeatable Chadwicks.

"I wish to see a list of all of the contestants in tonight's pageant," I said to Betty once we were inside her Hover-Benz. I looked pointedly at her handbag.

Betty placed a hand over the protruding clipboard. "No."

"Don't you want me to find the scepter? The pageant is in—" I checked my wristwatch "—only five hours. Don't you have the best interests of the pageant at heart?"

"Of course I do!"

"Then allow me to see the list."

"Golf." Betty was unscrewing her flask. "I was supposed to buy *that*? That bastard will use any excuse not to get in bed with me." She tipped the flask and suckled.

I took the opportunity to seize Betty's clipboard.

"Hey!" she said, but halfheartedly.

I flicked through the pages and found a list of the competing couples—seven in all. Seven! Where to begin? Tykes' Story Hour does not run *itself*, you realize.

"You don't need to bother with all of the contestants," Betty said, staring at nothing through the windshield. "Most are in awe of the Chadwicks. They know they don't stand a chance of winning. They only compete for the fun of it, and out of a sense of town pride and Christmas spirit." She swiveled to face me, her face crooked, eyes moist, mascara smudged. "*No one* can compete with Merton and Mary Chadwick."

"Wait," I said. "You say *most* of the contestants are in awe of them?"

"The only couple who stands a chance is Jackson and Ginger Dubonnet. They're new to town, but Dr. Cornelius thinks they are a spectacular specimen of an all-New American Territories sort of married couple. I heard him say as much."

"To whom?"

"I don't recall." Betty cranked her reactor and reversed out of the Steak Cave parking lot without even looking behind her. We lurched forward onto the highway.

"Where are we going?" I asked, clinging to the door.

"To the Dubonnet residence, silly."

The Dubonnet house was, like the Chadwicks', a grandiose mock Tudor, but its laurel hedges were immature and the ivy had crept only a foot up the side. No hovermobiles sat in the long brick driveway, but Betty and I went to the front door, anyway. I knocked. A wreath of rubtex candy canes decorated the door. With a *psssssst* it wafted sweet peppermint.

My spirits lifted. Perhaps I'd find the scepter here. Why ever not?

A small, black-haired maid answered the door. Betty and I learned that Ginger Dubonnet was not at home but booked into the Splendid Boudoir Beauty Parlor.

Minutes later, Betty had lodged her Hover-Benz in a mound of snow next to the Splendid Boudoir on Main Street. We were about to go inside when Dr. Cornelius, in a wool coat and a fedora, stopped. "Miss Pynne, good afternoon."

"Oh, hello, Doctor," I said. Why did my voice sound so *mewling*?

Dr. Cornelius's eyes were on Betty. "Mrs. Glover, I wasn't aware that you were a library-goer."

"Oh, I've only just met Miss Pynne today," Betty said. Her eyes flicked around, and she lowered her voice. "Dr. Cornelius, what will we do at the pageant if *it* isn't recovered?"

"We will carry on," he said. "Mistlehurst *needs* the pageant. Mr. and Mrs. Mistletoe are the irreplaceable torch-bearers of our town's brighter tomorrow. The scepter is a mere emblem. I believed, Mrs. Glover, that I was the only person who knew of the scepter's disappearance."

"Oh, no. Mrs. Chadwick talkaphoned me *promptly* this morning—perhaps even before she talkaphoned you."

"I find that difficult to imagine," Dr. Cornelius said.

A woman pushing a double-seater pram stopped beside us. "Hello, Mrs. Glover," she said with a smile. "You haven't seen the twins yet."

"Mrs. Killigan, how nice to see you. Let me at the little sweetie-pies." Betty bent over the pram and began coochie-cooing.

"Miss Pynne," Dr. Cornelius said to me in an undertone, drawing me aside, "I am most disappointed in you."

My neck prickled. "She—I'm only—"

"I suggested that you look into this matter as a way for you to take your degenerating health into your own hands. Enlisting the help of a woman like Mrs. Glover is, in fact, contraindicated in the cure."

"I did not enlist her, precisely. She elbowed in and I—"

"Do not share *anything* you learn with her—you haven't, have you?"

"No." Well, I *hadn't* in point of fact. Not deliberately.

"What have you learned?"

"Nothing." Yes, that was a lie but only because I saw Dr. Cornelius's pulse in a vein on his forehead.

"I feel it is only right to tell you, in the strictest confidence," he said, "that Mrs. Glover is not stable."

"Is it female prohenteriariosis?"

"I am afraid so."

We both looked at Betty tickling one of the twins. She *did* have a frenzied edge, but I had chalked it up to her tippling.

Dr. Cornelius looked at the twins with paternal pride. "I delivered those boys into the world. Fine little specimens, aren't they? Thick hair. Big hands. Nice broad foreheads."

"Oh, indeed," I said. The twins looked to *me* like unbaked bread rolls.

"I would advise you not to believe a word that Mrs. Glover says, Miss Pynne. She is *unreliable*, and what is more, she is a snoop. Why, quite recently I opened the door of my private office at my practice to find her listening at my key-hole. I must be going—I am expected at the hospital. It's Mrs. Knightley, two days early. Talkaphone Miss Gint at the practice the minute you learn anything about the scepter." Dr. Cornelius tipped his fedora and trundled away.

Betty bade farewell to the mother and her babies. "Dr. Cornelius didn't even say goodbye to me? Snob," she said to me. Her lipstick had bled into the lines around her lips. "Just between you and me, Miss Pynne, I think he's *up to something.*"

"I really don't—"

"Last month, I happened to overhear him on the talkaphone with Dr. Pater in Laurel Hill."

Laurel Hill was a neighboring town as richly treed and moneyed as Mistlehurst. "With your ear to the keyhole?"

"No! Did he tell you that?" Betty turned puce. "I had only bent to retrieve my dropped earring in the vicinity of his keyhole."

"Oh, I see."

"And, well...." Betty leaned in. I smelled vodka. "*I think Dr. Cornelius is conducting medical experiments on the townspeople.*"

"I beg your pardon?"

"You heard me."

"What evidence have you of this?"

"When he was on the talkaphone with Dr. Pater he said, clear as day, something about *town specimens.*"

"That could mean anything. That could mean, well, urine samples, to be terribly coarse."

"He also said that the Dubonnets are a marvelous specimen of an all-New American Territories married couple. Mark my words, there was something sinister about it. I think Dr. Cornelius is collecting our skin cells or hairs or something. I don't know. Maybe he's run out of mice for his laboratory."

"What laboratory?"

Betty tapped the side of her nose. "I'm seeing Dr. Frost in Pennyton now." She tottered into the Splendid Boudoir.

I followed, passing beneath a ball of mistletoe.

Did you know that mistletoe is a parasite? It lives high in the branches of host trees and attaches a little root onto a branch of its host, through which it steals water and nutrients. Quite like an umbilical cord, actually.

271

This was my first time inside the Splendid Boudoir, since I have my hair trimmed every four months at Ethel Strong's Hair Salon.

"Yes?" a girl said to Betty and me from her seat at the shrimp pink reception desk.

"I wish to speak with Mrs. Dubonnet," I said.

The girl blinked. "We do not allow persons off the street to interrupt our clients while they're in the middle of a treatment."

"I have an appointment for a Wasp-Waisting at three o'clock," Betty said. "I'm early, but I'd *so* enjoy a cup of tea and a magazine and a footstool."

The girl looked like she would have liked to refuse, but she nodded.

I said, "And *I* would like to book an appointment. Immediately. For a simple hair trim." I was nearly due for one, anyway.

"The hair cutter is booked solid, I'm sorry to say."

"What have you available?"

The girl studied her appointment book. "There is nothing left today except for one appointment in ten minutes with Mr. Guy for a Hair Rejuvenation Treatment."

"All right. I'll take that." Surely *hair rejuvenation* was nothing but a frivolous name for a trim.

Another girl in a shrimp pink smock emerged and led Betty and me into the Splendid Boudoir's inner sanctum. A bouquet of white rubtex roses went *psssssssssst* as we were led through. For a moment, I felt airy and feminine—*most* disconcerting—but thankfully the sentiment passed.

A few minutes later, Betty and I emerged from our separate changing rooms attired in the mandatory shrimp pink nyluxe robes and slippers. I was whisked away by Mr. Guy for my treatment. Evidently he was hard of hearing—

perhaps as the result of excessively long sideburns—because he did not hear when I said, "Just a trim, please."

I watched with horror in the mirror as Mr. Guy applied a pungent frosting of chemicals to my hair, yet I felt powerless to stop him. Through the hair chemicals I smelled rubtex roses. After every fragrant *psssst* I reminded myself it was best not to interrupt a man at his work.

Mr. Guy wrapped my head in flexi-metal and said, "Now then, seet in lounge for twenty meenoots."

I went to the lounge.

"Miss Pynne," Betty called from a pink chaise, "I would like to introduce you to Mrs. Dubonnet."

I went over and shook Ginger Dubonnet's hand. "Mrs. Dubonnet, I'm Miss Pynne, the town librarian."

"Call me Ginger." Ginger's voice sounded stuffy because of the white surgical rubber sling across her face. "Caught you looking at my nose, Miss Pynne. I'm getting the Temporary Nose Shaping. Ski jump style 2.b. I thought 2.b would be swell for the pageant tonight. Cute but classy at the same time. Jackson said he thought it'd go real nice with the scepter we're gonna win." Ginger laughed. She had white-blond waves and a dewy, film ingénue appearance, but her laugh called to mind a beery roadside tavern.

"You are quite confident of winning, then," I said.

"Course. I've met all the contestants. No one stands a chance except the Chadwicks, and let's face it, they're over the hill. The wrinkles on Mrs. Chadwick! Looks like someone skied across her face."

"Have you seen the scepter?" I asked.

"Not in person—I mean, why would I go into the Chadwicks' bedroom? Ick. Course, I *coulda* snuck off to their bedroom on account of the hullaballoo when Betty here sloshed her pink squirrel all over Mrs. Chadwick's white velvet couch."

"Mrs. Chadwick is very particular about her upholstery," Betty said.

"That was some swell distraction you made, Mrs. Glover," Ginger said. "*I* always use my hips, but we just work with what we've got, right?"

"It was not a deliberate spill," Betty said stiffly.

"Suit yourself." Ginger turned to me. "I never saw the scepter for real, but I've seen plenty of pictures."

Either Ginger didn't know the scepter had been stolen, or she was pretending not to know.

"Mrs. Glover?" a smocked attendant called from the doorway.

"Oh, fudge," Betty said. "Time for my Wasp-Waisting already." She gulped the rest of her tea—which emitted biting fumes—and swayed off.

Ginger put a conspiratorial hand on my sleeve. "I'm *so* glad Mrs. Glover's gone, because, well, I didn't want to say this in front of her on account of she's the pageant committee chairlady, and I wouldn't want to get anyone into *trouble*, but seeing as you're asking about things, Miss Lynn—"

"Miss Pynne."

"I think the Chadwicks are going to be disqualified tonight."

Here was something. "Oh? Why?"

"Because Jackson and me studied the pageant rulebook from cover to cover, and there's this bylaw in there, see, that says that if you don't take care of the scepter, then you're out on your ear."

"Then you *do* know that the scepter is gone."

Ginger smushed her lips. "It's gone?"

Oh, dear. "I mean to say, the scepter is—well, I'm sure it *will* be gone from the Chadwicks' possession and in your home by tomorrow, Mrs. Dubonnet."

"Okay," Ginger said doubtfully.

"Go on, what were you saying about the bylaws?"

"Well, the rules state plain and simple that you're supposed to take care of the scepter and never let it out of its special case. The winners are supposed to keep it in their bedroom, too."

"Why?"

"Don't know. Anyway, I saw the scepter *out of place* a couple weeks ago."

"Where?"

"It's like this: I went to test-drive a new hovermobile because Jackson promised me once he got that big promotion and we moved to Mistlehurst, he'd buy me a big white Hover-Benz. Well, I took one for a spin out at Chadwick's Fine Hovermobiles—Merton Chadwick was along—and when I got out I happened to glance into the backseat, and I saw the pageant scepter just *lying* there."

"Good heavens, how very peculiar."

"That's what I thought."

"When was this?"

"Oh, about three weeks ago."

"Before the Chadwicks' cocktail party?"

"Yes."

"And you didn't say a word to Mr. Chadwick at the time?"

"Nope. I was just opening my trap to ask him about it when he sort of stuffed the scepter, all secret-like, under the seat and slammed the door. Hiding it, you know. So I decided not to say anything. Well, I told my Jackson about it, and *he* said we oughta tell the pageant committee, but *I* said, why don't we keep it up our sleeves and wait and see how it all pans out?"

"But why? Wouldn't it have been nice to have the Chadwicks disqualified before the pageant so you might enjoy yourselves, assured of a win?"

"Naw. Jackson and me, we're fighters, see. We want to compete with the Chadwicks and show everyone we can outshine 'em onstage. We couldn't do that unless we were all up there onstage together tonight, neck and neck." Ginger smirked. "Course, *some* of us has got stringier necks than others. But I've got to hand it to Mary, she can still reel 'em in."

"Reel what in?"

"The men."

"You speak of her husband?"

"Haw! Merton? No. I just wonder if the pageant judges have got double standards, because at my physical examination—it's required to enter the pageant, you know— Dr. Cornelius strictly warned me about having anything to do with subpars, now that I've arrived in Mistlehurst. He said I wouldn't want to hurt my chances of becoming Mrs. Mistletoe."

"What have subpars to do with the pageant?"

Ginger shrugged. "Got to keep up appearances, is what I figured. But Mary Chadwick, well, I saw *her* with her subpar gardener in the back of his Helper Hack and let me tell you, they weren't having a businesslike chat back there. Not with her in that lacy—"

I coughed. "Mrs. Dubonnet, please." I didn't wish to hear lurid details, yet there *was* something important in this. I couldn't say precisely what. Mary Chadwick consorting with her handsome gardener, Wen? Nothing startling there. And why did my mind keep returning to those almond-eyed quintuplets in that pram? Those babies resembled Wen, I realized, but they were Mrs. Pitridge's babies, not Mary's. Perhaps Wen was some sort of gigolo.

"Sorry," Ginger said. "Betty told me you're a spinster. Don't know much about the birds and the bees, is that it?"

"You would be simply amazed by what one might read about in books," I said. "About the spilled pink squirrel. Why did you suggest that Mrs. Glover wished to create a distraction?"

Ginger giggled. "Well, isn't it obvious? So she could get herself a chance to flirt with Merton Chadwick while Mary was running around screaming and blotting soda water on the stain. *Everyone* adores Merton."

I thought of Betty's face when Merton had said that he'd been playing squish, not golf, with her husband. Things were not adding up correctly....

I sank back in the chaise. Rose-scented oxygen spritzed me from all sides, and my eyelids drooped.

Presently, Mr. Guy installed me beneath a whizdri dome. The sound was deafening; I could not think. Then he teased, snipped, and scraped at my hair, and whirled me around to face the mirror.

I screamed. "What have you *done*?" My neat, gray-threaded bun had been supplanted by guinea pig whorls of platinum blonde.

"You look like movie star, darlink," Mr. Guy said. He arranged a curl across my forehead.

No, I did *not* look like a movie star. I resembled a bespectacled goat in a movie star wig. There *is* a difference.

"All you require is a nice leepsteek and a Better-in-a-Sweater Suction Treatment," Mr. Guy said. "You make appointment now?"

"No, thank you," I said, standing. "I believe you've done enough, Mr. Guy."

I would be late for Tykes' Story Hour, but I was so very disgusted with everything that I opted to walk the six blocks to the library rather than ask Betty—wherever she was—for a lift.

As I walked, I attempted to formulate a theory as to who had stolen the scepter. I gave up. During the course of the day I'd assembled a lot of unrelated nonsense—Mistlehurst's dirty laundry, really—but nothing more.

I was only five minutes late to the library. I removed my coat, settled onto my stool, and read "The Night Before Christmas" aloud to the tykes and their teacher, Mrs. Klegg. Mrs. Klegg surreptitiously studied my new hairdo.

As I gazed upon the little sea of five-year-old cherubic towheads, I noticed for the first time that they looked as though they could've all been siblings.

Mrs. Klegg and the children left. Evening fell. The library was empty, dim, and cold. I shelved four carts of books. I would talkaphone Dr. Cornelius and inform him that I'd failed to find the scepter and pick up my prescription at Huxley Pharmacy. Then I would go home to eat my froze-in megavision dinner on my sofa tray next to Mother. And yes, I would decay with female prohenteriariosis like a forgotten, mildewed book, but in the larger scheme of things that was perfectly irrelevant.

I put on my coat and hat and reached for the black talkaphone on my desk.

It rang.

I jumped back as though burned. My heart shuddered.

It rang again.

I picked up the receiver. "Hello?"

An unfamiliar man's voice said, "Miss Pynne, the scepter will arrive, unharmed, at the pageant tonight."

"Who is this?" I asked.

Dial tone.

With a trembling hand I replaced the receiver. Should I tell the police? Should I tell Dr. Cornelius?

No.

Something unfamiliar bloomed in my chest, something red and tremulous like an unfurling poinsettia.

No. I wouldn't tell Dr. Cornelius about the talkaphone call; I'd go to the pageant, capture the scepter, deliver it to Dr. Cornelius, and *prove there was nothing the matter with me.* After that, I would demand that he tell me precisely what sort of tinkering he was doing with the wombs of the ladies of Mistlehurst.

Mr. & Mrs. Mistletoe 1957! SOLD OUT! read the marquee at the Mistlehurst Civic Auditorium. Christmas trees twinkled on the sidewalk. Shiny hovermobiles left couples at the curb, the men in overcoats and fedoras, the ladies in high heels and furs. A queue snaked away from the box office.

Tickets. I didn't have a ticket, and if the pageant was sold out, then I couldn't purchase one.

I went around to a slushy alleyway and found the side entrance. I know my way around the auditorium because I have judged the Mistlehurst Spelling Bee on a multitude of occasions. Not that I enjoy *boasting.*

Inside, I found my way to the lobby. I could only hope that the anonymous man on the talkaphone would be in the lobby, too. He was clearly someone who knew I was looking into the matter of the stolen scepter, but after my day of snooping about town, that could be anyone.

Mistletoe swayed from the lobby light fixtures, and everyone had a drink in hand. Voices droned. Perfume swirled. My neck itched. There were perhaps fifty men in here; how could I possibly discern which one had the scepter? Then there were the male pageant contestants backstage. Oughtn't I check on them, too?

"Miss Pynne," someone said. "I almost didn't recognize you in that...coif."

I spun around. "Oh. Dr. Cornelius."

"Why didn't you talkaphone?"

"I—"

"That shade doesn't suit you," Dr. Cornelius said, inspecting my platinum tufts. "A fawn tint would have been more appropriate."

"I thought a change was in order."

"Ah." Dr. Cornelius's eyes were sad. "Extreme behavior such as this" —he gestured to my hair— "causes me to wonder if your prohenteriariosis is more advanced than I previously thought."

"I don't care," I snapped.

His bushy white eyebrows knitted. "Have I asked too much of you, Miss Pynne?"

"No, you haven't."

"But you haven't located the scepter, have you? You do realize the implications, don't you? Mr. and Mrs. Chadwick will not be able to compete tonight because of the bylaw which—"

"I've found it."

"Oh. Well then, where is it?"

"It—it hasn't arrived yet. But it *will* be here."

"Who has it?"

I couldn't bear to say I didn't know, so I backed into the crowd and then hurried toward the auditorium.

"Miss Pynne!" someone shrieked over the hubbub. Betty Glover blocked my path in a clinging red gown and all lit up with vodka. "Why'd you sneak off like that from the Splendid Boudoir? Look at my wasp waist—isn't it teeny?"

"Well—"

"Where's your drink? Everyone's drinking. Let me fetch you a filthy martini."

"I—"

"Where are you sitting? Have you a ticket? No? How did you get in, then? Oh, never mind—I've got an extra because Bert's sister was going to come along only she can't make it because she's got one in the oven and her feet are swollen up like a couple of hams. Bert's going to be late because he hovered all the way to Laurel Hill to collect her and then he got roped into having dessert. Bert can't ever say no to dessert, especially Lauren's pineapple gel pyramids." Betty dug a ticket from her sequined clutch and passed it to me.

I was in.

The pageant began. From my seat between Betty and a tall, dark man—a stranger—we watched Round One: Evening Clothes. Husbands and wives paraded in complicated routes across the stage. The men wore tuxedos and the women wore evening gowns of scarlet, pine green, gold, and snowy white. Hair pomade, teeth, patent leather, and lipstick gleamed in the spotlights.

Due to Betty's status as pageant chairlady, I supposed, our seats were directly behind the judges' table. Dr. Cornelius hunched over his papers, scribbling. I was close enough to see flaked skin on his bald spot. The other judges had been introduced as Mrs. Gill of Mrs. Gill's Academy of Dance, and Robert M. Hanstan, a prominent Mistlehurst attorney.

Next came Round Two: Bathing Suits.

"Ginger looks a little too *orange*, don't you think?" Betty whispered moistly in my ear. "Although Jackson's bathing trunks are to die for."

Jackson Dubonnet's small red trunks were trimmed in white fur to match his wife's bathing suit.

After the Dubonnets had appeared in all their glossy-magazine glory, Merton and Mary Chadwick (in holly-print bathing suits) appeared stringy, dry, and inexplicably less appealing, like Thanksgiving leftovers.

"Lordy, there's Bert," Betty whispered.

Off to our left, Bert Glover was inching sideways to his seat. Everyone in the row swiveled their legs to let him pass. Betty slouched lower.

"Sorry I'm late," Bert whispered, huffing and puffing as he plopped into his seat. The seat hinges creaked.

Dr. Cornelius swiveled around, "Quiet, if you please," he whispered hotly. He didn't notice that his judging form had drifted from the table to the floor under his seat.

I bent and picked up the judging form. Betty was too busy scolding Bert to notice.

Dr. Cornelius's scrawl filled the margins of charts that resembled those butchers' diagrams with dashed lines dissecting cow or pig outlines into cuts of meat. Only these outlines weren't pigs or cows, but women and men. I stared blankly at the form. Shock, I suppose. In front of me, Dr. Cornelius was flipping through his papers on the judging table, searching for his missing form. Onstage, Mr. and Mrs. Fitzwilliam swiveled, doll-like, beneath the spotlight. As Dr. Cornelius's notes and arrows indicated, a "slight paunch" *did* hang over Mr. Fitzwilliam's waistband, and Mrs. Fitzwilliam's thighs *were* "dimpled 6/10."

My goodness me. Why hadn't I seen all of this earlier? Dr. Cornelius had told me that Mr. and Mrs. Mistletoe stood at the helm of Mistlehurst's future, which was to be filled with intelligent, well-proportioned families.

He had meant it to a tittle.

The reason that Mrs. Klegg's kindergarten class looked like siblings was because they *were* siblings. They were all little Chadwicks. Dr. Cornelius must be harvesting the Chadwicks' fertilized ovum at regular intervals. And now that the Chadwicks were looking a little dated, here were the fresh, beautiful Jackson and Ginger Dubonnet to take their places as the parents of new litters of Mistlehurstians. Mary Chadwick's contribution of ovum tainted by Wen—Mrs. Pitridge's quintuplets—was probably the reason Dr. Chadwick had warned Ginger Dubonnet to steer clear of subpars.

Dr. Cornelius bent to look for his missing form on the floor. I leaned forward and slipped it onto the judges' table. He found it and straightened.

So wrapped in thought was I, all the kissing around me did not at first register.

Yes, *kissing*. Two seats over, past that tall, dark stranger—who was rather handsome, I realized for the first time—a couple pretzeled together, groaning softly. Behind me came suctiony sounds, and when I turned I saw a man with his hand *quite* upon a woman's bosom. I will not tell you where *her* hand was. I was surrounded by a galaxy of kissing people. Fondling, moaning, writhing. I could not breathe; you must understand that I look away when there is even the *faintest* hint of an impending kiss on the cinema screen.

Onstage, Mr. and Mrs. Dixon paraded to a brassy rendition of "Let it Snow." Dr. Cornelius scribbled madly. That all seemed so dull, however, compared with the square lines of that handsome stranger's hand upon his knee, just next to me.

I glanced up into the stranger's face; he was already looking at me. Somewhere nearby I heard a *pssssssssst* and then, as one, the stranger and I lunged together, mouths open.

You couldn't have pried me from that delicious man with a spatula. My thoughts were fevered and bits of my body throbbed, bits that I didn't even know I *had*. His hand at the back of my skull—oh, the ecstasy.

And yet...there it was again. *Pssssssssssssst*.

I tore my lips from the man's. His eyes were briefly hurt before he turned to the woman on his other side and massaged her thigh, despite that she was already kissing someone else.

Psssssssssssssst.

Betty was kneeling on her seat and she had Bert by the lapels. "Come on, little Bertie," she said in a husky undertone, "why are you always holding out on me like this?"

Bert twisted sideways to get away, and his jacket fell open. In white-hot stage light, I saw it: the scepter. Its golden rod. Its green rubtex leaves.

Psssssssssst went the scepter.

The scepter emitted an odor, musky, blearily exciting, and it was making the entire audience mad with lust. *This* was why it was meant to be kept in Mr. and Mrs. Mistletoe's bedroom under that glass box with the little holes. It was designed to drive the pageant winners to bed.

Onstage, the curtains swished shut and the house lights went up for intermission. No applause—everyone was too busy necking. Bert floundered from his wife's grasp and stumbled away, over and around the legs of oblivious kissers. Dr. Cornelius swiveled around, eyes narrowed.

"Wait, Bertie!" Betty wailed.

I headed after Bert, treading on toes and bracing myself on shoulders and not even saying *excuse me*. I caught up to Bert on the steps leading up the side of the stage.

"Mr. Glover!" I said, panting.

He glanced over his shoulder and kept going. "Last thing I need is another dame cornering me," he said.

"It's not you that I want."

"Yeah, I heard that before, too." Bert disappeared behind the curtains.

I followed, glancing back to see Dr. Cornelius stomping, red-faced, up the steps behind me. Betty trailed in his wake, wailing "Bertie! It's been so long! Just one little kiss!"

Backstage was in commotion. Missuses and Misters darted around in bathing suits. Stagehands wheeled giant wooden teddy bears. Bert shouldered through, his brown jacket flapping. Up ahead, Merton Chadwick lounged against a wall in his holly-print bathing trunks, smoking. Bert rushed up to Merton and thrust the scepter in his hands.

"Thanks, Bert," Merton said, and with his cigarette dangling from his lip, he brushed the back of his hand tenderly down Bert's cheek.

"Oh no, you don't!" Betty shrieked. Her high heels clattered as she trotted past me. "Is *he* who's done it to you, Bert? The almighty Merton Chadwick? Is *he* why you say you're going golfing when really you're going to—to—? Is *he* why you won't kiss me anymore?"

"Now hold on there," Merton said in his newscaster's voice. "Bert here brought the scepter back as a favor to me, so I wouldn't be disqualified tonight. Said he found it in your dresser drawer, as a matter of fact. Why'd you steal it, Betty?"

"Shut up!" Betty screamed. She ripped the scepter from Merton's hand and hurried down the hallway toward the sign that said in glowing red, EXIT.

Dr. Cornelius and I broke into a run after her.

Dr. Cornelius wheezed as he ran. His beard bounced and his belly shook like a gel dessert. But I, with my spinster's shoes and no-nonsense limbs, clipped past him.

"Ha," I said.

"You'll die alone," Dr. Cornelius panted.

"But you'll die much sooner."

"You're diseased."

"There is no such thing as female prohenteriariosis. You made it up to manipulate me." I slammed out of the EXIT. Biting-cold air, starry sky. I faced the rear parking lot.

I heard a WHOOSH. There was Betty's white Hover-Benz, peeling out of a parking spot. I raced over and pounded on a rear window even though it was moving. "Betty!" I yelled.

Behind me, the EXIT door banged open. Dr. Cornelius.

Betty slammed on the brakes. The passenger door popped open. I dashed around and got in, and Betty whooshed out of the parking lot before I could even shut the door.

"This scepter's gotta go!" Betty said as we barreled down Main Street. The scepter was wedged between the two front seats. Betty was steering with one hand and tipping her flask with the other. "I'm going to throw it in the lake. Then all the man fish can go and kiss each other and the lady fish can sit home alone and cry."

Pssssssssssst went the scepter. I smelled a faint musky aroma, but I had no desire to kiss Betty.

"Why are you looking at me like that?" Betty asked.

"I suspect that, although the scepter's aroma inspires lust, it does not change one's natural inclinations."

"Baloney."

"Did you create a deliberate distraction by spilling the pink squirrel on Mary Chadwick's sofa?"

"I just couldn't stand it anymore, seeing my own hubby flirting with a—a fellow. Oh, God, what's wrong with *me*?"

"So you stole the scepter and took it home in the hopes that it would" —I coughed— "act as a marital aid?"

"Yes, but I thought it was broken, right up until Bert brought it into the auditorium."

"Why were the Chadwicks pretending that it had only been stolen yesterday or today?"

"Why? Ha! Because they were both using it for their own separate shenanigans, and half the time it probably wasn't even in their bedroom at all. Neither would've known someone had *stolen* it, you see."

Yes. And the self-assured Chadwicks probably didn't truly believe they'd be disqualified, no matter what the bylaws said.

Betty glanced in the rearview mirror. "Hell's bells. That's Dr. Cornelius's hovermobile." She stepped on the reactor pedal and we roared up Montcrest Avenue. Up ahead, bloated, glowing, moving forms loomed larger and larger.

I turned to see Dr. Cornelius's headlamps growing larger, too. "Faster," I said in spite of myself.

Betty went faster. And faster. My eyes were filled, blinded, by those headlamps—SMACK.

Nothing.

Nothing.

Then, rattling pain and a hissing, bent Hover-Benz hood. We'd hit a tree.

Dr. Cornelius's hovermobile was on the sidewalk just behind us. His headlamps blazed.

Pssssssssssst went the scepter.

"Goddam piece of junk," Betty said. She took a glug from her flask, tossed it in the backseat, snatched up the scepter, and jerked the door handle. Nothing; the door was smashed in, the window shattered.

Betty crawled out the window headfirst.

I climbed shakily out of my own door. We were in the Moores' yard. Silver rubtex snowflakes glittered on the roofline. Kyndlyke-Snow blanketed the lawn. The hot air balloon was completing a descent next to the driveway. Mrs. Claus waved.

"Stop!" Dr. Cornelius bellowed out his hovermobile's window.

Betty dashed to the balloon basket and clambered in. A second later, it was rising. Betty dumped Mrs. Claus overboard.

"Got you now!" Betty yelled down at Dr. Cornelius. "You'll never catch me!"

Dr. Cornelius revved the engine of his hovermobile. The hovermobile shuddered and the front end lifted.

"You're sick and crazy!" Betty screamed. "I heard you talking to Dr. Pater! I know what you're up to! I'm going to—to stuff this scepter down the chimney and let it *melt*!" The balloon had reached its zenith. Betty leaned out of the basket—it teetered—and dropped the scepter down the chimney.

Dr. Cornelius's hovermobile roared. In one ponderous arc it launched into the air. It landed on the rooftop and smashed to a final, sickening stop against the chimney. Shingles showered. Betty screamed. Dr. Cornelius slumped, unmoving, against the steering wheel. His white beard glowed.

The balloon completed its gentle descent to the Kyndlyke-Snow on the lawn. Betty was weeping. "I think

286

he's dead," she said, almost falling out of the basket. She was missing a shoe. "That's all right then, isn't it, Miss Pynne?"

"It's fine." I straightened my glasses. I looked around at the curve of decorated street, its fortresses of mock Tudor, its fleets of shine-in-the-dark hovermobiles. I looked further out, to the rolling dark hills all around twinkling with house lights, and beyond that other towns twinkling, too, just like Mistlehurst, each with their own pageant, their own doctor, their own litters and schools of cherubic blonde children. "We must keep our eyes open, Betty, and then perhaps it will all be just fine."

The town of Mistlehurst took root in my imagination during long midday dog walks in the Magnolia neighborhood of Seattle. The desolate landscape of mock Tudors and pruned yards populated by gardeners and nannies morphed into something rather sinister. It's possible that having to carry sacks of doggy-doo on my walks contributed to the sinister mood, as well.

Maia Chance

ACKNOLWEDGEMENTS

All four authors would like to thank the many people whose hands touched this book in some way, including our editor, Mimi the "Grammar Chick;" cover designer Andrea Orlic; and other folks who read early drafts during stressful times.

Maia Chance is eternally grateful to Zach, Jennifer, and all of her readers.

All of Janine A. Southard's books so far have been possible because of crowdsourced funds via Kickstarter. She owes great thanks to her many patrons of the arts who love a good science fiction adventure and believe in her ability to make that happen.

Raven Oak wishes many thanks to the *Ladies of the Write* (especially Kat Richardson) for their copious and detailed suggestions; to Editor Claire Eddy & the Cascade Writers for their copious feedback; and to contest winner, Charlene, for the use of her name. She also sends her thanks to her readers, friends, family, and last but not least, her husband.

G. Clemans gives many, many thanks to her wonderful family—Dave, Sam, and Charlotte—for their unwavering love, distracting silliness, and amazing plot-problem-solving skills. She is endlessly grateful to her extended family for their abundant support and more specifically grateful for the assistance with the German language offered by her father-in-law, Otto. Her first writing group, *Magnolia Chapter One*, deserves heaps of praise for helping her transition from non-fiction to fiction and for providing much needed instruction and affirmation along the way.

ABOUT THE AUTHORS

National bestselling author Maia Chance writes historical mysteries that are rife with absurd predicaments and romantic adventure. She is the author of *Snow White Red-Handed*, *Cinderella Six Feet Under*, and *Come Hell or Highball*. 2016 titles include *Beauty, Beast, and Belladonna* and *Teetotaled*.

Maia lives in Bellingham, WA, where she shakes a killer martini, grows a mean radish, and bakes mocha bundts to die for. She can be found on the web at:

Website:	www.maiachance.com
Facebook:	https://www.facebook.com/MaiaChance
Twitter:	https://twitter.com/maiachance
Goodreads:	http://bit.ly/maiagdrds

Janine A. Southard is the IPPY award-winning author of *Queen & Commander* (and other books in *The Hive Queen Saga*). She lives in Seattle, WA, where she writes speculative fiction novels, novellas, and short stories...and reads them aloud to her cat.

To get a free ebook, sign up for Janine A. Southard's newsletter (http://bit.ly/jasnews).

You'll then also be among the first to know when her latest book is released (or get fun release-related news like when her next Kickstarter project is coming). Usually, this is once a month or so, but sometimes goes longer or shorter. Your address will never be shared, and you can unsubscribe at any time. Plus: free eBook!

Website: www.janinesouthard.com
Twitter: https://twitter.com/jani_s
Goodreads: https://www.goodreads.com/jani_s

Raven Oak is the author of the bestselling fantasy novel *Amaskan's Blood*, the bestselling science fiction novella *Class-M Exile*, and the upcoming space opera *The Eldest Silence*. She spent most of her K-12 education doodling stories and 500-page monstrosities that are forever locked away in a filing cabinet.

When she's not writing, she's getting her game on with tabletop and console games, indulging in cartography, or staring at the ocean. She lives in Seattle, WA with her husband and their three kitties, who enjoy lounging across the keyboard when writing deadlines approach.

Raven is currently at work on *Amaskan's War* and *The Eldest Traitor*. You can *Join the Conspiracy*, her official mailing list to gain information and freebies at http://bit.ly/romaillist. Raven Oak can be found online at the following:

Website: www.ravenoak.net
Facebook: http://facebook.com/authorroak
Twitter: http://twitter.com/raven_oak
Goodreads: http://www.goodreads.com/raven_oak

Depending on the hour, G. Clemans might be writing about a post-apocalyptic world ravaged by lightning storms, teaching semiotics to twenty-year-olds, or squinting at art in a gallery.

Photo © Samantha Seaver

A founding instructor of Critical & Contextual Studies at Cornish College of the Arts, Clemans regularly contributes art criticism to *The Seattle Times*.

Clemans has only recently embarked on the wild ride of writing fiction. Inspired by her two daughters, she crafts real-world fantasies for young adults—stories that intermingle historical research with made-up mythologies.

For updates on her writing, please visit:

Website: www.gayleclemans.com
Facebook: https://www.facebook.com/gclemans
Twitter: http://twitter.com/gayleclemans

OTHER BOOKS BY...

Maia Chance

Fairy Tale Fatal Series
Snow White Red-Handed
Cinderella Six Feet Under
Beauty, Beast, and Belladonna*

The Discreet Retrieval Agency
Come Hell or Highball
Teetotaled*

Janine A. Southard

Hive Queen Saga
Queen & Commander
Hive & Heist

Cracked! A Magic iPhone Story
These Convergent Stars

Raven Oak

The Boahim Series
Amaskan's Blood
Amaskan's War*

The Xersian Struggle Series
The Eldest Silence*

Class-M Exile

G. Clemans

The Map as Art: Contemporary Artists Explore Cartography
(with Katharine Harmon)

* *Coming in 2016*

LIKE WHAT YOU READ?

Word of mouth is the number one **best** way to ensure that your favorite authors have continued success—better than any paid advertisement.

If you enjoyed this book, please consider leaving a **review** or starred ranking on Amazon, Barnes & Noble, Goodreads, and other retail or reviewer sites.

Your review is greatly appreciated.

CPSIA information can be obtained at www.ICGtesting.com
Printed in the USA
LVOW11s0858151115

462644LV00001B/49/P